TO CURSE A RIVAL

MAJESTIC MIDLIFE WITCH BOOK 2

N. Z. NASSER

CHAPTER I

As summer ripened into rotting fruit and a smattering of fallen leaves underfoot, the raja no longer kept us under lock and key in the palace turret. It pleased Prem Kumar that I'd returned freely to Jalapashu. In his mind, that could mean only one thing: I was as enamoured with him as he was with me. He had told me as much himself during a picnic under the stars: just me and him and a dozen servants. *We will be something special,* he said, while I tried not to choke on my samosa and wished for something stronger than passion fruit juice to wash it down with.

To the raja, I was a romantic challenge, not a threat. A trophy to claim. An exotic rose.

Who was I to stop a man from tripping over his own ego?

I smiled, even as the need for rebellion clawed at me. I clamped my lips shut from questioning whose orders had led to Sitara's death, why his people stole food, how a curse had trapped Deven in his human body and what had befallen the missing seer. I made grateful noises as the raja allocated me and Leena a small house in exchange for the promise of labour and taxes. I greeted neighbours and pretended to be meek. Even though gargoyles flocked to our roof from neighbouring houses in the dark. Gargoyles, whose ragged breath I heard through the crumbling red-brick walls, each inhale-exhale demanding I take action.

Nobody survived in Jalapashu without masking their true feelings. We were no exception.

The kingdom was full of marvels–garlanded elephants, rich foods, flowing silks, gleaming jewels and magic beyond all imagining–but it stank of decay. Though I stood on unfamiliar soil, I had no doubt: the rot stemmed from Prem Kumar's reign. Anger simmered at my core as Leena and I arranged our new home. Nestled in the heart of the kingdom, our single-storey house stood on a dusty road between the market and a temple. The gleaming white of the royal palace loomed in the distance.

At least we were out from under the raja's thumb.

Inside, weathered walls bore the marks of age, with crumbling patches and traces of faded paint. The air was already thick with the earthy scent of clay. Equipment from my workshop in Boundless Bay, brought by the general and his men, sat side by side with the kiln and tools inherited from Jalapashu's great pottery master, Vikram Reddy, who had created the gargoyles long ago. Sunlight streamed through the window, illuminating dust motes and casting warm hues on the potter's wheel and scattered tools I had yet to organise. The plate with our family's five entwined handprints on it–its broken parts reassembled and glued by Deven–had pride of place on a shelf.

I sighed. "It's just not home without our books and pottery."

"You're not doing that. You're not going to make me nostalgic for things. We're better than that. At least we don't need to bicker about how to arrange our books. By colour, obviously."

"That's fighting talk. Genre, every time."

"I miss my records and my clothes."

"Aanya can sing to you."

"Her repertoire is miles apart from my collection." Leena brightened. "But maybe I'll teach her some Amy Winehouse, Fleetwood Mac and Nina Simone. If she can do Springsteen, I'll melt."

"Aanya's voice is more honey than whiskey." Laughing, I dusted my hands on my trousers. "You didn't have to rush home from the clinic, you know. I could have handled it here."

Leena swept the floor. "Shame we couldn't get your gargoyle army to leap into action as our very own cleaning company."

"I'm pretty sure they're meant for more important things. That would be exploitation."

"Not if you fed them in cake… Anyway, it's not like I was doing much at the clinic. The setup is rudimentary, to say the least—barely any medicine. The locals gave up visiting it long ago. But there are some interesting plants around that help with minor ailments."

"That's great." Finding purpose in Jalapashu was part of our plan to cover up our real intentions. Leena was evidently taking work more seriously than me. I was setting up a pottery studio, but to me, it wasn't the real deal, even though customers had already begun enquiring about my wares, offering me Jalapashan coins, vegetables or garments as payment. Eventually, we'd find a way to preserve the best parts of our lives in Boundless Bay, and magic would be the cherry on the cake.

Leena laid the broom to one side. "Did you know? This house belonged to a weaver and his wife. Four nights ago, without a word of warning, they decided to move out. No one has heard from them since."

I paused from arranging my pots in the display window. A shiver ran up my spine. Is that why the raja had been able to find us a house with both living and working space so quickly? I hated the thought of us benefitting from another family's unhappiness. "Who told you that?"

"Farida. The one who wears so many bangles she sounds like a tambourine."

Sitara shimmered into being next to my potter's wheel, startling me. "That woman wears bangles so her cheating husband has enough warning to kick his mistress out of bed before she gets home. Like a cowbell except worse."

I tensed. "I wish you wouldn't lurk like that. Poor Farida. She'd probably rather we didn't know that."

"I'd wrench that man onto the street by the cojones, but this kingdom is full of people who have lost their fighting spirit." Sitara pursed her lips. "And Kiya, lurking is what ghosts do. It's an advantage given our current situation. You two give the appearance of normality, and I can rush about sticking my nose where it doesn't belong."

I muttered like an amateur puppeteer, taking care not to turn fully in her direction. Though barely visible at an arm's length, I didn't want nosy neighbours reporting back to the raja that our dead sister was very much still with us. "That's not going to work when a passerby catches you materialising in the display window and cashes in on that information." The house had a minuscule footprint compared to the home we'd left behind in Boundless Bay, split equally between the living, work quarters and a tiny garden. A display window invited passersby to glimpse my pottery. Part of me wondered whether we had been gifted this particular house because we were on display ourselves: exotic creatures behind shop front glass or strangers still under the microscope. Little did they know that the gargoyles breathed a warning whenever unfamiliar footfalls came our way.

"Nonsense." Sitara drew herself up to her full height. That is, she levitated for extra effect. Neither I nor the gargoyles could prevent my sister's wilful risk-taking. "No one is interested in us when they are in survival mode. They don't like the raja. They won't help him."

I made a strangled noise of impatience. "It doesn't matter what they think when spilling our secrets to the raja means their families will be fed."

Sitara had been ferreting for clues about Mahi's disappearance. So far, we'd not rocked any boats. Okay, that was a lie. We'd rocked plenty of boats but had not been caught red-handed by anyone other than the general. My heartbeat drummed faster just at the mere thought of Deven. I didn't know how much Deven would put his skin on the line for us or how disloyal he could be persuaded to be to his cousin, the raja. I didn't even know what we were to each other. After all, some people would write off a stolen kiss as nothing. A frisson of electricity didn't mean anything. Especially here in a kingdom full of strange magic, unfamiliar customs and double-dealing.

For all his sins, the raja trusted me.

The trust wasn't down to my cleverness. Yes, he feared our rising popularity after we leapt into the blood-spattered arena. Yes, he harboured romantic delusions about me. Mostly, however, the raja's trust in me was the result of his ego. Prem Kumar was so accustomed to being the most powerful man in the kingdom that he couldn't fathom being bested. Not by outsiders. Especially not by women. It suited him to swallow his suspicions about who had stolen the jewels from his bedroom. That way, he could pretend he was still fully on the throne: a man in control of the secrets and magic in Jalapashu.

He didn't know it yet, but he was slipping off that very throne.

There would come the day when we would push him right off.

My head jerked up at the sound of bells ringing at the nearby temple. On cue, a middle-aged man trundled past the window on his bicycle. I waved a hello and then continued to stack the shelf, willing Sitara to take the hint. To be subtle for once.

Sitara reared up in a spiral of cool air. "Why does it feel like we're playing house?"

Leena spluttered. "You've not lifted a finger."

A sly smile. "Technically, as a ghost, I don't *live* here. Besides, I'm still limited to brief touches like–"

She glided over to a shelf I had just arranged.

My eyebrows jackknifed. "Don't you dare!"

At Sitara's nudge, a pencil vase teetered on the edge before succumbing to gravity's pull with a resounding crash. Never one to truly let go in her lifetime, she was determined to wreak havoc on the other side of the veil. Our ghost sister was more impatient. More reckless. As if dying had eroded her understanding of risk and underlined the importance of living in the moment. She gave an impish grin. "Don't be mad, Kiya. It wasn't your best work. It probably belonged in the slop bucket anyway."

It turned out that death complicated feelings. I crouched to pick up the shards, wanting to kill her as much as I wanted to hug her.

Sitara skirted around me, a rippling, shifting figure comprised of mists and shadows, bringing the tang of her orange and magnolia perfume. "Sorry. Not sorry. All this power, yet we do nothing."

Wanting a rebellion was one thing; achieving it was another matter entirely.

Tossing the vase shards into the bin, I stepped out of the cold pocket of air that travelled where Sitara did, and hissed. "You're supposed to be the cautious one. You know we have to bide our time."

Secrets were woven deep into the fabric of life in Jala-pashu. I intended to take every precaution to protect ours. I ushered Leena behind the studio through a doorway, leaving

Sitara to follow us. Our living quarters consisted of a kitchen with a small table, a shower room and toilet, and a bedroom kitted out with soft quilts, embroidered curtains and two single beds. Luckily, ghosts had no need for human clutter or sleeping quarters, or we wouldn't have squeezed Sitara in.

Shutting the door, I blocked out the glaring patterns of the wallpaper and faced my sisters. I clenched and unclenched my fists, power coiling in me. Beneath my feet, I became aware of creaking floorboards and beyond, stone foundations, the soft embrace of fertile soil, the roots of plants, compacted earth holding the weight of centuries, the ground transitioning into cool rock, rising in heat to molten magma at the earth's core, a blazing cauldron of energy. "Don't you think I long to strike a blow?"

Leena shook her head. "Why are we holding back? Aanya's beside herself. We have to

find Mahi. The sooner we get rid of the raja, the sooner our friends will be safe."

I sucked in my breath. The thought of the seer's eerily empty house made my insides churn. "That's not fair. I've seen the suffering here. Empty pantries. Magic being used as a source of control rather than joy. Crimes committed in the name of the raja. But we have to plot our moves like it's a game of chess or Prem Kumar will crush us. He doesn't play by the rules."

A storm brewed in Sitara's voice. "It's not our friends or the kingdom I'm worried about. When Prem Kumar realises you two aren't as sweet and innocent as you seem, he's going to come for you. Yet here you are playing homemaker in a nest of vipers."

Leena looked from me to Sitara. As the youngest sibling, she hated conflict between us unless she caused it. "Aanya risked her position by searching the palace dungeons, but Mahi must be somewhere else. *You're* supposed to be the seeker of lost and found things, Sitara. So why can't you find Mahi?"

We'd had high hopes for Sitara's nightly wanderings and the clues she might uncover. Especially given the parrot had flown away at the first opportunity after Mahi's disappearance. There had to be some perks to being a ghost, given the downsides: no touch, no food and unfinished business.

Sitara threw up her hands, and her ghostly form flickered like the static on a television. "I had another grim night of disgruntled gargoyles, dank passages and parents whispering in bed that they can't stomach another day of pretending to adore the raja. Not to mention witnessing Farida's husband attempting to wax his own back hair. A rug, I tell you. I'm only one woman. This is supposed to be a coven." She glared at me. "What have you done to bring the seer home?"

The balance had shifted between us since we had gone against Sitara's wishes to run away from magic and the raja. Since she had realised the gargoyles answered to me. Sitara had abdicated responsibility. Her profile of being the eldest sister had been flipped inside out. Sitara hadn't relinquished her mortal concerns–in fact, Mahi would say that it was unhealthy for a ghost to not move on to the next realm–but she was no longer in the driving seat. My sisters readily provided their opinions, but I was suddenly the decision-maker of our trio.

To my surprise, I *really* liked being in charge.

"I sent Merlin after Babbu. He will have news soon, I'm sure."

We had barely glimpsed the parrot since freeing him from a chest in the seer's house the night of her disappearance. Without Mahi, Babbu had become untethered, losing all faith in mankind. His screeches of distress reverberated amidst distant treetops, but the citizens averted their eyes. No one wanted to acknowledge the seer's sudden absence. Their eyes glossed over at the empty space beside the raja where the seer had stood for decades. It was as if she had never existed, although her three-storey house remained in situ, a gloomy reminder that her power had been only second to the raja's.

I hadn't forgotten her. Her third eye haunted my dreams, violet and yawning.

Stepping over to the bottom kitchen drawer, where odd bits of paraphernalia swam, I pulled out a notepad and handed it to Leena. "I've been working up a list of who we can trust."

Leena flicked through the notebook and gave me a quizzical look. "Five names? You've marked Aanya and the chef from Biryani Junction as trustworthy, Deven and our grandmother as a maybe, and the court poet as definitely dodgy."

"The general and our grandmother are power brokers in this system. We can't take their alliance as a given." I shrugged. "And the court poet keeps passing off classic poetry as his own. That's a huge red flag."

"So you've been making lists." Sitara's green eyes glinted like dew-laden leaves. "We need to move faster."

Pottery needed preparation and patience. The feat before us wasn't any different. "We can't raise a rebellion overnight. This place is too unfamiliar. The raja is too strong. We don't have technology at our fingertips to rile the masses or a network to help us." A gentle breeze danced through the window, carrying whispers of secrets and dreams yet to be realised. "We have to hone our magic. Sitara's efforts have come to nothing, so we have to start whittling down who is with us and who is against us. Amongst the people but also the members of the royal court. Someone will know where Mahi is. We've been trapped by the past for too long. Her foresight can give us the edge. Then we spark our rebellion."

Leena nodded. "Aanya can help with making deeper inroads at court."

They'd been together scarcely a month, yet Leena brought Aanya into every conversation. Their eyes lit up in each other's company, and they couldn't help lingering touches in the most mundane moments. I couldn't have pulled Leena away from Jalapashu if I'd tried. It made the stakes for succeeding even higher.

Worse, my younger sister wasn't the only person who felt a magnetic pull to a citizen of Jalapashu. Not that I had allowed myself to thaw in the general's presence. Not after the kiss on the beach, when the world fell away, the ocean shrank to a point, and it was only his lips on mine in the murky drizzle.

In this monstrous kingdom, secrets would protect us. They would erect walls and keep us safe, wrapping around us like a cloak of invisibility. I was sure of it. Concealment was the key to surviving Jalapashu unscathed. I'd turned it over and over in my mind during the darkest part of the night when the gargoyles shuffled on our roof. By concealing our true intentions and desires, we'd remain one step ahead of the raja.

I turned to my sisters, and as the words flowed, a small internal voice asked where this version of myself had come from and why I had buried my authentic self. I silenced that voice. To survive, we needed to break out of our moulds. "Promise me. Sitara, no one can see you. And Leena, you won't let your mask slip. We'll guard our secrets, and we'll unravel each one of theirs and use it against them." My eyes widened as the gargoyles breathed a warning. Their eerie guttural grumble resonated through my bones. "Someone's coming."

The internal door rattled, and in flew Farida, our neighbour, in a jangle of bangles, arms flailing.

Our ghost sister dissolved into the air like a whisper carried away by the wind.

Farida frowned at the space where Sitara had been a moment before. The furrows on her temple deepened as she recalled the reason for tumbling into our house. "Ladies, there's jungle cats in the arena. And the general standing in the centre of it all! Everyone's heading up there." Her eyes filled with glee. The glee that came from witnessing ill fortune to others when you were usually the recipient of it. "Do you want to come?"

I gulped. *The general is standing at the centre of it all.* The general who was all too human after being cursed by the raja. My voice was thin and not my own. "We're coming."

Stone eyes bored into my back from every rooftop as I hastened with Leena and Farida towards the palace. A swell of loathing made me quake with magic. I was determined to hold it in check, whatever awaited us. Whatever Prem Kumar had manufactured against the man who I couldn't shake from my thoughts.

CHAPTER 2

We joined the crowds surging through the cobbled streets, through the palace gates and into the stands circling the arena. My feet stumbled, and my breath bottled in my chest as we took our seats. The murmur of the crowd enveloped me, a wall of noise that muddied my already spinning senses. Opposite me in the royal box, the raja waved a bejewelled hand. I nodded in acknowledgement, my lips stretching into a wooden smile in a vain attempt to mask my rising horror.

Farida ducked so close to me that her cloud of frizzy hair brushed my lips. "Now that's a man. If he had won the throne... but it was not to be."

A magnetic pull tugged my gaze to the sawdust-strewn ring.

The arena crackled with the fervour of competition. Bloodied silks, which I realised had come from the royal tailor's atelier, were strewn in the sawdust. Centre stage, a panther and a tiger encircled Deven. By the look of the jungle cats' crimson jowls, they'd already drawn blood. Deven's ornate dress coat lay discarded in a heap. He fought in a vest, his muscular frame slick with sweat. His trousers were shredded on one thigh by claws, and his dark hair curled against his forehead. Two small knives gleamed on his belt. They were nothing compared to the teeth and claws of his opponents.

Leena nudged me. "I'm scared for him."

My breath came in quick, shallow bursts. I could barely stand to watch.

Deven stood amidst the swirling chaos, utterly focused on the job at hand. I held my breath as the tiger inclined its head towards the panther as if sanctioning a manoeuvre. The panther leapt at Deven, a blur of velvet black sinew, nightmarish teeth and sharpened claws. With lightning speed, Deven ducked beneath the panther, his body coiling like a spring. He exuded a raw, untamed energy, matching the primal instincts of the beast. As the panther sailed over him, he delivered a sharp blow to its exposed underbelly. The panther sprawled across the sawdust, dazed.

The crowd applauded in machine-gun bursts, shuffling further and further to the edge of their seats.

Farida fanned her face. "I could watch this all day."

Leena murmured in my ear. "How long can he hang on?"

Not a second passed before the tiger launched an attack. Its striped golden flank rippled with muscles as it pounced. It flew through the air, an enormous paw extended to strike Deven's legs as if it could cut him down like a tree. But Deven moved with uncanny agility. The raja's curse had stolen his physical form, but he retained a jungle cat's grace. Somersaulting backwards to evade the tiger's claws, he landed with a thud. As the tiger lunged again, Deven threw himself sidewards, sweeping his leg up to bring the roaring beast crashing to the ground in a cloud of dust.

The tiger's guttural roar echoed through the arena, but the general didn't flinch. The controlled rhythm of his breathing melded with the symphony of the battle. The panther and tiger lunged and swiped, acting individually and as a pair to overcome him. Deven, in turn, parried and dodged, his coal-black eyes gleaming with intensity. He tucked a shredded sari into his waistband, unfurling it at opportune moments–contracting the cats' throats, momentarily retraining or subduing them when they threatened him–remaining cool despite the heat of battle. His body responded to their every move; he anticipated their advances as if this were more than a fight. As if it were a dance. God, he was beautiful. I caught glimpses of the tattoo snaking up his taut back. His sensual mouth was parted, and his cheekbones caught the glow of autumn light. Gasps and cheers filled the arena, and each blow and evasion met with rapturous applause. The crowd's cheers fuelled the energy of the battle.

I longed to repurpose their bloodlust against the raja.

But jungle cats were not mere playthings. They fought back with ferocity. One minute, the general was in control. The next, at the mercy of the beast. He evaded the panther's razor-sharp claws by mere inches. The crowd bellowed at the near miss, their excitement escalating. My heartbeat galloped at the primal energy in the air. The general's fist connected against the panther's flank, and I wondered why he didn't reach for his knives. How was he expected to end the fight with bare knuckles and sharp kicks? The tiger slashed its paw across Deven's arm. My chest constricted as the general staggered backwards, and a deep gash bloomed red. The tiger seemed to grin and held back a moment. It hung back while Deven snatched a shredded piece of fabric from the ground and wrapped it around his forearm. These weren't just jungle beasts. They were shifters, animals with human intellect that made them even more terrifying. I clenched my teeth with worry, flushing as I caught the raja's eyes on me.

Fighting to keep my composure, I gripped Leena. "He needs your help."

She tensed. "He needs to get the hell out of there."

Farida clapped her hands. "Isn't it exciting?"

I gave a cold smile. "Oh yes, bloodlust really gets me going."

Deven gritted his teeth and pressed on despite his injuries. I remembered the taste of his lips: saltwater and smoke and the taste of rain. It was stupid to care for someone in a place like this. Every fibre of my being willed him to succeed. I could help; I knew it. I could flex my hands and will the earth to open up beneath the beasts, but then the raja would know my magic wasn't piffling at all. It wasn't toy shop magic; it was world-reshaping magic. It was my magic he should fear.

My sister placed her hands on my balled fists. "Don't."

Despite the bruises, cuts and gashes that marred his body, Deven had an instinctual understanding of a predator's world. He didn't see how his six-year-old nephew Ishaan slipped from his mother's grasp and darted into the ring to distract the beasts from his beloved uncle. He faced down his opponents, his focus unbroken.

Until I leapt out of my seat with a sharp cry, "The boy!"

Deven's inky gaze flicked upwards, finding me. A frisson sparked between us, blocking out everything else. He wrenched his gaze from mine as the tiger raked his chest, tearing his vest. Paling, he delivered a precise blow to the tiger's jaw, causing it to reel back, disoriented. The crowd were on their feet, pointing at Ishaan, whose plump fists were raised. Deven spun, expression grim. Without hesitation, he intercepted the panther's charge seconds before it reached the child. Lassoing a swirling silk, Deven redirected the panther's momentum, sending it crashing into the arena wall. With a softness that made my gut twist, he placed his cheering nephew into the stands, wincing as he finally looked down at his chest.

Anger clouded his face–almost certainly because of the danger to Ishaan–and a new purpose filled his stride.

I sank into my seat as the crowd erupted in applause, my emotions spent.

A second more, and I would have unveiled the extent of my magic for all to see.

From the royal box, the raja's quizzical eyes, unfeeling and icy blue, bored into me.

Teeth gritted in pain, Deven balled the fabric poking out from his waistband and stuffed it into the panther's mouth, seeking to humiliate. The crowd chuckled in delight. As the beasts regained their senses, he yanked two frayed saris off the ground and jogged towards his opponents. A sea of aquamarine and violet meshed together as he entangled the tiger's front limbs, pulling a knot tight, then ensnaring the panther's hind legs in the fabric. The cats struggled and then collapsed in the dirt with pitiful mewls. A twisted smile flashed across Deven's haughty face before he laid his two knives in the sawdust–underlining his lack of reliance on the blades–and made a low bow to the raja.

The crowd went as wild as my heartbeat.

Leena shuddered. "Why doesn't he kill them?"

Farida grinned. "Because those are his men, silly. The general can't kill his own men."

"Not even if they attack him?" said Leena.

"He'd be court-martialled and lose everything," said Farida. "But if the men incapacitate the general, they claim his job."

My stomach hardened. "That doesn't seem fair."

Deven freed the beasts, and they transformed into bruised and shivering wrecks of men, who wrapped the saris around their nether regions and inclined their heads first to their general, then to the raja and the crowd.

"It's training. The soldiers have to stay sharp in case Jalapashu is attacked. Although it's unusual that the battles are so… invigorating. Luckily, Deven Kumar is our best warrior. Songs will be composed about how he saved the boy."

With the spectacle over, the crowd streamed from the arena.

An orgasmic shiver ran up Farida's body as she watched the general stoop low to collect his knives, his bloodied thigh bulging through his trousers, dust them off and slot them into his belt. "Even more of Jalapashu's women will be swooning over him after this show of heroics. Of course, he'd not been interested in anyone since his wife died."

I went still inside, my voice careful. The barrage of secrets was unrelenting. With each revelation, the battlefield grew bloodier. "The general was married?"

"He became a shadow of himself when he lost her. So many unanswered questions. He's more serious these days." Farida gave a wry smile to the heavens, where gunmetal clouds gathered in the autumn sky. "Life starts as a bed of roses, but soon enough, they wither. Still, he's a catch. You're not interested, are you?"

My words stuck in my throat. "Don't be silly."

Leena glanced at me, worry lines at the corners of her mouth. She knew about the kiss and that it had meant something, despite my attempts to brush it under the carpet. Sisters didn't need every emotion spelt out in words. They could tell what had unravelled by a slight stiffness in the body, an unanswered question or a fluctuation in mood.

"Phew. Because the raja has you marked out as his. He's not taken his eyes off you. What the raja wants, the raja gets." Farida clapped her hands in excitement. "Who knows, you might even be a future queen. Jalapashu is a place where men and women rise and fall in the blink of an eye."

Farida waggled her eyebrows. "As for you, Leena, you can't fool me. We might be sheltered here, but I know you have *other* tastes. It's quite okay. I'll keep your secret."

The polite smile slid off my face. Next to me, Leena had a choking fit. Neither of us realised that being in Jalapashu would mean coming out all over again. It was Leena's decision on how to navigate this, but a good wingwoman was always prepared with an exit strategy. I thumped my sister's back and hauled her to her feet. "It was lovely seeing you, Farida. Do pop into the studio whenever you like."

"Goodbye, my new friends," she called out after us.

We threaded our way to the edge of the ring, where Deven fielded congratulations from the townspeople, none more proud than his sister and nephew. There were women, too, fussing around him, and men giving him hearty claps on the back. My heart ricochetted in my chest at the sight of weeping wounds on his torso, thigh and arm. Swathes of colourful, torn saris lay abandoned in the sawdust. For all the beauty of this kingdom, it was normal to find silks soaking in blood and bones bending like boughs. To survive, my witch sisters and I had to buckle up and learn fast.

Leena leant up against the side barrier and waved to Deven. "Over here!"

I schooled my expression and prayed that he couldn't guess how I wanted to take him aside and tend to every wound. "General, perhaps Leena can offer some nursing aid?"

Weeks had passed with only fleeting glimpses of him. I didn't know if he was protecting himself from the raja's ire or was avoiding me. But my heart skipped a beat each time I spotted him in the market, commanding his men, or playing with his nephew. Somehow, he always picked me out of a crowd as if we were opposing magnets.

Deven extricated himself from well-wishers and strode towards us, frowning at my formality. "Did you enjoy the show?"

The air between us fizzed with energy. I bit my lip. "Hardly. Are you okay?"

In the royal box, flanked by court members, the raja watched with hooded eyes, then abruptly left his seat.

Deven's body language was stiff, and his lips were white,

though he tried to hide his pain. "It was a little scuffle, that's all."

He had been married before, and I hadn't known. The thought swirled in my head.

Leena's voice was matronly. "If you come with me to the clinic, I'll see to your wounds."

"I wouldn't want to waste your time stitching me up when I could be back in the ring tomorrow. The raja is fixated on testing my loyalty." His inky gaze never left my face.

There had been rumours that the raja was displeased with Deven. Stomach plummeting, I laid a hand on his arm. "Let Leena see to you."

Deven jerked back as if he had been scalded. "Don't."

I flushed. This man probably kissed any number of women. I had no claim to him.

Confusion marred my sister's brow as she looked between us. "General, you're seriously injured."

"I heal fast, and the physician has given me a surplus of ointments for this very reason." He glanced over our heads and gave a mocking bow. "Forgive me. It's time for me to retreat into a corner and lick my wounds."

Disappointment flared. I turned clumsily on my heel, slamming straight into a hard chest.

The raja steadied me with strong, bejewelled hands. A duo of soldiers stood discreetly to one side, tracking any threats. Prem's gold crown gleamed in the mellow afternoon sun as he stooped to kiss my cheek. Then he swivelled me to face the general. "Well played in the ring, cousin. It seems you continue to earn your place at my side.

A vein throbbed in Deven's jaw, and I realised that the general's mocking bow had been intended for his king. "You know me, Prem. I don't back down from a challenge."

The raja's blue eyes grew glacial. "Oh, but you did once, didn't you? Tell me, is it your intention to send women running away as fast as your enemies?" He waved a dismissive hand at the general and raised his eyebrow at us. "I'm surprised you two chose to sit in the stands when you have an open invitation to the royal box."

I ignored the general's retreating back with difficulty. "We were busy settling into our new home and arrived late, Prem-ji." How easily he had turfed Mahi from her elevated position despite years of service. A pause. "Did our house belong to a weaver family? We'd hate to have been the cause of distress."

The raja's smile sent shivers down my spine. "What weaver family? That house has been waiting for you to claim it. I trust it is to your liking? You could always move back into the palace."

Power curled within me. The only way I wanted to return to the palace was if he was not in it. I mimicked his smile and hoped it reached my eyes. "The house is perfect for us."

The raja nodded. "Excellent. My enforcer is doing the rounds this afternoon. My friends can always get a reprieve."

Leena gave a violent shake of her head. Each of us had paid our way in Boundless Bay. It wouldn't be any different here. "That won't be necessary. We're independent women, after all."

Prem flicked out dirt from his perfect fingernails. "Jalapashu is a dangerous place without the backing of a man."

A muscle jumped in my cheek. "Women are warriors, too."

"I've offended you." Prem chuckled. "There's fire at your core, Kiya Marlowe, and that excites me. I have no time for the meek."

Leena snorted. As a light drizzle fell, it was her turn to rescue me. She splayed her hands to the heavens despite her love of dancing in the rain. Her tone was so mild that only I could sense her scorn. "Goodness, will you look at that? No woman likes to be drenched. We wouldn't want to catch our deaths or, worse, a frizzy head of hair."

We took our leave. My legs were skittish as my sister hooked her arm through mine and guided me through the surge of people exiting the palace grounds. I risked a look over my shoulder, colouring at the sight of the raja staring after us.

A nervous laugh spilled from Leena. "You've become his favourite plaything."

"He's after a notch on his bedpost." I drew in a shuddering breath.

"He's after more than that, and you know it. You heard what Farida said. Either way, he's going to be disappointed. Your chemistry with the general was enough to set the palace alight."

My mouth was dry. As dry as when Deven had raced across the ring to rescue Ishaan. "He's in no fit state. I can't believe he didn't accept your help. Anyway, you've got it all wrong. He couldn't bear me to touch him."

Leena's spurt of laughter drew stares, and she dropped her voice to a whisper. "That's what you thought? That flame's not going out until you tear each other's clothes off. I can't wait to watch the fireworks."

My chest fluttered. "We have a thousand other things to worry about." Deven had been married before, and I wanted to tease his whole history out of him. I scrambled for something coherent to say to hide my rising blush. "I didn't believe a word of what Prem said about the weaver's family. Did you?"

"No, I didn't. And yes, we have work to do." My sister put her arm around me with a knowing chuckle. "But there's always time for what makes life worth living."

CHAPTER 3

The next day, a pastel sunset spun across the skies over Jalapashu, and a breeze carried the salty smell of the ocean to my nose. The kingdom's beauty couldn't chase my worries away. Merlin had been gone for days. Our time imprisoned in the palace turret had given me the false impression that he would always be at my side. Only in his absence did it hit home how much I missed his companionship, guidance, the intensity of his watchful liquid gold eyes and the comforting weight of his sooty body on my lap.

Once, I had considered the hare a nuisance; now I understood he was family.

Sitara assured me it was the hare's nature to roam far and wide. He always returned. By my calculations, the hare had navigated the paths of life for close to eighty years, and still, my mind dreamt up alternative scenarios. He might have gotten caught in a trap while searching for Babbu or lost in the marshes. Perhaps he lay whimpering and hurt in some dark place, waiting for me to rescue him.

I would only have to whisper to the gargoyles to find

him, and they would accomplish it. I no longer feared being able to wake them. With every day that I spent in Jalapashu, our bond grew stronger. The creaking of their stone bodies had become a soundtrack in my mind. If I so wished, they'd tear down the kingdom to find the seer. Their rasping breath told me as much. I resisted that misstep. Gargoyles were not a stealth weapon. We needed a gentle tug to unravel all Jalapashu's secrets, not an outright declaration of enmity.

Besides, commanding the gargoyles formed one segment of my witchcraft, not the entirety. Aanya kept insisting that wholeness was the essence of witchcraft. She disapproved of my intention to attend court, but it troubled her conscience to leave us unprepared. In the absence of Mahi and Merlin, she had stepped in to instruct us in the ways of being a witch.

"To have any hope of bringing Mahi home or defeating the raja, you'll need all your talents and knowledge." Dressed in her maid's uniform of a red cotton shirt and trousers, her doe-like eyes demanded our attention. "If Mahi were here, she'd tell you the same thing. Think of the lunar phases and the immense power that accompanies a full moon. Think of this process as adding ingredients to a cauldron. You'll need to blend the past and present. Add a generous sprinkling of collective wisdom, a bouquet of ancient tradition. Most importantly, your own intuition, innate skills and experiences."

I frowned as her words rushed over me, craving simple instructions, not a philosophy lesson.

Aanya raked her hand through her lank hair. Her fingernails were bitten to the quick. She was grieving, Leena said. Despite their age difference, Mahi was her best friend. "Don't hold back. Practice. Magic is about belief. It's about primal forces. The ease and flow of energy. Silence everyone else's expectations. Has doubt ever brought anything but pain? Cast away your limiting beliefs."

Leena rose to her feet from where she had been resting on the uneven ground, ready for another bout. "Your passion is lighting a fire in me."

Sitara tutted. "I doubt you're talking about intellectual curiosity."

Aanya stoically ignored them, her magic a radar for how I struggled with the simple tasks she had set me. I'd failed to retrieve a crystal she'd hidden in the earth, failed to shape the soil into a cylinder and failed to crumble a cracked brick to dust, though even human hands could have accomplished it. I worried my magic only answered my call when I was angry or grieving. How could I survive in the shadows of Jalapashu when my magic was unreliable?

Aanya's voice grew more melodic to soothe my creeping anxiety. "Mahi has so much faith in you. She believes you can make all the difference here. She's seen it in her visions."

My tone was gentle, but my words cut deep. They poisoned the air between us. "You're using the present tense. Can we be so sure she's alive?"

Leena folded her arms, disgruntled, as if voicing our fears might make them come true.

Aanya's undercut had grown out, and she hadn't re-shaved it, although this minor rebellion was important to her. As if the raja was already winning at chipping away individual power. "Of course, she's alive. A witch as powerful as Mahi doesn't just die without a whimper." She laid a hand on her breastbone. "I feel it here. She's alive. Don't you dare doubt *that*."

Nerves knotted my stomach. "Did Mahi tell you what she saw? Think back, Aanya. We must have missed something."

Shadows pooled across the angles of the maid's thin face. "You know better than that. She rarely shared her visions. Even the joyful ones. Marriages can be upended. Babies never born. Leaders are suddenly stable hands. Great feats of mankind dwindle into a hiccup of history. All because someone made a different decision when the road forked. Even the raja was only given snippets of her knowledge. But you. You brought the promise of hope, she said. Isn't that a beautiful thing?"

What was hope if not blind optimism, a silent prayer, a wistful whisper? No, we needed concrete answers: new information, steadfast allies, and reliable magic. I clenched and unclenched my fists as the beginnings of a migraine took root. "I don't know what I'm doing wrong."

"Stop thinking so much." Aanya hummed a ballad, pausing only to guide my hands towards the earth again, where the stump of an aspen tree required excavating, and all I managed was a feeble patch of upended earth.

A few paces away, Leena raised her hand. Her brow furrowed, and the bark of the dead tree turned from silvery-grey to a dark brown and sprouted a spray of shimmering yellow foliage. She'd come a long way from palm flowers.

"Show off," I muttered as Aanya threw her slight arms around Leena's waist in celebration.

Leena gave me an apologetic look. "Maybe your jewel is faulty."

I harrumphed. "The one hidden just below my pelvis? Why don't we dig it out and have a look? Then we can rummage around your upper arm and Sitara's heart space. I'm sure it will be a piece of cake, what with her being dead and all."

Leena's brows pulled up. "No need to be tart."

Three times, we'd met in our walled postage-stamp-sized garden, and three times, I'd failed to make any significant progress with my magic. After witnessing the raja's callous treatment of Deven in the arena, my hunger to be accomplished at magic was insatiable. But the more I yearned for it, the more resistance I encountered, as if I was stuck in a perpetual loop of wanting without receiving. As if the fibres of my being conspired against me with a stranglehold on the very magic I knew I was capable of.

On paper, I was the most powerful sister.

My mouth twisted. Life liked to play its little jokes on us.

Sitara had wiped our memories of the skirmish with the general and his soldiers at the Amber Hollows, but her recollections of the encounter enthralled me. Leena's snaking vines had felled battle-hardened men. I had crumbled cave walls and built them up again, all in the blink of an eye. She said I'd created sandmen that chased our foe away. Not three weeks ago, when the mists had surrounded us at the Maharaja's Summer Soiree, I'd unlocked the doors to allow the revellers to escape the heat of the raja's wrath. I had plucked spells from my mind and poured them into vessels I had made. I turned my hands over, studying them. The feats I'd achieved instinctively no longer seemed possible.

With every passing moment, I failed Mahi.

Aanya nudged me towards a mound of soil she wanted me to flatten. The evening rays illuminated the row of earrings on her cartilage and the oiliness of her unwashed hair. "Come, Kiya. Try again."

I bit down on my lip and got to work. At least my humiliation wasn't for public consumption. The secret of our magic was well preserved behind the high walls of our minuscule garden. We didn't need to worry about being overlooked. The two gargoyles stationed on our rooftop would provide ample warning of trespassers. However, any nosy parkers who did catch a glimpse of the garden might have scratched their heads in wonder at the transformation.

The weaver family had long since given up on tending to their little patch. Mere days ago, the garden had been unkempt and overrun by wild grasses and delicate weeds. Tangled vines criss-crossed over its central pathway. Moss carpeted worn stone steps, and a once-golden sundial was now grey with age. A gnarled rose bush sat withered in one corner adjacent to the mouldy, neglected fountain where water had once sprung from the trunk of a granite elephant.

Then, my sisters wielded their power. Sitara restored gushing water to the dry fountain. At her command, rivulets of water fed the rose bush and brought sustenance to its frail blossoms. Leena, too, excelled, her green witch powers sending clusters of fuchsia and sapphire wildflowers defiantly towards the marshmallow skies. A twist of her wrists and she brought order to the chaos, uncurling vines from the path, sending weeds back into the earth, coaxing blooms from long ravaged flowerbeds despite the onset of autumn. With their magic, the scent of decaying foliage was replaced by the smell of damp soil and delicate roses.

I was happy for their success and pressured by it.

"You've made remarkable progress." Aanya beamed at Leena. She pointed to a stack of bricks next to tall grasses. "It's time for more combat-focused training. As for you, Kiya, it could be that I'm not the mentor for you. I could always ask the general to help. You can trust him."

I piped up. "No. That's not necessary. I'll keep trying."

She shrugged and turned to Leena. "I've watched the soldiers train all my life. They always start with strength-building before honing their fighting skills. Start with moving the bricks to the opposite garden wall."

Leena snorted. "I get arm ache looking through clothing rails. There's no way I can lift those. Besides, I don't want to be Big Bicep Bertha."

Aayna hid her smile, removed a tiny hoop earring and balanced it on the edge of the sundial. She beckoned Sitara over in her lilting voice. "It's time for you to unlock how to move objects every time you try. Stop thinking about how you are a spirit attempting to move matter and focus on..."

I blocked them out. The mound of dirt taunted me with its stubbornness. I brushed a speck of dirt off my cheek, my dark hair tousled from my failed attempts. The heaped soil quivered but didn't do my bidding despite hand gestures, breathing exercises and wild incantations I threw at it. *Samatalayatu.* Nothing. "How hard can this be?"

"I think you've met your match." Sitara whooshed to my side. "Let your magic flow through you. Don't try so hard."

I attempted another spell. *Bhūmirbhavatu samatalā.* Nothing. The mound wobbled like jelly but refused to comply. I was a potter, and I couldn't even shape garden dirt. Spells always came more easily when Merlin was at my side. God, I hoped he was safe. Worry and exasperation made me waspish. "How is flattening earth going to help? This is ridiculous." I was sorely tempted to run at the mound—only a few metres, given the size of the garden—and flatten it with my plump bottom. It would be endlessly more satisfying than the frustration of my errant magic.

Aanya shook her head. "No, it's survival. I've spent most of my life within the palace walls, Kiya. No one knew better than me about the injustices and corruption within the court. How men and women are promoted not for their qualities and abilities but for their blind loyalty. I've served drinks and delicacies, listening to all manner of whispers and game-playing between court members. I can provide insider details about the palace and the raja's habits, but I can't physically protect you. They will not hesitate to expose vulnerabilities or play tricks on you. In Jalapahshu, magic is armour, and yours must be intact."

Leena gave me a worried glance in the waning light. "Maybe I should come with you. Sitara is right. You're wound as tightly as a spring. It's not conducive to magic."

My stomach was leaden. The occasional cawing of seagulls drifted inland from the coast, and I missed home bitterly. "So now you're an expert, too?" I regretted it the minute I lashed out.

"Don't be like that." Sitara's eyes were the mossy green of

a tranquil forest. Her sympathy shamed my petulance. "We're going to get through this together."

My nod was a lie. Why did it feel like I carried the world on my shoulders?

Leena reached out to me. "It's been a long day. Our fridge is woefully empty. If we're lucky, the kitchen at Biryani Junction will still be open. Fancy a bite?"

I didn't need much persuasion. We freshened up and, leaving our grumbling ghost sister behind, entered Jalapashu's most beloved restaurant fifteen minutes later. A cloud of spices hung in the air, and dishes sizzled in earthenware pots. I had grown as fond as the locals of the homey cuisine and open-armed welcome we received from the chefs Jilu and Radha. Aanya, Leena and I wove our way through the bustling restaurant and settled in at a small table at the window overlooking the kingdom. Though we were in public and nobody in the wider world knew of their relationship, Leena and Aanya played footsies under the table as if they were teenagers and not women in their forties. As if they ached for each other and nightfall gave them permission to cast away all the pretence of the day.

I scanned the restaurant, leaving them to their peace, the tender beginnings of connection that brought so much joy. It really was a lovely establishment. No technology intruded here. Mobile phones didn't form part of life in the kingdom, and I found I didn't miss mine at all. Being in Biryani Junction reminded me of simpler times when diners didn't break conversation to answer a message. When they savoured their food and didn't think to photograph it. It wasn't the sort of place that would feature in a Michelin-starred guide, though the food smacked of flavour and was beautifully presented. It was the sort of place that small towns did so well, that wrapped you in warm nostalgia and a sense of family and tradition—the beating heart of the community.

At the other side of the restaurant, Radha proudly

showed a diner the water jug I'd made for her and painted with cherries, her favourite fruit. A man formed a mound of rice and curry with his fingertips and funnelled it into his mouth before smacking his lips with satisfaction. His young companion slurped on a glass of mango lassi. I smiled at their gusto, feeling better already in the down-to-earth ambience that evoked memories of our mother. Only then did I notice the general eating alone in a shadowy corner.

A jolt of electricity went through me as our eyes met. His injuries seemed well enough healed for him to sit and eat without discomfort, although he held his fork a little stiffly perhaps, and his informal garb and the crescent shadows under his midnight eyes suggested he needed rest. His gaze lingered on my face, scrubbed clean of makeup, my simple Punjabi suit and the messy bun at my nape before dropping to my lips. I held my breath. When Jilu approached us, wearing an apron smeared with tomato paste, I jerked my attention back to our table.

"My favourite new guests." We knew full well that there was no competition in that category, given the kingdom seldom welcomed outsiders, but he charmed us nevertheless. He brought with him a generous portion of chickpea curry, a tower of buttered naan and a salad of pickled radishes and carrots, all balanced in his practised hands. "The kitchen has closed to orders, but I would have suggested this dish to you tonight anyway."

Leena ogled the feast before us. "This is just perfect."

"It's the least I can do. I slept soundly last night because of the sleeping draught you gave me. I've had such worries about keeping our pantry stocked." He handed out plates and placed a cup of cutlery on the table. "It is Radha's very best. Earthy chickpeas in a thick sauce with a touch of mellow sweetness. Enjoy."

"Thank you, Jilu." Every cell in my body was aware of the general across the room.

We ate, surrounded by the chatter of customers, the clinking of cutlery and the gentle sound of sitar music on playback. Leena and Aanya ate with a gusto that came at the end of a hard day, not noticing when I barely joined in the conversation. I was self-conscious as I tore pieces of my naan and scooped the curry into my mouth. Deven sipped a beer. He raised it in a silent toast to me. His coal-black eyes locked onto me in a way that sent tingles down my spine.

I cleared my throat to shake off the feeling of vulnerability and decided to use my cutlery. There was something strangely intimate about a man watching me eat with my fingers. Some sauce dribbled out of the corner of my mouth. I stole a glance at Deven. Heat rose in my cheeks as I used a napkin. "He must be heavily medicated to be staring at me like that."

"What?" Leena gave me a puzzled look. A slow grin spread across her face as she looked over her shoulder. "Oh no. Apparently, the court physician just gave him some salve. Here comes trouble. He looks like a different man out of uniform."

Diners made room for him as he crossed the floor to our table, raking a hand through his tousled hair. He wore a white T-shirt over blue jeans and flip-flops. Small bandages covered his arm and chest, but his health was a million times more robust than at the end of the fight. I supposed that was thanks to his shifter genes, despite the curse. Not that he looked happy about it.

The general's expression was fierce as he nodded a greeting at Leena and Aanya and leaned over our table. Stubble lined his jaw. "You've finished with your meal?"

His presence unnerved me. Notes of soap and antiseptic hit my nose. I raised an eyebrow. "You ruined my appetite."

A nerve pulsed in his jaw. "I need to talk to you outside." It wasn't a question. It was a command. He might be out of uniform but wore authority like a second skin.

I glared at him. "Fine. I'll see you at home, Leena."

My sister gave Deven a look that could curl toes, but it was all a performance. The corners of her mouth suggested she found my predicament highly amusing. "Okay."

I followed his ramrod-straight back outside as if I was a naughty schoolgirl, garnering sympathetic looks from diners who had obviously been hauled over the coals by him before.

The cool night air washed over me as he held the door open for me and guided me around the side of the building where there were no witnesses apart from a dog licking every inch of a takeaway container. Clusters of stars formed constellations above our heads. The general stood close enough for me to see the patterns of his irises and the silvery scar above his eyebrow. The clunking breathing of the gargoyles faded into the periphery of my mind.

There was a wall at my back, and suddenly, I didn't know whether I wanted to kiss him or shout at him for unsettling me. I only knew that I felt all alone, and it was somehow Deven's fault. My thoughts didn't make any sense at all, and so I gathered my wits–despite the impoliteness of him ruining my dinner–and asked, "Are you well?"

Incredulity chased across his face. His breath was warm on my face. I could almost taste the beer, but his eyes were clear. "Weeks without talking to each other, and that's all you have to say?"

I lifted my chin, fortifying my defences, even though with his injuries, his were still porous. "We don't know each other, Deven, and we certainly don't owe each other anything." Strictly speaking, the first half wasn't true. I knew about his love for his nephew and sister because I had witnessed it. I knew about his dead wife because Farida had told me. I knew he was as opposed to the raja as I was because he had protected me. I knew about his curse because he had told me himself, though he was a secretive, stern man. I knew he was in pain because he winced when he bent to pick dirt from my hair, which I had somehow missed.

But in Jalapashu, lies made you stronger.

He frowned. "You're angry. Kiya–"

"We can't be found like this. It'll ruin everything." A commotion sounded, and I turned towards it, ignoring the undercurrent of desire that simmered between us.

CHAPTER 4

I half expected the general to chase after me. He didn't. My disappointment was dulled only because of the commotion that had erupted from a quaint house nestled near the restaurant.

Cries and the sound of breaking glass echoed through the air, together with a baby's wails. A crowd had spilt out of Biryani Junction, and I pushed my way through it to Leena and Aanya's side. My stomach knotted at the sight of a young couple on the doorstep, flanked by my portly grandfather wearing the raja's colours of purple and blue, together with a group of armed soldiers. They didn't need their steel in a civilian setting. Their intrusion at this late hour was pure malice.

"What's going on?" I whispered.

My sister wrung her hands. "Grandfather is collecting taxes. It's their last warning."

"Prakash *Saheb* has been the raja's enforcer since your mother fled the kingdom. Some say he enjoys it, but I don't believe that," said Aanya.

My anger flared, igniting my magic deep within me. It didn't matter what my grandfather believed. It only mattered what he did. Only a monster would choose to terrify a family in the middle of the night. As the soldiers ransacked her simple home, the wife clung to their swaddled son, her nightdress wet with milk. The crowd stood silent and aghast as the soldiers overturned furniture, tossed crockery through the air and gleefully heaved a bookshelf to the floor. Terror made her husband's face its canvas as he pleaded with my grandfather, but the old man pulled down his bushy brows even further. His stern expression left no room for negotiation.

Clearly, the poor family did not have the money. Not for the first time since meeting my grandfather, I was bitterly ashamed of him. I scanned the crowd, searching for pockets of courage, but found only despair. They stood in eerie silence, eyes fixed on the unfolding scene. Fear hung thick in the air, suffocating any chance of dissent. They stood like statues, witnesses to the injustice, steeling themselves against the baby's wails and the wild destruction wrought by the raja's men. Not a soul met my eyes. The contrast with the jubilant spectators of the bloodshed in the arena couldn't have been any greater. How quickly a leader's malevolence contaminated the fabric of society.

My nails dug into my palms. "Surely someone has to intervene?"

"And face the raja's wrath?" Aanya's shoulders hunched. "Many advised Minesh and Nina not to have a baby. Three mouths are harder to feed than two."

Leena huddled closer. "What happens after the final warning?"

Aanya's voice held a haunting flatness, like a broken music box. "Seizure of the house, forced labour, public humiliation... it's dependent on the raja's mood."

Her words sank in as the soldiers left the house at last, unfazed by their brutality like they'd carried out similar orders a thousand times before. My grandfather completed his lecture over the hiccupping cries of the now exhausted baby. His cheeks grew ruddy as he caught sight of us in the crowd. I was pleased that he felt some shame. Less so when he puffed out his chest like a strutting rooster and addressed the crowd.

His voice boomed like a cannon through the silence. "Go home. Go home by the decree of the Maharaja of Jalapashu."

I contrasted his fat belly and self-certainty with the cowering frames and calloused hands of the onlookers. It hit me then that the raja wasn't just skimming fat off the top. He and his acolytes channelled funds from unfair taxation into the royal purse rather than back into the kingdom. Why else were the people impoverished?

I reacted instinctively, slipping out of Leena's lightning-quick grasp despite her sharp rebuke. The crowd took a step back as my footfalls echoed across the street towards the royal grouping. My thoughts tumbled like leaves in a gust, scattered and untethered. Outright rebellion seemed impossible, but what about small defiances? There had to be some advantage I could mine to help this family. On the rooftops, the gargoyles shifted. Their roar reverberated in my head. I willed them to be quiet and let me think. They mostly listened.

Two soldiers moved to block me, their movements nonchalant. To them, I wasn't a threat.

My grandfather motioned to them to allow me passage. He smelt of sweat and aged leather. His nostrils flared as he hissed at me, low enough for the conversation to remain between us. "Foolish girl. Do you want the same thing that happened to the seer to happen to you?"

"Girl? You missed my childhood, grandfather. You never knew me as a girl."

The soldiers openly stared at my audacity as if the challenge was a relic from days gone by. As if they would never dare to challenge the status quo themselves.

His bushy eyebrows knitted together. "If you live here, you live by Prem Kumar's rules."

Disappointment made me cruel. I wanted him to be someone I could be proud of. "How does it feel to sell your dignity for a few sacks of rice?"

He jerked back as if he'd been slapped, and I almost felt sorry for him. "You don't know what you're talking about. So be it. Act like a petulant child. I won't spare you."

Defiance blazed through my veins. I gave the distraught family an encouraging smile, then adopted a carefree tone for the crowd despite the tightness in my chest. "Yesterday, the raja offered my sister and me a reprieve on paying tax. We declined his generosity, but I'm passing his reprieve onto Minesh and Nina." A coquettish laugh fell from my lips. I prayed my acting had improved since my school nativity when I'd fluffed my Mary lines and dropped baby Jesus on his head. "I'm sure to please me, the raja will make the reprieve a permanent one."

To my astonishment, Minesh and Nina knelt at my feet, showering blessings on me. Whether prompted by kindness to strangers or the fragile roots of our new friendship, Jilu–still in his smeared chef's apron–hesitated before breaking into applause. Like a contagion, the applause cascaded through the onlookers. I urged the couple to their feet and caressed the bewildered baby's cheek, hoping that I hadn't misjudged the situation and that the raja could be shamed into delivering my promise.

"Maybe you're your mother's daughter after all." A wistful expression floated across my grandfather's face. Then, it hardened. "Let's hope that the raja reacts mildly to your interference because if your pledge turns out to be wrong, it won't just be Prem Kumar who turns on you."

"Is that a threat?"

"No, child. It's a warning."

I turned away from him and sought my sister's solace in

the crowd. Instead, I found the general leaning against the tired restaurant façade. His midnight eyes were unyielding, all softness and searching erased. He pushed himself off the wall with fluid grace and stalked into the night as if we were no longer allies. As if the sparks between us had withered to nothing. As if it was impossible for him to be allies with a woman who courted Prem Kumar's favour. I bit back the words on my tongue, reminding myself that we didn't owe each other any explanations.

In the velvet night sky, a luminous green parrot spiralled, calling out for his beloved owner.

I caught an iridescent feather like a falling star and found my sister. "Does this mean–?"

"Let's find out." Leena squeezed Aanya's hand to say goodbye, not even risking the briefest kiss.

When the maid spun away, she held Leena's parting gift to her nose–a daisy to represent new beginnings–and I understood my sister and her love had found a way to communicate truthfully despite the secrets that swirled all around.

We walked home through dusty streets as the hour struck eleven. My belly fluttered. Not from apprehension but from anticipation of a reunion with Merlin. Once, I would have thought twice about two women walking home in the dark. But now, no monster could harm us without being harmed itself. We were witches. Though we carried no weapons, there had never been a time that we'd been more formidable. We were the ones to be feared. I revelled in no longer being prey.

That is if my magic didn't flounder.

The pangs in my stomach came from anticipation of a reunion with Merlin. The moon had painted the kingdom in silvery brushstrokes. I toyed with the feather between my fingers, searching for the parrot in the skies and a hare's silhouette in the shifting darkness. Shadows twisted in patterns on the ground, creating shapes that played with my mind–the hare's slender ears, the contours of his hind legs–then dissolved into obscurity.

Leena's focus was elsewhere. "You were wonderful for standing up for that poor family. We all felt the injustice of it, but…"

I frowned, barely registering a shuffling on the roof. "But what?"

Somewhere, an elephant trumpeted, and a tiger roared.

"It's just that we don't have many family members left, and I don't want to burn bridges with our grandparents." She plucked Babbu's feather out of my hand–delicate hues of jade and emerald–and pursed her lips. "Not before we get to know them."

I snorted. "I think tonight taught us all we need to know about our grandfather." There was a beat of silence. I let her words sink in, not admitting out loud that our grandmother was worth knowing, and it wasn't fair to assume that Leena would distance herself from our grandparents just because I was wary. That was the thing about sisters. They let things pass in a way that friends didn't always. Tonight, when exhaustion seeped into my bones, and my heart was sore from my training failures and the run-in with the general, I was grateful for it.

Leena chided me playfully. "You know, you've left out the juiciest bit from tonight. What did Deven want?"

My emotions swirled. I hated him getting under my skin. "It was nothing. He was all stern and brooding. I was…"

She laughed. "All uptight about how you feel about him?"

"It's not like that." I'd shut him down like a nervous teen. In truth, I didn't really know what he wanted from me.

"The longer you run from it, the harder you'll fall. Besides, he's an ally, and we have precious few of those."

"Actually, I had him as a *maybe* on my list."

She pulled up at our house. "You know as well as I do that's a pile of bull."

I chewed the inside of my cheek, startling as a grinding sound came from the rooftop. I looked up to see a gargoyle ogling Leena. It spread its lips into an adoring albeit gruesome smile. I ribbed my sister. "Love is definitely in the air."

My sister gave a heavy sigh. "You again."

The gargoyle's stony facial flesh drooped. "Gargoyles might be servile, but we have an internal world too."

This one had been enamoured with Leena since she had protected her in the heat of battle. She was an awkward soul, not only short and squat like the other gargoyles but with a fishtail that dragged along the ground and bulbous lips that barely stretched over her crumbling teeth. Her deformed wings were frayed and worn as though they had weathered countless storms. Small arms extended from a squarish upper body. The shyness in her pale yellow eyes revealed a vulnerability that contrasted with the toughness of her stony flesh. According to Leena, who had been ambushed by her before, her grey, stony flesh was cold and rough to the touch. The ambushes had grown in number since Leena and Aanya had been together.

A passerby could easily have confused the gargoyle's voice with the creaking autumn branches as they shed the last of their golden leaves, but it still wasn't wise to be so conspicuous.

Leena fiddled with the lock, eager to get inside.

I craned my neck. "This can't keep happening. You must be patient."

"I'm sorry, mistress." A creak as she drank in the sight of Leena. "I wanted her to know my name."

Leena softened and arched backwards to give the gargoyle a gentle nod of acknowledgement. "Go ahead."

The fishtail gargoyle beamed and placed a stony hand on its chest. "Sindhuja. It means 'born of the ocean.'"

My sister strained to hear, but the words flowed unimpeded into my mind. "Sindhuja."

"Sindhuja," repeated my sister. "It's nice to meet you. But please know that you don't stand a chance with me."

The moon hid behind a bank of clouds, but the gargoyle's smile was a lantern in the night sky. I wondered if, as a species, they were hard of hearing. Sindhuja either didn't hear the tail end of my sister's words or chose not to accept them. She scurried across the rooftops with a soft scraping sound, achieving minimal lift with her frayed wings.

Not for the first time since our arrival in Jalapashu, Leena and I exchanged incredulous looks.

"I'm never going to let you live this down."

"Stop it." She pushed open the door and stepped into the veiled darkness of our new home.

Sitara didn't need light. An ethereal form, she traversed the gloom, passing through objects and navigating her surroundings with ease. For her, the absence of light was irrelevant because she was part of the shadows herself. It was another matter for me. Entering through the shop front, I slipped off my shoes while Leena closed the front door. I fumbled for and failed to find the light, then skirted around the potter's wheel only to stumble into the shelving unit. The crowning glory of a new autumn-inspired tea set teetered on the edge: an ivory mug adorned with burnished crimson and gold leaves concealing a miniature ceramic pumpkin within its cup.

No sooner had I steadied it did I yelp.

CHAPTER 5

Leena flooded the studio with light, holding Babbu's feather up like a weapon.

"What are you going to do? Tickle our intruders into submission?" I grinned and peeled the squashed cherry tomato out of my toes. Only that morning, they had been plump and rosy in our fridge.

Her brow furrowed at the trail of vegetables, but I knew their meaning. A half-gnawed cucumber lay limp and discoloured in front of the door connecting our living and work quarters. We found more tomatoes bruised and oozing their pulp onto the floor. I quickened my pace. Shredded salad leaves were strewn like confetti across the threadbare bedroom.

At the fridge, a hare munched on a carrot, his whiskers quivering with pleasure.

His name leapt off my tongue like a long-awaited melody. "Merlin!"

Merlin's sooty ears turned in our direction. When I crossed the floor to him and crouched down, he hopped into my arms–a warm, quivering bundle of black and tan fur–and nuzzled against my chest. "Not so tight."

I eased my grip and murmured into his fur. "I missed you." His body radiated comfort and security. Ours wasn't a casual bond. It was more than that. His loyalty to our family had spanned generations. With his return, I already felt bolder. All the stories I'd devoured as a girl, which spoke of the link between witch and familiar, suddenly seemed more than ink and imagination. This bond was as real to me as blood and bone and my own warm flesh.

Sitara glided over to us across smeared tomatoes. "She's not even mad at you for the mess."

"Welcome home, Merlin," said Leena wryly. "I'll grab the dustpan and brush."

I rubbed the hare's ears and murmured into his fur. The scent of damp earth, light rains and foraging in the wild washed over me. No wonder he'd been hungry. After decades in the wilderness, we'd made him soft by treating him as a pet. But he'd survived, as he always had, despite my agitation.

A hint of resignation laced Sitara's words. "That affection is more than you ever showed me, Merlin."

"There's more than enough bunny love to go around." His low, rumbling voice brought back the nights our mother would sit in her rocking chair and read us fairytales. "But Kiya's nature is tactile, so we are a better fit."

Leena swept up the mess with a titter. "And you give *me* grief for being blunt."

Sitara shimmered with impatience. "As amusing as this is, I've been playing hostess. Quite frankly, I didn't even enjoy hostessing when I was alive, so I'll hand the reins over to you."

I felt a pang, knowing this was just her reinforcing to us and even herself that she wasn't in charge anymore. That I was. I understood this formed as hard a transition for her as crossing from life into death. Her gaze, which had once reminded me of emerald forests but now brought the sense of mossy graveyards, flickered to the windowsill. There, a soft rustling sound made my ears prick.

Babbu tilted his head and squawked a greeting. "Dirty hare."

My brow furrowed. Funny, this time, it didn't sound like an insult. It sounded like an endearment.

The hare wriggled in my arms. "I should tell–"

I released him from my embrace. "We'll catch up in a minute, love." I approached the parrot with caution, not wanting to spook him. The open window meant he could fly away at any moment. I frowned at Sitara before realising that, of course, she couldn't close it herself. My confidence wavered as I edged closer to the bird. We'd heard his screeches of distress across Jalapashu, but nothing like this deterioration.

"Be careful," said Leena, behind me.

Something wasn't quite right.

Babbu's once vibrant green feathers were now faded, in disarray and dotted with bald patches. His red beak, which provided a striking contrast with his green plumage, showed signs of chipping. His beady, mischievous eyes were now vacant. All in the space of a few weeks. In Boundless Bay, we'd wrapped seagulls in towels when they needed help and taken them to the vet, but rolling up a magical parrot like a burrito seemed plain wrong.

My heart went out to him. "Poor thing. You must be distraught without Mahi." I held out my hand for him to sniff and withdrew it when I remembered he wasn't a dog.

Babbu cocked his head as if studying me intently. Cogs whirred in his mind; I was sure of it. Perhaps he recalled our previous encounters or assessed whether to trust me. I had no idea where parrots stood in the memory stakes: clearly above goldfish, but perhaps not as adept as elephants. Or perhaps he had trauma-associated memory loss. He was clearly wary of forming new connections. My preparation was sorely lacking. I didn't have any sunflower seeds or bird swings or whatever else it was that made parrots happy. With a flutter of his tattered wings, Babbu hopped closer to me as if drawn by an invisible force. His weary eyes softened as our eyes locked, and I was jubilant that we would unlock Mahi's whereabouts. He hunched over, about to impart his wisdom. Then, in a wanton frenzy, he pulled out a plume of his feathers and spat them into the air with a violent squall.

I sprang back as the scraggly feathers twirled like dervishes through the air. "Babbu, it's okay. You're amongst friends now."

The parrot's beady eyes darted around haphazardly. "You took my feathers."

I raised a single eyebrow. "I really didn't."

"Certain people are above the law." His beady eyes swivelled in my direction.

Leena took offence on my behalf despite prodding me about my tactics moments before. "I'll have you know, Kiya stood up for what was right today."

He screeched. "Avian ambush." He whirled around to the open window.

Against my better judgment, I leapt forward and tackled him to the ground with my cupped hands. His feathers were both scraggly and downy. His rapid heartbeat thumped against my palms. "Shut the window, Leena."

She lunged at the window sash, her golden hair an unruly cloud. In her haste and fatigue, she smacked her forehead against the pane, then closed the window with a groan.

In his own domain, Babbu's demeanour had exuded a tempered freedom. He'd torn through the gloomy, airless halls of the seer's house with reckless abandon, fiercely guarded her doorstep and danced with joy through the skies. Yet now he was wretched and befuddled.

"You're safe here." I cradled Babbu securely, willing him to be calm.

Even in his distress, the remnants of his beauty remained. Up close, his feathers held subtle variations in colour, from vibrant greens and yellows to hidden hints of blues and reds, like a masterpiece of nature painted on his body. When his claws gently grasped my fingers, relief flooded me. I'd finally withered his resistance. I gasped as he struck out, leaving a crimson gash on my palm. The flapping bird escaped me and looked mournfully at his failed escape route.

"This is going well," deadpanned Sitara.

Babbu strutted up and down the sill, staring at himself in the window with such suspicion that he quite possibly believed that his reflection was another bird. Only when Merlin made a soft chirping sound did he turn around and find ease from his frantic movements. "Dirty hare." He nestled on the sill and closed his eyes.

This time, I was certain: his term for the hare brimmed with affection, not scorn.

Somehow, my hare had become a crutch for the worried parrot.

Merlin sighed. "Now, can I fill you in?"

I spun to him, nursing my palm. "Merlin, you knew? You knew he was volatile."

"You told me to be quiet. I obliged." His nose twitched, and he dropped his voice. "The truth is I think we made a terrible mistake when assessing the bird's faculties. I say *bird* because it wouldn't do for him to cotton on. I don't want to hurt his feelings."

Leena urged me to the tap and washed off my palm before applying a plaster. "Get to the point."

"I spent days tracking him to his nest, and even when I found him, he wouldn't come down. At first, it was easy to confuse him for a spray of evergreen leaves. His green plumage glinted like emeralds in the dappled sunlight, adding to the enchantment of the chase. He fluttered amongst the treetops, his movements like quicksilver, muttering to himself. I beckoned to him, and he ignored me. I tried to tempt him with berries and seeds. My kindness infuriated him so much that he took dumps on me from a great height. So I attempted to dislodge him and arced sticks in his direction. My aim didn't hit him once. I know what you are thinking–hares are not known for throwing skills–but I might have succeeded had Babbu not woven through the foliage, disappearing momentarily only to reappear in a different spot. Hunters tried to capture us, but we evaded them well enough with Babbu's flight and my speed."

"Hunters?"

"I know their ilk. They weren't there for sport or food. They wanted coin." The hare grunted. "After they left, I tried promising Babbu that I would take him back to the seer's house, but that scared him all the more." One of his ears was turned towards the sleeping parrot as if he monitored his own offspring. "This morning, I gave up. I worried you'd be anxious without me. As anxious as a mouse in a room full of bats."

I frowned. "Cats, surely? Not bats."

The hare sniffed. "That's what I said. I worried about you even more than Babbu's bald patches. As soon as I turned my back, he swooped down from the branches and called me dirty hare. And it touched me."

Sitara's incredulity made her flicker like a lightbulb. "It touched you?"

"I fear I am the only friend he has left."

How I'd missed his dear face. I considered him my family. I hadn't given him enough credit for creating his own families, not by blood, but by loyalty. All this time, I'd wondered if Mum had picked well in her childhood, but maybe it was Merlin who had chosen her. Maybe he was drawn to the lonely, the misfits and the broken. I'd believed for so long that we were caring for him, but in reality, he had been caring for us. With my palm patched up, Leena and I sank onto the bed. "Don't stop."

"Within hours, it became clear to me…"

His molten gold eyes shimmered in the midnight hour. "We thought the parrot was wise, and he'd be able to help us in our quest for the seer. But in fact, he is, above all else, a creature of routine and repetition. When he said 'certain people are above the law', that is not a new thought. He is simply repeating what he has heard before. They are nothing more than echoes of the seer's teachings, ingrained in his memory. Strings of words that pleased him for their cadence. Words that painted a picture in his mind. Rhythmic patterns. Phrases associated with the seer's excitement. Those are the ones he mimics. He spits them out like fortune cookies popping open without warning."

Leena nodded. "So when he says *dirty hare*, someone must have referred to you as that."

Merlin's ears flattened against his head as if this had not occurred to him before. "Obviously, a fool who doesn't realise that hares are full of possibility."

My thoughts whirled. "Their loss."

The temperature suddenly cooled, and Sitara's anger distorted her voice like a car radio going through a bad patch. "Then we are no closer to finding the seer than on the night of her disappearance when we pledged to overthrow him."

I corrected my slouch, inspiration hitting me. "You're wrong. Just because Babbu isn't sharing any new thoughts, it doesn't mean he can't help us. Think about it. Surely Mahi, with all her visions and witchcraft, must have discerned her own fate? We assumed she didn't warn us because she didn't have a chance to. But what if she didn't warn us because she had already planted the knowledge we needed? Not in plain sight, but hidden in Babbu's mind, in her house, maybe even in the royal court itself." I dragged in a deep, healing breath as my resolve grew. "I'm going to court tomorrow, as we agreed. And one of you will be listening very carefully to Babbu's *bon mots*."

Molten gold eyes in a sooty face. "Kiya, that's not a good idea. Terrible things happened to your mother at court."

Sitara scowled. "She won't be told."

I shrugged. "Bad things happen all the time. I just have to be prepared."

"Then we won't sleep until you are ready," said the hare.

He kept his word. Sitara left us to go on her nightly wanderings, for our ghost sister wasn't as tethered to our world as she wanted us to believe. As the night passed its darkest point and began to lighten, Leena said goodnight, slipped off her clothes into a heap, and soon, her gentle snores reached us in the studio where we worked.

My frazzled mind knew the joy of my reunion with Merlin but also with time carved out for my passion for clay. Though night wrapped around us, my time at the potter's wheel healed my soul as much as sleep healed my body. My injured palm caused me no bother. Leena had wrapped it well, and clay was forgiving. I leaned forward over the wheel, a smile on my face. My foot worked the pedal. Outside, the stars shone. Everything fell away: the gargoyle's breathing, my false bravado about what lay ahead, my guilt about Mahi's long wait for her rescue, my angst about the raja's reaction to my interference in tax matters, even the swirling cauldron of emotions I harboured for the general. It all fell away, a great shedding and cleansing as my fingers touched the spinning clay, shaping vessel after vessel that I filled with spells.

The spells came more easily with Merlin at my side. Our connection stemmed from truth and generosity. It was impossible to distinguish where my thoughts ended and the hare's began. I didn't stop to think. Vowels tumbled together. There was *tyāga* and *tvamapaśya*, which I'd used before. New spells came to me unbidden–*krodho nivartatām, mohitaḥ bhava, vismar* and *mayi premaṃ patiṣyasi*–nebulous threads that I coaxed into being. My mind folded and crumpled and was remade anew. All the while, my hands worked, and the potter's wheel whirled. The power intoxicated me. Magic was flowing with instinct, breath and play. It was energy tangling and rhythms weaving. It was darkened canopies, trails of luminescence and mystical maps I trusted but couldn't yet follow. Invisible beneath my skin on my left thigh, an inch below the pelvic bone, the topaz jewel–the legacy of my ancestors, hidden by the seer–burned hot.

The hare stood vigil, his chest puffed with pride.

When we had finished our work, and the kiln hummed its familiar song, I washed up in the studio to the sound of Merlin's gentle grumbling and crept into the living quarters to sweep the parrot's scraggly emerald feathers into a cardboard box. It didn't seem right to discard parts of him when he was so vulnerable. That seemed akin to giving up on Babbu, and I wanted with all my heart to see him return to his glorious, maddening, unencumbered self. I crawled on my hands and knees, collecting the feathers, then tore a tatty scarf into strips before transferring the makeshift nest to a safe spot on the kitchen counter. With a wry glance at my injured palm, I placed the napping parrot in it while Merlin made soft chirping sounds.

At long last, with the spells still turning over in my mind, I stripped off my clothes, turned out the lamp Leena had left burning and crawled into the remaining single bed. The mattress sagged beneath me. I sighed as Merlin laid his soft body against the back of my bare legs.

Within seconds, the curtain of sleep fell.

CHAPTER 6

Tranquillity ebbed away, replaced by the vibrant chaos of mornings in the kingdom. Calls of market vendors, the clatter of pots and pans and the chatter of neighbours slipped past the single windowpanes. I pushed away an object that scratched the soft flesh of my upper arm and peeled open my eyes. The parrot perched on my headboard, his scraggly body hanging downwards 180 degrees so that his sharp beak and beady eyes loomed millimetres from my head.

He squawked at me. "Melon."

I made a hasty retreat from my bed. Little harbinger of doom. Even his breakfast request sounded ominous. "Men barking orders at women went out of fashion with corsets and powdered wigs." I leaned over warily to straighten the covers. My heart skipped a beat.

"Actually, corsets are back in fashion." Leena approached with two mugs of tea. "What's wrong?"

The bed looked like a chaotic battlefield. The thin mattress bore imprints of my sleeping body, the covers twisted in disarray and balls of fluff from Merlin's coat. What gave me real cause for concern were dozens of Babbu's tatty feathers scattered across the bed. They lay askew and crumpled as if I had crushed them with my body. I scanned the parrot for signs of further anxiety attacks, but his balding spots had not grown. Inexplicably, he had ferried the feathers from his makeshift cardboard box nest to my mattress.

Babbu cocked his head. "Melon."

Leena pressed the mug into my hand. "He's an odd one, all right."

"I'm out of my depth." I gave her a wry smile. "Thanks for the tea."

Deep brown eyes met my hazel ones. "You're not alone, you know. We'll work this out together."

The tea burned a trail down my throat. My eyes drifted across the chaotic jumble of our new home. If I allowed the disarray of our surroundings to consume me, how could I ever summon the strength to face the difficult challenges that lay ahead?

My sister looped her arm around my waist. "Don't let small things derail you. Let me worry about the mess today. Don't think I didn't notice all those vessels in the studio this morning. You and Merlin have been hard at work."

I gave her a weak smile. "Where is he?"

"Trying to get hold of melon for Babbu. Underneath that roaming, guileful, sometimes petulant personality is a real sense of attachment to those who need him." She took my mug as soon as I finished it. "Given you've made up your mind about court today, I asked Lokesh *Saheb* to help you dress the part. Pockets included, of course. You have an appointment with him at 10 o'clock."

I glanced at our tired old wall clock. "That's in half an hour."

"You'd better get a wriggle on then." Her nose wrinkled. "And Kiya? Take a shower. Our house smells like a farm right now, and you need to be your ravishing self."

MISTIMING HAIR WASH DAY WAS TYPICAL OF ME. I RUSHED towards the palace in leggings and a T-shirt, calling out muffled hellos to curious neighbours. The scent of fallen leaves and earthy musk wafted into my nose. My wet hair clung to my back like seaweed adorning a rock. On my shoulder, a bag clanked with an array of small vessels that an unseasoned observer might have confused for make-up containers, perfume bottles or a portable apothecary. I crossed my fingers that the royal tailor would hide them within my skirts without becoming suspicious. The crisp air blew goosebumps up my arms and damp back as I pushed on towards his atelier, through dusty streets clogged with market stalls where the aroma of freshly brewed chai mixed with the scent of flatbreads and lime chutneys and tables of vibrant textiles and bowls of trinkets gleamed in the autumn sun.

On the rooftops, the gargoyles pivoted their stone necks to an imperceptible degree to track my progress. Even if I hadn't sensed their scrutiny, the soft grinding in my mind would have revealed their keen interest. *I am a witch*, sang my interval voice, foolish glee fountaining at my core. I fought my hubris. My witchcraft was just beginning. I was untested and unmoored, as unsure of myself as I was of my magic. What good was power unless you knew how to use it?

Leena's idea to book me a coveted appointment with Lokesh *Saheb* had been inspired. She had a natural flair for fashion; I did not. Leena took pleasure from playing with colour and form, whereas I favoured practicality and earth-toned attire. As a ghost, Sitara's attire never changed. She wore the same linen shift dress in faded orange she had worn the day she raised a tempest from our kitchen sink. The day she died. But in life, her fashion choices had reflected her disciplined and structured nature, tailored to fit her curvy figure. In my twenties, I'd found myself plain and dowdy in comparison to my sisters. In time, I understood beauty wasn't limited to a single definition. It could be many things: seduction, self-expression, simplicity, glamour, professionalism, authenticity, elegance. We were simply ourselves.

"No whalebone corset today?" I asked at the sight of the options the tailor had prepared for me.

"You're already anxious enough," said Lokesh *Saheb*.

I blew out a breath. I'd been sure I'd masked my emotions. But Lokesh *Saheb* didn't care. He was already deeply involved in my transformation. I gave myself over to the poking, prodding and squeezing of him and his assistant, trusting that by the time he had finished, I would blend seamlessly into courtly life. Forty minutes in his atelier was enough for a complete transformation. When he was done, and his assistant had cleared away the blow drier and the trolley of make-up and hairpins, the tailor patted me with his brightly-feathered walking stick and urged me towards the cheval mirror.

The woman in the mirror was me, but not me. Lokesh *Saheb* had managed to mask my flaws and highlight my beauty. But it was more than that. He'd intrinsically understood the parts of my body I disliked and the parts I secretly loved but had never voiced out loud for fear of seeming arrogant.

Gone were the shadows under my eyes, the wet mop of hair, the love handles and the stress blemish on my chin. A *salwar kameez* in rich maroon fabric draped my curves with finesse. Gold embroidery traced delicate patterns along the deep neckline and knee-length hem. Three-quarter sleeves added a touch of sophistication, revealing stacks of slim gold bangles around my wrists. Beneath the *kameez*, palazzo trousers in a matching hue and soft billowing fabric left my movements unrestricted. A gold gauze *dupatta* looped across my breasts and cascaded from my shoulders, obscuring the bulging vessels in my generous pockets. Simple studs and mid-heeled strappy sandals completed the ensemble. My dark hair, now dry, had been teased into a chignon and secured with decorative gemstone hairpins. Lokesh *Saheb*'s assistant had applied simple make-up: smoky eyeliner, bronze eyeshadow and mascara to accentuate the depth of my hazel eyes, and a hint of blush and dusty rose lipstick restored a freshness to my face that tiredness had chased away.

For a moment, I almost didn't miss my clay-splattered overalls.

I turned to the tailor with a soft voice, gratitude swelling, "How can I repay you?"

Shrewd eyes twinkled beneath a silken black turban. "My dear, your attire is borrowed, not gifted. Besides, I have an inkling that my generosity will pay for itself in kind when the gentlemen of the court are enthralled, and ladies flock to me demanding the same result without the same canvas."

I flushed. If the courtiers looked at me, it was because I was an outsider. "You tease me."

The old man gave a staccato tap of his walking stick on the sprung floor. "I do not. Just be sure to greet Prem Kumar before all others. It is good for your well-being and my business to know which side your bread is buttered on."

I nodded, wondering where he would stand on my list. Whether, in time, he would be a trustworthy member of our rebellion or the raja's stooge like my grandfather. I bit my lip. Our brief encounters had made me fond of him, but the tailor had an enviable position in the life of the kingdom. He was one of the rare non-magicals with a home in the palace, with skilled work that was central to courtly life, and removed from all the pettiness of court politics.

Lokesh *Saheb* smiled. "What makes you think I don't have magic?"

My eyes widened. I stumbled on my heels, mortified that I'd not been more careful. "I'm sorry–"

He steadied me despite his frailty. Then he removed a pocket watch and chain from his lapel and opened its back to show me a tiny topaz jewel embedded in the clockwork. His eyes gleamed with amusement.

"I thought it was customary in Jalapashu to wear topaz openly to denote belonging to the highest class of citizens, as a sign of power and magic?"

"I've never needed to show evidence of my worth. Let them think that I am beneath them even when they beg for an appointment." He chuckled. "Reading their minds without them knowing keeps me safe. Why do you think I've lasted so long in this palace, let alone in fashion? In all these years, only three people within these walls have known my secret, Kiya. I'll take your secrets to the grave if you keep mine."

I sucked in my breath, instinctively driving my hand to my pockets, where my fingers found the shape of the tapered vessel with a forgetfulness spell. In our brief moments together, how many secrets had he unravelled with his telepathy? My deepest insecurities, hidden desires, buried regrets, haunting trauma, my ambitions for Jalapashu or maybe even secrets swirling in my subconscious I hadn't even admitted to myself.

The tailor laid a hand on my arm, all the while peering at my pockets. "I'm no threat to you. We all do what we must to thrive."

"Can you help me find out what happened to the seer?"

"I don't get involved in inter-court warfare. I'd like to keep my head on my shoulders."

At that moment, his assistant returned, and Lokesh *Saheb* resumed his persona as an uncompromising artisan, interested only in the running of his studio and the waves his creations would make at court.

I loosened my grip on the tapered vessel, praying I'd made the right decision. "Thank you for today."

He gave me the slightest nod. It was as much a dismissal as an acknowledgement.

I steeled myself and descended the cool, winding stairs to the ground floor. The querying glances of servants followed me through the myriad of corridors leading to the throne room, and I missed my sisters and Merlin fiercely. There was no turning back when I reached the carved doors, and a horn player signalled my arrival.

With a ragged breath, I lifted my chin and sashayed into the throne room. My breathing quickened as its occupants swivelled in interest. Sunlight streamed through tall arched windows, caressing the polished marble columns and casting a sun-kissed glow on murals of epic battles and courtly life. Courtiers mingled in clusters, perhaps fifty in total, sipping fruit-infused water in varying hues from elegant crystal glasses. The aroma of freshly cut flowers in ornate vases filled the air. With each step, the heels of my sandals drove into the wool carpet.

The ruby-and-emerald-encrusted throne stood empty, but by the way the court flocked to his side, it was easy to locate Prem. He wore a turquoise *kurta* and trousers and artfully dishevelled shoulder-length hair. His beard and the angle of his crown gave him the look of a rogue despite his riches.

I held my head up and inserted an extra sway into my walk as I passed column after column. Seduction wasn't my intention; rather, I wanted to obscure my silhouette with the flowing fabric, lest eagle eyes catch onto the contents of my pockets. I wasn't the only exotic creature in the room. Gilded cages held unassuming songbirds chirping impossibly intricate melodies. Silvery fish swam backwards in small, glowing tanks. Rabbits with horns and luminescent fur hopped through elaborate runs. Courtiers gathered around, spellbound and hastening for pouches of coin.

Whispers rose like the tide as I made my way to the raja's side. Aanya, serving wine from a carafe in the midst of a small group, gave me an encouraging smile. I spotted my grandparents: her all dolled up in a *sari* and flushed with happiness, him scowling as though a raccoon had raided his well-stocked pantry. The general lingered by a marble pillar, resplendent in his military uniform, his starched saffron cuffs and high collar contrasting with his hooded obsidian gaze. I hadn't told him I was coming. It wasn't his business. His presence made me feel both safe and in freefall. My breath bottled as I walked towards the man at the centre of it all.

At my approach, the raja's striking blue eyes grew glacial, and he whispered to an aide.

My stomach clenched, but I forced myself to give him a radiant smile. I'd seen countless men use this blustering tactic over the years. I didn't see why it shouldn't work for me.

Confusion marred his features, then, with a glimmer of a reciprocal smile, he held out his hand for mine as I reached him. "There had been whispers that you wouldn't fit in at court. That your parents had pushed your English heritage but neglected your Indian one." His blue eyes travelled over my body as his thumb stroked the back of my hand. "The naysayers were wrong. Confidence emanates from your every pore. You wear traditional clothing, yet you sparkle with modernity. You are the queen I have been waiting for."

The air was still, laced with danger until I let a soft laugh fall from my lips. I withdrew my hand and smoothed my outfit, drawing his gaze. "Aren't you a charmer? I am no queen, and I certainly don't seek a throne." Perhaps I was a better actress than I had given myself credit for. Maybe authenticity and deceit weren't natural qualities but rather learned and practised, and it was becoming easier for me to lie. Easier to find the dark side of myself in a world of shadows.

Prem's smile faltered for a moment, but he quickly recovered. After all, the court watched, and Aanya told me that courtly life was all about charades and intrigues and ostentatious displays of love and lust, cruelty and wit, art and wealth. He fixed his smile back in place, and within the glint in his icy eyes, I noticed once again how intriguing he found my defiance. That he was a man who loved the chase but perhaps not the courting. That maybe he would toy with me and skip straight to the kill. That his tiger side held sway even when he walked in his human form.

He turned to the court with a sweeping gesture. "A woman who shuns power. That only makes her more alluring."

A chorus of amusement echoed through the courtiers. Even the sternest faces chuckled. I was under no illusions that they accepted me. They smiled because the raja willed it. He was a master manipulator, skilled in the art of bending people to his will. Here, every smile, every gesture was a transaction.

Underneath my honeyed exterior, a storm brewed. I longed to spring a trap: to plunge the courtiers into a pit of their own deceit, to root Prem to the ground, to make him as immovable as ancient oaks, to crumble his façade like dry desert sand succumbing to the wind, to build a new unsullied kingdom from what remained.

He raised a hand, and in the corner of the throne room, a musical ensemble started up, consisting of a *sitar*, *tabla* drums, and a lute-like instrument called the *sarod*. The trio of instruments filled the room, creating a tapestry of soul-stirring sounds that sent the caged animals into a frenzy.

The raja ignored them. "Tell me, have you and your sister made any progress with those quaint powers of yours?"

I prayed he couldn't read the telltale signs of my lies: my sweaty palms, the slight tremor in my voice, my pounding heart, and the way my gaze flickered away from his. "No. They tell me magic takes a long time to flourish."

"That is true. My people are descendants of the founders of Jalapashu. Technically, they could all have magic, but I am choosy about who I give the gems to. After all, I only have a limited supply." He paused. "I *could* gift you one."

Had he really convinced himself that we were so inno-cent? Or did he enjoy playing with his prey? "That's not necessary."

"Of course, it would only be appropriate under certain circumstances." His eyes flicked to the dais, where the throne sat. "My queen will be as powerful as me."

My body tensed. "She would be a lucky woman."

"I could arrange for you to have a mentor. Perhaps your grandfather. It would be a chance for old wounds to heal, perhaps."

I wondered bitterly if this particular track had been my grandfather's doing. If he had been too cowardly to make inroads himself. He had asked the raja to command me when an apology would have sufficed. "Our estrangement is diffi-cult to breach."

Prem compressed his lips. "You will make efforts because it pleases me. After all, your sister is already making strides in that respect."

I frowned. "You must be mistaken."

"A raja has eyes and ears everywhere. But you, Kiya, you can't hope to know everything that goes on in Jalapashu." There was an unmistakable edge to his tone that sent a chill through me. "Which brings me to an altogether different matter. My courtiers tell me the talk on the streets is that Jala-pashu has found a new heroine."

I struggled to maintain my composure. How dare he try to turn Leena and me against each other? He would have no qualms about casting us adrift into a stormy ocean, far from the shore, or locking us away in the darkest dungeons of the palace, or throwing us into the arena to partake in a ruthless contest for entertainment. He was power and wrath and vanity, and I hated him. He would think nothing of placing us where the light never reached, and the air was thick with despair, hollowed-out dreams and haunting laments until nothing was left of us except powdery bones.

His manicured hands told me that he wouldn't even get his hands dirty.

Why, then, did we risk it all when fear gnawed at the edges of my mind? When lesson after lesson showed me the colours of the raja's soul? He was a monster who had set in motion Sitara's death. He had all but confirmed his complicity in the seer's disappearance by erasing her name from the lips of the people who had lived side by side with her all her life. He didn't hesitate to turn Jalapashan families out of their homes if it suited him.

Yet I couldn't turn away. This was a story begun long ago by my mother and continued by Sitara—a story of our ancestral magic and the pursuit of justice. Even now, my magic resonated through my being, like the whisper of wind on a crisp autumn day, carrying the wisdom of ages and the echoes of ancient incantations. Its current told me I could overpower Prem Kumar. The way he underestimated me told me I could outwit him. As long as I held my nerve.

A shiver went up my spine as I stepped closer and laid a hand on his breast. He smelt of sandalwood, musk and clove. Under other circumstances, the contours of his body, the brilliance of his eyes and the power he emanated might have been intoxicating. "What do you think of this new heroine, Prem-ji?"

Underneath my palm, his heartbeat was slow and steady: a king comfortable in his power.

"I'm intrigued, of course. But heroes and heroines tend to be reckless. One wrong move and..." He trailed a bejewelled finger across his neck and down the length of my arm.

The weight of his words tightened like a noose tightening around my neck. I shivered, my mind siphoning through the little grenades in my pocket: the potent spells held in pretty vessels.

He seemed to translate the shiver as pleasure. His eyes dropped to my lips.

I murmured. "Perhaps the people would respond to a softer touch."

Prem's lips curled into a mirthless smile. His eyes didn't leave mine, and his voice was low and velvety. "Power is not about what the people want. It's about control and maintaining order. The people may desire softness, but they need strength."

Despite the melodies woven by the ensemble, the courtiers' interest remained wholly with us. They weighed every look, word and gesture that passed between the raja and me. Some had pigeon-holed me as a plaything. Others looked amused. A few cast me pitying looks. Only the general and my grandfather glowered as if I had intruded somewhere I didn't belong, and they wanted to smack my behind and tuck me up into bed.

Watch, I thought. *Watch all you hangers-on, craven pawns and faithless bystanders. You're so content to revel in this rotting kingdom as long as your share of power and privilege remains intact. Chalk me up as an inexperienced gauche. I will take your secrets and find my friend.*

I kept my voice soft and teasing, though inside, I burned with resolve. "Is that right? It's a shame I'm not a heroine, then. They tend to inspire change."

Prem chuckled softly. "You have spirit, Kiya Marlowe. I'm charmed. I'm sure that was your intention."

The idea crossed my mind to confront him directly about Mahi's whereabouts. Could I shame him into revealing the truth? Maybe the attraction he felt for me could translate into something useful. But opting for truth rather than playing the game of lies would be a perilous gamble. I needed to be cautious and strategic, using every ounce of wit and magic I possessed. Prem Kumar was more than a man and more than a raja. He was a wild beast. I'd witnessed the gouges on the thick carpet in his chambers and the claw marks in the drapes. He appeared docile for a moment, but his primal instincts would resurface.

"I have business to attend to now," said the raja. "Mingle, my dear. One day, these courtiers may be attending to you, too. But be sure to come and see me before evening falls. I have a favour to ask of you. After all, you did use my name without permission." He turned his back, calling out over his shoulder. His crown caught the autumn light. "And Kiya?"

My stomach fell like a stone. "Yes, Prem-ji?"

A hard smile. "Never interfere in taxation matters again."

CHAPTER 7

Smarting at the raja's rebuke, I surrendered myself to the pulsating rhythm of court life. As a natural introvert, I preferred the solitude of my pottery studio to crowds. The admiring gazes I drew added to my vulnerability. I longed for my sisters' company as a crutch, even though one sister was dead and the other babysat the seer's unhinged parrot. The goosebumps chasing up my arms were nothing to do with Sitara. She was more unbiddable as a ghost than she had been in real life, and that was saying something.

There was no option but to execute my plan.

Scanning the throne room to get my bearings, I steeled my nerves. The raja and his entourage peered into the songbird cages and marvelled at the horned rabbits. Courtiers flitted about like butterflies in jewel-toned turbans, intricate *saris* and embroidered *sherwanis*. The air was infused with the scent of food and flowers. Bouquets of vivid marigolds, unfurled lilies and crimson rosebuds caught my eye. Servers dressed in simple cotton clothing circulated with canapés. At the edges of the room, silk curtains fluttered in a barely-there breeze.

The music held an air of unpredictability that mirrored the court's dynamics. The *sitar's* lilting strings and the *sarod's* sweetness, mixed with the *tabla's* rhythmic beats, stirred a primal urge to dance. I wanted to give in. I wanted to be merry and dance and allow myself to drink in the sights, sounds and tastes of what my mother had experienced long ago.

But I had a job to do.

With deft fingers, I checked the vessels in my pocket. Their various shapes, sizes and textures allowed me to distinguish between them even without looking. I pulled out one that resembled a perfume bottle, with a slender neck, delicate etchings and a cork lid. Its unassuming appearance disguised the powerful enchantment it contained. *I am a witch*. The thought spun in my head, mingling with the vowels and consonants of the confusion spell as I brought the bottle to my pulse points. *Mohitaḥ bhava*. Merlin had assured me that a simple intention would activate the spell.

My plans had been carefully laid. After all, the rumours I intended to spread couldn't be pinpointed back to me. That would jeopardise everything.

Deven lingered in the shadows, his face brooding.

I turned my face away, ignoring the jump of my pulse. My clothes swished, and my feet protested in the heeled sandals as I wove through the clusters of courtiers. At court, artifice was armour. But I was here for the whispers of long-held ambitions, clandestine romances and covert plots. I was confident I could siphon clues about Mahi's disappearance from the atmosphere of rivalry and confessions. A potter paid attention to fine details and surface cracks. Like clay, people were malleable and yielding, shaped by their interactions. Like clay, people had the capacity to harden over time.

Here goes nothing. I smiled warmly at Bhavesh, one of the trio of sorcerers who had unleashed a searching fog at Prem's command during the Maharaja's Summer Soiree. "Sorcerer, how wonderful to see you again."

A calculating smile played on his lips beneath his wiry moustache. "You have a talent for finding your way into places you don't belong. Much like I did at your age."

My laugh tinkled. "If curiosity is a vice, Bhavesh *Saheb*, then I am guilty. I have never seen such sights."

His smile widened a fraction. "My old man's eyes grow tired of marvels. I find the arrival of new blood far more enchanting."

I sensed my opening and seized it. "New arrivals must be the topic of the day. I just heard the seer has been sighted at a remote temple on the outskirts of the kingdom. I do wish she'd said goodbye."

A glint of interest sparked in his milky eyes. He leaned closer, close enough for me to release the confusion spell. "Is that so?"

Mohitaḥ bhava. My magic flowed like a soft gust of wind brushing against my skin. There was a subtle shift in the air. "Of course, keep it to yourself. You know how rumours spread."

Bewilderment clouded his gaze as if he struggled to piece together the fragments of our conversation. Giddy relief flooded me, but I kept my face as still as a porcelain mask. How easy to pull the wool of a sorcerer's eyes when he believed my magic was nothing compared to his.

"I won't keep you any longer, Bhavesh *Saheb*. I'm sure you have your own intrigues to attend to."

He nodded and moved away to tend to his affairs, a faint flicker of confusion lingering on his brow. The rumours would soon ignite like wildfire precisely because I had asked him not to utter them further. Rumours were the engine of places such as these. They were currency: a commodity to be traded and manipulated for personal gain, holding the power to build alliances or destroy reputations, sway opinions or incite rebellion.

Rebellion. The word became a chant in my head, looping like a mantra.

I made my way deeper into the sea of vibrant colours. Food formed an integral part of court life. The canapés made my stomach rumble: crisp vegetable *pakoras*, cucumber cups with a blend of seasoned chickpeas and tangy tamarind sauce, skewers of marinated paneer and charred bell peppers drizzled with honey, spicy potato cutlets dotted with green chutney and miniature *samosas* with glistening golden pastry. On a circular tiered dessert table, rose-flavoured gulab *jamuns*, golden *jalebis*, cascading pyramids of lychees, and pineapple orbs sparkled like jewels in the afternoon light. The middle tier held fruit tarts with shiny glazes sprinkled with edible flowers and almond-studded *barfis*. At the pinnacle of the display, flutes of passion fruit juice, flavoured water and fragrant saffron *lassis* beckoned with their intense hues.

How wasteful the extravagant spread was when everyday people in Jalapashu struggled to feed their families.

I frowned as a change of musical rhythm resulted in a strange wave of euphoria from the munching courtiers. Only then did it occur to me that the music wasn't any old ensemble. It was magic: sensory manipulation that intensified flavours and evoked memories of cherished meals from years past. Snippets of conversation reached me of street food in Kolkata, dance festivals in Punjab, bustling bazaars in Mumbai and family meals in Delhi. I clamped my lips shut, vowing not to sample a morsel in case my judgment, too, was clouded. In case I lost track of my goals.

But Aanya had other ideas. She found me and pushed a pomegranate tartlet towards me. "Eat. One bite will ward off the musical spell. More than one will muddy your mind and sweep you along in your bliss. I won't take no for an answer."

I bit into the tartlet. The sharpness of the pomegranate and the sweetness of honey drizzle danced on my tongue like a spring breeze.

Aanya handed me a napkin. "It's good, isn't it?"

"Like nothing I've tasted in this world." I eyed up her platter.

She inched it away, her face tight with worry. "Have you had any luck?"

A shake of my head. "I'm planting seeds. Who knows what I will sow."

Her singsong voice eased the tightness in my chest. "I've been keeping my eyes and ears peeled. Your grandfather seems highly strung. It's unusual for him. He usually plays the game well."

I spotted him in the crowd, ruddy-faced and bristling. "He can't stomach my presence here. He'd rather we were meek and grateful. Or maybe he'd rather we disappear from Jalapashu altogether."

"Family is complicated. Perhaps there's still a way to bridge the gap between you." Her doe eyes on mine. "Be careful, or your sister will never forgive me."

She moved on with her platter to the next courtier, leaving me to wonder whether the family complications referred to her own or ours or whether, in a world like this, friendship surpassed biological bonds. My grandfather barrelled towards me, his lips pressed into a thin line, but I darted towards a courtesan standing alone, whose dancing had mesmerised me at the Summer Soiree. He was too proud to interrupt me.

The courtesan's pretty face shuttered at the sight of me. "Kiya. We have yet to be formally introduced. I'm Lata."

I offered her a smile, plotting which morsel I would share. "You look beautiful. One of Lokesh *Saheb*'s creations?"

A topaz jewel shone like a star on her forehead. She gave me a pointed stare. "I'm his muse, he says. Although perhaps he has found another one."

I preferred sisterhood to rivalry. Self-deprecation was an easy way to connect with her. "Hardly. Do you know how much work this took?"

Lata flashed a sweet smile, placated. "Beauty might seem effortless, but we all know it takes diligent application."

Pity welled up inside me, suspecting that she'd never known the freedom of venturing into public in her pyjamas or lounging in bed with a lover without a full face of make-up, or going a week without wearing a bra just for the free-wheeling joy of it.

Was I as bad as the raja for manipulating her? I took a cleansing breath and swallowed my guilt about the lies I told. I had no choice but to involve her in my schemes.

Dipping my voice, I leaned closer. "Some aren't interested in the shackles of society. A close confidante of the raja told me that Mahi withdrew from court so she could live a secluded, peaceful life as a hermit."

Lata's eyebrows knitted together in surprise, but she quickly composed herself. "That can't be true. The seer revelled in her power."

"Apparently, she packed a bag before she vanished." I shrugged before grasping her hands and placing a kiss on her cheek. "You smell as wonderful as you look."

Mohitaḥ bhava. The spell drifted into the air.

A look of befuddlement passed over her dainty features before a tinge of pleasure coloured her cheeks. For a moment, I glimpsed the person beneath the veneer of courtly etiquette. "It's my own concoction. A blend of rose petals, wild lavender and a few drops of citrus."

"You must be quite the alchemist."

"I like science."

"Yet you became a dancer."

"My face was like a flower, so I found myself at court."

She had buried her authentic self. For what? With the echoes of rebellion chanting in my heart, I said goodbye, hoping that meeting Leena could rekindle Lata's scientific passions when this was all over.

The general watched from afar, tracking my every move.

The court poet came next. His love of stories made him a prime target. Then, the sorceress with the *jhumka* earrings. I smiled warmly and asked about their families and for tips on fitting in at court. It was easy to feign innocence, easier than I thought. The lies spilt from my lips, on and on until they sickened me.

"Word has it that the seer was spotted near the ancient banyan tree, sharing cryptic messages with a cloaked figure. A clandestine meeting, it seems."

"I heard the seer travelled to a distant land to study ancient healing techniques."

"Mahi disappeared into a book of ancient spells written by a long-forgotten wizard."

"The seer took refuge in the Amber Hollows and will return with a wheelbarrow of jewels."

The afternoon slowed and stretched, seeming both fleeting and eternal, and time reeled away like a ribbon. Every now and then, Prem smiled at me from across the room. He was occupied, ostensibly so as if he revelled in the trappings and machinations of courtly life. His court was a battlefield of ambition and aspiration. His attention and favour were the ultimate prizes.

Not everyone welcomed me. Some viewed me as a threat or with suspicion. Some noticed my presence in their midst and chose to speak Hindi, Urdu or Gujarati instead of English just to freeze me out. Once, it would have killed me to let a false narrative about myself stand. Now, I didn't care what they chose to believe. It served my purpose to let the court think that I had no grasp of my mother tongue when, in fact, our mother had insisted on grounding us in it through chatter, Bollywood movies and songs.

Over and over, I sowed seeds of deception. Over and over, I released the *mohitaḥ bhava* spell. My initial glee at my mastery of the spellwork morphed into silt on my soul. Eventually, as Merlin had forewarned, the time came when the spell fizzed but no longer delivered. I'd drained the vessel of its magic, and to recast it, I would need to return to the potter's wheel because my magic was rooted in earth and clay. It didn't matter; I felt in my bones that the landscape had already shifted.

After all, lies could cause ruptures as potently as weapons.

By the time the sun began its descent, the whispers had marinated and taken on new forms. Conversations flowed like a river around me. Conflicting accounts took root, and soon, the court buzzed with intrigue. Some paid rapt attention, and others concealed their curiosity behind masked expressions. Some showed discomfort, and most were so engorged with the thrill of gossip that they continued the chain of retellings. The raja was oblivious. He sat high and mighty on his throne, encircled by courtiers who–judging by their raised index fingers and quick-fire outbursts–seemed to be haggling, their voices intermingling like a tapestry of negotiation and commerce.

When I could no longer stomach another moment, I stood against a cool pillar near the throne, feet sore and mouth dry, to observe the reactions. Despite the tailor's skill, my clothes hung heavy on my body, and I longed for simpler garments.

Footsteps sounded behind me, and a none-too-gentle grip tightened around my elbow.

My heartbeat drummed. I swivelled and looked up. "What the–?"

Inky eyes stared down at me. His neck was corded, and his Adam's apple bobbed in his throat. "What are you doing here, Kiya? Hours I've watched you circle through this room, oblivious to the shark-infested waters. I didn't take you for such a talker."

I jerked my head back. If he knew anything about me, he would know that talking depleted my energy, and my mouth was as dry as a dessert. "Arrogant much? I don't answer to you, Deven."

His touch ricochetted up my arm, sending colour to my face and heat to my core. "You should have stayed away. You gain nothing by coming here. There's only gossip and intrigue, alliances and betrayals. Is it power you covet? You don't know these people like I do. If you come here, every move is scrutinised. Every word carries weight."

I swallowed hard and pulled my arm away. My voice was barely audible. "How quick you are to paint me as naïve, General. Not power. *Justice.* I want the seer back. I want the raja gone. And I'm going to use every skill in my arsenal to make it happen."

A storm passed over his features, but he was too adept in this environment to let it linger when every expression was read and decoded. He plucked a flute of sherbet from a passing server and pressed it into my hand. "Then we are still on the same page. You don't think I want that, too?"

I released a breath I didn't know I'd been holding and drank from the glass, letting it quench my parched throat. The music whirled around us. "You distanced yourself from me."

He scoffed. "I distanced myself? You're the one who ran from me when we spoke outside Biryani Junction. You're the one who has been using Prem's name as currency and batting your eyelashes at him for all the court to see."

I gritted my teeth. "I need him to think he has a chance with me. Just for now." I felt dirty even saying it.

He scowled. "That doesn't explain why you ran from me. Am I really that intimidating?"

My breath caught in my chest. "Don't flatter yourself."

He hitched an eyebrow. "Then tell me."

I hoped to hell I hadn't misread the current between us. "Romance isn't my priority."

A sigh of frustration. "Nor is it mine. I want to help you. Tell me your schemes."

I turned back to my task, surveying the courtiers bathed in the soft hues of the evening light.

His voice was gravelly in my ear. "You can't do this alone. It's too dangerous. You need me."

I huffed out a breath. "If you must know, I've been spreading rumours. Boundless Bay is a small town. I know how communities work. Rumours provoke chain reactions. Now we simply listen for wisps of information, decode expressions and search for signs of unease and guilt."

The general's coal-black eyes widened. The twitch in the corner of his mouth showed he'd noted the *we* and how he'd finally whittled down my barriers. "You started rumours to ferret out where the seer is? Didn't it cross your mind that someone will identify you as the troublemaker?"

"I used a confusion spell to mask my involvement."

A bark of laughter. "I'm impressed. But your efforts might come to nothing or take too long. I'm not sure how much time the seer has."

I glared at him. Failure would be a bitter pill to swallow. "Aanya's position as a maid means she can listen out even if nothing transpires today." I didn't mention how helpful Sitara's nightly wanderings were. It tickled me that her ghost self was still a secret from him. We could have a bit of fun with that. Especially since he'd pooh-poohed my plan. "What have *you* been doing? She's your friend, too."

His eyes narrowed. "Later. Look."

My grandfather and the court mystic were embroiled in a war of words directly beneath an enormous painting. They faced each other, expressions tense and voices raised in an intense exchange of words. My grandfather's wide stance, forward-learning pose and tight-lipped grimace revealed his displeasure. The mystic elucidated his points with animated hand gestures, his pale green eyes blazing with conviction. When the music stuttered to a halt, the two men didn't even notice. Their clash of perspectives ignited the air around them, drawing stares and hushed speculation from fellow courtiers.

My pulse raced. "Can you make out their words?"

"No. But it can't be a coincidence that they keep looking at that painting."

I followed his rapt gaze. In the painting, two people stood side by side in an apple orchard, bathed in the violet glow of dusk. The trees reached skywards, and I blinked as their weighted branches swayed in the wind. The two were alike in stature and colouring, although the man was a fraction taller. The woman wore a flowing *salwar kameez* shimmering with magic. Her thick dark hair had been cropped into an elfin cut. Her hands reached out to the man beside her. This wasn't a romantic pairing, of that I was certain. The man was dressed in a deep amethyst tunic embellished with gold. His head was slightly turned away from hers. They wore matching topaz medallions.

I inhaled sharply as my eyes settled on their faces.

At first, I thought perhaps time had ravaged the original beauty of the painting, but the damage appeared to be deliberate. While the wider landscape held exquisite detail–the rippling of individual grass stems, the glow of the red apples, the embroidery on the Indian clothing– the features of the pair had been shrouded by crudely applied additional brushstrokes. The additional layer of colour on the faces was dull and smudged rather than vibrant and intricate as if someone sought to erase the past. Despite the original beauty of the painting, it now exuded quiet horror.

I couldn't tear my eyes away, nor could my grandfather

or the mystic. They peppered their disagreement with sly glances at the portrait.

"Who are the two people in the painting?" I whispered to the general.

"Mahi and her twin brother Menon."

A chill laced up my spine. "Mahi had a twin?"

"He walked these very halls. He was Prem's favourite sorcerer."

A jolt of realisation. "My grandfather and the mystic know where she is."

His chiselled face was grim. "I've been suspicious of Prakash and Qasim's alliance for weeks. One day, and you've managed to confirm their involvement."

The air crackled with tension as the men continued their heated argument. I longed to dig out a spell from my pocket to make the walls grow ears or allow me to borrow the senses of one of the caged creatures. To deepen my witchcraft so that spell casting would be as simple as linking my intention to a click of my fingers or the blink of my eyes. But witchcraft stemmed from profound knowledge, not short-cuts, and the spells in my pocket were simple. So, I joined the rest of the court in watching the fireworks. Each word fanned the flames of their disagreement until the irritated raja flew off his throne to intervene.

Prem's commanding presence hushed the warring men, and his biting words made it clear that he would not tolerate any further discord in his court. He addressed my grandfather alone, and a shiver crawled up my spine as I read my name on Prem's lips. An undercurrent of understanding passed between the two men. Then, the raja called for the music to start once more and returned to his throne. Court life churned again: the murmur of secrets and concealed alliances forming an undercurrent beneath overt exchanges. I craved the simplicity of my own house with its bare furnishings and art, sloshing tea and honest food, and getting out of my fancy clothes.

Deven scanned my expression. "I warned you."

"Yeah, well. We do what we have to. Would you rather I hid away?"

His eyebrow arched. "It would be safer." A sigh. "But we have a starting point."

I grinned. "Good, because I can't wait to get out of these shoes."

We watched as my grandmother rushed towards her husband, fretting and fussing. My grandfather cast her aside, his hands gentle but his face resolute. I baulked as shrewd eyes fell on me. There were half a dozen metres between us.

The general's long fingers curled around mine and tugged me after him. "Come. We've both had enough. Let me save you from this encounter."

I resisted, even though his skin warmed mine, and I wanted more. "I've got this."

He frowned as my grandfather caught up to us, shielded from onlookers between two pillars as the sky darkened outside. Perhaps my anger about my grandfather's cruelty as the raja's enforcer drove me to do it. Or how since we met, Prakash Malini—one of my only living maternal elders—had treated me like I was little more than the shit on his shoe. Or how it transpired, he was involved in the disappearance of our friend. Or maybe it was simply because Mum had run away from this kingdom when she was scarcely a child, and my grandfather hadn't even bothered to try to bring her back. I took all those reasons into the cauldron of my mind and plucked a vessel from my pocket. It was round and squat, and I knew it held the forgetting spell. With a flick of my fingers, I uncorked it, released the spell into the air and blew it like a kiss towards my grandfather, willing him to forget I was ever at court that day. *Vismar.* I willed a chasm in his mind, and though I'd never used the spell, I experienced deja vu. The currents in the air and the vowels that swirled were disconcertingly familiar to me. Yet I doubled down. *Vismar, vismar, vismar.* The chant didn't gain in power.

"Kiya–" the general warned.

My grandfather's face contorted. "Stupid girl. I'm a sorcerer. You think I haven't warded off such manipulation."

I'm in midlife, not infancy. A small smile drifted across my lips. He was so pompous, so full of his own self-importance that perhaps he'd made an oversight. Perhaps he'd only accounted for powerful spells and not simple ones. Simple ones that I had mastered with more ease than grand spells that teased me and slipped through my fingers like nebula or cumulous clouds or sands on distant shores.

My grandfather reached for me, and the general stepped forward as if he were my bodyguard.

"Wait." Shoving clumsy fingers into my pocket, I retrieved an oval vial marked with the etching of an eye with a diagonal slash through it. My heart pounded as I uncorked the spell I'd used before on guards the night my sisters and I had decided to stay in Jalapashu. *Tvamapaśya.* I felt the thrill of it unwinding on my tongue and tipped the glimmer across my grandfather's plum-coloured *kurta.* The glimmer evaporated, leaving a faint trace on his brooch. *Tvamapaśya.* Magic coalesced around me. My grandfather's face was painted in surprise as the vowels stretched and contracted like a living, breathing organism in my mind. I felt a rush of joy at my natural talent. No, the ancestral talent that had come down Prakash Malini's line and boomeranged back at him. *Tvamapaśya.* The consonants snapped like twigs, and I released my spell, willing him not to see me.

Prakash's outrage melted away. He looked through us, his face blank, brushed off his jacket and turned back into the room.

"You've been here mere weeks, and you did that?" said the general.

A smile played on my lips. "Watch and learn." I sauntered past him towards the carved doors out of the throne room, thrilled by my success, only to come face to face with soldiers guarding the exits. I reached into my pocket, weighing up the few options I had left. A simple *tyāga* would make them leave their posts. However, that might look conspicuous to the other guests.

Deven stayed my hand. His purr in my ear made me shiver. "Easy there, little witch."

The guards parted at his nod, and we escaped the throne room at last.

CHAPTER 8

The general and I stepped into a forsaken corridor where no other soul ventured. It wasn't a service galley or main thoroughfare, simply unused and unloved. When Deven wordlessly took my hand in his, I didn't resist. Our footsteps clipped the floor. His grip was relaxed, our fingers interlocked like a zip, but it felt unnatural. Neither of us dared to move. As if we didn't know what was permissible or ridiculous. As if we'd rather stumble through the dark with heat rising in our cheeks than talk about what transpired between us.

My sore feet longed for the cool marble against my skin, so I paused to take off my sandals. "Where are you taking me?"

Wall lamps cast shadows across his face. "To my quarters, so we can unravel this all."

"Lead the way, but don't think I'm going to let my guard down."

Our eyes locked, and there was an electric tension in the air, drawing our bodies together. The flicker in his dark eyes told me he felt it, too. His eyes dropped to my lips, and then he crouched to pick up the sandals, and I felt cheated out of his touch. There had to be a spell to get a grip on myself because being at court hadn't felt as dangerous as being in this tight corridor with him.

The marble soothed the soles of my feet, and my clothes swished in his wake. Deven's quarters lay less than twenty paces further on the ground floor, tucked away from the more opulent side of the palace. Almost as if the raja had placed him here as a deliberate slight. The door was unadorned and unlocked, but then, who would be foolish enough to steal from the General of Jalapashu?

He twisted the handle, pushed the door open and switched on the light, a wrought iron chandelier with exposed bulbs giving it an industrial feel. "After you."

I swept my gaze around his quarters, unapologetically curious. He had two rooms separated by an archway. His living room exuded a humble charm. It had no windows and was tidy, a reflection of his disciplined and orderly nature. The furniture was sparse. A desk with curved legs stood against one wall. His two chairs were low and boxy, with backrests that featured carvings of lotus flowers and cushioned seats covered in earth-toned fabric. A narrow bookshelf filled with histories, biographies, thrillers and mystery novels. The overall impression was unpretentious, a stark contrast to the lavish decor of the raja's quarters and the turquoise chamber, where we had been imprisoned on our arrival in Jalapashu. Its simplicity, compared to the rest of the palace, felt like either a deliberate slight from the raja or a determined choice by the general.

Only the bookshelf marked Deven out as privileged. Aanya lamented that ordinary Jalapashans didn't have the wider world contacts to obtain books of their own. The vast majority of books in the kingdom were held in the palace library with limited access.

I looked at him in wonder. "You're a reader."

He lined up my sandals neatly by the door and gave me an easy smile. "You're surprised?"

"Most men I know choose the pub and computer games over books." I glanced at a tarnished silver frame on his desk, propped up next to an antique lamp.

"Books are how I travel." He flipped the frame onto its face.

I had already clocked the photograph of a woman in her early thirties wearing a forest green sari. She had wide brown eyes and hair that cascaded in soft waves around her shoulders. His dead wife. He tensed, so I averted my eyes to a delicate painting of a crescent moon.

"My mother's," he said.

"It's beautiful. Are your parents still alive?"

"It's just me and Nisha's family now."

"Your sister?" It touched me that he cherished his sister as much as I cherished mine.

He nodded and went beyond the archway into the bedroom to open the terrace doors. Then he sat on the bed, unlaced his shoes and shrugged off his jacket. I couldn't help admiring the planes of his face. I wanted to borrow one of his T-shirts from his wardrobe, but that would be over-familiar. Taking my time, I admired his paintings: a landscape of lush forests spreading across misty rolling Jalapashan hills and a close-up of a wrinkled elephant with magnificent tusks in the palace gardens. I inhaled sharply at a piece I recognised from an artist friend in Boundless Bay, golden sands stretching into a foaming shore and a dark smudge of black revealing the looming Amber Hollows.

I followed him into his bedroom unthinkingly, past more artwork and books on his bedside table, past a small wardrobe that no doubt held little else than his military uniform, past a double bed comprised of a sturdy wooden frame with clean lines and a dark mahogany finish, dressed in crisp white linens.

Terrace doors, framed by drapes in thick charcoal grey fabric, beckoned me. They opened up to the moonlit night, bringing in the earthy aroma of elephant dung intermingled with the sweet fragrance of jasmine blossoms. I gasped at the silhouette of an elephant passing a stone's throw away. It trumpeted, acknowledging our presence, before roaming further away.

There was beauty in this kingdom when you peeled back the decay. I yearned for the tranquil embrace of nature, the soft rustle of leaves, the soothing whispers of the wind, a walk in the gardens under a radiant moon and the fragrant petals of night-blooming flowers.

Deven drew the drapes across the opening so only a slither of fresh air snaked its way into the room. His mouth twisted. "You learn to be cautious here."

There was no denying he was handsome. He wore only a vest over black trousers. The edges of his geometric tattoo trailed along his muscular shoulders. I retraced my steps back to the living room, calling over my shoulder. "Have you ever lived outside these walls?"

"Once long ago, when I had a family of my own." Anguish crossed his face before it shuttered. "We must be quick, Kiya, before we are missed at court."

We sat primly opposite each other in his boxy chairs, but I was aware of the bed in the periphery of my vision. The incessant clamour of the court had frayed my nerves, but here, the cocoon of silence weighed down on me, making me too aware of him. In the quiet, I realised that I couldn't hear the creaking stone of the gargoyles. Perhaps they didn't consider the general a threat.

At least, not to me.

The warm light from the lamps played upon his dusky skin. "That was brave of you tonight."

My breath quickened. *Get a grip on yourself.* I cast my mind back to the painting in the throne room and tripped over my tongue. "Why did Mahi never speak of her twin?"

He raised a quizzical eyebrow at my tongue gymnastics. "I suppose she felt abandoned."

I could well believe it. Despite her power, the seer had cut a lonely figure. My sisters would never abandon me. We were as snugly woven as a patchwork quilt. "I still don't understand why someone vandalised the painting."

A wry twist to his mouth. "No, Kiya. Not vandalised. Changes commissioned by Prem himself. It's a reminder to us all not to cross him."

The recent past flooded my mind like a tumultuous wave: the blood in the arena, the fog at the soiree, the families terrorised in their homes, Sitara's limp body on the kitchen floor, and soon thereafter, on her funeral pyre. My gut twisted. "Where did Menon go? Did someone smuggle him out? Did he leave magic behind?"

Deven grunted. "Your guess is as good as mine. Mahi has been searching for answers ever since. They had fallen out, but she vowed he'd never have left without saying goodbye."

"She was wise to be suspicious." A whirlwind of thoughts in my mind. "I didn't think the raja simply allowed people to leave Jalapashu."

His obsidian eyes met mine. "He doesn't."

"Why didn't you help Mahi find her brother? Surely, she would have appreciated your help."

His expression grew cold, forbidding me to delve any deeper. "I had my reasons." I opened my mouth to protest, but his eyes hardened. "Some wounds are too painful to unpick."

So be it. I took a deep breath. "So we're agreed? My grandfather and the mystic are involved in the disappearance."

His topaz ring glinted. "They wouldn't dare to touch a hair on the seer's head without Prem's say-so."

I rubbed my scalp where the hairpins pinched. The ring

was useless while his magic was impeded, but he still wore it. As if he was drawn to symbols. As if, like his tattoo, it was a symbol of what he had lost and a challenge to fix it. "Is it the curse that makes you hate him?"

He gave a soft shake of his head. "There is more to this story than you know, little witch. It's personal, yes. But it's political, too. I thought he could be a good leader. It's all he ever wanted. But he cares nothing if the people suffer. Hell, he cares nothing if he *causes* suffering. What heart he had calcified long ago. What kind of king dines in a palace while his people eat crusts with their chai for days on end? What kind of man orders the removal of innocent creatures from their natural habitat and trades them for coin? What kind of king holds women against their will?" His black eyes sparked with quiet rage, and I knew the women he talked of were us and that, in his own way, he'd tried to protect us.

My list floated into my mind. Of course, he was an ally. How had I ever doubted it?

Rather, why had I feared opening myself up to him?

My brows pulled in. "Wait. That was what was going on at court? Animal trading?"

"Yes, Kiya. That's exactly what it was."

My body went cold. "I thought..."

"That they were there as an exhibit. Clandestine trading is Prem's way. If it wasn't this exchange of power and secrets, it would just be something else." He raked a hand through his hair. "Mahi has wanted me to challenge Prem for years. She said I was the only one who could hold his power in check until..."

I pursed my lips. "Until?"

"Until you came along. She'd seen you in her visions. But the future is elusive, even for a seer. It's an ever-changing mosaic, an endless ripple effect of events. Emotions, intentions and desires are volatile." He gave a harsh laugh. "I've never seen Prem as enchanted by a woman as by you.

Perhaps you are the one who transforms him into the man he's supposed to be."

"No. Just, no." The notion filled me with self-loathing. Bile rose up my throat. Far better to be an advisor in Prem Kumar's inner circle than to be his wife. A smile tugged at the corner of my lips. Not a loyal advisor, obviously. I'd keep him on the throne and manipulate him with my spell work. I was becoming rather good at that.

Deven's eyes narrowed. "You're plotting something."

I grinned. "I'm not."

"You don't really think we can win this? That we can take Prem's throne? Now Mahi's gone, we have even less power to wield against him than before. I saw you once, in your element, at the Amber Hollows. You made short work of us all. It was extraordinary. This soft, beautiful woman, new to magic, acting on pure instinct. But you haven't found the core of your essence again." His voice was monotone. "And the curse binds me from being myself."

My words weren't meant to wound, but he flinched all the same. "You sound defeated."

His jaw tensed, and the incomplete tattoo on his back–the one that symbolised his promise to break the curse–glimmered in the half-light. "Not defeated. A general waits for the right time. The right strategy. If the jewel fragments you stole that night–"

I quirked an eyebrow. "Not stolen. They were ours."

He snorted. "If *your* jewel fragments didn't amplify your magic, then we'll find another way."

I couldn't help it. There was something about the intimacy of being in his quarters, the crackle of electricity between us, and the way he put his own skin on the line for me despite not being wholly himself. I rose from my chair, feet padding against the cool floor. Time slowed to a crawl, and the world ceased to exist. The bustling court, the grandeur of the palace, and the weight of our goals dissolved, leaving us in suspended reality. There was nothing and no one but us.

His obsidian eyes unnerved me and simultaneously drew me in. As if we teetered on the precipice of something beautiful. Something dangerous. But he didn't move.

I could have walked out the door, but of course I didn't.

I stood between his knees and picked up his hand. Then I pressed it against my upper thigh, where Mahi had hidden the jewel fragment with her witchcraft.

He held our eye contact, and it was electric.

"The jewel worked, General. I hear the gargoyles."

"The gargoyles have slept for decades, yet they answer to you, just as the seer promised they would."

"They wait for my command. My spell casting is effective. More than that. It is powerful. The earth moves at my will."

His eyes hooded. "Call me Deven, little witch."

"But my magic isn't as strong as it has been. I need to be stronger, Deven."

He pulled me closer, and his thighs closed around me. "I will help you."

I sank into his lap. "Are you completely healed?"

"Yes. Now kiss me."

My lips parted. "Yes, Deven."

I leaned in and let my scarf fall to the ground. His hands settled around my waist, and our bodies fused together. The vessels in my pocket impeded us, so he pulled me sidewards onto his lap. Our first kiss on the rainy beach on Boundless Bay had been undemanding. This one plundered. My fingers entwined in his hair, and his hands caressed the small of my back. His tongue found mine, and our bodies ignited with intoxicating chemistry.

"I know this dance," he murmured against my lips.

My lips were bruised with his touch, but I wanted more. "Stop talking."

A playful tone laced his gravelly voice. "So I am the object of your fantasies."

"Deven," I pleaded, but he held me back, his eyes roaming over my face and reading the need there.

A slow smile tugged at his lips. In the lamplight, the silvery scar on his eyebrow shimmered like a celestial mark. I chided myself for falling too hard, too quickly, before his touch chased all thoughts from my mind. His fingers found my nape, and then he pulled back for a moment to remove the hairpins that made my scalp so sore. The heavy curtain of my dark hair fell across my shoulders, and he shuddered in response, then jerked me forward again. I didn't feel self-conscious about the weight of my body on his lap, the wildness of my hair or the smudges of makeup on his thumbs from where he traced the contours of my lips. The gallop of his heartbeat matched the rhythm of my own. Warmth spread through my veins as I melted into him. Only when familiar goosebumps trailed up my arms did I pull back from Deven and stumble off his lap, though he grumbled.

Sitara materialised in his living room—the utter passion killer.

Her mossy eyes twinkled. "You scrub up well, little sis. And that extra attention you're getting is making you glow. Don't mind me. I'll just hover around here until you're done."

A blush crept up my cheeks. I calmed my raged breathing and shot her a death stare before giving Deven a bewildered look. He wasn't bothered. He didn't jump out of his skin at my ghost sister's appearance or shout for help. In fact, he leaned back in his chair with a self-satisfied smirk and smoothed out my scarf on his knee.

I signalled from Sitara to him. "Deven?"

He looked right at Sitara's ethereal incarnation. "Oh, I can see her and hear her. Mahi told me everything." His brow furrowed. "And I'm sorry for what happened on my watch."

Sitara lifted her chin. "That's a start."

"You knew. You knew she was a ghost. You could have saved me the pretence."

I still felt the heat of his lips on mine and would be having words with Sitara about her timing. Although I was starting to realise that ghosts didn't have a good sense of timing at all. The world of the living and the world of the dead were not mirrors but distinct realms. Sitara walked the borderlands between life and death, fully anchored in neither.

He leaned back, at ease and in control. "You seem to be revelling in the charade."

"He's not wrong." Sitara folded her arms. "I died a virgin, you know. It's very sad."

I scoffed. "No, you didn't."

"No, I didn't. But the men I slept with were so bad at it, they're best forgotten." Sitara's playful tone shifted into a turbulent storm that brewed within her very being. A cloud of frustration settled over her features. "You didn't really think I'd let you swan off to court without checking in on you, did you? I couldn't show myself, but you must have sensed me. Those lies, Kiya... I'm furious at you. Lies consume everything in their path. My lies led to my destruction. I don't want you to make the same mistake."

Her criticism stung. "You can't be serious. The lies I told tonight were white lies. They didn't really do any harm. But in return, we know now Grandfather and the mystic are involved in Mahi's disappearance. If it's my safety you're worried about, then I have it covered. My spells were effective. And besides, I have the gargoyles and my earth magic. I'll be fine."

Deven rose out of his chair. "And I thought my sister got serious really quickly."

"Stay there. This won't take long." Sitara's mossy eyes flashed as if she held back a tidal wave of emotions. "There's no such thing as white lies. Didn't I think I was helping by hiding the truth about our magical heritage from you? A white lie is lying about someone looking beautiful when they look like a donkey's arse to make them happy. That lie is a closed circle. But the ones you told tonight were arrows across a crowded field. Are you so sure that one novice witch can prevent consequences from spiralling out of control? That smacks of hubris, Kiya. You're gentle and honest. Don't forget yourself just because you're in a different world. Go back to the wheel. Remember how a potter's craft embodies honesty, never seeking to deceive or impose. Your work and your identity have always been about connection. I fear for you."

"I'll give you some space." Deven walked to his bedroom and dipped behind the drapes onto the terrace.

I watched him go, stunned by Sitara's attack. I hadn't enjoyed the lies, but I had felt their power. Navigating the throne room had been like an intricate game. The stories I had crafted were so convincing that I even began to believe them myself. I could picture Mahi with a packed suitcase. I could picture her meeting with a shadowy figure under a banyan tree or living as a hermit far away from Jalapashu. I could even picture her being absorbed into an ancient spell book. The lies had come to me easily, tripping off my tongue full of vitality and meaning. I'd felt sick, yes, but I also felt a surge of satisfaction in each brushstroke of deception I painted upon the canvas of reality.

The court deserved it. The raja deserved it.

They had hurt my family and friends. They had hurt me.

Each and every one of them was complicit.

I balled my fists. "They deserve everything that is coming to them."

Sitara's icy coolness made me shiver. "Because winning is all that matters, right?"

Shards of glass in my throat. "Yes! It's all that matters. I admit I'm stooping to their level. But the throne is within reach, Sitara. I can feel it. Then we can make this kingdom everything it has the potential to be."

"Listen to yourself. Mum and Dad would turn in their graves." She flickered and vanished from sight.

The remnants of her presence lingered in the air–a palpable aura of disapproval–as if the very walls whispered their judgement.

CHAPTER 9

I reeled from our clash. There was an inherent vulnerability in arguments between sisters because they know your deepest fears and wildest dreams. They had glimpsed your potential and foibles, so criticism carried an extra sting. Deven remained on his terrace, eager to give me the privacy I needed with my sister. How embarrassing that he had witnessed the spat.

Closing my eyes, I replayed her words in the tape deck of my mind. The growing chasm between us unsettled me. A chasm that was inevitable, given Sitara had passed over to the world of the dead. The divide became more pronounced with each passing day.

A persistent knock echoed through the room, pulling me back to the present. I took a steadying breath to compose myself and answered the door. My fingers delved into my pocket for the remaining spells. I'd show them. I could handle anything that came my way.

In my haste, I forgot that in this culture, it was improper for a woman to be in a man's quarters. Especially at this late hour, in a room cast in the soft glow of lamplight with my scarf on the floor. Especially when the man in question was a highly-respected widowed general, and I was a stranger. Especially when the raja's penchant for me was the talk of both the town and the servants' galleys.

The servant's eyes widened, but he greeted me with a bow. "*Memsaheb,* I have Deven-*ji*'s evening tea." He was little more than a child in a man's crisp uniform with a finely tuned radar for impropriety. He had mousey brown hair and the first scratchings of a moustache on his upper lip. His darting eyes told me he considered making a hasty retreat. "I am very sorry to bother you. Let me fetch you another cup, *memsaheb.* It won't take me long." Curiosity lingered in his eyes.

"How kind. Another cup won't be necessary." I mulled over my options and found the *tvamapaśya* spell I had used on my grandfather. The scent of jasmine wafted from the tea. I tapped the remnants of the spell into my palm and blew it towards him like a kiss. In my mind, the spell bloomed. *Tvamapaśya,* like the roots of a tree spreading and twigs sprouting. "Let me take that from you."

The servant frowned, but he relinquished his hold on his tray. It had been polished to a shine and held a teapot I would have been proud to have made myself and a single teacup. The teapot was painted with an image of the palace against a backdrop of a starlit sky and a crescent moon: domes and minarets in shimmering gold brushstrokes and lush gardens filled with flowering plants.

His face was blank before he turned away.

I manoeuvred the door shut with my elbow and carried the tray a few steps into the general's quarters, only to come face to face with him, his expression etched with anger.

He took the tray and set it down on his desk, where his wife's picture faced down. "That was beneath you. Yuvan has worked for me since he was a boy, and he's under my protection, and I trust him. You've got to rein in that recklessness. You can't just use magic like confetti. In Mahi's absence, I'll mentor you."

I shifted uncomfortably under his watchful gaze. "I'd like that."

His shoulders relaxed. He held out a hand to me and pulled me closer. "That's decided, then. What else have you got in that pocket of yours, little witch?"

I showed him the vessels and told him about *tyāga*, *tvamapaśya* and *vismar*, and about *krodho nivartatām* and *mohitaḥ bhava*. When I uttered the incantations within my thoughts, they danced with familiarity, like slipping into a well-worn groove or onto a sofa moulded to my shape. But speaking the Sanskrit out loud proved to be a different challenge altogether. My mouth faltered over the blend of vowels and consonants as if the spells needed wrangling, lassoing, smoothing and coaxing. The rhythm and cadence of the words required a harmony that was just beyond my reach. They were a complex symphony in untrained hands. Without Merlin at my side, the fear of mispronunciation or misinterpretation lurked at the edge of my consciousness.

Desire crackled between us, but it was tempered by the irritation that lingered about the spell I cast on the servant. My instincts told me to skirt over the last spell I had prepared. But when Deven plucked the last vial from my pocket, a triangular prism with a tubular neck and a simple L etching on its body, I had no choice but to elucidate.

"That's *mayi premaṃ patiṣyasi*."

He turned it over in the palm of his hand, where lines crossed his skin like rivers on a map. The vessel exuded an earthy aroma reminiscent of freshly turned soil after a gentle rain. "And what does it do?"

"It's a spell to make someone fall in love. The perfect defence, Merlin said."

His neck corded. "I'd call it the perfect attack." His voice was the quiet whisper of whiskey on a man's lips before he picks up a revolver. "Did you use this spell on me?"

I baulked at the accusation, my heart pounding against my ribcage. I tried to find the right words to reassure him, but his piercing gaze made it hard to form coherent sentences. "Of course not. I haven't used it. It was a last resort. I didn't even want it."

He searched my eyes for any hint of deception on a day when he'd watched me tell a thousand lies. His jaw tensed. There was a flicker of hurt in his eyes. "You're just like her."

I frowned. "What?"

He masked his pain with a veil of resignation. "We'll find Mahi together and take Prem's throne. But I can't be anything other than a mentor and a collaborator to you."

I reached out to touch his hand. It struck me then that I cared for him. That I wanted to understand his past, be part of his future, and feel the thrill of his touch. I'd blown it. "I would never use magic to manipulate someone's feelings." *Especially not yours.*

His tone was strained. "Prove it."

My stomach dropped. "I can't."

"Why didn't you just go and live your life when you had the chance?"

"Because although this place isn't mine, I feel it could be. Because the raja spoils it. Because of my heritage. Because when you find a place where the earth sings at your touch, why would you turn away from that magic?"

He massaged his temples and pinched the bridge of his nose. "This is what's going to happen. You'll stay so we can plot our next steps. Then, you'll leave the palace through the terrace. It's safer that way."

I wanted to hide, but I lifted my chin. The floor was littered with pins that he'd plucked from my hair. The tea grew cold in its pot as we made our plan. A short while later, the general waited while I collected my things and accompanied me to the terrace doors. He expanded on his curt goodbye only to advise me to choose the long route to the gates so nobody guessed where I'd come from. Then he pushed the drapes aside as silhouettes of an elephant pair roamed in the distance and turned me into the deepening night. I waited, the night breeze ruffling my hair, as he sank onto his bed with a book.

The creaking of the rooftop gargoyles filled my mind as I made my way at last through the gardens, past the yellow roses my mother had loved, gurgling fountains and verdant lawns chirping with crickets. The moon illuminated my path to the palace gates, where sleepy guards languished. I had learned that the court was in session for as long as the raja willed it, and still, courtiers tumbled into the night. Some went to their apartments in the palace, drunk on their closeness to power and tittering about the sights they had seen and the gossip they had learned. Others went to their homes outside the gates.

I pressed on, my feet aching, smarting from Sitara's intervention and Deven's coldness. A coldness that was entirely my fault. A few streets from home, someone called my name, and I turned to find my grandmother, bright-eyed and straight-backed despite the late hour and her age.

She stopped under a street lantern. "Kiya, won't you accompany an old lady home? Prakash is still engrossed with matters of court." There was not a hair out of place in her henna-coloured beehive, and her sari folds hung elegantly from her birdlike frame. There was no slippage or crumples in sight, although it had been hours since she dressed.

I approached warily and offered her my arm. "Of course, Grandmother."

Kavita beamed and tucked her arm through mine. Luminous eyes found mine that seemed to hold a thousand secrets of their own. "You disappeared in the middle of court. Wherever did you go?"

I hoped her attention to my whereabouts was a sign of her affection and not an indication of my carelessness. My voice wavered. "The library."

"That's odd," said my grandmother mildly. "The library is usually closed when the court convenes. I must say, you were very busy today. A veritable social butterfly, just like me in my prime."

I concentrated on guiding us through a cobbled walkway, deliberately skimming over the implication in her words that she was wise to my actions. "Are you no longer as sociable as you were in your youth?"

"I learned with age that real friendship is a precious gem amidst the sea of rituals. Most interactions are shallow exchanges of pleasantries. Trite phrases repeated. A curious focus on a kilo lost or a kilo gained, as if outer shells are more fascinating than inner worlds. All scripted. All tedious. Actual friendship involves listening more than speaking. I find I recognise it mostly in shared silences over freshly brewed tea."

I smiled, recognising a kindred spirit and decided the moment of my grandmother's insightfulness had passed in favour of philosophical musings until gnarled fingers squeezed my arm.

She checked over her shoulder for passersby, but quiet reined in the dusty streets. Admiration filled her gentle voice. "You're an effortless spell caster. The only giveaway is the slight movement of your lips. I recognised it because I had the same habit myself in my early witching days." Her bird-like shoulders squeezed upwards with joy. "It must be genetic."

I froze, thoughts ricocheting. For the first time, I wondered if I could make it through the minefield of traps at court and come out unharmed. But when I read the lines on her face, it shone with goodwill. Even leaving my grandfather's harmful choices aside, I wasn't ready to fully trust her—

not after how she had treated my parents–but I could listen. I wanted to listen. "You keep reaching out, but I don't know how to give you what you want. And I can't fathom why you would be with such a man as my grandfather. He's the raja's enforcer."

Fierce loyalty lit up her face like a flare. "He's much more than that, Kiya. I'm with him because I love him. We've been married for nearly sixty years. No one has ever loved me more than Prakash. And no one has ever tried so hard to protect me. He is not perfect, and neither am I." Her eyes reflected the shadows of bygone days.

"I'm sorry."

"It's okay. The young don't always understand the old."

My chest was tight. "This kingdom. Is it worth saving?"

Her words lingered in the air between us as we shuffled along. "Only you can decide that. Those who have lived behind a wall all their lives see differently from those who see the open horizon before them. I'm in my twilight years. I've lived through the collapse of an empire, the birth of this kingdom, the turning tides of royalty. I've seen magic–with all its marvellous potential–destroy my family. I want so much more for you."

She felt like true family in that moment and filled the void that Sitara had left: the tender care of an older relative. Why, then, had she never taken an interest in us before our accidental arrival in Jalapashu? "My mother never spoke of you."

"I loved my daughter deeply. She was the light of my life. But love alone cannot shield us from the mistakes we make. When she chose a path different from the one we had envisioned for her, my heart broke. I revisit those choices sometimes at twilight when the world is quiet, and my regrets won't sleep. A mother stays a mother. Even when their child is gone." Her voice was tender with longing. "I doubt she even thought of returning. On her last day here, there was so much anger, and Prakash wouldn't still his tongue. His bark is far worse than his bite. But words leave their mark. Sometimes deeper than the lash."

Her hurt was a salted wound. "I'm sorry."

"Don't be. I'm so proud of what she built. I'd hear snippets of information from time to time from returning scouts. My cakes would tempt them to my kitchen table, and they would tell me what my heart longed to hear. A happy marriage. Three beautiful girls. I was so proud of her for living on her terms. I wish I'd had the chance to tell her." She gave a watery smile. "I bitterly regret not mending the rift. I have told Prakash that I won't let it happen again. He refuses to hear me. But he will."

I took a deep breath. "I cast a spell on Grandfather tonight."

"You managed to get one over that wizened old sorcerer?" Kavita's lips quirked. "He probably deserved it. It's nothing I haven't done a dozen times. He really is the most infuriating man."

I stared at her. "You did?" She had steel in her core, I hadn't expected. I'd expected her to be soft and yielding like the petals of a rose. Instead, she was a fortress, strong and resilient, weathering the tides of life.

"Of course." Her laughter was like a gentle melody, filling the air with nostalgia and comfort. "I've kept him on his toes all his life. I can see in your face what you think of him. You leave him to me. I know how to reach my husband. He'll come around."

It was hard to believe she knew of his involvement with Mahi's disappearance. But I had to nudge. I couldn't just trust her blindly. She was so loyal to her husband that I tried a different tack.

"What is your sense about the court mystic? I saw how he behaved with Grandfather. He was rude and out of control."

She waved a dismissive hand. "Nonsense. They were as

bad as each other. But that sly old Qasim is up to something." A shadow passed over her face. "He and Prakash are the raja's new favourites, and that never bodes well. Better to fly under the radar and find small happinesses than to fly too close to the sun… I'm old enough to know that the darkness comes in cycles. It's arrived. I feel it here." She held her hand to the centre of her chest, with its barely there rise and fall, and her fragility made me think she was made of glass, not bone. "I'd tell you to run away, but my cleansing rituals haven't worked. It's too late to run. The shadows grow longer. The magic is already swirling. And when there's a surge in magic, pain is never far behind." She didn't seem a harbinger of doom. There was real fear in her eyes.

A chill ran up my spine. "You don't need to worry about me."

"I hope so, child. I'd hate to lose you too."

"Does my grandfather know what I did today?"

Her laugh filled the night air like a bloom. "I'm not going to tell him. He doesn't need another reason to ban me from seeing you."

I cleared my throat. "Actually, the raja insists I should spend more time with you both."

"Wonderful. What the raja says holds more sway than a wife's pleas. You must visit us for lunch tomorrow. Ask anyone for the address, and they'll point you in the right direction."

Her eyes flickered, and I wondered if it was true that Leena had visited her before. In any case, she was too polite to mention it and put a wedge amongst sisters, so I followed her dance of politeness. "I wouldn't want to trouble you." Visiting them was a double-edged sword: socially awkward but a rare opportunity to obtain a closer glimpse of my grandfather's affairs.

"Trouble?" Kavita slipped her arm from mine with the jittering movements of a butterfly. "It will fill me with pure joy to fuss over you. I'll expect you and Leena at one o'clock. Tell Leena she can bring Aanya if she likes. I know they're friends."

I hugged her, and it felt right. Like maybe in another universe, she could have been the sort of grandmother who baked me cookies, pinched my cheeks and made messy art with me. It comforted me that despite the complexities of our family history, we could find a fragile sense of belonging with each other. Particularly given the clumsy errors I'd made in my relationships that day.

"Shouldn't I walk you home?"

Kavita leaned into the hug as if she had been waiting for it all her life. "That was just a ploy to talk to you. I know the contours of each paving stone. No harm will come to me here." She walked into the night's embrace. The curve of her neck and the sway in her step reminded me of my mother.

The eerie murmur of rooftop gargoyles accompanied me home.

CHAPTER 10

Merlin approached his role of looking after the parrot with unwavering dedication. Somehow, during the days in the forests of Jalapashu, when hunters had tried in vain to capture them, they'd forged a bond. In Babbu's hour of need, the two familiars had turned a corner from the frosty beginnings of their friendship, and the hare became akin to a surrogate parent.

Mahi had raised the parrot with a sense of freedom, allowing him to roam the dark corridors of her home and leaving her front door ajar so he could come and go as he pleased. He rarely strayed far. While I was at court, Babbu had repeatedly flown into the pane of glass. The third attempt resulted in a beak injury that Leena tended to. After that, it took only a little persuasion from Merlin to convince her to leave the window open. He argued that Babbu's anxiety would be soothed by the gentle caress of the wind and the option to fly away.

It was an astute move.

The parrot's attachment to Merlin meant he didn't venture far. He flew outside to do his business or to stretch his wings, but he always returned. The hare created a cosy corner in the kitchen, complete with a comfortable perch and a sensory toy stolen from an unsuspecting child visiting the market. Their routine was a dance of companionship. When Babbu bobbed his head a certain way or emitted a specific sound, Merlin recognised his signals for fresh water or a medley of seeds or leafy vegetables they enjoyed together. The parrot mimicked the hare's chatter and added his own commentary in the form of muted squawks. The great feather eviction continued, but Merlin distracted Babbu with displays of tap-dancing that combined swift and precise foot-work with gliding grace that made the parrot caw with delight. It was the equivalent of putting a baby in front of *Sesame Street*. In thanks, Babbu often nuzzled against the hare, and sometimes, Merlin stroked the parrot's feathers, carefully avoiding the bald parts. The hare's gruff nature belied his soft heart.

He really was a keeper of lost things.

All was fine and dandy, but the melons pushed me over the edge. Colossal watermelons that made me stub my toe when I reached home, my sole intention to face-plant into bed.

Exasperation washed over me as the morning light unveiled the full absurdity of the situation. The worktop of our small kitchen had been so overwhelmed with fruit that some had rolled onto the floor. Coupled with the strewn feathers, our home looked like a barnyard gone awry. It was a good thing that the house was already in a state of disre-pair, or I would have lost my rag. "I still don't understand why you brought home so many, Merlin."

The hare huffed softly before responding. "Babbu kept saying the word. I didn't know what else to do. How was I to know that he meant *Menon,* not melon? It's been an age since that wizard lived in Jalapashu. I feel very stupid for not having thought of it." Liquid gold eyes surveyed the parrot with suspicion. "This friendship hasn't been very good for my brain."

Babbu paused his rhythmic pecking of a succulent wedge and fixed his beady eyes on me. "Melon." Then he unhooked his claws from the melon and nudged it off the counter.

I threw up my hands as the pulp decorated the floor like an abstract painting. "For heaven's sake."

Merlin hopped three paces in alarm. "Come on, Babbu, time for some fresh air."

The parrot's loving squawk filled the air. "Dirty hare."

My blood pressure eased as the parrot flew out of the window, his trajectory haphazard due to his unbalanced plumage. "Thank you for building a rapport with him," I murmured to Merlin as I lifted his silken body onto the sill. "But next time, remember that one melon would have been plenty."

The hare laid his cheek against mine. "It's much easier reading books than deciphering the mind of a deranged parrot."

"He didn't give you any more clues?"

He flattened his ears against his head and made a low, guttural grunt. "Nothing. It was like babysitting a toddler. Not one squawk of interest, despite all my coaxing. Just pulp and feathers and ill-judged flights into windowpanes."

I recalled the songbirds and the luminescent fur balls at court. "Merlin, you were right about the hunters. Be careful."

His watchful liquid gold eyes met mine. "Of course." With that, he followed his friend off the ledge.

I turned back to Leena with a wry smile. "You were supposed to be in charge. How a parrot of Babbu's stature was supposed to eat this much fruit, I do not know."

Together, we started the clean-up operation. Leena couldn't resist the odd bite.

"It looks like a fruity commotion, but I'm sure we can find uses for it. Juices, salads, cocktails, maybe even skincare. We both could use something cooling on our eye-bags." Leena assessed a half-imploded watermelon. "I know you've been working hard to make this place look homey. For what it's worth, I was called over to the clinic to help a poor kid who'd fallen into a patch of nettles and then got distracted by Sitara's tale of woe. She's worried about you."

I grimaced. "I hate fighting with her. I pushed back harder than I should have, but what I did was for the right reasons. I thought Sitara was going to step back and let me make my own decisions."

"I *love* that we have a lead on Mahi." Leena blew out her cheeks. "But Sitara wasn't wrong. We all need someone to remind us when we've forgotten who we are."

"I know who I am."

"Good. So we can move on." She rubbed her hands on her jeans and pulled her golden hair over one shoulder. "Then tell me about what you were doing in Deven's room. Did you get it on? Sitara said she definitely disturbed you."

I hesitated a moment, then blurted out. "That man can kiss." My mind flashed back to his lips on mine, like the first touch of flame to dry leaves, his fingers grazing my skin. Telling myself that we wouldn't have worked out together under the raja's nose was cold comfort.

Leena's triumphant fist cut through the air. "I *knew* it. I sniffed that chemistry out a mile off. You two are like a fireworks display."

"Yeah, well, it's over. At least romantically."

"Oh. That was quick." She shrugged. "Well, at least he's out of your system."

Grasping at straws to change the subject, I recalled the raja's words. *You will make efforts to see your grandparents because it pleases me. After all, your sister is already making strides in that respect.* My chest tightened. "Why didn't you tell me that you've been seeing our grandparents?"

She bowed her head. "I'm so sorry. I should have told

you. I hinted. I was going to tell you the night you showed us your list of who you trust. But I just couldn't disappoint you." A heavy sadness hung in her voice. "But we don't have much family left, Kiya. And I don't think Mum harboured any bitterness towards them. She was happy with her choices, and she wouldn't want her choices to bind ours. Remember that Maya Angelou quote she loved?"

I went quiet inside. My memories echoed with the wisps of Mum's voice. "'Life loves the person who dares to live it.'"

Leena released a pent-up breath. "Yes, that's it. My heart is wide open, Kiya. Is yours? Don't even answer that. You're like brittle clay fired in a kiln, prone to crack."

My eyebrow arced. "I can't believe you used a pottery metaphor against me. That's a low blow. You can't tell me you like Grandfather."

"Course not. He's a dickhead of the highest order, but Grandmother is special. I felt welcome the moment I stepped over her doorstep. It felt like home."

I laughed. "Okay, okay. Stop coming at me so hard. You've convinced me. And as it happens, we're invited to their house for lunch. Aanya, too, if she wants to come." Goosebumps trailed up my arms that sometimes heralded our ghost sister's arrival, but she didn't materialise. "What about Sitara?"

"She flounced off. It's her new modus operandi. Have you noticed? She'll be back."

I nodded, hoping that our ghost sister would stay away until the meal was over. It seemed unkind to have a family reunion she was incapable of being a real part of. She could hide in the shadows while we ate and talked, but it was cruel to relegate her to the darkness, detached and unseen. She didn't belong in the void; she belonged at the table with us.

No, lunch with our grandparents was just another secret we had to keep.

The secrets were piling up too fast for me to keep track of.

"I DON'T SEE WHY I CAN'T COME," SAID MERLIN. "THEIR HOUSE used to be my home once."

I hated to disappoint him. He'd borrowed a little taupe bowtie from Ishaan, who happened to come by the pottery studio midmorning. But I couldn't take any chances. After all, the hare had been a gift to my mother as a child and had sided fully with her when she had fled Jalapashu.

I knelt down to him. "You haven't been invited, and I don't know them well enough to impose. Besides, with Sitara in the wind, I need you here to keep an eye on Babbu. I can depend on you, can't I?"

The hare puffed out his chest. "Of course." He escaped back into the house, avoiding children who ooh-ed and aah-ed over his appearance and begged to stroke him.

Leena and I had dressed in embroidered tunics over *churidar* trousers that we'd picked up at the market in exchange for a few gold coins we'd earned at the clinic and pottery studio. How odd to be hidden within the borders of England and using a different currency. The coins glistened like captured sunlight in our palms. One side showed the raja's image in profile. The lines of his regal turban hinted at power and tradition, and his piercing eyes gazed into the distance as if foreseeing the destiny of his kingdom. As though ascending to the throne was alchemy that blurred the lines between human and deity.

I wrinkled my nose at his image. Jerk. Was it fawning courtiers, the grandeur of poet's verses and artists' portraits and high palace walls that made monarchs believe their own myth?

It was the flip slide of the coin that captured my imagination. This side bore the seal of the kingdom: the sacred banyan tree, which provided shade and shelter to market traders. The tree was beloved by Jalapashans and featured heavily in their oral histories and stories. A focal point for meetings and celebrations, the banyan tree could often be found decorated with ribbons, silk scarves, oil lamps or offerings of small trinkets. I spotted its canopy on our way to lunch.

Leena navigated through the dusty streets with the confidence of repeat visits. She didn't sense my agitation, but Aanya did. The maid hummed a calming tune under her breath as we strode along, clutching a small bouquet of goldenrods, asters, and fireweed bound with twine as a thank-you for the invitation. A few streets away from the seer's house, Leena came to a stop outside a wrought iron gate.

My breathing slowed. "This is it?"

The gate's hinges groaned as Leena pushed it open. "The very one. Come on." Her fingers floundered in the air for a moment as she reached to take Aanya's hand but thought better of it.

We followed her down the shingle path that meandered from the wrought iron gate to the front door. Built on a wide plot and two storeys high, the house was grander than its neighbours, though not as tall as the seer's towering topsy-turvy home. The exterior was painted in a warm shade of ochre, its walls adorned with delicate floral motifs that added a touch of whimsy to the façade. Sky blue curtains framed its large windows, and no gargoyles sat atop the sloping roof. Despite the season, an array of pots spilt over with aromatic herbs on either side of the path: basil, rosemary, chamomile and lemon mint. A wooden bench sat beneath a gnarled tree, a perfect spot for tea.

A vivid image spiralled from my imagination: my mother on the bench, with her nose in her book and a glass of lychee juice at her side. But she'd never divulged those memories to me, so it was constructed nostalgia that might never have happened at all.

What if Kavita was as complicit as Prakash? My mind

flooded with all the stories of evil grandmothers I had consumed as a child: Baba Yaga, Yama Uba and the wolf in disguise as the grandmother in *Little Red Riding Hood*. "I don't know if I can do this."

Leena gave me a sympathetic look. "I was a wreck the first time I came."

"What can go wrong when you have each other?" said Aanya. "If it's too much, we leave."

I sucked in a ragged breath and grasped the door knocker. Sculpted with meticulous detail, it comprised of a winding vine and intricate leaf, with a blooming rose nestled between them. The handle met the door in a decisive knock.

The sound lingered for a moment, then footsteps approached.

When she opened the door, Kavita Malini's smile was like the sun breaking through the clouds on a chilly morning. Her voice cracked with emotion. "I've been waiting for this moment for so long." She wore an unadorned olive *salwar kameez* that exuded comfort as if she embraced a simple life away from the royal court. Around her waist was an apron, and on her shoulder, a tea towel flecked with brown sauce. Her dyed hair, with its telltale tinge of henna orange, fell in a thin plait down her back. She greeted us each in turn, placing dry kisses on our cheeks and remarking about the sheen of my hair, the fragrance Leena wore and Aanya's shy smile. "Prakash isn't home yet. Lucky for me, or he'd complain about how I always underestimate how long it takes me to cook. Of course, I could serve him beans on toast like the English." She chuckled. "How about you explore while I finish up in the kitchen? This was your mother's home, after all."

We took off our shoes as a mark of respect. The scent of freshly ground spices—cumin, coriander, and cardamom—travelled through the house after us. We wandered past a rustic dining room, its wooden table adorned with a vase of wildflowers and a spotless bathroom with an array of scented soaps. A portrait of my mother hung above the mantelpiece in the living room, younger than the picture in the library. The painter depicted her on a garden swing at the age of about eleven. Her hair was the colour of sun-kissed earth, and her soft brown eyes showed no hint of the strong-willed woman she would become. From the window, we surveyed the tranquil garden, where herbs burst forth from neatly tended beds and bundles of drying herbs hung beneath a canopy. I cast my eyes over a trickling fountain, whimsical wind chimes and a rusted swing that I recognised from my mother's portrait, its chains wrapped in ivy. It was the closed study door I was most interested in.

Leena turned shining eyes on me and Aanya. "Isn't it beautiful?"

"All these homey touches and all her capacity for love, with no one to expend it on but Grandfather." I dropped my voice to a murmur. "There's never going to be a better moment to sneak into his office." I cringed even saying it. I'd never been good at games of stealth and surprise. In my childhood, even playing Knock-A-Door Run had given me palpitations. I was the sort of woman who got jittery about train inspectors even when I had a ticket.

The colour drained from my sister's face. "That's why you agreed to come, isn't it? No. That's out of the question. You can't sneak around their house. It breaks all the rules of hospitality. Tell her, Aanya."

Aanya pulled at her hoop earrings, solemn and awkward. "It is impolite–"

Leena gave a triumphant smile. "See."

"–but I don't care if it helps Mahi."

My sister's face fell. "Oh. Well, I'm outnumbered then."

We retraced our steps to outside the study, where a series of elegant silver-framed botanical watercolours adorned the wall: a posy of lavender blossoms, tendrils of rosemary, a spray of deep green basil, delicate thyme leaves in varying shades, and mint leaves that seemed almost three-dimensional. The door to the study loomed before us, daring me to be brave. From the kitchen came the sizzle of frying.

"If you must do this, go now. Aanya and I will pretend to admire these and keep watch." My sister pressed her lips together. "But don't ruin this, Kiya. Be quick about it. This relationship is important to me."

With a nod, my mouth dry, I twisted the doorknob into the enforcer's study and stepped inside. Then I closed the door gently behind me and faced the darkness. It was an odd, windowless room that kept the daylight at bay. Heart pounding, I fumbled to light an oil lamp that cast elongated shadows across a room full of old-world charm. The scent of aged paper, ink and tobacco filled the air. In the middle of the room stood an oak desk polished to a lustrous sheen. It was cluttered with mounds of papers, quills, inkwells and a weathered pipe. The walls held nothing but a portrait of my grandmother. I scanned the room, looking past the shelves of dusty books and a prayer plant that curled on a side table. An imposing filing cabinet drew my attention. It might have stood in any household had it not been secured by a bolt that threaded through the front of its five drawers.

I tiptoed across the room towards it, though my grandmother couldn't have heard me over the clamour of cooking. The parquet floorboards creaked a warning that I was an intruder. The cabinet's metallic surface was dull and dented in the lamplight. My stomach quivered at the realisation that the bolt didn't travel through brackets but was stuck fast. In fact, it was so resistant to my ludicrous, heaving attempts to dislodge it that it must have been the work of magic.

That wily old sorcerer. But my grandfather wasn't the only one with magic.

I glanced furtively over my shoulder, pulse racing, and brushed my fingertips across the cabinet's dented surface and the bolt. When I reached for my magic, it refused to answer. Panic rising, I tried again. It was hard to find my belief when I'd crossed wires with everyone dear to me, and I was here, in my mother's home, again choosing the path of shadows over an honest question to my grandfather about his involvement. My magic was dormant and unreachable. It was an untapped mine; I was the trapped canary.

I jumped as the door edged open.

My sister peeked through. "You're giving me a heart attack, Kiya. And there's not even a proper hospital to save it. I mean it. Hurry."

"I'll be right out." I'd managed to undo locks at the crowded soiree. Why wasn't it working? Determination flaring, I filled my lungs with air, pushing out my anxiety, and focused on the cycle of breath. Minutes past. Long minutes in which my sister fretted outside. But for a moment, I held all expectations at bay and tuned into the energy of the world beneath my feet. My bare soles tracked the vibrations through the wood flooring, the concrete foundations, the soil beneath it with its echoes of life and endless renewal, burrowing creatures and the pulse of the land. A shiver of recognition chased up my spine as the hum within my veins became a chorus, and my intention synchronised with my ability. With each breath, I drew the energy of the earth upwards, magic spiralling through me. The prayer plant turned my way. With a clunk, the bolt yielded to my touch, breaking my grandfather's spell.

My stomach churned as I tugged the heavy drawers open, unveiling a collection of records in alphabetical order. Pulling out a name I recognised, I sifted through its contents, surprised to find an entry on Farida's husband's affair laid bare and his drunk and disorderly behaviour. I replaced the file. The records went on, chronicling a tapestry of human flaws and transgressions. I chose another and another, my heart in my mouth, taking care to replace each one. There were records of Jilu and Radha's dreams of opening a string of Indian restaurants in England and Deven's sister speaking out against the state. There, etched in damning detail, was a list of Mustachio's betrayals and killings. There were files on both commoners and courtiers. Files on those who had stolen food or jewels, who had shown cowardice in the arena, whose magic showed promise and who owed debts–tales of crimes and betrayals, yes, but also tales of simple foibles and dreams–collected by my grandfather, the enforcer, and now exposed to my gaze.

In exposing Jalapashu's underbelly, he had only reflected the darkness of his own soul.

Every shuffle of paper felt like an echo in the silence, magnifying the weight of my intrusion. But I hadn't yet found what I was looking for. Despite my frayed nerves, I couldn't stop without the answers I needed. Limbs shaking, I hunted through the *M* section of the cabinet and retrieved the seer's heavy file.

All the records were divided into sections: *identity, lineage, networks, magic, occupation, transgressions* and *punishment*. My jittery fingers traced the black ink. I read through a series of observations chronicling Mahi's transformation from fierce critic of the young raja to staunch ally following her twin's disappearance. The entries were dense: snippets of private conversations with names blacked out, glimpses of visions Mahi had reported to the court, allegations of bias towards the general and a few refusals to carry out the raja's requests, communicated to him privately. There was also a clear sense that she was invaluable to him. She had never failed tests of loyalty.

That changed with our arrival in Jalapashu.

The most recent entries were written in hasty script, detailing the time Mahi had spent with Leena and me, how she might not have told the truth about our magic, how she seemed not wholly honest during her regular seer's consultations with the raja and how he felt placated rather than served. My stomach turned at a note stating how Mahi refused to collude with Prem to magically secure my affections. Suspicions about her had been cemented when, at the soiree, she stood with the people against him–publicly–to ask him to deescalate his actions and warned him of rebellion. Evidently, Mahi had crossed a line.

In stark black ink on pale parchment was the royal decree: the seer would not live to see another sunset in Jalapashu.

The lingering stench of tobacco suffocated me. Was our friend imprisoned in darkness? Had she been sent into exile? Had the raja sanctioned her killing?

Voices sounded outside the study, and my unease rocketed. I switched off the lamp and scurried behind the desk, clutching the file, blood rushing to my ears. I'd had no time to close the cabinet. Shame made my body heat rise. I didn't know what I would do if either Kavita or Prakash caught me here red-handed. Would I conjure a believable excuse on the spot or stammer over my words? Would I care if they ostracised me? Leena would never forgive me.

My grandmother's muffled voice came through the door. "I always forget to water the prayer plant in there. It really is a beauty. Would you mind?"

The door handle swivelled. I prayed my thin breathing couldn't be heard in the stillness of the room. The approaching footfalls echoed in my chest like a heartbeat. But the step was youthful, not old. The flash of navy trousers was Aanya's, not Kavita's. I collapsed with relief as Aanya passed me with a watering can and tended to the prayer plant. She side-eyed me as she left the room. Beads of sweat had sprung up on my brow.

"Where's Kiya?" asked my grandmother.

"She needed the toilet," said Leena. "Let's give her some space. It usually takes her a while."

Grandmother harrumphed. "Well, she's probably a thorough hand washer. I wouldn't have it any other way."

Their voices drifted off, and the drumbeat of my heart eased. I didn't dare to turn on the light again. My mind a blur, I turned to the *punishment* section of Mahi's file, squinting at it in the dark. There were two pages of drawings rendered in rich browns and soft greens. The largest was a grouping of concentric circles that resembled the ripples on a pond after a stone was cast. Another blink and the drawing became a complex array of lines and shapes that intertwined in a bewildering dance. Suddenly, the lines shifted, and a web-like pattern stretched across the page. Overleaf were sketches in pencil that made the hair on my nape stand on end: elongated figures with angular features, sinister faces made from curls of smoke and wraiths with contorted expressions.

I needed to know what the sketches meant. I couldn't rest until I knew what had happened to Mahi.

But I knew what kind of person my grandfather was. He was a man of the raja's ilk: devious, power-hungry and willing to collect secrets on his friends and colleagues. Here I was, about to break bread with him.

With deft hands, I ripped out the final two sheets and returned the rest of the file to the cabinet. With a last check to ensure I had left no evidence of my presence behind, I closed the cabinet, taking care to replace the bolt. As the world spun, the sun blazed, and the stars hid in the daytime sky, my magic drove the bolt back into its place.

Folding the stolen sheets, I slipped them into my bra, readjusted my tunic and ventured out to join my family.

CHAPTER 11

Making a show of drying my hands on my trousers, I headed into the kitchen. Leena and Aanya ogled the bowls of piping hot delicacies on the counter. A sideboard stacked with jars of herbs dwarfed the simple stove and dented sink. My grandmother stood before a weathered table adorned with an assortment of herbs and flowers, conducting some sort of ritual.

My sister came to my side with a hiss. "I'm going to kill you."

"Thanks for covering for me."

Leena stared at me. "You found something."

I nodded. "I think so."

"Oh, hell." She passed me a napkin and turned loving eyes on our grandmother, leaving me under no illusions about her priorities. "Wipe the sweat from your brow. Can you at least have a sunny attitude at lunch?"

"Don't mind me, Kiya. I'll be finished in a moment." With deft hands, Kavita tied together a bundle of sage, rosemary, lavender and eucalyptus leaves. She set it alight, then closed her eyes, profound concentration settling over her features. Her hands moved in deliberate, choreographed circles as she distributed the curls of smoke around the kitchen and then beyond into the dining room, ending at the portrait of Mum. Finally, she stood still, her palms pressed together in reverence.

My eyes widened. "You're a kitchen witch."

"Why, of course." Kavita left the burning sage in the hearth. "I've been a kitchen witch all my life. I thought I mentioned it."

Leena gave a soft smile. "She's been helping me catalogue some of the herbs I've spotted so I can understand their uses better."

Aanya laughed. "You're a quick learner. The court physician is quite upset at how quickly his years of learning have been replaced by an upstart."

"Well, as far as learning goes, he's a dinosaur. I'll get him and the clinic whipped into shape."

"Kavita-*ji*, maybe you could teach me some of your recipes," said Aanya, admiring radish and coriander. "The cooks at the palace don't like me looking over their shoulders."

"I'd be glad to have you in my kitchen." My grandmother filled a jug of water and dropped in some mint leaves. "Are you well, Kiya? You look quite pale. I could steep some chamomile and ginger root for you and add a touch of honey. That should make you feel better."

I shook my head. "I'm fine, thank you." I barely caught the threads of their conversation. My findings consumed me. I wanted to pore over the stolen pages with Merlin and decode their meaning. I wanted to be somewhere safe, away from people who sought to harm us. I didn't want to pretend anymore that everything was okay just to keep up appearances. I wanted to talk frankly and shout from the rooftops and town squares and the foot of the banyan tree about the corruption in the kingdom. I wanted everyone to know how good people suffered at the hands of monsters. But I didn't, of course. A promise was a promise, and Leena deserved more than me spiralling out of control. She deserved a chance to build bridges here.

"Bring those in, will you?" Kavita led the way, and together, the four of us carried the bowls of mango chutney, tamarind sauce and lime pickle, and platters of *samosas*, *pakoras* and fried *mogo* into the dining room. She directed us like an orchestra conductor until the dishes were arranged to her liking around Aanya's bouquet of goldenrods at the centre of the table.

The sizzling plates of food should have made my mouth water, but my stomach churned. "We'll wait for Grandfather."

She ushered us into the high-backed chairs. "Certainly not. Prakash has no concept of timing where work is concerned. It's best we get started. I wouldn't want the food to get cold." She filled our plates, ignoring our protests about *too much* and *later*, content to watch us eat our fill while taking bird bites herself. Her eyes rested on me a moment. "I really am glad you came."

Leena elbowed me.

I sucked in a breath. "Tell us about the kingdom. Is it strange to have lived your whole life here?"

Kavita's thoughts meandered through the rich brew of her experiences. "Jalapashu is so much more than magic. As a child, I dreamt of the wide world beyond our borders, but as a grown woman, I appreciate our sense of community. We sing, eat, pray and celebrate together. The women here scrub and rinse our clothes together, side by side. We look after each other's children and rally around during ill health. Our elders–I guess that's me now–are always on hand with wisdom and advice."

I put a dollop of chutney on my plate, unable to marry her words with my own perceptions. To avoid being contrary, I chose to be trite. "I'm *not* enjoying washing our clothes by hand."

Her words flowed like honey from a comb. "We had washing machines for a while, but everyone felt lonely. We prefer talking to friends as we scrub our clothes clean. The children, too, missed their mischief amongst long laundry lines."

A wistful smile drifted over Aanya's face. "Oh yes, those are some of my favourite mornings."

Leena snorted. "You need to get out more love."

My grandmother's gnarled fingers traced the intricate patterns on the armrest of her chair. "The bonds here are strong. I remember when Prakash was a young man, before he joined the royal court, how he'd toil in the fields from dawn until dusk, sweat mingling with the earth. He'd gather with his friends some evenings in the shade of the banyan tree, sharing tales of the day's work and dreams for the future. He was more carefree then."

I played with my fork, thinking of the gladiatorial feats in the area and the fact my mother hadn't found a way to be happy here. I thought of the reams of files in my grandfather's study that told a story of betrayal, not friendship.

Kavita's hand brushed mine as she piled more food onto our plates. "Jalapashu is a place where anything is possible, Kiya. Anything you can imagine. In this kingdom, leaders aren't determined by genealogy, brute strength, divine right or marriage. Leaders in Jalapashu can be raised in the dirt but still rise to the throne."

Leena nodded. "But all leaders must have magic to rule, is that right?"

Kavita smoothed her plait. "We're all descended from the same five ruling families. We *do* all have magic, though some do not have access to topaz of their own. An injustice that Prakash has long wanted to correct. Aanya, how good are you at your history? Do you remember Prem Kumar's beginnings?"

"His family were potato farmers."

"Indeed. His father was in love with my Hansa, but when she spurned him, he married another. It was a marriage of practicality rather than love. Soon after marriage, Prem was born, but their luck ran out with his birth. Harvest after harvest, the crop failed. They barely made a profit. In England, the farmers have the help of mechanical and technological advances, but not in Jalapashu. Their backs bowed under the weight of years of toil. The once-fluid movements gave way to a snail's pace. Their calloused hands became crooked, and their magic was too meagre to be of use. It didn't do Prem any good to see how they worked themselves to the bone. His magic and ambition, but most importantly, his experiences, propelled him to the throne. He was determined never to be poor again."

I tensed at how she painted the raja sympathetically, the chutney souring in my mouth. "Does his history excuse his choices?"

Kavita blew out her wrinkled cheeks. "We're all changed by the situations we find ourselves in."

She'd had a ringside seat to the raja's atrocities. Was her love for us worth less because she found it in her heart to love a corrupt man? I couldn't figure out whether her fighting spirit had been dulled by the years or whether she was too forgiving. Was an unlimited well of forgiveness a good trait? Perhaps my grandmother had lived through worse injustices that made her write these off. Perhaps she was reluctant to put in the boot because she benefited from my grandfather's proximity to power.

I suspected she only had a soft slipper anyway, and maybe that was okay.

Except, sitting there at my grandparents' dining table, I knew it wasn't. Kavita Malini hadn't raised her voice for our mother when it counted, and I really wanted her to use it for us.

"Last night, you said the magic is already swirling, and pain is never far behind. What did you mean by that?"

Her eyes took on a faraway look. "A long time ago, in my youth, the Rani of Jalapashu called the great pottery master Vikram Reddy to the palace. The people were turning against her. She flattered his ego, telling him he was a man of revered talents and she needed his help. Vikram-*ji* loved his queen. In fact, he was *in* love with her. He returned to his studio and worked for five days and nights until clay crusted his skin and his kilns burned hot."

Leena took a bite of samosa. "What did he make for her?"

"He made gargoyles," I said quietly.

"That's right. Who told you the story?" My grandmother didn't wait for an answer. "The gargoyles were gruesome creatures that emerged from rough blocks of clay. Their faces were a fusion of human and beast, twisted into grotesque masks that hinted at the lurking darkness—contorted bodies captured in a moment of eerie animation. My parents told me of wings made of intricate patterns of veined stone. Exquisite details from sinewy muscles to clawed hands and chiselled scales. You can see them on the rooftops today, but their details have been partially eroded by the wind and rain."

Leena pushed her plate aside. "What did the rani want with the gargoyles?"

Kavita was a natural storyteller. Her Indian accent made for elongated vowels and rolled Rs, making her words a pleasure to listen to. Her voice rose and fell like a melody, carrying us through the highs and lows of her memory. I almost forgot we still sat at the dining table.

"You're catching on, Kiya. I can see it in your face. Vikram-*ji* should have asked what they intended them for, but he didn't. He wasn't a violent man. Perhaps he thought the gargoyles would stand sentinel, and the rani would use them to inspire obedience. He delivered them to the rani with a deep bow and woke them from their slumber before her very eyes."

I swallowed hard. "Was she pleased?"

"She thanked him," said our grandmother. "Then she found a small imperfection in the fishtail of one of the gargoyles."

"How rude!" My sister might have spurned Sindhuja's affections, but woe betide anyone who criticised her.

Our grandmother's brow furrowed at the overreaction. "Disappointed by the underwhelming response to his artistry, Vikram-*ji* went home to clean his studio. Mere hours later, the rani unleashed his gargoyles upon the people, and bodies rained down from the skies. Blood-curdling screams of grown men grew silent. With horror, he realised his terrible error of judgement. He watched from afar as the gargoyles he'd created turned against his friends and neighbours."

"The palace library holds a collection of diaries from that time." Aanya's sing-song voice was monotone. "My parents told me that children cowered together and begged their fathers to stay inside and not to fight the beasts. They'd never seen the gargoyles before. No one could imagine what damage they'd do."

Our grandmother nodded. "Simple weapons and soft flesh stand no chance against stone and claws and teeth. The rebellion was quelled. Those who tried to flee across the intersecting membrane of Jalapashu and Boundless Bay were crushed. The rest fled into their houses. Only then did the rani command the gargoyles to return to the palace."

My heartbeat was sluggish, my fingers cold as they gripped my glass despite the warmth of the food.

"Vikram-*ji* was only in his forties then, but some say the last of his youth fled that night. He knew the magic that lay within his hands. He had the power not just to shape clay but also to shape destinies. With a determined glint in his eye, he returned to his studio; his mind focused on a singular purpose. Days turned into nights, and nights into days. His fingers danced over the clay. The magic swirled as never before in Jalapashu. When he had finished, he called a wagon to take his masterpiece to the palace and presented it at court. The rani was amazed to find a lifelike statue of herself under the shroud. She had a cold beauty and an imperious stance. He'd managed to capture her down to the smallest nuance of her expression."

"Some say, in that moment, she returned his love," said Aanya.

My grandmother nodded. "I think they were right. I think in that moment she loved him. For a cold woman, that was something."

I puckered my lips. "I don't understand. The people of Jalapashu were dying, and in response, the great pottery master made the rani a statue to stroke her vanity?"

"What made the statue remarkable was that it was not made of clay alone. Vikram-*ji* mixed the clay with the very essence of the land–the soil, the water and the air–infusing it with a potent magic. The court was hushed in anticipation as the rani reached out to touch the statue. In that instant, a shockwave of energy rippled through the palace. The rani's form shifted, her mouth first, so she called for the gargoyles, but they were loyal first and foremost to the pottery master. Her body transformed into clay that crumbled and melded with the statue, bringing an end to the bloodshed."

Leena shuddered. "She became one with the representation of her arrogance."

My heart pounded. "What happened to the statue?"

"Initially, the next raja intended to keep the statue as a reminder of the consequences of hubris and the power of artistry." My grandmother tried to put a handful of crispy *mogo* on Aanya's plate.

Aanya whipped her plate out of reach. "But the people were terrified of the statue. Even today, palace staff tell stories of how evil seeped from it. So the raja commanded soldiers to take the statue to Boundless Bay and toss it into the ocean."

"Some say what happened broke Vikram-*ji*'s heart. He never spoke of it again, even though he became a legend. He instructed the gargoyles to take up positions in the quiet corners of the palace gardens and on the kingdom rooftops. They've slept there ever since. Even today, those creatures, born of Vikram-*ji*'s skill and the rani's dark purpose, with their long shadows stretching over the town, chill me to the bone. In a way, I was relieved when Vikram-ji died. The very same day, a scout brought news from Jalapashu that you had been born." My grandmother frowned. "I pray that the gargoyles never find breath again."

Leena's gaze flicked to mine, but she and Aanya didn't divulge my secrets. Could it really be that I was the pottery master's heir apparent? When I closed my eyes, the gargoyles' creaking breath filled my consciousness.

I didn't hear my grandfather come in. The air grew still, like the moments before a thunderstorm, as he entered the dining room in his socked feet. His bushy brows were already pulled down into his perpetual scowl. Despite his size, there was a tenseness about him, a tightly coiled energy that revealed his controlling nature. "Why are you bringing out these stories from the time capsule of history, Kavita?" He sighed. "It's been a long morning. I hope you have left enough food for me."

My grandmother rose to lay a chaste kiss on her husband's cheek. "Of course, darling."

We followed suit and stood at his arrival. I kicked myself for being a lemming and hastily sat down again.

With a low grunt, Prakash settled into the chair at the head of the table, bringing the scent of old leather with him.

Only when he glanced at Kavita did his eyes soften, a rare crack in his gruff exterior. Kavita plated up his food for him, knowing after years of marriage what his likes and dislikes were, which foods reacted badly with his digestion and which he would only eat in the morning and never at night.

He ate a mouthful and then sighed with satisfaction. Her Indian accent was thicker than his, but she had a deeper grasp of the English language. "Did you enjoy Kavita's cooking?"

"It was delicious, Grandfather," said Leena. "You do know Aanya from the palace?"

"Yes, of course. A marvellous voice," he said, as if that was all she was good for. Frowning, he turned to me.

I held my breath, hoping he didn't remember the spell I had cast to make him leave me and the general alone. Hoping he couldn't tell that I had rummaged through his study and stolen from him. The documents scratched against my breast.

He broke apart a *pakora* with his fingers. "I'm glad you didn't bring the hare. He is not welcome here."

My grandmother gave him a rueful look. "Prakash is not good at small talk. I've been trying to teach him for years."

Usually, I gravitated towards people who couldn't do small talk. It tired me out. But I stiffened at the insult towards Merlin. "He wanted to come but said you might still hold a grudge for him facilitating Mother's escape."

"I do. He filled her head with nonsense. She might have stayed without him."

Leena and I exchanged glances. He preferred to picture Mother as his little girl than a woman with her own desires and needs. It was easier for him to blame Merlin than to admit his own failings.

"How much headway have you made with your magic?" asked our grandfather.

I met his gaze. "Mahi was mentoring us, but she left without saying goodbye. Do you know what happened?"

His eyes flickered. "No idea. She was always unpredictable. Perhaps I can be of service?"

Hell, no. I smiled sweetly, thinking of the shadowy drawings in my bra. "Oh no, we've both had a better offer."

Aanya followed our back and forth like a game of tennis, whereas Leena sat stock still, mouth drooping.

My grandmother piped up. "Isn't it wonderful how Leena has found love with Aanya here in Jalapashu, Prakash? Back in our day, women couldn't be anything more than friends. You don't mind me saying, do you, Leena and Aanya? I find it's much better to define the things that are important to us."

My grandfather's scowl deepened. "What are you talking about, Kavita?"

Aanya choked on her water as lunch descended into a farce. "You told them?"

"Oh dear." My grandmother swept some imaginary crumbs off the table.

The dining table should have been a symbol of unity, not a battleground where words were hurled like verbal artillery. There was a reason why family gatherings ended in fireworks. Beneath the veneer of celebratory togetherness simmered a complex web of unresolved conflicts and clashing personalities. Unspoken grievances and long-held grudges fuelled patterns of friction. Innocuous comments held the potential to spark explosive arguments. But my sister was kind and honest in her relationships, and she had supported friends and lovers through the process of coming out, and she remembered what it had been like herself.

"Oh, darling. I'm sorry. I didn't tell them anything," said Leena. "I promise we can take this as slow as you need to."

"What are you sorry about?" asked my grandfather.

"I'm not sorry about *that*." Leena flushed. "I'm sorry it came out before you're ready."

"Well, it's not out. I was just confirming a rumour," said my grandmother. "I'm not the only one here who knows how useful rumours are. They get a bad rap, but they are the oldest way of spreading news. They're how we receive information before checking it. And Prakash is much better when he's out in front of secrets rather than the last one to know. And we are *very* happy for you both and won't tell a soul until you are ready."

Aanya floundered and looked down at the table. "Kavita-*ji*, this is new for me. I'm afraid the townsfolk will look at me badly."

My grandmother lifted her chin. "People always look at us badly for one reason or another. At my age, you learn it's more to do with them than you. Whenever you are ready, we will be in your corner. Won't we, Prakash?"

My grandfather grumbled and squeezed out a yes, realising he'd been outmanoeuvred. Leena gave our grandmother a grateful glance. All the time I had been stewing over my grandfather, I hadn't stopped long enough to admire my grandmother's qualities. Even closed off from the rest of the world, Kavita had managed to retain a softness and fluidity of thought that meant she could bridge the gap between old and new, tradition and change.

But Prakash still bristled at me. Since his arrival, lunch had felt like avoiding potholes in the road rather than a joyous countryside drive. He was, quite simply, utterly assured of his own importance and incapable of finding common ground or even showing any natural interest in us. There were a thousand topics of conversation he could have raised with us and a thousand more we would have happily listened to, but instead, he said, "You are more complicated than your sister."

"Actually, I'm pretty complicated," said Leena.

Prakash grunted. "That's why Prem-*ji* is fascinated by you. But you must tread carefully and agree to his every whim. If your mother had known how to fall into line, she could have been a rani."

"Our daughter didn't care for palaces or politics," said my grandmother. "What Prakash means is–"

He pinched the bridge of his nose. "I mean that when the raja makes requests of us, we say yes. That's how we keep safe. It is not an option to fall into his bad books."

For a split second, my breathing was suspended, but I couldn't help myself. My words were like a runaway train. "*We* are not a part of this family. Family isn't made overnight."

Leena's expression was stony. "Biology would beg to differ."

"Those bonds are earned by valuing and tending to each other day after day."

A storm gathered on Prakash's brow. "You're like your mother. Headstrong, rash, oblivious to the consequences of your actions."

My sister shrank beside me. "Stop it, Kiya."

"A potter is the opposite of rash." I balled my fists. "I know what *you* are." The silence stretched, a battlefield of unspoken words. I suddenly realised how it must have felt for my mother to battle her father as a teenager. Only, I was a grown woman.

His eyes were like polished stones, cold and unfeeling. "And what's that?"

"Prakash, please." said my grandmother. "We're a family. Finish your meal. I'll get the pudding, and perhaps Aanya can sing us a song."

Aanya nodded, her eyes like saucers. "It would be my pleasure."

But I didn't want it. I didn't want her dulcet tones to soothe away my anger, and neither did my grandfather. We wanted to stay angry at each other. That much was clear by the way he wiped his napkin across his ruddy face and stood up. The air was thick with unsaid words.

"I have matters to attend to in my office." His hand on my shoulder surprised me. "Families fight. It's the nature of things."

He walked out to his study, leaving my grandmother to make apologies for his behaviour when he and I had been as bad as each other, and shame prickled behind my watery smile of thanks. We helped my grandmother clear the table and soaked the used plates in soapy suds. Though my heart was heavy, the tension had lifted from Leena and Aanya, and there was a freeness to their interaction that I had only witnessed behind our own walls. Leena draped her arm around Aanya's waist, and Aanya's brown eyes radiated with the happiness that came from the liberation of living her truth. Unchained from secrecy, our grandparents' house had become a sanctuary from them. Whereas for me, it had become a hall of mirrors, reflecting the fractures within our family.

In the hallway, Kavita's delicate fingers intertwined with mine, an outer fragility that belied her emotional resilience. "Come again. Anytime. Don't let Prakash's prickles chase you away."

I kissed her papery cheek and caught the scent of the musky perfume dotted behind her ear. "Thank you for today. It was ungracious of me to argue."

"Don't be silly. Is it ever ungracious to speak from the heart? Better that than staying silent, placating or being inauthentic." Her gaze flickered to my tunic. She probably thought I stuffed my bra and was too polite to say. "The two of you will find a way to each other. Some bonds take longer to ferment."

I shifted uncomfortably. "I don't want to disappoint you."

"You could never do that, Kiya. Every moment I get to

experience with the two of you is a gift. Perhaps you can come to temple with us."

"Actually, it's not our thing." It sounded harsh saying it out loud, and I almost wished I'd lied.

I stood aside as my grandmother said her goodbyes to Leena and Aanya. It was much lighter in tone than ours, their embrace warm and without formality. Turning my face away, I glimpsed my grandfather behind his lamplit desk through the sliver of the door opening. His pipe hung from his mouth, and the smoke curled into the air like whispered secrets, leaving the room in a haze. A breeze brushed against my skin from the direction of the windowless, stuffy study. Only when the smoke cleared enough for me to make out a faded orange slip dress and a mass of midnight hair did I clock Sitara, encased in her ethereal glow. I swallowed a gasp.

My ghost sister was deep in conversation with the enforcer.

I strained to listen, but I couldn't make out their words. She had preached to me about honesty, yet here she was going behind our backs.

"Kiya? Are you okay?" asked my grandmother.

My gut wrenched. "Yes. Thanks again."

I followed Leena and Aanya out of the door into the early evening light, leaving Sitara behind. We walked a few paces through withered leaves under skies heavy with gunmetal clouds. When grandmother no longer lingered on her threshold, Leena turned to me.

"That was a freewheeling mess. I asked for sunshine. You gave me a storm."

I exhaled a sigh. "I was out of line."

"You're afraid of connection."

"Kavita is kind." I squeezed her hand. "And you both handled the situation gracefully."

Leena gave Aanya a soft smile. "It does feel rather wonderful, doesn't it?"

When the rhythmic drumming of raindrops began, Leena and Aanya twirled, unburdened by cares. Aanya wasn't ready to draw attention to their romantic relationship in public, but in a few short hours, she had gained confidence. Her laughter rang out like music as if with every twirl, she flung off the weight of the world. Their footsteps made ripples in the puddles as if the rain washed away their inhibitions.

I sheltered under a tree, soaking up the sight of my sister's joy to the soundtrack of the rain's gentle percussion. I loved seeing Leena happy. There was an ease in their relationship that I wanted for myself.

On the rooftop, Sindhuja, the fishtail gargoyle–whom the ancient rani of Jalapashu had judged to be imperfect–watched Leena dance with Aanya; her lips stretched into a smile. As if, despite her own desires, it was enough to admire Leena from afar. As if she desired Leena's happiness rather than to conquer her. My sister noticed her new friend balancing on the rooftop in the driving rain and waved.

By the time Leena and Aanya came to a stop with a final flourish, I was long gone.

CHAPTER 12

I didn't want to go home. I didn't want to dampen Leena's happiness with my bitterness about our grandfather, and I didn't want to argue with Sitara again. We were fortunate to have this time together; no one could guess how long it would last. Her return as a ghost should have been a chance for us to mend the fractures in our relationship. Instead, our differences expanded like fault lines in the earth.

But I had other plans anyway. It wasn't difficult to find my way when the seer's house stood out like a mountain peak amongst plains.

I walked through the empty streets as the rain eased, soaked to the bone. My hands shielded the papers I had smuggled from my grandparents' house. It had only been yesterday that I'd seen the general, only yesterday that we'd made our plans. A quiver of anticipation rippled through me as a memory unfurled of him drawing me onto his lap, his demanding lips bruising mine. Although he couldn't have felt the same way, not given his accusation that I had used spells to manipulate his feelings.

I was grateful to the general for our alliance but under no illusions that we could be anything more. The beginnings of attraction were as brittle as a glass sculpture. There was no room for errors. Whereas familial love and friendships had an inherent resilience, early attraction was like positioning a sculpture on a narrow ledge. It lacked a built-in buffer for mistakes. Instead, it was a balancing act of vulnerability and performance; each word and action weighed up and magnified. Not for the first time in my life, I'd crashed gracelessly to the ground.

Not that I blamed him. I'd allowed my mistrust of the raja and the environment to taint my character. Now, I was too entangled in the machinations of court to extricate myself.

With a sigh, I crept down the rain-washed stone of Mahi's alleyway, wrinkling my nose against the undertone of cow dung. It was dangerous being here. Loyal citizens knew better than to remember the seer existed. I kept close to one wall as Deven had advised, the gargoyles' breath a roar in my mind. A wave of trepidation came over me at the sight of the leaning, three-storey house. Its balcony plants were now shrivelled to a black husk. The slightest touch would crumble them. But it was the thick chains around her house that made my adrenalin spike, a metallic lattice that symbolised the raja's power. They emitted an eerie chime at my approach that almost made me turn back.

Mahi's woodworm-ridden door opened a crack, and Deven beckoned me inside, his index finger on his lips.

Wary of latent magic, I assessed the gaps between the chains like a seasoned mathematician. But there was a reason I was a potter. I raised one foot, testing my agility and cursed myself for not taking the time to stretch that morning. My long hair risked getting entangled in the lattice, so I tied it up, ignoring Deven's amusement. I needed to squeeze through a gap of half a metre squared, and I wasn't sure if my hips would cleanly make it. I considered diving through, but in the end, I fed one leg through and then the other, my body contorting in ways that would have made a yoga instructor proud.

Once I was safely over the threshold, the general closed the door, trapping us in the gloom of Mahi's house. Only his torch illuminated the darkness.

Triumph coursed through me. "I didn't think I would make it."

Deven bit his lip to hide a smile. "It isn't magical. It's just a chain."

"What? It was humming. Like this–" I made a weird high-pitched noise. "It was definitely magical."

His voice was velvet and smooth, although the seer's house was sharp with magic. "Nope. Mahi was too powerful for simple chains to contain even her residual power. The chains are just theatrics to dissuade people from coming inside."

Humiliation sent a crimson tide to my cheeks, but there was something about this dance that was as old as time: the teasing, the undercurrent of pleasure that made my breath thinner, the way I was aware of the glint in his eyes, the fall of his hair and the way his jumper moulded to his body. *Pull yourself together, Kiya.* "Why did you let me go through that?"

He grinned. "It was very endearing. Your flexibility needs work, though." Despite his casual clothing, he wore his belt of daggers, and his topaz ring gleamed on his finger. He handed me a second torch.

"Thanks. Did you really need to bring the daggers?"

"I don't go anywhere in Jalapashu without my knives. Come on. We have work to do."

"About last time–"

"It's in the past."

I didn't want our kiss to be in the past.

"You got caught in the rain. Shall we find you some clothes first?"

"I'm fine. I'm sure Mahi's very protective about her stash of eighties T-shirts."

This time, he laughed out loud.

We ventured into the house. The chapel-like windows were closed, just as Mahi had liked. I scrunched my nose against the stagnant air, sweeping my torch across her home. I didn't admit it to the general, but I found myself affected by Mahi's house in the same way as his men. It didn't seem right to be there without her pottering about and the parrot swooping past in flashes of green and crimson. Every creak of the floorboards and rustle of my clothes sparked my imagination. Even long after she had disappeared, the subtle vibration of the seer's lingering magic kissed my skin and settled on my tongue. As if even in the absence of the seer herself, the mirrored burgundy walls possessed an uncanny ability to draw out concealed truth.

"You think it's possible that whoever combed through Mahi's things missed something?"

"I know the men that came in here. They didn't dare rummage through her belongings. They said she would know. That it would be bad luck."

We conducted a thorough search of the ground floor. Mahi's shelves drooped under the tools of her witchcraft: tarot decks, oracle cards, scrolls, magnifying glasses, crystal and half-used pillar candles, their wax trickling down in frozen rivulets. When we entered the kitchen, I shuddered at the memory of the topaz fragment sizzling and steaming against my skin, driving deep into my thigh. The kitchen needed a deep clean. Unwashed utensils and gleaming animal bones cluttered the work surfaces. I gagged at the pungent tang of fermenting herbs and mildew seeping from mason jars, thinking how quickly a home lost its vibrancy when left untended.

I picked up a jar of tea leaves covered in a thick layer of dust. "It's hopeless. We don't know what we're looking for."

Deven rubbed his hand over his face. "Mahi is too clever to be blindsided by Prem."

"You were friends for much longer than I knew her. Why didn't she warn you?"

"She sees fragmented puzzle pieces, not the whole jigsaw. They arrive in a kaleidoscope of time without the convenience of chronological order. Sometimes, they don't come to fruition at all. What she is most afraid of is influencing the natural outcome. But I know how her mind works. Mahi is always prepared. There is something here, I'm sure of it."

I cleared my throat. "I found papers this afternoon. You should take a look."

He came to my side, coal-black eyes intense, as by torchlight, I reached underneath my tunic and unfolded the documents I'd hidden there. "Where did you get those?"

I pushed aside some clutter and smoothed out the sheets on the counter. They were warm and damp from my skin. "I took them from my grandfather's study this morning."

His eyebrow scar glinted silver in the torchlight. "You stole from the raja's enforcer?"

"I did." I wondered if he'd think poorly of me.

A softness coloured his tone when I'd expected chastisement. "You're making a habit of surprising me."

"Just a few pages in the *punishment* section of her file."

Sorrow clouded his face, but a soldier's stoicism replaced it a second later. "So they do have her." Both of us knew just how proficient the raja was at clearing obstacles from his path. Deven himself had been the victim of that. Why else had he been cursed if not to emasculate him somehow in this society where violence was often the answer?

"I hope she's still alive."

"You and me both, little witch. Let me see the pages."

A thrill chased up my spine when his arm brushed mine.

We placed the torches on a table, gingerly turning the pages as we pored over the documents. His breath hitched as he studied the drawings. The intricate composition of concentric circles sometimes morphed into angles, adding unexpected dimensions to the pattern as if created by an illusionist. Deven muttered to himself at the sight of the malevolent, twisted visages on the page, each more disturbing than the last. Even though I'd seen them before, the otherworldly agony of the drawings spoke of a realm beyond mortal comprehension. Fear settled like a stone in my stomach.

I searched his face. "Do you know what they mean?"

"They're unlike anything I've ever seen." His inky eyes snagged on a symbol. "Some of these are familiar, but I'd have to cross-reference with ancient texts. The ghoulish faces are siphoned straight from nightmares."

My skin crawled. "I hope Mahi is nowhere near them."

A shadow drifted across his rugged face. "She may well be, Kiya. But she's strong."

"I hoped the drawings would be easy to interpret."

"Sure. By the person who created them." Deven scrubbed a hand over his face. "I'm going to make a replica. And then, I'm going to use the resources available to me in my role as general to find out what these symbols and figures mean. I'll have to be careful, but there's a few people I can ask for insights."

"Has my grandfather always been a jerk?"

"Not always. By all accounts, he changed when your mother left."

"What if he realises I stole from him?"

"Then he'll have to decide whose side he's really on." He grasped my chin, and his inky eyes probed mine. "This is a turning point. Mahi's not going to be lost to us forever. Because of you, we'll bring her home." He averted his eyes, and his downcast expression made me realise he meant her body for closure, not a reunion.

I swallowed hard. "Let's try upstairs."

The narrow staircase creaked beneath us as we took the

stairs, our torches low. His breath was steady behind me, a far cry from my own galloping heartbeat. The upper floors of the seer's house were like a warren, each room with a distinct purpose and aura: a library without bookshelves, towers of books and parchment piled high from floor to ceiling; an apothecary with bottles of various shades and sizes, marked with labels that read *chin hair remedy* and *be gone varicose veins*; a meditation room with an altar and geometric symbols on the walls; a room full of bird cages that lacked doors; a chamber filled with curiosities from around the world despite the fact she had never left the kingdom; a room of cracked mirrors; a room with a carpet of soil, full of withered snake plants, peace lilies, pothos vines and dracaena; and, at the very top of the house, an observatory that contained three telescopes and a ceiling painted with constellations.

My frustration climbed with every trinket and relic I examined. "Maybe we were wrong."

"Just this door left." The general entered Mahi's bedroom and swung his torch in a circle. "Good god, there's a lot of furniture in here."

With a resigned sigh, I followed him inside. The sea of furniture was such that there was barely room for two people to negotiate the space sufficiently. Shuttered balcony doors made the room even more claustrophobic. Throughout the rest of the house, there was no evidence of Babbu's excessive shedding, but in the bedroom, his feathers clustered in tufts. Pushing back his sleeves, exuding a soldier's calm and focus, Deven sifted through the room. He was undeterred by layers of dust. His fingers trailed along the edges of ornate chests, lingering over intricate carvings and ornamental handles. Crouching down to examine the dark recesses of Mahi's wardrobes, he explored every nook and cranny for hidden compartments. A current passed between me and Deven with each accidental touch. His sudden stillness was the only hint that he noticed it, too, but we pressed on all the same. I examined the upholstery of the chaise lounges by torchlight, my movements sluggish, and turned my attention to her bedside cabinets, the scent of aged wood filling my nostrils as I sorted through drawers filled with trinkets.

"I'm done." Flushing, I shut a drawer crammed with garters and packs of condoms from the 1970s.

"Find anything interesting?"

"More like a trip down memory lane," I responded with a grin.

He looked deflated. "I need a rest." He sat on Mahi's unmade bed, with its blankets in clashing patterns spilling unevenly over the sides. But he had no idea it was a waterbed. He dropped his torch as the bed swayed like a boat rocked by currents and almost swallowed his tall, muscular frame. He struggled upright, but the bed responded by shifting to even the subtlest pressure, and he flatlined into it before righting himself again.

Laughter laced my words. "The bed's taken a liking to you."

His charcoal eyes narrowed. "Navigating enemy territory is easier than this bed. Care to try?" He reached forward, closed firm fingers around mine and yanked.

My eyes widened as I flew forward into the devilish bed. "You've got some nerve." I slammed against his chest, about as elegant as a marionette with tangled strings.

He curved his body slightly away to protect me from his belt of daggers, though they were sheathed. "That was an exquisite landing," he deadpanned in a low murmur as his hands gripped my waist.

Suddenly, I wasn't angry anymore or even tired. A charged silence enveloped us as I lay on top of him, my thighs entwined with his, my back arched away. I wanted to bend down and taste his whiskey lips here in the tangled sheets of the seer's forsaken house. Time was suspended. His thumb caressed my skin where my tunic had risen. My breath quickened. I could hear the rhythm of his heartbeat.

Then he pulled away, his voice gruff. "We can't–" A pause. "There's something underneath me."

His tone was like a cold shower. When my attempt to stand up failed, I rolled off the bed and fumbled to find a torch on the floor. I lifted it and shone it in the general's direction, my nerve endings still tingling.

His brow furrowed as his fingers encountered a solid object beneath the covers. He delved beneath the mismatched blankets, brushing away a mound of feathers, and pulled out a small book: some sort of compendium of animals. The worn pages parted, bookmarked by the sleeve of the Eurythmics' *Sweet Dreams* album, to reveal a familiar image. He tensed. "This is it. This is what she left for us."

"Here." I planted my feet and hauled him up out of the clutches of the wobbly bed. His breath warmed my cheek for an instant before we both peered at the entry in the book. My heartbeat slowed. "That's Babbu."

He strained to make out the cursive lettering. The significance of Babbu's feathers slowly unravelled before us. "It says here that magical parrots are born once a generation." He frowned. "I thought Babbu was just an ordinary, frankly annoying parrot Mahi chose for companionship. I remember her choosing this scraggly, devilish bird over a sweet cockatoo."

I pointed to beneath a diagram of a feather. "Read this bit. It says that the feathers are more than just adornments or components of flight." I was alert with excitement now. "It says if we burn a feather–at the foot of a banyan tree under a blood moon–we can traverse dimensions. A portal will open."

"Portals are impossible. They're an invention for children's stories."

"This is why Prem is interested in Babbu." I tapped the page. "Why else did Mahi bookmark this?"

A vein throbbed in his jaw. "Look there. The feathers need to be newly harvested. The seer's parrot was seen flitting about in the trees but hasn't been seen for weeks. A good thing, too, given the hunters are out in force on the raja's orders. If he were to get into the wrong hands…"

"He is in my hands," I said quietly.

His voice was low, dangerous. "What do you mean?"

"Merlin found him a few weeks ago. He's at our house." I choked back a laugh. "I thought he was anxious. But he's actually been trying to give us the gift of his feathers."

Deven's mood blackened, and he gripped my shoulders. "You're gambling with your life. Don't you understand that? I've lived in Jalapashu all my life. I have context and experience and a position at court, and even I don't understand what is going on here. What makes you think you can come here, Kiya, and survive a clash with the raja with your body and mind intact?" He shuddered. "I can weather his cruelty, but are you sure you can?"

If he wanted to scare me, it wasn't working. I was too far along this path. "I can handle myself."

He lashed out like a whip. "I saw you in Boundless Bay with your sister. You were magnificent. But you aren't that strong anymore. You haven't reached those heights again."

"I can. I will, General." I had never been as sure of anything before. However hard my road, carving out a better future for Jalapashu was my destiny. It was my birthright.

His hands tightened around my shoulders. "I told you to call me Deven."

I didn't flinch. "I can handle myself."

"It's not just about handling yourself. There are dangers you can't predict, threats that go beyond what you're used to dealing with."

"I have my sisters. I have you."

"Dammit, Kiya. You're not listening. Sometimes that's not enough."

"I thought you would do anything for this kingdom."

A shadow passed over his face as the edges of his anger softened. "Yes. But not at the expense of you."

I reeled with new understanding. "You care for me."

His carefully guarded exterior crumbled. "What if I do, little witch?"

A shiver ran up my spine at his nickname for me, but there was something else, too: an eerie rush of the gargoyles' whispers crescendoed in my head. Their whispers–indecipherable as always–conveyed a tone of disquiet and warning rather than spelling out a threat. It can't have been Deven. I had been with him for hours, and the gargoyles hadn't seen fit to warn me about him.

No, another threat loomed. I knew by how the hair on my nape stirred. We'd been in Mahi's house for so long that I'd become attuned to the atmosphere. The subtlety of her residual magic had grown denser, taking on a palpable weight. With each inhale, my senses sharpened. The creaking of floorboards and the rustling of drapes went beyond the mundane.

We were no longer alone.

I was sure of it.

A silent look of acknowledgement passed between us as we both switched off our torches. Deven slid Mahi's book into his pocket and held his finger to his lips. Not that I had any inclination to speak. My mouth was desert dry. His posture shifted, and he reached for a dagger as he scanned the enveloping gloom. The air grew heavy still, there in the seer's bedroom, with her ridiculous waterbed and endless secrets, as if the very walls of the house bristled with an awareness. A realisation that danger had arrived on the doorstep without the squawking parrot's warnings and the seer's protection.

It started from the door to Mahi's bedroom. I blinked, heart pounding, as the shape of the darkness shifted and contorted. The dark slithered and curled. It elongated and retracted as if it was feeling its way. As if the dark had eyes. As if the dark could hear. As if the dark could hurt us. As if it was sentient.

A primal scream built in my throat as the shadows advanced. They weren't governed by the rules of science. The sun had disappeared beneath the horizon. No moonlight snuck through the windows. All torches, lamps and candles had been snuffed out. The darkness moved of its own accord, with an unsettling autonomy that defied any logical explanation.

That reeked of magic. Black magic.

Dread clawed at me as Deven cursed softly and tightened his grip around his blade. He knew as well as I did that he couldn't cut through something that was devoid of substance.

I froze as the shadows stopped their searching. Perhaps they heard his curse or the soft swish of his blade. Perhaps the darkness sensed our quickened pulses. It didn't matter. At that moment, the shadows converged on us with malevolent intent, and I remembered.

I remembered I had magic, too. I remembered that darkness needed crevices to creep into.

But I was an earth witch, and I could build walls so dense that not even a chink of light or gasp of breath or slither of shadow could find a way through.

Deven stepped forward, but I had already uncurled my fists, centred my breathing and kicked off my sandals so my soles connected with the ground. It didn't matter that we weren't outside. I called forth magic through the walls and foundations, connecting with the pulse of the earth beneath the house and with the carpet of soil in Mahi's neighbouring plant room.

The darkness hesitated as if sensing my magic.

I envisioned the earth weaving through the air, forming an impenetrable barrier against the encroaching darkness. When the darkness clawed forward, seeking us in its grip, I made a sweeping motion with my outstretched hands and released the magic I had harnessed. Soil streamed towards me in rivulets that became a rampart. It formed a barrier between us and the shadows and grew, solidifying, widening, pulsating, even as the darkness sought to penetrate it. Even as it writhed and hissed.

Every fibre of my being strained as I maintained my focus, strengthening the foundations and reinforcing the structure against the insidious nature of the shadows. When the darkness clawed at the edges of the barricade, I stumbled, but Deven's warm hand at the small of my back steadied me. His touch grounded me, a reminder that I wasn't alone. I stole a glance at him.

His jaw was set, and his eyes focused on the shifting darkness. He whispered in my ear, "Now."

With a final surge of my magic, the barrier expanded and reached the ceiling, casting back the shadows and securing our safety.

My body sagged as exhilaration and relief flooded through me.

Deven's expression mirrored my own astonishment. But he gestured for me to remain quiet.

Footsteps approached on the other side of my handiwork. "Those who navigate the abyss often fall into it," said an unfamiliar voice. "I'll find out who you are. It's only a matter of time before even the most carefully constructed walls crumble."

Deven stiffened. Then he opened the shuttered doors to Mahi's balcony and ushered me out.

A muffled gasp escaped me as two gargoyles seized us and carried us across the moonlit rooftops of the kingdom.

Their wings sliced through the night air as the world blurred around us. They had come for me without an explicit command as if our fates were tied. I didn't fight them. I didn't fear them.

Exhausted, I closed my eyes and gave myself into their care.

CHAPTER 13

"Kiya, wake up." Deven's voice was urgent. Calloused fingers brushed my cheek.

I stirred from sleep and found myself cushioned on cool, soft grass, propped up against him.

The rugged contours of his face came into bleary focus. "Thank god."

"Hey." I shifted slightly, trying to get a better sense of our surroundings.

We were in a meadow on the outskirts of the kingdom. The moon hung like a pale disc in the indigo sky. It bathed the landscape in shades of silver and grey. The air carried a subtle hint of dew and the earthy aroma of soil. It calmed me to be outside after the intensity of what had unfolded in Mahi's bedroom. Even so, an unsettling stillness cloaked the kingdom as if the shadows had gained a foothold and everything that was kind and good had retreated. A pervasive feeling niggled at me that evil lingered just beyond the edges of my perception. The symphony of nocturnal creatures had faded, replaced by an unnerving silence broken only by the rustle of leaves or the distant hoot of an owl. It took me a minute to tune into what Deven was saying.

"Kiya?" he repeated. "It was so hard to wake you that I thought you'd gone too far with the magic."

My mind was still hazy. "I'm sorry. I haven't done that before. It must have drained me."

Concern filled Deven's obsidian eyes, eclipsing the admiration there. "What you did back there rivalled the power of the greatest sorcerers at court."

"Well, that's good."

"Is it?" he asked quietly.

I was too tired to decode his meaning. I didn't want more conflict; I wanted peace.

Frowning, I rubbed my shoulders where a gargoyle had grasped me. "I ache all over." The gargoyles' whispers told me they were near. Looking around, I recognised Sindhuja's silhouette against the horizon, next to the lion-maned gargoyle leader, Harya, who had been the first to declare loyalty to me the night we stole back our jewels. They stood, silent sentinels, about ten paces away. "They must have brought us here for safekeeping."

Sindhuja gave me a shy little wave, then resumed her guard alongside Harya, whose ridged tail slashed from side to side.

Deven scanned the meadow, ever the soldier, then shifted his gaze back to me. "I knew you commanded them–in theory–but experiencing that... I can hardly believe what happened. The gargoyles of Jalapashu are legendary, Kiya." His face twisted. "They may have protected us tonight, but they are the destroyers of Jalapashu."

My stomach knotted. "I hear their murmurs, if not their words. I know their story, Deven, but I also know that they're not inherently evil. They were merely the tools of a corrupt rani. They are as complex as you or I. They can rewrite their story."

His face tightened, and I longed to caress the lines away. "How can flesh made from stone be complex? I trust my soldiers, Kiya, but I don't trust them. Do they have our emotions? Do they have our wisdom?"

The coolness of the grass seeped through the fabric of my clothes. "I don't know. But they have witnessed the suffering. Through wind and rain, they stayed in Jalapashu. They didn't desert it."

He stood abruptly and glared down at me. "Then why haven't they woken to protect the people? Why did they stay silent? What if Prem gains control of them?"

I tucked my legs up against my chest. "Keep your voice down. You'll upset them, and we don't have time for a gargoyle therapy circle."

His frustration mingled with a flicker of a smile. "You're worried about gargoyle sensitivities?" He sighed. "You should go to them. They were unimpressed by my title and refused to go away until they spoke to you. They wouldn't believe me when I said you were sleeping. The one with the fishtail kept prodding you." He offered me a hand.

Heat radiated through me as I accepted it, and he pulled me to my feet. "She cares. She seems to go that extra mile to show it."

"Be careful." He moved to accompany me.

"It's okay. They won't hurt me." I padded towards the gargoyles, caution ringing in my ears.

Sindhuja and Harya turned to face me with a slight grinding noise. Half my height, they bowed, deep and low, their gesture reverent even though it was they who had saved us. They waited for me to speak.

"Thank you for what you did tonight." On impulse, I reached out and touched the battle-hardened skin of their small arms–I wasn't sure about a handshake with their claws–to show my gratitude. After all, it was not long since Sindhuja had spoken of the internal worlds of gargoyles, and I thought she might appreciate the gesture.

For humans, touch was a tactile language that bridged

gaps. We tended to respond to affection with a reciprocal gesture. But the gargoyles remained unchanged, their forms rigid and unyielding. Even Sindhuja froze, her pale yellow fish eyes darting from side to side.

Harya's lion face had a piercing intensity that made me squirm. His deep voice rumbled like distant thunder. "We are glad to be of service, mistress. We have been waiting, but you have not called us."

I gave him a blank look. I wasn't their general. I didn't even have my own bearings yet.

"We have been sleeping for so long that there are those of us who crave action," said Harya. "We crave war. To stretch our wings and limbs and soak our teeth in blood. To win back our honour after the failures of the past."

"Those failures were not yours," I said. "The failure–the moral bankruptcy–belonged to the rani."

Harya's stony face was expressionless. "We cannot sleep when the city suffers, mistress. It is cowardice."

I pinched my lips together. Though small, their strange brutishness intimidated me. I didn't let them see it. "The great pottery master responded in haste to the rani's command, then repented at leisure. It is not cowardly to gather complete information. Acting too quickly can lead to unintended consequences."

Sindhuja took an involuntary step closer to me, and I imagined the creaking of her bones. "It's good not to be hasty. The gargoyles have failed Jalapashu once before. We don't mean for it to happen again, but some of our numbers say you do not have the strength of the great pottery master. But we will tell them what we saw tonight."

Harya grumbled. "Vikram-*ji* worked endless days and nights. *He* did not need to sleep. I say this not to cause offence. Only to caution you to build more muscle."

His understanding of human physiology was obviously limited.

Sindhuja blew out her stony cheeks, making her bulbous lips wobble. "Forgive me, but I do not think muscle has much to do with anything. There are some of our kind with more muscle than me, yet it was my will that enabled these withered wings to lift the general over the rooftops of Jalapashu. And he is a hunk. I mean a chunk."

"You embarrass us, Fishtail," said Harya, and it suddenly became clear to me why it was so important for Sindhuja that Leena knew her name. "We will take our leave now. Goodnight, mistress."

With that, they spread their wings and propelled themselves upwards into the night sky. Sindhuja struggled to gain the same elevation as Harya. She arced unevenly after him through the star-studded expanse. The night sky swallowed them, leaving me alone with the general.

The wind sighed through the trees like a haunting refrain as I returned to Deven's side. He stood beneath the golden-leaved canopy of a beech tree. His gaze followed the fading shapes of the gargoyles. As I approached him, he released a heavy breath, his concern subsiding into a tense resolve.

"We can't afford to let them fall into the wrong hands."

I liked the sound of *we* on his lips. But goodness, I was tired. "I know."

"Come. Sit with me." He sat on the ground and beckoned me to follow suit. "The gargoyles waking drives home the gravity of what's at stake here. Dammit, Kiya, it drives home how much you can achieve here."

I knelt down opposite him and, with great relief, removed the drawings from my bra and set them down between us. "Then why can I hear hesitation in your voice? You doubt me."

"Not doubt. I worry for you. Do you blame me? Too often, you act as if you're alone in this." He retrieved the animal compendium from his pocket and placed it beside the drawings. "We were lucky to escape tonight. Qasim is a formidable foe. He met his match in you tonight. But as the court mystic, he has the means to uncover our identities. It won't be long."

A shudder ran through me as I recalled my grandmother's words. *It's too late to run. The shadows grow longer. The magic is already swirling.* "The shifting darkness. That's what's depicted in the drawings."

His jaw clenched. "I agree."

"But to use black magic. Why would he do that?"

"Qasim's most defining trait is his thirst for power. He must see Mahi's absence as a golden opportunity. He's calculated that Prem will tolerate any methods to retain control."

My brow furrowed in thought. "I think she's alive, or Qasim wouldn't have fought so hard tonight."

He absorbed my words. "You're right. She's a formidable adversary. He doesn't want her to reemerge."

I nodded slowly. "She's in the portal, and Babbu's feathers are how we get to her. Maybe she even locked him in the chest herself to keep him safe from the hunters."

His inky eyes gleamed as he leaned closer, his breath mingling with mine. "Mahi said the potter would piece things together. I thought she meant the kingdom. I didn't realise she meant you would piece me together, too."

A jolt of pleasure ran through me. I was hyper aware of his body and mine. But when he threaded his hands through my hair, I stalled, resisting his kiss. "You said we wouldn't do this. You said that you didn't trust that I had manipulated your feelings. You said we should only be collaborators. That it was safer that way."

He trailed his thumb across my bottom lip, his voice raspy. "I don't care what I said. I don't care if you manipulated me. I don't care if your pockets are full of spells. It's been so long since I felt this way." He leaned in.

But it wasn't enough. I still hesitated. "Why? Why do you worry about me, Deven?"

I knew why. I knew why because, just before all hell broke loose in Mahi's bedroom, he'd admitted he cared for me. But I needed to hear him say it. I wanted so much to savour it.

He looked out across the meadow as if seeking answers in the moonlight, and when his gaze returned to mine, it was clear as crystal waters on a still morning. "You matter to me. More than I thought possible."

My chest fluttered. Still, I challenged him. I needed us both to be sure. "You said that the raja wanted me."

His jaw clenched. "He can't have you. Only I can have you."

My eyes dropped to his lips. Whatever was happening between us was just one more secret to keep. I leaned into his touch, and when our lips met, he groaned deep in his throat. He pushed the drawings and the book aside, kissing me all the while as if he couldn't bear a moment of separation. As if he yearned for me as deeply as I yearned for him. His anger dissipated at our first touch, and the soft brush of his lips against mine made my core smoulder.

The world around us faded into insignificance. The mystic, the gargoyles, the information we had won.

None of it mattered except this moment of need—him and me, an island in the strangeness of this magical kingdom.

But the kisses weren't enough. We both longed for more. He shifted beneath me to unclasp his dagger belt and flung it aside. He held my face, searching my eyes to check if this was okay, if I was okay, if we should stop or give in. I caught his lips in answer. Strong arms looped around me. The ragged rhythm of our breath mingled in the night air. He couldn't stop touching me, even though he tried to slow the pace of our desire. He lifted my top, stroking the skin at my waistband–the tiniest brush of my skin–making me moan for more. I straddled him, rocking a little, knowing I was a tease and wanting him to beg.

I wriggled out of my tunic and reached back to undo my bra.

His lips parted, and he reached up to cup me.

"No. Not yet." I shook out my hair and let it fall across my moonlit shoulders.

"Careful, little witch. I can play the same game."

I bit my lip, and he followed every movement of my tongue. "Take off your jumper."

He peeled it off. His hair was mussed, and his eyes fiery with desire. I ran my hands over his chest. The rhythmic rise and fall of his breath highlighted his strength, each contour and curve an ode to his physical prowess. I leaned forward, tracing the scars from the battles he'd fought, wriggling out of his way when he raised his hands to caress my breasts and pressed myself against his chest instead. I enjoyed every groan, every whisper of my name as I flicked my tongue over his nipples and trailed kisses down to his navel.

"You're beautiful," he said, and it was an accusation.

The vulnerability in his gaze mirrored the turmoil within him.

Only when my own ache grew too strong to ignore did I let him return my touch. He rolled me onto my back with deft hands, intent deep in his eyes. The grass was cool against my warm skin, and the beech tree scattered its copper leaves in the breeze. He cupped my cheek, tugged my ear with his teeth, tangled his tongue with mine, and dipped his head to place rough kisses on my nape that made me wild. I closed my eyes as he kneaded me, exploring every inch of my skin. He took first my left and then my right breast in his mouth, sucking as I gasped, taking his sweet time, placing kisses on my soft peaks while I drove my hands through his tousled hair, needing more, so much more.

"Are you sure?" He threw me a questioning glance. At my nod, he frowned. "Say it."

I quivered, parting my legs and urging him closer. "I'm sure."

He gave me a slow, lop-sided smile that made my heart somersault. Then he slid my trousers over my hips, taking my knickers with them. When he took off his own trousers, I gripped his buttocks, revelling in the sensation of his strong thighs against my soft ones. It was clear he wanted me. Clear from the way his kiss plundered, the way he paid attention to every part of my body, dipping his fingers into me, knowing how to build me to my wildness. Clear from how he wrapped a silken strand of my hair around his finger, slowing our passion and kissing me with soft abandon as he slid into me. I wrapped my legs around him as our bodies moulded together, and we discovered a rhythm that was entirely ours and rode to the stars.

Afterwards, he took me in his arms under the canopy of the beech tree, with the moon as our witness, and we were both quiet for a while. When he noticed goosebumps trailing up my skin, he covered me with his jumper that smelt of him—of sunlit forests and warm earth—and tucked me into the nook of his arm.

"I didn't cast a spell on you."

Laughter rumbled through his chest. "Yes, you did. The moment I saw you."

I swatted him. "I mean, these feelings between us. They're honest."

"I know, little witch. I trust you. I trusted you the other night, too. It's just that—"

I reached up to trace the edges of his tattoo, the silver scar on his eyebrow and the bend on the bridge of his nose where it had been broken sometime in his past. "You've been hurt before."

He knew I didn't mean physical injury, so he simply said, "I lost someone, and I barely survived it."

"Your wife," I said softly.

Anguish flashed across his face. "Yes. My wife."

"I'm sorry." I meant it. I meant it even though it felt strange that another woman had been the centre of his world when I was starting to imagine myself there.

He usually held his cards close to his chest, but there was an openness in his expression that I'd not seen before. An openness that had perhaps disappeared when his wife died. So I dared to ask him the question that had been on the tip of my tongue since he'd told me the meaning of his tattoo. Since he'd told me about the curse that prevented him from shifting.

"Deven, why did Prem curse you?"

His brow furrowed, and he traced small circles on the small of my back as he talked. "When it is time for a new raja to be appointed, anyone can challenge for the throne. Young and old, men and women, all line up to test their wits and strength against each other in a magical contest. It's all fun and games until it gets down to the last two." He sighed. "We were young men, beloved cousins. We egged each other on, neither of us thinking that we would be the last two standing."

My pulse sped. "Prem didn't want to back down?"

"Prem *couldn't* back down. His personality and the rules prevented him from doing so. You see, his parents had been too proud for help but dirt poor. And it gave Prem a steely core. I didn't see it then, not until it was too late. When we got that far, he decided he wanted to win. He *had* to win. Even though the rules of the contest stated that the winner of the throne must kill the challenger."

My eyes widened. "But you are cousins. And you survived."

"It's a spiritual killing, little witch."

I sucked in my breath. "What did he do?"

"He persuaded Menon to curse me in exchange for a position as his most trusted advisor."

"Mahi's brother?" My chest constricted. That's why he'd never helped Mahi to find her missing twin. The man had caused him profound suffering–splintering his identity–all for power.

"But you were family."

There was a sharp edge to his voice. "I was stupid."

Surely, he couldn't blame himself? "Did you consider taking the throne for yourself? Sometimes, a smaller evil is necessary to stop a bigger one."

"Sometimes, I think about whether the trajectory of this kingdom would have been better without him. I wonder whether this is all my fault." His body tensed. "I could have overpowered Prem physically. That might have been enough. I could have sought the support of another courtier–your grandfather, for example–but my heart wasn't in it. I didn't care to be raja. And I refused to hurt my cousin. That would have meant I was the same as him."

I didn't know how it was possible for him to keep his moral compass after all he had been through. Hearing his story renewed my sense that Prem didn't deserve mercy, and in the stillness of Deven's eyes, I read his doubts about his decision.

He should have killed Prem. Neither of us said it out loud.

"The raja hasn't truly trusted you since then, even though he limited your magic."

"No, he hasn't. He sees me as soft. Why do you think he took Mustachio aside, though I led that mission to Boundless Bay and told him to retrieve the jewel at all costs from Sitara?" His heart pounded beneath my ear. "After all I've done for him."

I had feigned ambivalence toward him for so long that it

surprised me how keenly I felt his pain. "He wants to keep you small."

"He succeeded."

"No, he didn't. We can still win."

He let out a long exhale. "Yes, maybe we can," he said as if he had never really considered it. Never really believed it. "We can't rush into this blindly. We have to trust each other. And make sure the gargoyles don't switch their allegiance."

It seemed like an enormous feat, but it wasn't impossible. Nothing was impossible. I clung to that fact. "We'll enjoy tonight. In the morning, no one can know that this happened. It would be foolish to anger the raja."

A spark of anger. "It's not the first time he's meddled in my relationships."

My breath bottled. I lifted my head to look into his inky eyes, and they deepened with lust all over again. "Deven, what are we to each other?"

"In private? Whatever we want to be."

His words lingered in the air between us.

"You will train me as you promised? So I'm ready?"

He smoothed the hair back from my face and traced the silvery patterns of moonlight on my skin. "Yes, Kiya, I'll train you. As long as you agree not to go this alone."

The warmth of our tangled bodies lulled me into a blissful haze. My eyelids drooped. "I promise."

"We start tomorrow. The blood moon is in three days. That's our chance to get Mahi."

I couldn't keep my exhaustion at bay any longer, and my body grew heavy against him.

He shifted me into a more comfortable position, cocooning me from the breeze. "Rest awhile, and I'll keep watch."

In that moment, it felt like there was nothing we couldn't do together. Syncing my breathing to his, I slept in his arms–

my first sound night's sleep in the kingdom—as the first hues of pink and rose gold crept into the sky.

CHAPTER 14

The next morning, as the sun found its way into our house, Babbu perched beside the window, his vibrant plumage illuminated by the soft, golden light. His anxiety had melted away once he learned that it might be possible to bring Mahi home. It pleased him that we'd unravelled the meaning of his feather loss: he was the key to finding his beloved seer.

We shut the windows and ensured no neighbours poked their noses into our living quarters, even when Ishaan tumbled through the door and pleaded with us to see Merlin. There was so much at stake, so many secrets to keep under wraps, and I'd promised Deven to be careful. So I sent the boy away with promises of a future visit.

The parrot's transformation was a marvel to behold. The melon mayhem was behind us. A sprightly serenity had replaced his once agitated movements. He pecked at his breakfast, savouring his seeds with relish. The uneven, haphazard fluttering of his wings had become a graceful and purposeful glide. He looped through the air with newfound confidence, skimming the ground and the ceiling until I couldn't watch any more for fear of injury that he narrowly avoided. He hopped from the windowsill to the bed and kitchen counter and back again with newfound ease. His chattering washed over us, fragments of ominous phrases. "Blood moon. Celestial tune. Secrets old and true."

Most strikingly, while his beak had not yet fully healed from his unfortunate meeting with the windowpane, Babbu's plumage was no longer patchy. Thanks to Leena, his green feathers shimmered like a canvas reflecting the brilliance of a new day.

Only Merlin soured at the parrot's flights, playful hops, and vibrant calls. His black and tan body hunched. "I tried everything to make him happy."

"You did more than make him happy, Merl. You kept him safe while we were figuring this out." I crouched to comfort him and then turned to Leena with a slow, disbelieving shake of the head. "I don't know how you managed to rejuvenate his feathers. You weren't even trying to heal him."

"Well, it made sense to me," said Leena. "The animal compendium says that the feathers have to be newly harvested, and we know we need to keep Babbu hidden. The mountain of expelled feathers is a liability. We have to get rid of them. I figured we can't just toss them into the bin. Burying them is too risky as some cretin might dig them up. So burning was the only way."

"Show me again."

She grinned. "Watch that remaining sore spot near the crown of his head."

With a glint in her eye, she gingerly picked up a feather that had fluttered to the ground. Beside her, a simple matchstick awaited its purpose. She struck the match against the rough edge of the matchbox and lit a flame. Then she held it to the feather's emerald tip. A sharp and acrid aroma, akin to gasoline, saturated the room. Babbu cocked his head with keen interest, though Leena had repeated this process over and over in the hours since waking. The feather caught fire, but as it burned, it didn't disintegrate into ashes like ordinary matter. Instead, the flame merged with the feather instead of devouring it, emitting a small sphere of radiance.

Then, something remarkable happened.

The feather's strange glow intensified, and a faint shimmering pattern appeared on the crown of the parrot's head. My eyes widened as the feather weaved itself back into Babbu's being. His bald patch diminished as a feather emerged. With a final flicker of brilliance, the burning feather in Leena's hand dissipated in a cascade of sparks.

I looked from her to Babbu in awe. "God, that's brilliant."

Babbu gazed at Merlin with one beady eye. "Dirty hare."

This time, the parrot sounded more like himself: sharp rather than submissive. As if recovering his health and his hopes had restored his defiance. By the looks of Merlin's forlorn expression, he preferred the other version of his friend.

Leena's eyes shone with satisfaction. "I wonder if the same process could work for menopausal hair fall or receding hairlines. It could be our little side venture."

"More lucrative than a nurse's salary or pottery, I expect."

Merlin tore his gaze away from the parrot. "You are relaxed considering what faces us, Kiya."

"He's right." Leena gave me the eye. "You were with him last night, weren't you? The general? That's why your cheeks are rosy. That's why the servant from the palace brought you that package."

I grinned. "I might even give you all the delicious details."

Her voice rose in pitch. "I knew it! You slept with him. Oh, Kiya, you hussy. I love that for you. How was it? I can almost smell the pheromones on you. Let's put the kettle on."

The hare's liquid gold eyes flickered like the flare of the match. "I like a good rumble in the hay, too, but now's not the time for distraction. Things hover just outside our perception. I can feel them when I spring through the grass and cower in the gaps between the rising shadows."

I gathered up the last few errant feathers and scooped Merlin into my arms. "Merl, I know you're scared, but we're not being reckless. We're taking calculated risks for the greater good. We're gathering as much information as we can, and I need your help."

The hare nuzzled his silken head against me. He cared for our safety more than the future of the kingdom, and his cautious nature paralysed him. "Name it."

"We have three days until the blood moon. I'm just trying to keep sane."

"You can sneak into places we can't. I need you to slip into the library and do some research. Try and find out what we're up against. Qasim used a kind of spreading, sentient darkness, but there are other symbols in the drawings we don't yet understand."

Merlin puffed out his chest. Libraries made him feel at home. "It would be my honour."

"That's settled then. You'll go to the library. Leena and I are due to train with the general."

"What about Babbu?" asked the hare.

Leena put the matches back in the kitchen drawer and swept the ash flakes into her palm. "We should ask Grandmother to ward our living quarters as an extra precaution."

Shame gnawed at me. Kavita might have discovered my snooping by now. She had been so kind, and whichever way I turned it, I couldn't defend my behaviour. "No, let's just leave this between us. The gargoyles can ensure Babbu stays inside while we're gone, and I have other precautions in mind."

Merlin didn't look very convinced that the gargoyles would cope with the parrot, but he had been shunned by my grandparents, so he didn't speak for them. Instead, he wriggled free and bounded to the ground. "Shouldn't Sitara be here with us?"

My stomach clenched. "Yes, Merl. She should. It's strained between us at the moment."

Could the secret lunch at our grandparents' house have provoked Sitara's absence? Weren't we equally justified in feeling annoyed about her clandestine conversation with Grandfather, considering he was aligned with the raja's interests? How was it possible to love someone so much but repeatedly clash?

"Ordinary sisterly grievances don't matter anymore," said Leena. "You're losing your internal compass, Kiya. I don't know what it is. I don't know if it's being away from home, the darkness in this kingdom, or the fact that you haven't been in your studio–"

"That's not fair." Her words made me reel. She wasn't far off the mark. Sitara calling me out had been uncomfortable because I didn't want to fall in her eyes. And I didn't know how it was possible to overthrow a corrupt raja without becoming corrupt myself.

But Leena wasn't concerned with the kingdom. She was concerned with individual relationships. "Sitara's changing, have you noticed? She's not as attached to us anymore. She's distant and preoccupied. Like she's lingering at the edges of our lives rather than central to it. And the awful thing is... This is normal. It's what death is. It's absence." Her words hung in the air, tinged with the gentle sorrow of a nurse who had witnessed the coming of death in its various guises and understood its quiet inevitability.

Sitara had been more absent. The outline of Sitara's ghost self wavered like a mist dissipating under the warmth of the sun. Occasionally, she flickered like a fading light, indicating her gradual detachment from the tangible world and from us. My gut twisted at the thought that she might already have slipped beyond our grasp. At the thought that Sitara, made now of shadows herself, might have been swallowed by the darkness that had crept into Jalapashu. But the thought was too horrible to give credence to, so I pushed it to the back of my mind.

I wrung my hands together. "I've noticed it too. When she's back, I'll set things right."

Merlin's ears flattened against his head. His deep voice echoed with knowledge of ancient woodlands. "You must. The three of you know the pain that comes with abrupt endings. The unresolved feelings. Your parents wouldn't want that for you."

"She's hanging on to the earthly plane for us. I know this pattern so well from the hospital, Kiya. It's a fragile thread that can so easily fray and unravel. And then Sitara will be adrift without us in the afterlife." Leena bit her lip. "A good ending matters. An ending full of love and without judgement. Whatever is happening in Jalapashu, our sisterhood comes first."

"Yes, of course it does. Our sisterhood comes first."

But as the parrot flapped his feathers in my peripheral vision, the pang in my heart space told me I wanted both: to put things right with my sisters and address the wrongs in Jalapashu.

BEFORE OUR TRAINING SESSION WITH THE GENERAL, I MADE MY way to the studio. Our success hinged on keeping Babbu safe. Though it made sense to keep our magic hidden a little longer, after our clash with Qasim's shadows, it didn't hurt to be extra prepared.

Merlin sat, nestled against my legs, a wordless comfort, as the wheel spun and I shaped vessel after vessel. The clay took on a muted, ethereal glow, each vessel a conduit for my magic. With the touch of an artist and the heart of a witch, I breathed spells into them, aided by the hare: *tava atītaṃ bhakṣayatu, tvayā hatānāṃ bhayaḥ* and *tvayā abhimāno nāśaḥ*. Spells that jarred, and I wrenched out of myself. Spells like shards of obsidian that clung to the corners of my mind and resisted birth, like thorny vines reluctant to be uprooted. Spells that oozed with defiance and hate, like caustic elixirs staining my tongue. Spells that left nothing but ashes in their wake, toxic brews that seethed with rebellion. Ravenously hungry spells that obliterated everything they came into contact with, leaving smouldering ruins in their wake. I infused the clay with my intentions, my desires, my hatred. As the sinister rhythms of the incantations faded, I was left with a sense of twisted accomplishment.

Merlin's body hunched. "These dark spells can bring nothing but pain."

"Without a counterattack, we are sitting ducks."

"I am a hare, Kiya. See, the black magic already addles your brain. This much will always remain true–darkness begets darkness. If you wish to bring about change here, you must do it without losing the essence of what makes you strong and just."

When I didn't listen to his warnings, he left for the palace library, leaving the parrot so bereft that his feathers once again dwindled. Leena calmed him down with promises of the hare's return, then acquainted him with Sindhuja. The fishtail gargoyle, though not impressed with parrot-sitting duty, agreed to help, if only as an excuse to make lovey-dovey eyes at Leena.

Every now and then, I broke from my work to serve a customer or stare at the landscape I had first seen in the general's quarters. His servant Yuvan had delivered it that morning without a note: the sunlit sands of Boundless Bay with its foaming shoreline against the ominous speck of the Amber Hollows. The gesture was all the more romantic, given Deven's usual self-control. Last night, he had been a refuge.

Maybe it was inevitable to look for the solace of light where darkness swirled. Leena had done the same, but she had always been more open to vulnerability.

Lost in the sinuous vowels and jagged consonants of the spells that swirled in my mind, I filled the kiln with my creations. At first, I didn't tune into the gargoyle whispers in my subconscious that alerted me to the commotion on the street.

Shock pulsed through me as the raja strolled through the studio door.

An entourage of advisors and well-wishers rushed after him.

Prem Kumar lifted a bejewelled hand to signal they should wait outside. "I see why the weavers begged to remain here. It holds a certain crude charm."

My breath stalled as I greeted him. I prayed that Leena and Sindhuja could keep the parrot quiet and that I could mask the hate in my heart. "Good morning, Prem-*ji*. What a surprise."

It was uncommon for him to be here, in the heart of the city, without elephants and a procession to herald his arrival. His long hair was loose, and his beard had been trimmed to highlight the angles of his face. He wore a simple tunic over trousers and leather loafers, his attire comfortable and unpretentious for once. He had rolled up his sleeves, revealing well-defined forearms, but his forced body language told me that maybe he had posed in front of his mirror that morning, calculating how best to show his muscles off. Even if he hadn't exhibited poor morals and wrongdoing, his vanity alone would have made me cringe. True allure lay in authenticity and integrity. My job was to keep the tiger thinking he would get red meat without him feeding on my flesh.

Only the tiger in question didn't look particularly happy.

The raja cast his eye over the wares in my shop, and the wheels, and the kiln, and the tools of my trade, and the sink smeared with traces of clay. He hovered at the painting of Boundless Bay, then turned to face me, his blue eyes glacial. "A nice surprise, I presume?"

The gargoyles roared in my head, urging me to unleash their fury.

My scalp prickled with danger. I could stop the raja now before he realised I was a threat. Here he was, away from the palace, away from his guards and allies, and so trusting of me. The vessels imbued with spells were still in the process of being fired in the kiln, but I wasn't defenceless. I could still harm or incapacitate him. Beneath my feet, the earth pulsed, ready to hear my call. I could summon the gargoyles. I could sweep the raja off the throne and be done with it. Wasn't this everything I had waited for?

But then I would lose the element of surprise, and we might never get Mahi back. The people would not have time to pick a side or be persuaded. They might paint me as a villain, or I might become one.

What was more, I could only destroy him if I knew what came next.

If Prem Kumar was no longer raja, another equally corrupt courtier could take his place.

My sisters wanted me to be myself, but how could we win without playing a little dirty? So, I washed the clay off my hands and decided to keep playing the game. "I hardly look my best."

He seemed pleased that my vanity apparently matched his own. "I didn't want to wait any longer. We could be enjoying each other's company, Kiya, yet here you are, engrossed with lumps of clay. Did you not listen when I said we could be something special? Did you not hear when I told you at court to come and see me before evening fell?"

I felt trapped. This wasn't an innocuous visit; Prem suspected us.

Even if Leena were to release Babbu from the window, the agitated parrot couldn't be relied upon to make a quiet escape. Nor could we trust him to remain absent until the threat had passed. The noise of the crowd might mask his squawks, or someone might spot him.

Prem took small steps towards me, his eyes never moving from my face, as if my future teetered in the balance. "Was your avoidance of me a deliberate slight?"

Curious onlookers pressed their noses against the window glass, reading every expression. Sweet smiles told me they presumed this was a romantic visit.

My mouth went dry. Prem Kumar outsourced his violence. Only rare individuals had seen him shift. But still, I couldn't help the morbid thought of him shifting into his tiger form if he were displeased with me. My mind painted vivid scenes of rippling muscles, tawny fur striped with obsidian darkness, the pulse of his power radiating from every footfall, every snap of his jaw. A witch stood no chance against such a primal beast. The uneasy drum of my heartbeat contrasted with the rapt faces of our audience, our neighbour Farida amongst them. Could they really be that naive? By the looks of it, they expected us to fall into Bollywood mode and run towards each other through a field of flowers or dance to a soaring ballad.

He still wanted me. I could see it in the deepening of his eyes. Something else lurked in his irises, too: it turned him on to think of himself as the predator and me as the prey.

I found my voice, but it didn't sound like my own. "Maybe I wanted you to chase me so you understand my worth. Tell me, when was the last time you chased something worth winning, Prem-*ji*?"

His eyes glinted dangerously. "When I won the throne, I did things even the bravest refused."

I arched an eyebrow, unimpressed by how he repackaged the merciless treatment of his cousin to make himself sound heroic. "Are you proud of those things?"

"I came from nothing. The decisions I made were easy in comparison to what I endured." His confidence radiated like a dark cloud. "I have not given up hope of mining more jewels from the Amber Hollows, Kiya. Each morning, my mystic reads the tarot. His readings always point to you. To our entwined fates. He tells me you are the key to unlocking the kingdom's future. He tells me I am the catalyst to all the power you could imagine." When he stepped closer, I could smell the clove and cinnamon from his morning *chai* on his breath. "You need me."

Perhaps we all needed opposition to rise and be our best selves, but that wasn't his intended meaning.

My throat filled with bile, but I kept my voice soft. "Maybe I do."

His eyes were the frosted blue of a winter lake. "But today, I need you to prove your loyalty."

My pulse was a hummingbird in my throat. It was still possible to avert danger with a convincing performance. I didn't flinch from the raja's gaze. "Do you doubt me?"

His face shuttered, and there was nothing left in his expression: no desire, no ambition, just the neutrality of a man who put his own neck first. "There are some that do. Tread carefully. I gave you access to my kingdom. If you move against me, you will not get off lightly."

The gargoyle whispers in my mind stirred, urging me to be wary. When the door rattled, my blood cooled at the sight of the thin, pale-eyed mystic stepping out of a light autumn drizzle. At the window, the buoyant mood of the onlookers had been replaced by mute distress. It was clear to all that the arrival of the mystic didn't bode well for me. A small child at the window mimed a hangman's noose, his head lolling to the side. Far away, I heard the parrot's squawk, and fear crawled up my spine.

A sly smile graced Prem's lips. "I understand you know Qasim? He's my most important advisor."

I remembered when that role was Mahi's. Though my heartbeat raced, I schooled my expression. "Actually, we've never met."

"You're mistaken, Kiya." The talismans around the mystic's neck clanged as he leaned forward. He reached out and folded my hands in his. The tip of each nail was pointed and dark, like polished onyx. "Our paths have brushed a number of times. I've been looking forward to a proper introduction."

"Kiya is, of course, Prakash's granddaughter. Although it is my hope that one day she will be much more," said Prem as if I had no agency over my own future. As if women could only ever be defined in relation to men.

The mystic's pale green eyes burned into me. "That is certain. The cards tell me you are the wild card in the deck. Unlike your grandfather, you have it in you to transcend the confines of convention."

I squared my shoulders. "Your divinations don't dictate my worth. I forge my own way."

Qasim's voice was deathly quiet. "Is that what you did last night?"

My belly knotted, and my magic swelled in my veins. Even if I could match these men in power, they outmatched me in intent. They were both willing to go harder and further in pursuit of their goals, whereas there were lines that I would not breach. "I have no idea what you're talking about."

"A simple rebuttal is not enough." The raja pursed his lips. "I was forced to waylay my plans to accompany the hunters to trap the seer's parrot today. But no matter, Qasim will have caught the traitors before the day's end, and then I can resume preparations for the trade fair."

My breathing thinned. Babbu was no safer inside with us than outside if the hunters roamed. "Traitors? Goodness. What did they do?"

"They entered the seer's house last night. One had unexpectedly powerful earth magic, which was a surprise, but a raja's reign is full of these challenges." Prem's cerulean eyes stormed with excitement. This was a man who would never be content as a family man in a respectable job. He wasn't even content to enjoy his riches. He was thrilled by blood lust. "Usually, such power resides at court. It's highly unusual for magic to be hidden from me, and indeed, such power, if hidden, presents a threat to the crown. The search should have been easy. The woman left behind shoes, but they were unlike the ones the seer favoured for her monstrous hooves."

My mouth turned sour. "Mahi was your friend once, Prem-*ji*."

A cold warning laced the raja's smile. "Friendship demands loyalty. When the seer spoke against me, she lost my protection."

I hid my angst beneath lowered lids. "Did you find the owner of the shoes?"

"Lokesh was unable to pinpoint who they belonged to," said the raja.

I sent my gratitude to the tailor, who almost certainly could remember who had worn and borrowed every single item of apparel he had provided.

He spoke of loyalty, but he showed allegiance to none but himself. True loyalty was a quiet commitment to others, unmarred by personal agendas. Prem Kumar thought nothing of sacrificing his people on the altar of his desires, and I hated him for it.

My blood pounded in my ears. "Have I lost your protection, too?"

"Protection has to be earned." The raja gave a curt nod to Qasim.

The talismans around the mystic's neck glowed, amongst them a topaz stone that channelled his power. Though the hazy orb of the autumn sun was at its highest peak, shadows uncoupled themselves from the mystic's gown like serpents awakening from a slumber. "You will forgive the intrusion, but we must rule out every possible traitor, even in those cases where the raja insists on their innocence." The ambience in my studio shifted, the air growing denser as the shadows spread their inky fingers across the floor, as though the world had momentarily shifted, bending its rules to accommodate his black magic.

A scream built in me as sinuous tendrils of darkness slinked beneath the door to our living quarters with an eerie grace.

CHAPTER 15

The world tilted on its axis, and a thousand thoughts converged in my mind like arrows in flight. We should have found a safer hiding place for Babbu. We had failed Mahi. My grandmother would know loss again, and I hadn't let her in. I might have had a chance to be happy with Deven. Mum ran from this place. Sitara died for it. Leena found love in it. I had found endless possibilities here.

Our stories, hopes and losses echoed within me as Qasim's slithering shadows searched for treachery.

If Prem found Babbu, it would cost us our safety and our hopes.

A spark of defiance ignited in me. I bitterly regretted that my spells weren't yet ready. I longed to fill my pockets with the vessels like tiny grenades. The gargoyles rumbled in my head, but commanding them seemed too big for me. A feat reserved for the legendary pottery master. Yes, it was unwise to reveal my power, but what choice did I have? So I slipped off my shoes and turned my attention to my breathing. With every inhale-exhale, nature's heartbeat intertwined with my own, reminding me that once I released this energy, the world would shift in response. Sending a silent prayer to my ancestors and the universe, I drew strength from every root, every layer of the earth, every whisper of the land's history. At my sides, my fingers curled like the roots of ancient trees anchoring deep within the soil.

As the mystic walked to the dividing door, like an undertaker at a funeral, I gathered my earth magic at my core. My fingers trembled, not from fear but from the intensity of the power I prepared to channel. I frowned as a new cadence of gargoyle whispers filled my thoughts. Until now, they had been a discordant chorus of voices: some gravelly and low, like fragments of memories buried deep within the stone. Others high-pitched and sharp, like the chisels that had sculpted the gargoyles into existence. Some carried an air of mischief and loftiness, echoing the lofty perches from which they kept their vigil. All combined to form a peculiar symphony of half-formed thoughts, ancient chants, and echoes of the living world observed from stony vantage points. But at that moment, the gargoyle voices swelled, and one soared high above the rest, enough for me to isolate Sindhuja's creaking whispers.

Stay your hand. The green witch distracts the shadows, and the bird is safe within me.

I pinned my hands behind my back and went still, desperately trying to respond to Sindhuja, but there was nothing. There was no response from the gargoyle who loved Leena and had been kind to me—only the mournful echo in my mind of her kin.

She is gone. He will not allow it. She is lost. Cracked open. She is dust. She is unmade.

Their voices whirled. A cacophony within my mind, like tolling bells, lamentations, shattered glass, an unravelling, a tempest of grief that I couldn't differentiate from my own emotions. Then Prem put his hand on the small of my back, and I padded between him and Qasim through the dividing door to our living quarters.

My scalp prickled at the sight before us. "Leena!"

My spirited sister stood firm, fighting to shield our home from the malevolent forces that tried to claim it. My memories sprang backwards to the pugnacious toddler she had been, the combative teenager and then forwards again to the uninhibited adult who never backed down from a challenge or from learning or giving selflessly of herself. She spun her green witch magic with wild abandon. Our drab home was rich with the scent of life, as though nature itself had responded to Leena's call. Her vines and flowers stretched and twined, driving back the insidious advance of the darkness. Bursts of vibrant colour and life contrasted with the murky gloom, petals radiant in the face of shadows that coiled like serpents. As if the dark could never taint the natural world.

But Leena's body curved like a willow bow, and beads of sweat clung to her forehead. And as she tired, Qasim's shadows crept through the cracks between the leaves and petals. Their magic was a battle of opposition; Leena replenished her magic, but she was no match for the mystic. Her greenery wilted at their touch. The vines stretched and coiled, but the shadows twisted in response, draining the life they encountered. Each pulse of darkness eroded the colours a little more, turning vibrant greens into muted greys and transforming blooming petals into fragile husks. Leena's ashen face told me she couldn't last much longer, but she'd achieved her aim: to distract from Sindhuja and the parrot.

I spun to Prem, my fists curling with magic, logic warring with my emotions. "Call them off!"

He barked an order. The mystic breathed a word of magic. Like a tide receding from the shore, the darkness rolled back, folding in on itself as if drawn by some invisible force. It retreated up his wide sorcerer's sleeves, leaving behind a trail of wisp-like remnants that dissipated into nothingness.

"Is this what you faced in the seer's house, Qasim?" asked Prem.

"Almost certainly." A triumphant smirk played on the mystic's lips. "I told you it would be easy."

Neither man noticed Sindhuja's stone form in the kitchen, draped with threadbare bath towels from our morning showers. There was no sign of Babbu–in feathers or otherwise–but the fishtail gargoyle's words echoed in my mind. *The green witch distracts the shadows, and the bird is safe within me.* Of course. Natural law determined that shadows could not penetrate stone. While shadows could be cast onto stone surfaces, they could not physically permeate the material itself. Sindhuja's stone form was a boundary the shadows couldn't breach. It was this fact–together with Leena's brave decoy strategy–that had saved us.

I pulled Leena into my arms, and she nestled there on a wilted bed of tulips and hydrangeas, her chest rising and falling like she had run a great distance. I stroked her hair. "It's all my fault."

Her lashes fluttered against her cheeks. Her murmur was for me and me alone. "It's done now. Keep your magic hidden. Promise me."

Prem's words cut through the air like a blade. "Magic such as your sister's can't exist beyond my purview. It is an impossibility without a topaz stone of her own. I don't know how, but she violates the rules of Jalapashu."

My mind flashed back to the bitter, gritty taste of Mahi's crimson mixture coating my throat and the jagged gemstone, already tinged black with my magic, pressing deep into the skin below my pelvic bone. Whether prompted by her visions or by her knowledge of the raja's foibles, Mahi had already outsmarted him multiple times. My thoughts churned. I had to believe we could do it again. That Sindhuja had truly kept the parrot safe, and we had a chance to win. But not at the expense of my sister.

Anger mushroomed in my belly. "You gave us this home, but what is a home if even the king–who should model exemplary values–storms in here and sanctions the use of black magic against us? I don't know what you meant to prove, but my sister was defending herself."

The gargoyle chants in my head were insistent. *Fishtail is unmade. We must seek vengeance—flesh for stone.*

The mystic's pale green eyes lingered on my sister. "We witnessed your magic with our own eyes, witch. Admit your culpability. The raja demands it."

"As you wish." Leena peeled herself off my lap and rose to her feet. "I was in the seer's house."

Coldness hit me at my core. I looked at Leena, aghast. "What are you doing?"

But she stared past me, her chin held high, her gold hair mussed, and her eyes tender and defiant.

Keep your magic hidden. Promise me. It was my job to protect her, but I had been trapped by my own lies. "That's not true." Heat and fear simmered in my body, building to a cauldron's boiling point.

"Good. Very good," said the raja. "And what did you seek in the seer's house?"

"A stash of 1980s pop culture T-shirts," said Leena. "Especially the *James Bond 007* one where Bo Derek is coming out of the water. She's smoking hot."

Prem frowned at Qasim. "Her confession is enough." He gave me a tiger's smile. He brushed off his clothes like he was nearly finished with our unsavoury encounter, even though our trials had barely begun. "Though I am loathe to do it, your sister leaves me with no choice." He paused for effect. "I sentence Leena Marlowe to imprisonment in the kingdom's dungeons as punishment for using magic against a member of the royal court and for the possession of extraordinary, unwarranted power until a time as we can fathom the origin of said power."

His words struck like a physical blow against the desolate canvas of my mind. The raja had already taken one sister from me. Even the gargoyles were suddenly silent as if uncertain how to respond. As if they stood at a crossroads and every path would lead to defeat. As if Sindhuja would be trapped forever in her stone form, Mahi would never be found, and my sister and I would languish in a Jalapashan prison and join the skulls and bones that littered the palace passageways.

But Leena was composed. "It's been a while since I've had time to binge-watch a series." She reached out to gently squeeze my hand as if to urge caution and reason over the catharsis of a battle that my every cell cried out for.

Prem's gaze held a calculated intensity. "Your sister must be punished, but there is a way for you to win back her freedom. Marry me. Become my queen."

"Excuse me?" The colour drained from my face.

"It's what I intended to propose the night you were at court. Although it seems I have leverage now."

"Good god," said Leena. "The man's a lunatic."

"Such arrangements aren't as unusual as they seem. Not in royal circles and not in our culture."

He spoke as if he were a seasoned diplomat or shrewd businessman addressing a matter of strategic importance rather than proposing to intertwine our lives, body and soul, joy and sorrows. He spoke as if our union was a profit-and-loss calculation.

Leena rolled her eyes. "What a romantic."

Prem's cerulean gaze locked on to me to the exclusion of the others. "I've made no secret of my romantic interest in you. I find you attractive and intriguing. I watched how you coped with Sitara's death and adapted to our society. I watched how you navigated the waters at court. Our marriage would be an alliance that would reshape the fabric of this kingdom."

"Nothing says eternal love like the romantic flair of a spreadsheet," deadpanned Leena. "I thought romance was all about candlelit dinners, sweet nothings and the occasional grand gesture. Silly me."

My heart raced as he glanced around our home, skirting past the stone gargoyle. How long could Babbu survive in there? "You want this only because of what Qasim has read in the tarot. You want me because your father couldn't have my mother." Vainglorious bastard. My skin crawled.

The raja's eyes flickered with a truth that lay just beyond my reach. "What does it matter, given this is a shortcut to the same endpoint? I am the most eligible bachelor in this kingdom. In return, you would win power. You would win riches. Marry me, and on our wedding day, Leena walks free."

He was so sure he had won. He knew that with Leena's fate at risk, he had me cornered. It was a master move. My mind flashed back to the closeness with the general in a distant meadow. Hot skin and breath mingled, and our bodies entwined until the stars blurred. What choice did I have? I needed him gone to free the parrot from Sindhuja's stone embrace. I needed Leena safe.

The words were thick and sickening on my tongue. "Yes. I'll marry you."

Leena startled. "You can't be serious."

The raja's eyes gleamed with satisfaction. "The court had its hesitations about this plan, but I knew you couldn't refuse me. Your service has been invaluable today, Qasim. Your readings and your suggestion to come here were most helpful."

Qasim's enigmatic smile grew wider. "Destiny has woven a tapestry that the heavens can't ignore."

Prem took my limp hands in his. "Our engagement will take place in two nights' time when the blood moon rises."

I nodded. The day the portal could be opened. "So be it."

The world blurred around me, the gargoyle voices in uproar in my head as the raja and his mystic marched Leena out of our living quarters, through the studio onto the rain-kissed street. She turned suddenly at the door and mouthed our dead sister's name to me, but I could not answer, for grief engulfed me like a raging river. I followed in her wake, my steps heavy with dread through umbrellas that blossomed like flowers under the darkening skies. Some of the crowd sheltered from the rain under awnings and eaves, but most had stayed to witness our predicament. Confusion swelled on their faces. They hadn't known us long, but they liked us. Leena had tended to some of them in the clinic, and they had seen us speak for them. But they weren't brave enough to speak for us. When Prem waved to them, most bellowed their allegiance even though it was a performance. Even though I could see the defeat in their eyes and the slumping of their shoulders. This is what happened when the powerful exerted their might over the powerless.

Leena's story didn't really matter. Neither did the depths of her compassion nor the wellspring of kindness that was as natural to her as breathing. They didn't know that this was all my fault. Nor did they care that my sister had accepted my crime as hers or that she had bought me time to find the seer so we could challenge the raja.

In Jalapashu, under Prem Kumar's reign, misfortune was commonplace.

The people had been cowed into submission. Others indulged their baser instincts.

Under a sky veiled in shades of grey, a woman hurled a tomato at Leena. It found its mark, hitting her in the cheek, and the red pulp dripped down. Leena's fingers rose to her face, touching the sticky smear left behind, her expression stunned. A black and tan hare hopped through the crowd after her. And there was tearful Aanya, scolding the woman with the basket of tomatoes.

I couldn't watch anymore. I tilted my face to the rain, letting it wash my tears. Then I turned back into the studio, stomach heaving and spat bile onto the floor. As the kiln cycle ended, I made my way back into our kitchen, where the stone gargoyle waited amidst the wreckage of our home.

When I slid the sopping towels from Sindhuja's stone form, her bulging eyes and grimacing lips revealed the depth of her sorrow, as if it had been a wrench to turn to stone in the midst of Leena's battle. I peered at her awkward gait, quite unlike her rooftop pose. Her lower fishtail composition left no room to hide the parrot between her limbs. Neither could her small arms form a cocoon large enough for her purpose. But Sindhuja had found a way not to fail us. Usually, her wings framed her like tattered banners, their edges reminiscent of weathered parchment; now, they were fused at her back. She had enclosed Babbu within their stony embrace.

"Great thinking," I whispered to her as I leaned my ear against the cool surface of her shredded wings, hoping for a sign of life.

Knowing nothing of gargoyle anatomy, I thought at first that the rhythmic sound was Sindhuja's heartbeat. Eventually, I made out a muffled chirping that resonated through the stone. With a sharp inhale of breath, my fingertips brushed against the coarse stone. There was room for neither doubt nor hesitation. Leena had sacrificed her freedom to this end. Reverence and gratitude filled my heart as I willed the gargoyle to become flesh.

In that suspended moment, an almost imperceptible shift occurred. The stone grew marginally warmer beneath my touch as the gargoyle's stony exterior thawed. Delicate vibrations, like a hushed whisper of energy, leapt through my fingers as Sindhuja stirred to life. Slowly, the contours of stone began to soften, the rigid lines giving way to a more supple form. With a grace that defied the constraints of her stone prison, Sindhuja unfurled herself from her protective stance. A creaking breath, like the sound of ancient hinges being coaxed to movement, escaped her bulbous lips as she transitioned from the stillness of stone to the realm of the living.

She opened her pale yellow eyes. Once reserved and shy, they now held a quiet pride. "You asked me to guard the parrot, mistress, but I failed Leena."

"You didn't fail her. I did, with all my sneaking about. I tried to beat the raja at his own game, but I tied myself in knots. It's time to put my faith in you all. Did you keep Babbu safe?"

The gargoyle nodded. With a great sigh, she released her wings from their unnatural position.

A soft movement stirred at her back, and Babbu emerged in a machine-gun burst of squawking, blinking at his newfound freedom, his emerald plumage a dazzling display against the wilted backdrop of the room. He whistled happily, unaffected by being encased in stone, free-wheeling through the air as if his most arduous trial was behind him. As if Mahi had prepared him for this very moment. As if he had experienced a sense of safety, not trauma, within Sindhuja's rigid form.

Fishtail lives. The bird is safe. The seer waits sounded the chorus of gargoyle voices in my head.

Later, I would need a paracetamol, but for now, I wanted to celebrate Fishtail. "You did so well." I hugged her.

This time, Sindhuja didn't freeze at my touch. Her aloofness gave way to a subtle yielding as if the walls she had built around herself were slowly crumbling. She surrendered to my embrace with awkward, jerking movements. It lasted only a second before her fumbling retreat.

She sighed with pleasure. "You called me a good thinker."

"I did." Fear dispersed in my belly at Leena's sacrifice. "It is not easy to fool the raja."

"My heart is light," she said, although her heart was made of stone. "I've been waiting centuries to make this impact. You bring much-needed change, mistress. But you must learn to command us."

My heart pounded to the rhythm of my intentions as I tuned into a lineage of magic that flowed like molten clay through generations. I visualised my pottery wheel, the steady rotation of clay beneath my hands and moulding raw material into intricate forms. I stood at the precipice of power, a vessel of tradition and innovation, history and possibility. I was a witch who had come into her own–driven by necessity, belief and intent–I channelled my magic into a command. A simple command but an important one nonetheless because if I were to lead the gargoyles, I would be just and cautious. "My first command is that all gargoyles know your name."

Sindhuja, Sindhuja, Sindhuja, the gargoyles' voices rose in chorus, merging with the rustling leaves and the whispering wind.

By the wistful smile on her stone lips, I knew she heard them, too.

"Some embrace war for power. Leena embraced it because of love," said Sindhuja.

"Yes, I think she did." My younger sister's example and sacrifice reverberated through my mind, illuminating my own possibilities. "I need you to protect the parrot until I call you."

She jerked her hand to her chest. "Come, bird. I will be your temporary home."

The parrot rushed towards her with an exuberant hop, as if he had full faith in her, regardless of whether she was a cold stone prison or tepid, inflexible flesh. His feathers were a riot of colour against the weathered skin as he landed on the gargoyle's outstretched wing. Sindhuja checked for onlookers at the window, but the crowd had followed my sister. Then she cupped him in her hands and made her haphazard flight through the tumbling crimson and mustard leaves of the wet autumn afternoon.

CHAPTER 16

As the daylight waned and gave way to the cool fingers of twilight, Merlin returned to me. His presence was a steady anchor in the midst of jeopardy.

"I did as you asked at the library but would have served you better here."

The soft texture of his fur grounded me. "Did you see Leena?"

"She is in the dungeons beneath the palace. Aanya is with her, singing her magic to calm her nerves."

A bleak dullness in my chest. "What have I done?"

His voice resonated with the wisdom of a creature who had seen the plains, trees and skies turn through endless seasons. "You've made mistakes, but this was Leena's choice. She believes you will find your way. Your inner compass is your own. Jalapashu, for all its shadows, cannot sully its true north."

His words were a lifeline amidst my restless thoughts. "Did you find anything?"

The hare's tone was sombre. "The symbol you could not decipher on the stolen papers is a labyrinth. I've heard stories of such things emerging during rare alignments of the celestial sky during the reigns of long-dead rajas and ranis. A challenge reserved for the most heinous criminals or the most formidable adversaries. As old as the shadows themselves, the labyrinth is a construct of trials and choices."

I inhaled sharply. "Did you find reports of how others have escaped it in the library?"

Merlin's silken ears drooped. "There are no records of anyone succeeding."

"But we have Sitara who can pass through walls and you who can burrow beneath them. And we have the gargoyles and Babbu who can fly above them. We might not have Leena's green witch magic, but we have my earth magic. This feat must be possible."

"Anything is possible. But the labyrinth is not merely a physical maze. It's a manifestation of the psyche," cautioned the hare. "Those who dare to enter must confront their deepest fears and desires. It's a place where illusions can deceive, and truths can be obscured. Each turn, each choice, can lead the seeker closer to their goals or deeper into the recesses of their own doubts. If you pursue this goal, it will be a test of your mettle, your morality and your cunning."

My stomach churned. "So that is what we face in the portal."

He inclined his sweet head. "We face much more besides. Your engagement. Leena's imprisonment. Sitara's absence." A sniff. "And the parrot's constant replacement of me as a surrogate."

"Then let us get to work." I caressed his ears. "I am tired of losing. In two nights' time, we will have turned the tables. Come, I need your help."

He hopped along beside me as I returned to the potter's wheel to rid myself of the taint of the black magic and, instead, return to my intuitive self. When the wheel began to whirl, it was like dancing with an old friend. The rhythmic motion of my hands was a soothing cadence, a dance that had been imprinted into my muscle memory. The smooth surface of the wheel greeted my palms with a sense of reassurance. It was flow, meditation, and therapy. It was intuitive. This is what Leena had implored me to revisit.

I poured my intention and warmth into every curve and contour of the clay, infusing the shapeless lumps with a sense of love and magic. With a protection spell that swelled on my tongue, each syllable like a shield woven from the fibres of ancient oak trees. *Tamaso nivāraya. Tamaso nivāraya. Tamaso nivāraya.* I repeated the incantation over and over, and as I did, it was as if a warm hearth was kindled within me. This spell came more easily, like following a well-lit path through the darkest of forests, reading a map drawn by the stars or tracing the course of a river back to its source. Worries and uncertainties faded, and I knew that I had it within me to protect those I loved. Beside me, the hare exuded the serenity of a tranquil meadow, and the spell reverberated from and around us and merged with and brimmed into the clay.

Two hours later, I had a hundred simple egg cups that glimmered with the aura of the protection spell, enough for every household in the kingdom. I left aside four for Ishaan as I had promised, slightly different to the others, small and delicate, perfectly suited for a child's hands. Then, I batched them up for firing in the kiln. I intended to leave them all plain with the exception of Ishaan's, which I would glaze in sage green and paint with black and tan hares, given his fondness for Merlin.

Merlin looked at me approvingly. "If you had not taken this step, I would have left a tower of droppings in your bed. I am pleased that it did not come to uncouth behaviour."

"Over the next two days, I need you to deliver an egg cup to every household in Jalapashu. Can you manage that?"

He sighed. "Fine. I'll play the Easter Bunny for you, though it is November, not April."

"You'll have to be careful to avoid the hunters."

"I am quick and adept at hiding, in case you hadn't noticed." His nose twitched. "There is one thing you have left to address before we can proceed."

I wiped my hands on my apron. "I know."

He nuzzled against me. "Then what are you waiting for?"

I tidied away as best I could, buzzing with nervous energy. We returned to the back of the house, where I replenished the drinking water in Merlin's bowl, the drum of the water against the dish strangely amplified in my ears. I laid out a handful of clover and thistle for Merlin to eat despite his playful curiosity for the vines untouched by the darkness.

"You're delaying," said the hare.

Sitara had always been there for me in one way or another, ever since I had drawn breath. She always came when I needed her. It pained me to think it might be different this time. "What if she doesn't come? What if the shadows have swallowed her?"

Liquid gold eyes found mine. "Have faith."

I picked my way across the room and sat on my bed. There, I folded my hands in my lap, allowed my eyes to close and turned inward. I didn't need to speak out loud. My ghost sister didn't hear in the same way that we did. Not anymore. She no longer perceived the world through the lenses of the senses like I did. Her perception of sound had become subtler, tied to the currents of energy that whispered between worlds. I reached out with my thoughts–*Sitara, Sitara, Sitara,* her name a prayer–and could sense her presence brushing against my consciousness before chill air chased goosebumps up my skin.

My heart skipped a beat when I opened my eyes and saw her—or something that resembled her.

Sitara stood before me, her human self almost entirely

erased. Her mossy green eyes had undergone a further trans-formation. Tinges of heather framed her irises, their hue now resembling the twilight hues of a realm untouched by daylight, as if she were now truly a creature of the unseen world. Her body, once so familiar to me with its soft curves, was constantly in flux as if reality itself couldn't quite contain her. Her tangerine shift dress had faded to grey, and her physical form, woven from mist and shadow, held an air of delicate instability as if she could traverse the liminal space between worlds. Every movement she made caused a ripple in the very air, a subtle distortion that showed she was a creature of both light and shadow. Her existence defied reason.

I stared at this altered version of my sister with awe and unease but mostly love.

My heart burst at its seams to see her again, in whatever form. She was still my beloved sister.

Sitara's otherworldly eyes found mine. "What took you so long to call me?"

"Stubbornness. Fear." I bit my lip. "What took you so long to come?"

"Compassion. I made mistakes. You should have the space to make yours. You should have space to discover your authentic self when the ground shifts beneath your feet."

"You warned me that someone would get hurt."

Her mossy-heather eyes flared. "I did."

I leaned closer into the cool pocket of her translucent mists. "Do you forgive me?"

"Of course. Humans are fallible."

"And spirits?"

"We have a wider perspective but limited agency. The universe has a sense of humour."

My throat constricted. "Leena is in the dungeons. I will get her out."

"I know. I trust you. Our little sister has made herself a

bed with her magic. Daisies for a pillow and buttercups for the mattress." Sitara gave a watery smile. "She is convincing herself that this is a prime time to nap."

"Anything for a glowing complexion."

"Of course, it helps that once Aanya's song brought her calm, she worked out that she can use her vines as a tug rope and to strangle and to climb. She could escape the minute she wants to." Sitara tossed the black mass of her silver-speckled hair. "Did you assume she couldn't protect herself? You might be the strongest of us now, Kiya, but don't underestimate your allies or the power of alliances."

The clamp around my heart eased. "I'm learning that… Sitara, why did you go to Grandfather?"

"As a failsafe. I'm not long for this temporary world. If you look clearly, his compass is like ours. He puts family first."

I grimaced. "No, that's not who he is."

"You never took the time to understand him. Instead of underhand means, you could have built alliances. You see, Mum might have made a choice to leave, but she never doubted that Grandfather wanted the best for her. It's just that their versions of her best future were completely opposed. But absence is a harsh teacher. On the surface, Prakash Malini is the raja's stooge, but everything he has ever done has been for family. To keep his daughter safe. To keep his wife safe. He is ripe for change. What makes you think he wouldn't put himself on the line for you?"

"He can't even forgive Merlin for going against his wishes. How could he ever forgive me?"

"This isn't about forgiveness, Kiya. It's about absolution for the past. It's about love. And love has a way of building bridges, even across death and grief." The mists grew speckled. "As we prepare for the labyrinth, it is essential to remember one thing."

"You know about the labyrinth?"

"Of course, just because I've been out of your line of sight, it doesn't mean I've been entirely missing. My essence is changing. You might only perceive me sporadically, in the rising of the fine hairs on your nape, for example, but I can be found in the fleeting gust of wind against your skin, in the glimmer of light when doubts cross your mind, in the moonlit patterns spiralling across pavements and in the autumn leaves as they propel through the air." The mists grew speckled again, and her voice grew thin and distant. "What Merlin failed to convey in his report about the labyrinth can be distilled from a bedtime story Mum used to tell us. "The labyrinth in Jalapashan legend was a way to determine true intent. It was a means of assessing the hearts of those who wished to govern the kingdom. I have found a map in the mystic's quarters. It might help, but I won't be able to retrieve it alone."

A map of the labyrinth would lessen the risks we were taking. If one existed, getting it was essential. I barely registered the crescendo of gargoyle voices in my head.

I feared she might disappear again. I wanted her so much to stay. "Sitara? Where are you when you aren't with us?"

"In the vast expanse where the whispers of one world blend with the echoes of another. I am a wanderer between worlds, in a place where moments stretch and contract like the threads of a cosmic loom. I've danced with energies that pulse like heartbeats."

My heart contracted. "You aren't entirely you anymore."

Sitara's mossy eyes bloomed with the heather of wild salt-air meadows. "No, Kiya. I am both a memory and a presence. An echo of what I once was and a reflection of what endures."

Why did this feel like a goodbye? "If I call you again, will you come?"

Light filtered through her, like the evaporation of

morning mists when touched by the sun's rays. "For as long as I can."

Then she was gone. The imprint of her essence lingered.

Though I hadn't told her I loved her, I think she knew.

HOURS AFTER OUR AGREED MEETING TIME, I SET OFF TO MEET THE general. I chose a route away from the main thoroughfares, determined to evade unwanted attention. My steps led me down quiet alleys, where the shadows of buildings provided a cloak of anonymity. The hum of distant conversations and the buzz of activity receded into the background, replaced by my hushed footfalls over damp leaves, the chimes of temple bells and the remote strain of an accordion player in the market square. Perched on rooftops and nestled within nooks, the stone eyes of the gargoyles–frozen in eternal vigil–followed my progress across the kingdom, attuned to my purpose. Guardians of history. Fearsome warriors. Silent companions. With each corner I turned, each cobblestone I skimmed across, their gaze shifted.

Tomorrow, the blood moon rises. The portal opens. The earth witch is promised to the raja, chanted the gargoyles.

A shiver of dread raced through me, but I pressed on. Ribbons of burnt orange and deep crimson stretched across the horizon, mingling with the fading remnants of daylight. The first stars blinked to life, emerging like tiny lanterns against the deepening indigo and for a moment, I thought I recognised Sindhuja's erratic, endearingly clumsy flight and a flash of green at the furthest edges of my vision.

Nestled on the outskirts of Jalapashu, the general's training facility was essentially a vast warehouse with ample grounds, allowing his soldiers to hone their skills in a setting that afforded privacy and the equipment needed to prevent the army's skills from becoming rusty when it was seldom called up. Tall trees stood sentinel around a vast field, their leaves casting dappled shadows that danced across the earth below. A well-worn path meandered through the grounds, flanked by meticulously maintained training equipment, an array of wooden dummies and practice targets bearing the scars of countless strikes. Tucked amidst the field were clusters of seating, providing soldiers with a place to rest and strategise between drills. A stout, unassuming building, the main structure was a two-storey warehouse, its outer walls painted with faded murals of battles. The entrance was marked by a pair of weathered banners bearing the emblem of the kingdom: the sacred banyan tree.

Deven had promised to meet me here, but I wouldn't have blamed him if he had given up the wait. When I turned the sturdy iron handle on the aged wooden double doors, they swung open with a subtle creak. I peeked inside, suddenly tongue-tied at the thought of seeing the general again. Inside the lower storey of the warehouse, a vast space unfolded before me, divided into distinct sections, each a canvas for soldiers to test their techniques. The air carried the lingering aroma of determination and sweat.

Training dummies were arranged in strategic formations. Racks of weapons lined the walls: gleaming swords, rugged axes, spears with finely crafted tips and serrated daggers with handles of supple leather. Tucked away in one corner was a small kitchen with a bowl of bruised fruit and little else besides. The central area was a vast space filled with training mats for combat drills and sparring circles. A mirrored wall spanned one side of the building. Alongside it, there were pommel horses, topped with well-worn leather, flanked by parallel bars and gymnastics rings. I spotted sturdy benches, rudimentary treadmills, stationary cycles and rowing machines. Barbells and dumbbells stood in regimented rows, dully gleaming. Normally alive with the clash of steel and the grunts of soldiers, the training facility was steeped in silence.

With the exception of the general's breathing.

He stood alone amidst the quiet expanse of the training facility, lifting a pair of weights. Twilight infused the room through the narrow windows and bathed him in a soft light. He had discarded his T-shirt, giving me a full view of his unfinished back tattoo. Muscles, taut and defined, thrummed beneath his skin with each repetition of his bicep curls. His bare torso shone with beads of sweat, and his joggers hung low on his hips, revealing the contours of his pelvic bone. Each lift and controlled descent radiated a quiet power. His breath synchronised with the rhythm of his movements, steady and measured.

My voice was scarcely a whisper. "Deven."

His head of tousled curls flicked up, and our gazes met in the mirror reflection. Electricity sparked between us. He put down his weights on the mat with a muted thud and came towards me. "I thought you had changed your mind."

We were mere centimetres apart. I could almost taste the tang of his sweat. "About coming?"

"About us," he said softly.

A palpable silence hung between us. "Prem came to my house with Qasim this morning."

His coal-black eyes ignited like a furnace. "Did they hurt you?"

I shook my head. "The parrot is safe, but Prem sentenced Leena to prison."

Deven's eyes darkened. "For what?"

"She showed the extent of her magic." A tremor laced my voice. "I agreed to marry him. The engagement coincides with the blood moon."

He closed the distance between us. His fingers, warm and calloused, slid into the hair at my nape, and he tilted my head back. His words were a quiet murmur, but an intense storm brewed in his gaze. "It's clear why he asked you. What's unclear is whether you wish to be rani. Well, do you, Kiya?"

Still, he said my name like a prayer. My breath bottled. "I said yes in exchange for Leena's freedom."

He released a jagged breath. "Good. Because you're mine."

Then his lips found mine in a searing kiss, a fusion of desire and urgency that sent a shockwave through my body. The salty taste of his lips and the press of his body against mine left me weak with longing. When he pulled away, I blinked, my lips still tingling from the contact, and reached for him.

His eyes dropped to my bruised lips, but his jaw was set. "First work, then pleasure. You came here so we could train. I need to make sure that whatever happens tomorrow night, you can protect yourself."

I lifted my chin. "Fine. Have it your way."

Deven's lips quirked into a half smile. "You'll thank me later."

We moved to the centre of the training area. I kicked off my shoes to find the coolness of the mats underfoot. Then I stretched my back, my fingers interlocking behind me as I tilted my head to one side. "Don't look at me like that. You're all warmed up. If this middle-aged body goes right at it, I'll regret it for days."

His eyes lingered on where my breasts pushed out against my shirt. "You forget. I've seen you move. You're a natural."

Incorrigible flirt. I released my stretch. "Are you flattering me to boost my morale?"

"A little self-belief goes a long way in combat. I'm just making sure you start off on the right foot."

I feigned exaggerated discomfort. "Be prepared for a show-stopping performance."

"Try not to make too much of a mess, little witch."

At his nod, we engaged, our bodies moving in a series of tussles that shifted from playful to focused in an instant. Deven, with his years of experience, was the stronger and more skilled fighter, but he went easy on me, and I used his reluctance to hurt me to my advantage. He attempted to tumble me gently to the ground, but I drew from the energy of the earth, finding stability in the very ground beneath me and used the momentum to catch him off guard and send him stumbling backwards.

He righted himself swiftly, his eyes dancing with mischief. "Is that all you've got?"

I dashed towards the weapons wall, the cool metal handles of two daggers fitting snugly into my grasp, my body flowing with a grace that surprised even me. It was as if the earth's essence had intertwined with my movements, making me more agile and more resilient. "Watch and learn." I'd played darts in my favourite pub in Boundless Bay, albeit as drunk as a skunk. That counted as target practice as far as I was concerned. How hard could the upgrade from darts to daggers be? Daggers in hand, I turned to face Deven. With a flick of my wrists, I sent the daggers spinning through the air, the blades catching the ambient light and flashing like shards of silver in the half-light of the training centre.

His attention sharpened as he followed their trajectory, evading the first dagger's path with a well-timed step. The second dagger came closer, but he deflected it with a swift movement of his arm. "Not bad. Remind me not to get on your bad side. A fair bit of luck, I'd say, given you winced and shut your eyes as you threw them." He stalked closer, and for the first time, I noticed the predator in him, the tiger trapped by the raja's curse. His inky eyes flashed a challenge.

"I could get used to throwing them. I'll work on my form." I adjusted my stance and threw a punch.

"Form is important, but it's your instincts that matter

most in the heat of battle." The impact of his counterattack sent a jolt of force through my arm as I blocked him. His restraint hurt my pride, and I shifted my weight and let loose my fists. Our bodies moved in a dance of anticipation and response. His movements were a masterclass in precision, showcasing the fine line between offence and defence.

"You've done this before."

"I took a class in my twenties."

"Good. I'd tell you to avoid dangerous situations wherever possible, but it's too late for that. We don't have time to increase your endurance, but your muscle memory from back then will help. Use your body to complement your magic. Concentrate on balance, footwork and using momentum, especially when facing opponents stronger than you."

I evaded his attempted strike with a nimble sidestep.

He gave a grunt of approval. "You're agile and quick on your feet. Use that to your advantage." He effortlessly dodged a sweep of my leg and then swiftly countered, his movements seamless and precise. "Stay alert and aware. Observe your opponent's patterns. Every opening is an opportunity."

Noticing a momentary lapse in his defence, I seized the opportunity to launch a counterattack, aimed a kick at his nether regions and missed.

The general laughed, and I wondered how I had found him so stern at first and uncompromising. "Keep exploiting those weaknesses whenever you can. Quick thinking and adaptability can turn the tide of battle."

With a grin, I broke away from him and sprinted to the field outside, where the last rays of the sun painted the sky in hues of lavender and apricot. His footfalls echoed behind me, his steady rhythm blending with the wild thump of my heart.

Deven had warned me not to make a mess but also wanted me to play to my strengths. I was strongest outside in the elements, where I could sense the earth's molten core, the layers of rock and sediment and the intricate web of roots within the soil. Days ago, in our garden, even the smallest tasks had eluded me. Yet now, despite swirling uncertainties–Leena's imprisonment, Sitara's withdrawal and the looming shadow of an unwanted engagement to a despicable man–an unexpected synergy warmed my core: a melding of purpose and intuition.

With every stride, my anticipation grew.

I'd wanted to control my magic, to harness its unpredictable currents and bend them to my will. As the earth responded to my every thought and emotion, I understood that true mastery lay in surrender. My bare feet pressed against the cool mulch of leaves, grass and twigs in the field. I found my breath and gave in to my instincts. With a surge of energy akin to a burst of electricity through my veins, I commanded the earth to rise. The ground beneath me trembled, answering the call of my magic. Exhilaration and freedom coursed through me. Slowly, a series of hillocks and mounds formed, disrupting the even terrain and sending his combat equipment tumbling. The earth curved and swelled, reshaping the terrain into an unpredictable battleground shaped by my command. I breathed in the heady scent of the disturbed earth and directed the landscape to shift further, creating rises and falls that mimicked the ebb and flow of my magic, emulating soaring cliffs and concave valleys.

Turning, I found Deven standing between the weathered banners of the sacred banyan tree, his hands deep in the pocket of his joggers, his stance relaxed and commanding. "You're ready. You've broken through whatever was holding you back. It doesn't get better than this."

"Yes, it does." I smoothed the terrain with a gesture of my hands, restoring it to its previous state as if I were ironing out the creases in a bedsheet. No one would ever know how I had rumpled the earth with little more than a flick of my hands and a mere thought. The earth's ripples and folds were erased. Even the grasses rebounded, reinvigorated, and made anew. Only the scattered equipment remained as a reminder of what had occurred. Satisfied, I walked past him into the training facility. With each step, I peeled off my clothes, leaving a trail of discarded garments in my wake. "Are you coming?"

He didn't need a second invitation.

CHAPTER 17

Our lovemaking had a different kind of choreography to our combat training. Our naked bodies melding together held a tantalising newness–there was none of the complacency or comfort of long-time lovers–but the general was a quick learner: he already knew the pressure points that elicited a gasp from me, the spots that ignited a shiver. Our movements were no longer fumbling or uncertain. We had both stopped hiding from our desires, but each touch was tinged with bittersweet yearning. The blood moon loomed as a symbol of the unknown, casting a shadow over our hopes. Neither knew if the raja would still hold Mahi and Leena captive or secure me as his unwilling bride.

Deven held me as if the memory of our touch would anchor us in the storm to come. We kissed with tender urgency, me reaching upwards, him bending down, a silent plea to dissolve the distance between us. My breasts grazed his chest as we moved past the weapons wall and sparring circles, past the daggers I had thrown, towards the mirrored gym end of the room. He grunted with impatience and lifted me so my legs wrapped around his waist, and his hands splayed my bottom. I didn't care about the dirty soles of my feet, the beads of perspiration that glistened on my skin from our training, or the tiny flaws women viewed as chasms. I forgot it all. In his arms, I threaded my fingers through his unruly hair as if anchoring myself to him, planted sweet kisses across his jawline and sucked his ear. I writhed against him as he took one breast in his mouth and then the other. The chemistry between us seared me, and my breath came in pants as he lowered me gently to my feet and turned me to the mirror, his engorged member pressing against my back.

Our eyes met in the mirror, a collision of gazes that spoke volumes without a single word being uttered. His gaze travelled over me, studying every curve as if committing each one to memory. With infinite tenderness, he brushed a strand of hair behind my ear that had escaped my ponytail. His hands lingered on my shoulders, fingers tracing the line of my collarbone with a delicate reverence.

When I rocked my bottom against him, Deven groaned. "No, little witch. This is payback."

He clasped my fingers and lifted my hand above my head, leading me in a simple turn as if I were a ballerina figurine in a music box. With a playful spirit, I went onto my tiptoes and completed the pirouette. His laughter was a low rumble through the air, and his calloused fingers brushed my skin as he turned me around, sending a cascade of sensations through me. Then he knelt before me with his tattooed back to the mirror, holding my wrists as he kissed and sucked every part of me, from the peaks of my breasts to the valley between them, down to my navel and the soft petals of flesh between my legs. In the mirror, my half-closed eyes burned with exquisite pleasure, and my parted mouth and arched body looked wild with abandon. He almost brought me to my heights but stopped short.

I complained and wriggled my wrists free from his hold, needing to touch him, to run my hands over his chest and taste the earthiness of him, but when I tried to coax him down onto the mat with me, he beckoned me over to the pommel horse. My pulse quickened as his hands settled on my hips, lifting me as if I were as weightless as a wisp of air. The worn leather of the pommel horse was cool beneath me, a contrast to the heat that pooled between us. I reached out for him, heart racing, pulling him closer until there was barely a breath of space between us.

His eyes crinkled as he straddled me. "This is kinder on the knees."

"Oh?" I teased. "Are you still recovering from our last bout?"

"I haven't stopped thinking about it." He traced a feathery path along my skin, leaving a trail of goosebumps in his wake. His deepening kiss was a promise of what was to come, his tongue playing with mine. His eyes were dark with need. "I want you, Kiya."

"Then take me," I breathed, craven with desire.

His body aligned with mine, and the edges of my vision blurred as he entered me. My fingers raked his back, and my feet found purchase on the pommel horse as I tilted my pelvis, encouraging him to go deeper. We found our rhythm, and his hunger matched my own. I clung to him as the long shadows spiralled around us. The scent of him enveloped me, a heady mixture of summer woods and worn leather, salt and sweat. We slotted together like jigsaw pieces, though we came from different worlds. Here and now, we existed solely for this stolen moment of love. My orgasm wiped every thought from my mind.

Afterwards, the intensity of our yearning and release lingered in the air. A hot blush filled my cheeks as he helped me down from the pommel horse, which bore the imprint of our bodies, and when the heat loss after we were untangled and the cooler night air made me shiver, he brought me his T-shirt. I put it on, and it fell just above my knees. He held out his arms, and I went to him.

"Well, that was certainly payback," I said shyly.

"I much preferred your moans to the grunting and swearing of my men." The softness in his inky eyes made my heart flutter. "I could get used to sleeping with you every night."

I was still getting used to the flare of my own emotions. "Was it ever like this with her? With your wife?" I wanted to spool the words back because they came out all wrong. I hadn't meant to draw comparisons. I was just trying to unravel if he'd ever felt this way before. It hadn't been this way for me, not even with Tommy, who had filled my soul in many ways.

"No, little witch," he said. "It wasn't like this."

The thoughts in my head were too unwieldy for me to articulate, and so I didn't try, and neither did he. As the curtain of night dropped over the training facility, we slept a while on the thin mats meant for combat. The stars had emerged like diamonds against a velvet backdrop. I extricated myself from his arms and padded over to the kitchen to pour a glass of water. The cool liquid soothed my parched throat, and I passed the glass to Deven, who had followed me to the sink in his boxers and looped his arms around me as if we were bonded magnets.

We sat on a bench, and I remembered the landscape that his servant Yuvan had brought to the studio.

"Thank you," I said, "for the gift of your painting."

"I've loved it since I set eyes on it. It made sense for it to be yours."

"Merlin deciphered the last drawing. It's a labyrinth."

His eyes hooded. "I don't like the sound of this. I should go in alone. I'm a soldier, and–"

"I'm just as powerful as you."

He exhaled slowly. "Yes. You are."

I gave into my urge to trace his tattoo, marvelling at the precise geometry that adorned his skin. It was an intricate mandala design, symmetrical but unfinished. Woven from an elaborate interplay of shapes, angles and intersecting lines reminiscent of leaves and the rays of the sun. The ink was dark and rich against his bronze skin. The lines were crisp and exact, raised etchings I could feel even with my eyes shut. Although the tattoo had been added to piecemeal–each section marking a further year that Deven had suffered his curse–the ink flowed smoothly, and I could not tell where the joins lay. He had called it his hidden sign of rebellion. The tattoo began at the base of his neck, sprawling across his back and one broad shoulder. His other shoulder was partially bare, like a canvas awaiting the final brushstrokes of a masterpiece. My fingertips roamed over the paths of the tattoo, each line leading to another, creating a harmonious whole.

To me, the tattoo seemed a fusion of the mathematical and the spiritual. It was a testament to Deven's capacity to endure and his commitment to breaking the curse before his back was entirely covered; it was also a symbol of his yearning for his shifter identity and how, even suppressed, that part of him would always be essential to his wholeness. I wondered what he had been like before he started inking himself: if he had been an idealist more than a pragmatist, if he had known more joy than grief.

He shivered at my touch and caught my hand with his, his eyes unreadable as if this interaction between us made him more vulnerable than what had gone before.

I wanted so much to understand him. I couldn't imagine him in a body other than this one. I couldn't imagine the depth of his emptiness without access to that part of himself. Or the strength it took to be civil to Prem, obedient even. Or whether the topaz ring that channelled his magic–with its speckles of midnight–felt obsolete on his finger. "You must miss it… becoming your other self. Merlin told me you are a tiger."

His response held a raw edge, and he fixated on a distant point, somewhere near the weights. "Yes. That much is true. I miss it. I could shift into my tiger body from when I was a young child. Far earlier than Prem, even though we are of a similar age. Sometimes, I wonder if his rivalry with me started back then. It hurt him to see me inhabit the form when he longed for his own transformation."

I could almost envision a young Deven alight with the wonder of his first change. "What is it like? Being that way?"

"It's like nothing you've ever imagined. In some ways, I was more at home in that body. A tiger is solitary and aloof by nature. He doesn't need to fit in." There was a trace of a smile in his voice. "Prowling through moonlit forests. Running through the undergrowth. Feeling the rush of wind against my fur and the rhythm of the earth beneath my paws. The exhilaration of the chase. Embracing my primal power. Kiya, those experiences are etched into me. I'm like an addict who has had his last hit. I dream of those highs again. Prem took them from me. Just because he is petty. I loved my cousin enough to let him take the throne. He loved me so little that he split me in two."

I reached out for him, but his body was unyielding. "Betrayal is a common theme for Prem."

Deven's lips parted slightly as if there were words on the tip of his tongue, but he said only, "You can't marry him."

"I know." A pause. "How could I tell your tiger forms apart?"

He glanced at me in surprise and twisted the topaz ring on his finger as he talked. "We are as different as beasts as we are as men. We are both Bengals, but he is bigger than me, with colossal strength, fiery orange with thick stripes and icy blue eyes. I am..." He struggled for a moment. "I *was* sleeker as a tiger, built for agility and speed. My coat was a mosaic of rich earth tones, ambers, golds and browns, and my eyes were black as night, just as they are now."

I shifted on the bench and murmured. "Will you tell me how the curse happened?"

"I've only ever recounted it to my sister." He dragged in a breath. His posture was erect, and his shoulders squared in defiance. The words came readily as if he'd been over the event a thousand times in his mind. "Prem burst into my chambers that morning, demanding we pit ourselves against each other on a hunt. It buoys his ego to pit himself against other men, even if his superiority is an illusion. It is worth a man's life to hurt Prem's pride. We ventured alone into the ancient woods, with only his wizard Menon for company, who had made himself indispensable to Prem."

My pulse drummed in my throat. "Mahi's twin?"

Deven nodded. "It irritated Prem to hunt with me. We know each other's physical strengths and weaknesses too well to be fooled by acting. I should have realised then that he had an ulterior motive for luring me out there. He tried to draw my true strength out, time and again, but I knew his pettiness and manipulative tendencies too well to fall into the trap. I held back when his arrows and axes found their targets in animals the gamekeepers had herded into our path for the purpose. Prem's arrogant laughter echoed through the woods as stags and rabbits alike fell before his skill. We hunted for hours, pushing further and further into the ancient woods to a great English oak–that was his great joke, a little nod to the empire–and he dismounted from his horse." He closed his eyes and shuddered. "I remember it now... his boots meeting the ground, a faint cloud of dust swirling on that November day. Why didn't I carry on riding? Why did I feel obliged to stay?"

I swallowed the lump in my throat. "Because you could never imagine the lows he would stoop to."

His fingers, strong and calloused, clasped and unclasped, a mirror of his turmoil. "The wizard and I dismounted. That oak stood as a titan amongst the trees. Its gnarled branches soared skyward. Its russet and gold leaves carpeted the ground. Its aged trunk bore the scars of time like a story-teller's skin etched with memories. Moss and lichen clung to its bark." He met my eyes, which brimmed with a blend of fatigue and inexhaustible anger. "I didn't know anything so majestic could be so evil. It's not the first time I've made that mistake."

I laid my hand unobtrusively against the small of his back, hoping to bring him solace.

His fingers grazed the coarse surface of the bench as he continued. "Prem's small smile was odd. Then Menon's eyes, usually veiled, locked onto me. His lips moved, whispering an incantation as old as the land itself. I'd heard spells before, but this one writhed with dark magic. The sort of magic Mahi had been warning him against. When the oak began to tremble, my horse bolted. I tried to shift and escape, but my body resisted. The curse was already taking effect. My bones bent like boughs trying to shift into my tiger self. It was agony. Not only the physical pain but to realise I couldn't do what had so long been natural to me."

Angry tears welled in my eyes. I hated Prem with a passion.

His body bowed. "My vision blurred, and my limbs grew heavy with an unnatural weight. I don't know how I ended up so near the tree. It was as if the oak's branches became fingers. It enclosed me in its grip, and the coarse bark pressed into my skin. My heart raced, not just from the physical restraint, but from the overwhelming surge of magic that surged through the very fibres of my being."

"Oh, Deven." How could they have been so cruel?

"Menon's incantation hung in the air like a tangible thread." He paused, his hands unconsciously clenching as he relived that memory. "And then, as Menon's incantation reached its crescendo, an eerie light—a dark radiance, if that makes sense—emanated from the oak's core. As though the tree itself was channelling the malevolent energy of his spell. A torrent of energy cascaded through me that left me gasping for breath. It was a moment of profound surrender. For me. A general who teaches my soldiers never to give up the fight. To always press on. To always struggle. I was at the mercy of forces beyond my understanding. I must have blacked out. Time warped. I don't know how long I lay there. When I woke, all I knew was that a chill had seeped into my body during that November night, and something in me had been deliberately broken by Menon's dark magic. By Prem, who was my cousin and my king. Eventually, as if I emerged from a fog, I realised that the shouts I heard were my own. I dragged myself up and somehow managed to reach Nisha's ranch. A few days later, I returned with my brother-in-law, cut down that oak and lit a bonfire with the wood."

I couldn't find the words to respond, so I simply said, "Thank you for trusting me."

"Does my story make me pathetic in your eyes? The General of Jalapashu not even able to protect himself. Not even able to protect my..." His words trailed off.

"No, Deven. How is any of this your fault? You have always been the better man." I didn't dare touch him in his pain, but I wanted him to know he wasn't alone. "We should break your curse."

His voice carried a hint of sharpness. "Don't you think I've tried? It's impossible. Menon is long gone from the king-dom, and without the wizard, the curse can't be broken."

"Let me help you." I didn't know how, but I wanted to try.

"The hope has nearly crushed me, little witch. Besides, a

man can solve his own problems." He stood up to collect my strewn clothes from around the training facility like the conversation was over.

I decided I couldn't stay out of it. "What's one more problem to add to the list?"

He spun to face me in his boxers and bare feet, his stance fierce, as if I were his enemy, but his words smacked of protection, not battle. "I don't want you to risk yourself for me."

I bit my lip and drew blood. "Why are you like this? What happened to your wife, Deven? Before, in your quarters, you said something strange. You said, *you're just like her.* What did you mean?"

He threw down his topaz ring in a fit of anger, and it skittered across the floor, landing somewhere near the training dummies. Then his anger was gone, and he was kneeling before me, holding my hands. "Stop it, little witch, please. It's me who does the saving."

I frowned, not understanding. But I nodded all the same.

He briefly closed his eyes, and when he opened them, he had regained his composure. "I'm supposed to meet my sister's family tonight for dinner at Biryani Junction. Would you like to join us?"

My stomach rumbled. "Won't that raise eyebrows?"

"It's not common knowledge yet that you are engaged to Prem. Besides, Jalapashu is not so backwards that men and women can't enjoy each other's company as friends."

"Is that what we are?" I asked, looping my arms around his neck.

A growl laced his voice. "We are much more than that."

"I need to visit Leena." I planted a kiss on his cheek.

Not satisfied with meagre affection, he grasped my chin and kissed me deeply, washing away the sourness of our disagreement. "Leena's not in any danger. You need to eat."

We moved with a quiet intimacy. Deven picked up his

ring and brought me my clothes. I returned his T-shirt, and we dressed–him in a crisp shirt and jeans and me in the tunic and leggings I had arrived in–and attempted to hide the tell-tale signs of our exertions. Then he locked up. Elongated shadows ventured out into the night, almost as if they had a life of their own.

I didn't give them a second thought.

CHAPTER 18

The clock hands had passed ten in the evening by the time we arrived at Biryani Junction, yet the glow of the restaurant welcomed us. We stopped in the alley beside the restaurant, and the gargoyles were a silent murmur in my head, warning me of the coming perils, chanting about Sindhuja and the parrot, and the hare who could read, the ghost sister who grew ever distant and the green witch who kissed her lover in the palace dungeons.

"You go in first. I'll follow a few minutes later," said Deven. "Just as a precaution. My sister, brother-in-law and Ishaan will be sitting at our usual table. It's the back left table, nearest the kitchen."

"But she's not expecting me."

"Nisha is wise. She'll play along."

When I pushed open the door, a wave of warmth embraced me. Even at this late hour, the kitchen was still open. The air was alive with the fragrant spices of simmering dishes, and steam spiralled from the kitchen. Wooden tables bathed in ambient lighting remained abuzz with patrons savouring every bite. When they noticed me, the clinking of cutlery and laughter halted as if a gust of wind had swept through the room. Conversations dwindled to whispers, and curious gazes turned towards me. There were faces here that had witnessed Leena's arrest, but no one dared to question me about it.

Her imprisonment hung in the air like a storm cloud—a reminder of the fragility of life.

I fixed a neutral expression on my face and made my way to the table Deven had described, nodding at those who thanked me for the gift of the egg cup. Though by their expression, my gift was an oddity. Indeed, a toilet roll would be more useful than a single egg cup, whispered one uncle. Especially as Indians preferred spiced omelettes to boiled eggs. I stopped only for Radha's kind greeting, her gentle enquiry after Leena, and her insistence that I try a skewer of chilli *paneer* fresh from the kitchen.

Nisha's brown eyes flickered with surprise as I approached their table. She and her husband stood to greet me, leaving six-year-old Ishaan absorbed in his colouring. "Kiya. How lovely."

I leaned in to hug her and whispered in her ear, conscious of how I remained the centre of attention even though conversation and dining resumed around us. "Deven said it would be okay to join you."

"I am so glad you accepted our invitation. How silly of us to forget to ask for another chair." She returned my hug like we were long-lost friends. "Of course, you know Ashwin?"

Her husband gave a wry smile and clasped my hands warmly. "All we hear at home is how much Ishaan would like a hare. Sit, Kiya. My wife hints that I should find another chair amidst the rabble here tonight. After fifteen years of marriage, she doesn't even have to kick me under the table for me to comply."

Nisha swatted him, but her fond gaze followed him as he walked away. "We have an awful habit in this family of dining too late. Ishaan is used to it by now." She ruffled her son's hair as she sat down. "Aren't you going to greet your auntie?" It was Indian custom to label elders Auntie or Uncle as a sign of respect, regardless of biological ties.

In her late thirties, Nisha had a round face and kind almond eyes. She was dressed in khaki pants and a cotton shirt, deliberately practical in a town where most women emphasised the feminine. She'd tied her hair in a practical bun and had short nails. She bore only a passing resemblance to Deven, but like her brother, she had an aura of quiet strength.

I gave her a grateful smile as I took my seat and scooted closer to Ishaan. "Hi. Can I help you with your colouring?"

He glanced at me, his brow furrowed with suspicion. "Do you know how to colour in the lines?"

I hid a smile. "I can try."

"If you had brought Merlin with you, I would have said yes."

"Ishaan!" scolded his mother. "That's no way to treat our guest."

The little boy sighed. "Okay. You can colour with me." He pointed a chubby index finger at the page. "But only the ear of the ox. And then I decide if you can do any more."

I nodded solemnly as Ashwin reappeared with a chair. "That sounds fair to me," I said to Ishaan. "You know, I am preparing a gift for you." The thought of the egg cups made my protection spell bloom in my head. *Tamaso nivāraya.* I whispered it over the boy.

Ishaan gave me an impressed look. "What is it? It would have been better to bring it tonight."

His mother gave a long-suffering sigh. "My son is still learning his manners."

"If only adults would be so frank." I smiled shyly at her. "Thanks for not minding that I tagged along. I don't mean to intrude."

She poured me a glass of water and pushed it over to me,

a soft smile tugging at the corners of her mouth. "It's no intrusion. I'm starting to understand the reason for my brother's happiness."

I had coloured in the ox ear in magenta and olive tones and received a nod of approval from Ishaan. When the general entered the restaurant, my gaze lifted, drawn to him even amidst the clamour, as if we had the gravitational pull of a planet and its stars. Or the sun and the moon. Jilu and Radha rushed to greet him, and Deven chatted with them for a few minutes before weaving his way over to our table. He greeted me with a perfunctory nod as if we hadn't just spent hours tangled in each other's arms, but when he settled into his seat, he squeezed my thigh under the table.

The glint of amusement in Nisha's eyes showed she had caught him in the act. "You do the ordering, Dev. You spend enough money in Biryani Junction; you might as well take the reins and choose what we eat."

"Always the horse metaphors with you." Deven reached beneath the table to retrieve a fallen pencil for his nephew. "Your mummy tells me you'd much rather have hares, Ishaan."

"Yes, Uncle. I bet a hare could outrace Papa's best horse."

"Unlikely, *beta*. We rear horses on the outskirts of the kingdom," Ashwin explained, folding his arms across his chest. "It's a good, honest life. But sometimes I think my wife thinks she's the stud and I'm the mare."

Nisha rolled her eyes. "Oh, please. He's just being dramatic."

I locked eyes with Deven. "How is it that you spend a lot of money here? I thought Yuvan would bring you food from the palace kitchens." I winced at my slip of the tongue. Mentioning his servant showed a familiarity I was supposed to be hiding.

Nisha exchanged an *I told you so* glance with her husband. "It's not that. Jilu and Radha are known for their generous spirit. So long as there is still food in the saucepans, no one leaves this restaurant hungry, whether they can pay or not. They stretch each ingredient to its fullest potential, but it hits them in the wallet." She swatted Ishaan's hand away from the salt. "Dev eats here often and always leaves enough coin to cover his bill and a dozen more. So, to my mind, he should choose tonight's menu and every night in Biryani Junction after that."

"You can order if you want, Ash." Deven's grin was infectious. "I won't let a little thing like that emasculate me."

His brother-in-law gave him a mock glare. "We will settle this on horseback with swords at dawn."

Nisha's eyes twinkled. "Don't let them fool you. They are more likely to take a scenic horseback ride at sunset, complete with a basket of beer, than duel."

As the evening continued, I soaked up the sense of a family that enjoyed each other's company and siblings who had a deep friendship. Deven's demeanour shifted subtly in Ishaan's presence, his usual guardedness giving way to easy smiles. They exchanged playful jabs, and he made ships for his nephew from paper napkins when the food came, and Ishaan was too tired or restless to concentrate on his meal.

We ate a hearty meal, and Radha fussed around us, showering more attention on our table than any other, not because the General of Jalapashu sat there, but because of his quiet actions in supporting the restaurant and, in turn, her family and the community. The food was more than just flavours and nutrition. To eat in their restaurant was to be served dishes of love and blessings. Nisha needn't have worried about what we ordered because Radha brought us far more in variety and amount than we could ever have eaten. There were the chilli *paneer* skewers and crispy *samosas*, their golden-brown pastry cradling a savoury mixture of spiced potatoes and peas. There was saffron-infused rice, spinach and *paneer* curry served with saffron-infused rice and a trio of *dals*, their velvety lentils infused with the warmth of cumin and turmeric. We scooped up the *dals* with pillowy *naan* bread filled with coconut, with a slight char from the tandoor oven and washed down our food with pulpy mango juice. When I thought I couldn't eat any more, Jilu strode out of the kitchen with a tray of pistachio-studded *kulfi*, insisting every customer try one. Its rich creaminess carried a hint of cardamom, and Deven's inky gaze lingered on the remnants at the corner of my mouth before I blotted my lips clean.

"Uncle never looks at girls, but he looks at you," said Ishaan.

Ashwin spluttered on his mango juice and pulled a ball out of his pocket. "That's it, you; come on. Let's go outside and let everyone finish their meal in peace. He needs some air, Nisha."

Ishaan pouted and darted a glance at Deven. "I'm not going anywhere without Uncle. Uncle keeps promising to play cricket with me, but he's always too busy."

Deven grabbed him and tickled him under the armpits until the little boy gasped for mercy. "I'm never too busy for you. It's not my fault that you like cricket more than you like hares."

"Not true," squealed Ishaan, drawing smiles from nearby tables.

Nisha frowned as Deven hauled his nephew over his shoulder. "I don't know about playing cricket on the street at this hour. We should take Ishu home."

"That's not fair," said her son. "Uncle was going to play."

Deven won a giggle by pretending to drop the boy. "Be kind to your Mama. She just wants to keep you safe."

"But Uncle, I'm safe with you and Papa. Remember? You saved me from the panther and tiger."

Ashwin stood up and tucked his chair in. "Eat your *kulfi* in peace, Nisha."

Deven's eyes met mine. "Goodnight, Kiya."

Within their depths, I found galaxies: shooting stars and glimmering constellations but also swirling pockets of nebulous darkness and black holes threatening to eclipse the light. "Goodnight, General."

The men left with Ishaan, and Nisha turned to me. "He's right, you know."

I gave her a look of confusion. "Sorry. I was miles away."

"I joked with Ishaan the other day that mothers would keep their children in their womb forever if it meant keeping them safe. I've been holding on to him too tightly since he leapt into that ring. I thought my heart would stop seeing him there. Of course, Deven would never let anything happen to him. But I can't stop imagining the *what-ifs*. Jalapashu can be a dark place."

I set aside my dessert. "He's a beautiful little boy. Full of energy and curiosity."

"Yes, he is. But look at me, getting all morbid after such a lovely evening." She clapped her hand over her mouth. "How thoughtless of me to go on about myself when you recently lost your sister, and Leena has been taken." Her brown eyes sparked with venom. "Prem Kumar really is a pig."

"What he did to your brother..."

She gave me a look of surprise. "Deven told you?"

By now, the restaurant had emptied, and our voices carried. I glanced furtively around us, knowing Deven was intensely private. Though he trusted us, he wouldn't want anyone to overhear. "I can't even begin to imagine the pain he's endured."

Nisha reached for a napkin and trumpeted into it. "It's been such a lonely battle for him. He's fallen for his own myth. The General of Jalapashu is stoic and strong. He follows orders without complaint. My brother is so focused on protecting his loved ones that he forgets the cracks in his own psyche."

I flushed as the movie reel of my mind rewound to his hot skin on mine, his hands splaying my legs, his head dipping down. Sleeping with the raja's betrothed wasn't exactly following orders. It seemed to me the general was learning to fight back against the one man who had always tried to keep him under his thumb. I just hoped that–despite the growing shadows and Prem's violent bullishness–we didn't regret our push during the blood moon. All it would take was a little nudge for the stars to align for us.

Strange how we often truncated our own power and hushed our own intuition, thinking those we loved would be safer that way when tyrants didn't operate within any fixed-rules system. When they merely followed their whims.

Outside on the street, Deven, Ashwin and Ishaan's spirited game of cricket continued beneath the intermittent glow of street lamps. Silent, vigilant gargoyles watched from the rooftops.

I shuddered. "It's horrifying imagining what he went through. That ancient oak gripping him like a monstrous hand. The dreadful, inexplicable magic that contorted his very nature. I can't imagine what the immediate aftermath was like. The anger he must have felt. The need to retaliate."

Nisha's brow furrowed. "But surely you know it wasn't just the curse? Surely you know about Roshni?"

I held my breath. The weight of secrets hung in the air. *Roshni.* Such a beautiful name. I had long suspected a darkness lurked in his past, too agonising for him to dredge up. A darkness that had altered him in profound ways. I'd known from the minute our neighbour Farida had told me about his marriage that his trauma was deeply entwined with the death of his beloved wife. Why else had he guarded his solitude with such fervour? Why else did he keep a framed picture of Roshni in his quarters, even after all these years? The answers to those questions remained locked in him despite my probing. I could have stopped his sister in her tracks, but I didn't. I wanted to see past his emotional walls. As Nisha's kind eyes met mine, an unspoken understanding bridged the gap between us: we both wanted to shield Deven from further pain.

"He must have loved her very much."

She raised her beautifully threaded eyebrows. "Maybe he could have grown to love her. But how can you love someone who enters into marriage to manipulate you." Nisha rubbed a tired hand over her face. "Roshni was exquisitely beautiful, with skin as smooth and lustrous as sun-kissed olives, a cascade of ebony hair and impossibly long lashes. If I'm a workhorse, she was a gazelle. Everyone loved her for her beauty, but Deven was unmoved."

I feigned an air of nonchalance, but my heart betrayed me with its erratic dance. "It wasn't a love match?"

"No. He'd had other flames but hadn't ever considered Roshni that way. She was Prem's best friend, you see." She grimaced. "Even before he ascended to the throne, Prem would mark his possessions like a dog in heat. He considered Roshni one of his possessions. She had been his girlfriend once, and he kept her in his orbit. She still had her uses. There were rumours she returned to his bed whenever he felt the whim and that he'd send her a tray of cherries via a discreet servant to signal his need." She gave a self-conscious laugh. "Look at me gossiping. What must you think of me?"

I frowned. "But I don't understand. Why did Deven marry her?"

By now, only a few tables remained occupied in Biryani Junction. Jilu and Radha had retreated to the kitchen to clean up for the night after bringing us *chai* and a little pot of *sopari*: reddish-brown seeds of betel nut interspersed with tiny sweets, as a digestive aid and to freshen our mouths, that we poured into our hands and sucked straight from our palms.

"First, you have to understand Roshni's relationship to Prem. She could never say no to him. I don't know why. It wasn't the riches he gave her when he was in a good mood. She had a simple elegance and never wore the grand jewellery he gave her. It was more a kind of interdependence borne of the fact they both lost their parents so early." Nisha's eyes darkened as she toyed with her dessert spoon. "And when Prem asked Roshni to marry Dev, she didn't contemplate saying no. It was just another way of pleasing him and not a hardship at all. My brother has always had women throwing themselves at his feet. Who would say no to the General of Jalapashu?"

My stomach churned. "But why would Prem, who was so possessive over Roshni, want her to marry Deven, of all people?" I knew the answer before she articulated it.

Her voice dripped with contempt. "To widen his sphere of influence. He was always jealous of my brother, but after Dev refused to take the throne by force, Prem has always felt like the lesser man. What better way to win one over on your rival than poisoning his home life."

A chill ran through me despite the warmth of the *chai* cup nestled between my hands. "But why did Deven agree? Surely you tried to stop it?"

"Who would have her when she was rumoured to carry the raja's child? No one but my fool of a brother, with his odd sense of chivalry. He never had great expectations of love, and it suited him well enough to marry Roshni once it was presented to him. She had a laugh like a river's song, a simplicity that he liked well enough, and she didn't resent how much time he spends with his soldiers." Nisha's mouth twisted. "Of course, it came out after the wedding that she wasn't pregnant at all. It had all been a ruse to ensnare my brother."

I wrapped my arms around myself. "Goodness, that's despicable."

Nisha nodded. "They were married for a little under a year. All of this came out over the fullness of time. Little confessions from my sister-in-law. The confidences she had betrayed. The little mind games that Prem put her up to. It's hard to be machiavellian to a husband who is unfailingly kind."

"So they fell in love? Is that why he keeps a picture of her in his quarters?"

"No, Kiya. Maybe, given time, they *could* have grown to love each other. To be man and wife in reality, with all that entails." She sighed. "Dev didn't go home the night Menon cursed him. He came to me. And Roshni knew something was wrong. She'd sent him on the hunt. She'd heard Prem's and Menon's whispers. So when Dev didn't go home, she ran to the palace and demanded the guards let her into the raja's chambers." A shudder ran through her. "We don't know what happened that night. Maybe Roshni came to her senses and told Prem she wouldn't play his games anymore. Maybe Prem rubbed salt in the wound and told her what he had done to my brother. Or maybe the raja simply couldn't accept that Roshni–after a lifetime of agreeing to his every whim, never challenging him, and soothing his ego and bodily needs–wanted out… Her screams carried on the winds across the kingdom. Some say the gargoyles moved that night. All I know is that my feverish brother called her name. And that there was nothing of her to cremate. Nothing recognisable, at least. Only chunks of flesh mauled by a tiger."

Shards of glass in my chest. "Prem killed her?"

"He discarded her like she was nothing more than roadkill."

Now you know. Now you know what Prem Kumar is capable of. Raja after raja after rani. None as black-hearted as the tiger king. The gargoyle chorus became a tempest in my mind. *Sindhuja waits for the blood moon. While the luminous bird longs for his seer.*

My head reeled. The raja had killed his closest friend–and his cousin's wife–with relish and impunity. There it was in black and white. He was capable of limitless evil. Not only had he killed Roshni, who had trusted him, but he'd committed the crime with the full knowledge that his palace staff would be aware of it. He had not poisoned her or made her death quick. He had torn her limb from limb with his tombstone tiger's teeth and licked her blood from his lips. He had not given her family the comfort of seeing her face again during her funeral.

And I was to be his wife. Bile rose in my throat, threatening to spill out.

Nisha looked out onto the street. It was almost midnight, and the little boy flagged. His father swept him into his arms while Deven collected the errant ball. "My brother keeps her picture not because he loved her as a man should love his wife, but to fuel his anger against Prem Kumar."

Such openness and generosity demanded reciprocal honesty. What is more, I liked her. I didn't want to jeopardise the fragile beginnings of a new friendship. "Tomorrow night, I'm getting engaged to the raja."

She flinched, and then acute understanding fired in her eyes. "Is that why you and Dev put up such a theatre tonight?" she asked quietly.

Embarrassment heated my cheeks. "I don't know what you mean."

"Sure you do. All those longing gazes, the touches under the table, the palpable chemistry. You reminded me of my early days with Ashwin before I was a tired mother, when we couldn't get enough of each other." Her voice was wry. "Of course, now it's the suggestion of a night to myself that makes me quiver with excitement."

"I had to agree to Prem's proposal. I had no other way to keep my sister safe."

"Then you care for my brother?" She took her time studying the nuances of my expression, and I had the sense that she was using her horse training skills–the ability to assess subtleties in a horse's demeanour–to gauge my temperament and honesty.

I met her eyes. "Yes. Yes, I do."

A shadow of concern crossed Nisha's face. "You realise Prem's proposal to you–notwithstanding your many qualities–is another way to get the better of my brother?"

I shook my head firmly. "He doesn't know about us."

"Are you so sure?" She picked up her son's colouring book and stuffed his pencils into their box. "I like you very much, Kiya. But everything I told you tonight is because I love my brother, and he has endured far more than any man should have to."

"He's lucky to have you in his corner."

"Isn't that what siblings are for?" A look of understanding passed between us, but it evaporated just as quickly. "Some people in this kingdom think you are a hero, Kiya. The way you and Leena jumped into the ring to save a dying man you scarcely knew when you first arrived in Jalapashu. The way Lokesh *Saheb* makes time for fittings with you when even the most important members of the court struggle to get an appointment. The way you command the raja's attention but also stand up to him. It's not gone unnoticed. But I don't believe in heroes. I believe only in family." Her brown eyes were pools of hope. "You won't hurt him, will you?"

"No," I said, understanding she meant Deven. "I won't hurt him."

But as the blood moon's arrival loomed–and with it elements that I didn't comprehend or couldn't fathom–I didn't know if I could keep my promise. I didn't know if the scales of the universe would tip against us and cause us even more pain. I only knew that my heart was a frightened bird in my chest and that a part of it now belonged to the general.

CHAPTER 19

I longed for sleep, but there was no point in trying. Sleep was impossible without checking on Leena. No sister worth her salt could sleep while the other was in pain. It had always been that way with us. As children, the three of us would sneak into each other's beds if one of us had a knee scrape and huddle together during fevers, ensuring the infection caught us all. Most of my friends had found adulthood diluted the richness of their sibling relationships. It was a common trend for marriage, children and careers to absorb the lion's share of attention, toppling siblings from the top of the pyramid of primary relationships. An incremental separation of diverging paths was far more palatable than the sharp cut of death that had taken Sitara from us.

My stomach roiled at how alone in the world I'd be without Leena. She brought sunshine wherever she went. Her vivacity was the counterpoint to my contemplative nature.

The oily silence tightened around me—so thick that I could almost taste its bleak weight—as the guard led me down slanted stone steps to the palace dungeons. But as we descended the last few stairs and the dungeons opened before me, I was almost sure I heard the distant ring of her laughter.

Their appearance differed from the horrors my mind had conjured up. This was not the prison of Jack the Ripper's London. It didn't have cold, grimy walls or iron bars that criss-crossed its windows. Its air was not heavy with the stench of poor sanitation and overcrowding. The walls of the dungeon, instead of being dank and covered in moss, were made of well-polished stone, their cool, beige surface hinting at the palace's opulence even in its depths. The space had been divided into six large cells, a central corridor and a prison guard lobby with a round table and two upholstered armchairs. The aroma of freshly cooked meals wafted through the dungeon corridors.

"Leena-*ji*. There's someone here to see you," said the guard, as if he were a butler announcing a surprise visitor at her house.

Against one wall of her cell stood a narrow, sturdy bed covered in clean linens. A small, barred window allowed a thin stream of natural light to filter in during the day. There was a small shelf for her belongings beneath it and a table with a small lamp. My sister lounged around the table, playing cards with our grandmother, Aanya and a handful of prisoners. Leena wore turquoise trousers and a shirt reminiscent of hospital scrubs. Her golden hair was in a simple plait down her back, and her makeup-free skin gleamed as if she had managed to find a luxurious moisturiser as prison contraband. She looked completely at ease.

Her expression brightened further when her eyes alighted on me. She leapt out of her chair and hugged me. "You must have been so worried, but look, it's not so bad here. We've got cards, camaraderie and a delicious supply of food from the palace kitchens."

Heat prickled behind my eyes as I held onto her, relieved she was well. I wondered if the cool pockets of air meant that Sitara was with us. "How on earth did it come to this?"

"I know. A few months ago, the thought of being indefinitely imprisoned would have hit differently. But I'm feeling quite zen about it." With a slight curl of her fingers, green shoots sprouted from her upper palm and filled the corner of her cell with a blackberry bush, complete with fully formed fruit. She casually offered me a handful of plump berries, then popped one in her mouth. Her eyes shone. "Not having to hide my magic has made it come on leaps and bounds. Just think of how I could put an end to the misery of empty bellies when I am out of here."

My eyes roamed over her for signs of maltreatment. "How are they treating you?"

"I didn't enjoy being frogmarched across the streets in the sight of all and sundry, but the guards are quite civil. None of them have god complexes, as far as I can tell, and there's no whipping or forced labour or solitary confinement. I take it the worst offenders don't end up in prison. They're dealt with by more brutal means."

The tartness of the berry surprised her, and a tiny dribble of dark juice escaped, clinging to her lower lip like a glossy gem. Aanya came over with a hello for me, and when the guard turned away, she gently kissed my sister's mouth, lingering at the crimson stain.

I gave them a moment of privacy and peered at the other prisoners, chatting to my grandmother. "What are they in for?" I asked, trying to discern how safe Leena was or whether the kingdom's mean-spirited criminals would cause her trouble.

"Virendra is a baker. He angered the royal court by making English scones rather than paratha," Aanya kept her voice light as the guards returned and a slight shimmer pervaded the air like she had cast a net of her contentment magic over the dungeon, leaving me uncertain as to whether the guards would have been as good-natured without it. "Shivani is... how do you say it? A treehugger who protested against the burning methods used by the hunters. Karthik is an inventor accused of making tools and gadgets from discarded metal scraps. Jalapashu has always been suspicious of technology, you see, and Prem-*ji* likes the old ways. He is antimodern. Oh, and Neha. She is very clever. Perhaps the cleverest woman in Jalapashu. She is a scholar of languages who is tired of learning from books and repeatedly attempted escape to practice her skills in the wider world."

"We can launch the rebellion right here," said Leena in a mock whisper.

The guards laughed uproariously as if she had just told the best joke in the world.

I was wound as tightly as a coil. Yet, despite our environment, my sister was as relaxed as a cat in a sunbeam. I narrowed my gaze at her. "Have you been drinking?"

"Well, we did have the vodka chaser the cook sent down to help us digest the *vindaloo*."

"What?" Her expression looked a little smug, and I remembered the little girl who had an uncanny knack for winning us over, not by bending the world to her will but by coaxing it with kindness.

Aanya gave a gentle smile. "The palace cook has suffered from wrist sprain from too many *chapatis* for many years. He's been so taken by Leena's physiotherapy skills that he sent down delicious morsels from the kitchens."

"I've been sending him back edible flowers in return," said Leena.

"Not only that," said Aanya. "But she has won over the prison guards by tending to minor ailments. They've agreed to leave the doors to the cells open as long as the prisoners don't attempt an escape. They're even bringing Leena a sofa for her cell."

I gawped at my sister, not knowing whether to laugh or cry.

"A little first aid plus Aanya's songbird voice go a long way. For the time being, visiting hours are a suggestion." My sister's brown eyes grew troubled. "Of course, it could be because Prem Kumar is bellowing orders at those arranging your engagement party. If you marry that swine, I'm abstaining from bridesmaid duties."

I lowered my voice. "I'm not marrying him. At least, not willingly. Leena… I'm in love with Deven."

Her eyes twinkled. "At last, you noticed. I thought I would have to lock the two of you in a hot yoga class together to get you over the line." She nodded over to where Kavita sat at the table. "Come on. We've got plenty to talk about."

My grandmother shuffled a deck of cards with the flourish of someone who was no stranger to gambling dens. Someone who could have been a card shark despite her otherwise mild ways. "Come and join us, Kiya. We're playing *Chor.*" She darted an apologetic look at the other prisoners. "Ladies, gentlemen, would you mind? My granddaughters, their friend and I have family matters to discuss." She signalled at me to sit down as Jalapshu's dissidents vacated the table. "I'll deal you in. You know this game?"

I wasn't in the mood, but there was a determined glint in Kavita's eyes and an edge to her tone, so I did as I was told.

"Sift out your pairs, pick a card from your neighbour, and rid yourself of all your cards," said Aanya. "If you're left with the joker, you're the *chor.* The thief."

I slid into the seat, fairly certain from her loving body language with Leena and the subtle tension between us that she knew of my shortcomings. Our parents had taught us our manners well enough for us to apologise for our errors without making excuses or trying to save our own skin. "I'm sorry for stealing from your house and not trusting you to ward our house."

Kavita lifted her chin and gave me a hard-eyed stare. "I knew the moment you entered Prakash's study."

I winced. "You did?"

"Of course. The prayer plant told me. You didn't think it was in there simply for decoration, did you? It was there for protection. It's the sort of magic you'll be capable of in time, Leena." Her eyes hardened as she turned back to me. "I would have been delighted to ward your house. I would have done the warding and brought you a bowl of *pani puri* for your lunch, too. Instead, you landed your sister in a difficult position."

"Did you know Sitara was at your house that day?"

Kavita nodded. "She was there to build bridges. That's possible even where differences exist, you know, *beta*."

I recognised the little slap of disapproval combined with the endearment *beta* from how our mother used to interact with us.

Leena tugged at her bottom lip. "The card game's over, isn't it?"

"Oh no," said Kavita. "We're going to lay all our cards out on the table. And no singing, Aanya. I've been waiting decades for this family not to mask our emotions. We're ready to come clean, isn't that right, Kiya? What we need is some good old catharsis."

Was there any match for an unbending old crone? Old women who don't engage in idle chitchat or sugarcoat their words. Old women don't feel the need to tiptoe around their convictions or apologise for the waves they make. Old women who have learned that time is too precious to waste on empty pleasantries. That sometimes wisdom means saying *take me as I am* and letting the world adjust around you. Yes, Kavita was a woman who knew her power, and I was more than glad she was family.

I was proud.

"Now look here." My grandmother's birdlike fingers manipulated the deck of cards. She shuffled them with finesse, and the worn edges of the cards rustled softly against each other. Splitting the deck, she swiftly bridged its two halves together. The cards merged, and she executed a series of intricate cuts and shuffles, weaving them into new configurations, mesmerising us. This was her sleight of hand, her way of distracting others in the dungeon from the intimacies of our conversation. "I'm not stupid. I know what you are planning during the blood moon. After all, I was young and brave once. I don't want you three putting yourselves in danger. But the danger of not following hearts is worse." Her eyes glazed over with the past suffering. "And the truth is I wish I had been less passive when your mother left. I have limited options to help you, but I have information, and I have my magic and my blessings. That will have to do."

My heart pounded. "But what about Grandfather?"

Her eyes softened. "Oh, that silly old fool. He hates being the raja's enforcer. Those poor families at tax collection time. All those sordid little secrets. Every time he comes home, I make him a pot of my best chamomile. Not that it helps. Maybe he won't ever be able to wipe his soul clean. All for me. All of it. He believes that by staying close to Prem Kumar and appearing loyal, he can shield me from harm. Which is nonsense, of course. That jungle cat has always bitten the hand that feeds him."

I thought of Roshni and how she had been betrayed in the most violent way. How her flesh had become Prem's next meal when he could have chosen a thousand other ways to let out his frustration or show his disappointment, which would have allowed her to live. But it would have made Deven a married man, not a widowed one—a man who belonged to Roshni and not me. The cauldron of my emotions bubbled: a mix of shame, love, fear and hope.

Sitara had been right about our grandfather. She had understood all along. "Grandfather's worry for you puts him at odds with our goals, Grandmother, and I can't ask you to decide between us."

"I can tell him the truth until my breath leaves my body, but he won't listen," continued our grandmother. "So before I came here, I wrote him a tersely worded letter. I took my time and wrote it in beautiful cursive writing with my fountain pen even though my vision is not what it was, and I struggle with a pincer grip."

My pulse raced. "What did you write?"

"I told him he didn't need to protect me. I would give up all my comfort for another day with our beloved Hansa. Just one more day." Her chest heaved beneath the thin cotton of her sari. "And as that isn't possible, I choose to support my granddaughters. Then I told him that I can meet with whoever I like and make all my own decisions for the rest of my life without his permission, or he'll be eating his dinner cold and wearing mismatched socks for the rest of his days. And that I'm thinking about getting a tattoo on my foot. A yellow rose from our family crest. And that if he didn't like it, he could lump it."

I shivered as I recalled the rose on her door handle and worn by Mum in her portrait in the palace library.

"More power to you, sister." Leena nodded approvingly. "I love a granny who uses her body as a canvas and can express herself. Brighton is full of them. I'll take you one day."

Aanya's eyes glowed. "Do you think he will listen, Kavita-*ji*? My mother tried independence once, and my father didn't speak to her for a month until she relented. Mother regretted not standing her ground as she enjoyed the peace."

"I've learned a trick or two over the years. It just takes a little prodding to unpeel Prakash's stubbornness and reach his sentimentality." Our grandmother patted her beehive. "I used the same ink and fountain from the days when we wrote love letters to one another. Only... I decided I had gone too far."

My belly knotted. "You toned it down?"

"No. I didn't want to cause him to have constipation or a blackout or, God forbid, a heart attack. You know, bodies are fragile at this age. So I ripped up the letter and put it in the wastepaper basket, then came here. Because I meant what I said. I've made up my mind."

A flower bloomed in Leena's palm: a tall gladiolus with trumpet-shaped flowers to represent bravery. She placed it in front of our grandmother. "Did you tell Grandfather you were coming here?"

"*Beta*, there are some things that a woman keeps secret from her husband for the betterment of the marriage." Her dark eyes gleamed as she fanned the cards through the air, and I thought of the myriad of possibilities that lay in front of us and how they might unfold. "But it's good we have this moment together. I have information that might be important."

The three of us leaned forward in our seats, and still, the cards arced and collapsed through the air. A sliver of cold wind ruffled my hair, and the bitter tang of orange and magnolia perfume found its way into the cell. The lamplight flickered across the smooth beige walls, and the nearby guards chewed their tobacco and allowed their bellies to strain against their tight khaki shirts.

"Prakash's work means he is needed at all hours of the night. Sometimes, when I am lonely, I go into his study for a little light reading." She gave me a disapproving glance. "Not to pry, of course. I share the burden of his secrets so his soul doesn't have to carry them alone. So I can share my light with him and protect him from his sins, even though in his mind he is *my* protector."

I bit my lip. "Grandmother, what is it that you know?"

She harrumphed. "If you had been brought up in Jala-pashu, you would be calling me Nani. But never mind. Listen, the three of you. When the blood moon rises, the portal will open at the foot of the sacred banyan tree. You know it, yes? God's shelter. The cosmic tree. The tree of blessings. India's national tree."

"It's in the market square," interjected Aanya. "The sprawling tree which provides shade to traders and meeting friends."

Leena nodded pensively. "Banyans actually fall under the category of *Strangler Figs* because they smother the new beginnings of other trees. Their dangling aerial roots sink into the earth to become branch-supporting pillars. A single tree spreads laterally to increase its footprint so it looks like a grove."

My stomach was weighted. "That's not creepy at all." I'd always liked the tree, but now I was daunted, and it loomed large in my head with its leathery leaves. It now seemed utterly fitting for it to be the entrance to the labyrinth.

"Actually, I've been learning about its many medicinal qualities. It can be used to treat diarrhoea, prevent tooth decay and alleviate depression," said Leena. "Although, in my humble opinion, all trees do that."

"Although its fruit is inedible. I had a classmate who missed school for a week after eating a piece." Kavita sighed. The flow of the playing cards through the air was now barely a whisper as she neared the end of her revelations. "You will find the portal there at the appointed time. Take the parrot's newly harvested feather. They are part of the puzzle and the reason why the seer found him long ago. She knew this day would come."

My brow furrowed. "So all this time, Mahi has been planning to ensure she escapes her prison?"

Kavita shook her head. "You misunderstand. The seer

outsmarted all the men around her. She *engineered* her imprisonment. What she has been planning is how to open the portal. It only opens for selfless reasons, and the seer's reasons are entirely self-interested."

"Why did Mahi need to open the portal? Why would she want to be imprisoned in there?"

"Because her brother is in the labyrinth, too," said Kavita. "And has been since the raja tired of him."

Aanya's anguish revealed itself in how she tugged at the piercings on her cartilage. "This is what my friend put herself in such danger for? For Menon? All her schemes just to free a brother who never loved her as much as she loved him. She warned him about black magic. She warned him." After Menon was gone, it was Aanya who had sanded Mahi's hard edges with her softness. It was Aanya who had broken down her sullen defensiveness and her reluctance to let anyone in.

Kavita looked down. "Aanya, Mahi didn't know why Menon disappeared. You know how rumours spread here. We all thought he left of his own accord. I think she must have glimpsed him in her visions and worked out a plan in secret, manoeuvring all the pieces into place. You see, Prakash confessed to me years later that Menon was punished for turning his back on black magic."

Shock spiralled across Aanya's plain face. "He listened to her?"

Kavita nodded. "It was far too late by then, of course. His soul had already been corrupted. Prakash thought it safer if he was gone. Then Mahi accepted Prem's offer of becoming court seer, though she despised that life. Prakash assumes it was to protect the people. The seer has great power, not only in her visions but her ability to gain trust and manipulate those around her to her ends. Mahi might be kinder and more just than her twin, but she is equally tricky. Her file shows that she was Prem's trusted ally for decades until recently. Until my granddaughters returned to Jalapashu. So you see, you have it in your power to right a great wrong. But it could be that you are pawns in a greater game."

"I trust her," said Aanya. "I trust Mahi with my life and the lives of those I love."

Leena observed Aanya for a moment, using her opinions as a gauge for shaping her own because love fosters hope, and logic can't compete with such a simple, potent force. "Then I trust her, too. I like her all the more for going to great lengths to save her brother, even if he wasn't perfect. Love doesn't demand equal stakes. Some give tenderness, and others give laughter, challenge, thoughtfulness, practical labour, steadfastness, or an example of what we don't want to be." My sister pressed her girlfriend's hand, rubbing her thumb over it in small, comforting circles. "Mahi loved her twin enough to go into the darkness for him. And maybe Menon has already served his penance in that forsaken place. Maybe Mahi went to these lengths because it was the only way she could be at peace with herself. I don't grudge her that. Kiya?"

Blinking, I focused on her. I'd heard their conversation not in stereo but as a kind of background buzz. My mind clouded as if I had retreated from the room, and my thoughts were solely for Deven and his curse that only the wizard could lift and how he didn't want to be saved but how it was in my power to save him. "I don't grudge her either. It will be okay. We will set this right."

"You must be careful. The wizard did unspeakable things. The mystic is cut from the same cloth." Our grandmother leaned back, nostalgia filling her eyes while the cards leapt between her bony fingers once more, there in the dungeons of Jalapashu beneath the midnight sky. "I feel much better getting that off my chest. It's what my Hansa would have wanted. Now let's play cards and find out who the *chor* is, shall we?"

Maybe Mum would have been glad Nani showed us

unconditional support despite the divergence in our opinions. As she finally dealt the cards, our grandmother did seem more at peace with herself, as if the string that held the marionette up had finally been severed, and she was free to move in the direction of her own choosing. But by the time we had been born, Mum had moved much closer to her position. After all, what mother wanted their child to choose danger over safety? What mother would choose the pursuit of lofty goals if it meant curtailing their child's future?

With every turn of the card, the weight of our decisions pressed down on me, and I didn't know if we were ready for the path we were about to walk. Only that in life, there were never any certainties. Sometimes, the storms we faced carved out the most beautiful landscapes, and sometimes, they left a trail of wreckage and desolation.

CHAPTER 20

Sitara had told me that she was with us in some way, even when we couldn't perceive her or overlooked the signs. She had said to me that she was a wanderer between worlds, both a memory and a presence, and something about a cosmic loom that I quite frankly didn't understand. Nor was I supposed to. Still, it made sense to pay attention to the small signs that showed she was near, like the cloud of her perfume in Leena's cell.

Especially since I had one more stop that night to make, for which Sitara was the perfect accomplice.

Time would tell whether the third accomplice was a mistake. Taking your grandmother on a heist was an unorthodox choice, but Nani's enthusiasm was undeniable.

Our grandmother guided the train of her *sari* around her back, tucked it into her waistband, and adjusted the bobby pins in her beehive. "Well, isn't this wonderful? We have our very own coven—a sacred circle harnessing the arcane forces of the universe. I can pass on my ancient rituals and spells to you while my brain is agile enough–that really has been a worry–and we can sip beautifully brewed teas together. We can do naked rain dances together like my own mother did in her native India during the monsoon. Although it would be much more in the natural order of things for me to be the ancestral spirit, Sitara."

We were in the dark passageways of the royal palace. Once inside the palace gates, security was fairly lax because I had asked Deven to arrange fewer patrols that night. The altered routine hadn't sparked any suspicion. The men were pleased to have a night off before the as-yet-secret festivities taking place during the blood moon. Besides, with so many magicals roaming the palace, there was a presumption of great defensive capability, even without organised patrols.

It was a classic example of man and his hubris.

It had been a cinch to slip behind a wall rug into the cool, dark confines of the hidden passageways, especially since Sitara's wanderings made her able to pinpoint each entry point and the destination of every internal twist and turn. She whooshed ahead of us, with our grandmother taking up the middle position and me in the rear. My nose wrinkled against the stale air, and I resisted the urge to ask Nani to keep her voice down.

"I never got to have this fun with your mother. She wasn't interested in using her magic. Just think of what fun we could have had with my kitchen witchery and her time magic. We could have baked *dhokla* or caramel pudding and gone back in time to eat them fresh out of the oven. We could have brewed a pot of tea, added a touch of time magic, and hosted tea parties with historical figures like Gandhi-*ji*, Rabindranath Tagore or Lata Mangeshkar. We could have dined with our ancestors in the flesh… forgive me, Sitara, but spirits do not have taste buds or digestive systems. Nor can they help with the washing up… and uncovered recipes lost to time. Imagine being able to eat our great-great ancestor's favourite dish." She sighed. "But you know how teenagers are. Hansa was more interested in going to *carrom* and *antak-*

shari competitions and sneaking into Boundless Bay than practising our magic together."

Sitara backtracked to our side, and though the mass of her mists had grown even more hollow, I still discerned the exasperation in her mossy-heather eyes. "Usually, on heists, there is less talking and more doing."

"Of course. Silly me." A wistful smile passed over our grandmother's lips. "It's just I have been having these conversations in my head for so long that spilling my thoughts to you is the most exquisite pleasure."

"Qasim's quarters are just a little further," said my ghost sister. "The map is towards the back of his chamber, wedged in the join of an old sideboard." She still hadn't cracked the knack of moving matter reliably. Sporadic bursts of energy sometimes worked, but prolonged contact had proved impossible for her.

We ventured deeper, and my pulse accelerated. I reached into my pocket, taking comfort from the dark magic spells I had brought along as a precaution and as comfort, even though I had promised Merlin and my sisters to avoid such impulses.

"Your aura is darkening, but you don't need to worry. Qasim will be at court until the early hours like all the other courtiers." My grandmother ducked under hosts of cobwebs and stepped over mounds of vertebrae and a cracked skull as if making judgements about cleanliness. "Prakash complained the raja wants everything perfect for your engagement party, Kiya, and he won't permit anyone to leave until he is satisfied."

"We retrieve any info on the labyrinth and go home to bed." I didn't want my bed, though; I wanted the warmth of Deven's arms.

After a myriad of convolutions through the tunnels, we came to a tapestry halfway down a passage that I might have missed had Sitara not drawn our attention to it. It was the same colour as the stone walls, its surface equally jagged and raised. Only when I brought an oil lamp closer and ran my hand over its surface did it begin to reveal its secrets. A series of protective runes and sigils encircled the outer border of the tapestry, and celestial glyphs were embedded at its centre.

Sitara recited an incantation that I could barely make out–*āmram naya* or *āmaram naya* or *āmram nayatu*–and her words cast a gentle glow across the tapestry. The runes and sigils began to shift and change, rippling like water, their lines dissolving into new configurations. A number of the spell bindings unravelled, releasing their enchantments into the surroundings, while others reconfigured into new spells. The protection wards pulsed with renewed vigour, but Sitara kept up her chant. Then our grandmother joined in, and I did too, at last settling upon the right words, testing them out on my tongue. *Āmram naya. Āmram naya. Āmram naya.* The thrill of our combined power surged through me, and it was enough to break the binds of Qasim's spell. Our incantations revealed a hidden latch, and a low chime echoed as the latch clicked open.

I held my breath as the tapestry swung forward like a door, revealing a hidden chamber beyond. But Sitara didn't wait. She whooshed in ahead to the mystic's quarters, eager for our prize. Veils of gossamer fabric adorned the walls. They swayed in an unseen breeze, creating an eerie, dream-like atmosphere. The bed was long and narrow, with a slight dip in the mattress. Shelves along one wall held an impressive collection of ancient tomes and scrolls of esoteric knowledge, their leather bindings bearing the imprint of heavy hands. Pillar candles burned at intervals around the room, but their light was muted. A workbench cluttered with peculiar instruments of divination and alchemy stood at the centre of the room, the tools stained with a curious black ooze. The air carried an unsettling, acrid aroma, like the metallic tang of freshly forged steel, hinting at smouldering herbs and dark rituals. I stared at a large, ornate mirror in one corner, its surface rippling with a kaleidoscope of colours that reminded me of the Northern Lights. Next to it was a rack filled with the mystic's robes in duplicate.

Nani was in overdrive. She cupped a small vial of pure water in her hands and murmured spells, whose vowels stretched around us in a protective cocoon and countered residual negative energy. When she sprinkled her enchanted water around the lair, each droplet fell in a shimmering cascade, bringing a sense of ease and balance.

Sitara was already at the sideboard, hissing for my attention, more snake than sister. "Hurry, unless you want me to die a second death."

I bit back a retort. It wasn't unusual for the eldest in the sibling hierarchy to wield tongues sharpened by experience and responsibility. "Coming."

My grandmother and I hurried over. The sideboard stood solid and imposing, crafted from rich red oak. Eerie wooden figurines carved from wood covered its surface, knots and grain patterns still visible. Their faces–carved in the likeness of court members–gave me a jolt of recognition. Their bodies had been captured in motion, wood forms frozen in the midst of escape. Nani cursed under her breath at the sight of a figurine depicting our grandfather and slipped it into her sari blouse. Its protruding leg altered the shape of her right bosom, giving it the form of a cone.

"There." Sitara pointed to a discreet seam in the wooden join of the sideboard's lower cabinet.

The seam was smooth to the touch, lacking any roughness or snagging that I expected from an antique piece of furniture. I traced it with my finger and gently pressed a faint catch. With trembling hands, I carefully extracted an aged parchment. The map was a mesmerising drawing of the labyrinth, depicting its entrance and exits. Emblazoned at the top were two circular symbols, with an eye nestled in each one. One eye was wide open; the other slightly hooded. My memory tugged as I remembered the portrait in the throne room.

Excitement rushed through me. "These symbols are familiar. They represent Mahi and Menon."

Nani nodded. "Then we have the right document. Now, let's leave. Something stirs."

The candles flickered, and Sitara, whose wispy form had been impatiently hovering around us, suddenly grew in form and stature. Her mossy, heather eyes shimmered with a radiant inner light. "Ah, this is why I'm still here." She spun to me. "Take Nani and go. And remember, I won't ever be completely gone."

The gargoyle chants in my head lamented my folly and hubris, wondering if I was a flawed leader, too. Like Prem Kumar. Like the rani who had turned them against the people and commanded blood to be spilt in meadows laden with fruit trees.

Dread gnawed at me, and I didn't understand what had elicited Sitara's words or the gargoyles' sorrow until I felt it too: a malevolent thickness filling the room, a tangible weight that crawled its way towards us, amplifying the oppressive atmosphere in the room. I cried out as the map to the labyrinth crumbled in my fingers and became ash, its edges curling inwards with such speed that I flung the remnants to the floor. Within a nanosecond, there was nothing left.

Only regret at this lost chance. Regret at how my sister was already rising to defend us.

That part of her DNA that protected us, despite the fact she was no longer flesh and was only spirit.

Hangers scraped the rack as–through some mystical art– shadows poured forth from the sleeves of Qasim's gowns. They twisted and writhed like dark tendrils, swimming towards us as if they were serpents in the inky depths of the ocean.

As panic rose through my chest, I scrambled for the black magic in my pocket, the vials that had still hardened in the kiln when I last encountered the shadows. I wrenched the spell out of myself, and it felt thick and charred on my tongue. So thick I almost choked on it. "*Tava atītaṃ bhakṣayatu.*" I repeated it once, twice, three times, the hard consonants toppling into each other like dominoes crashing down, like the crumbling of mountains. To my horror, my attempts deepened the darkness as if my black magic inadvertently fed the shadows.

My sister's voice was not her own; it was the ghoulish wind atop a gorge. "Run! There will not be another chance."

"Listen to the spirit. They are wiser than us." My grandmother dragged me back to the passageway. "What are mere mortals? Only spirit can fight shadow. And I am not leaving without you."

I looked over my shoulder as Nani urged me onwards. My sister unleashed her own magic. Was it water? Was it her essence? My mind struggled to comprehend what unfolded as her radiant light danced like an intricate ballet with the shadows. Sitara had now become something other than my sister. Her flowing, ebony hair had a luminescent quality, as if strands of moonlight were woven into its dark tresses. Her eyes held no colour at all, and yet they dazzled me as if they held entire galaxies. The lingering threads of her orange shift dress–the dress she had died in–pulsated with symbols I yearned to decipher.

I loved her. I loved her, and I wasn't ready to let go.

Even though I had been blessed to have this long goodbye.

That last glimpse of her stretched as if the world itself held its breath. As if the universe wanted this to be my last memory of her, not her bleeding out on the kitchen floor of our ramshackle house. She gave herself to the night for us.

Sitara, transformed into a radiant sentinel, faced the shadows with unwavering courage. Her movements were a breathtaking spectacle, a dance of light battling the abyss. With each graceful gesture, she summoned tendrils of pure energy that lashed out like celestial whips, striking at the encroaching darkness. The shadows recoiled and twisted, hissing as they were pushed back by her power. Her hands flowed like water. She spun and twirled, tracing intricate patterns in the air to channel the essence of the cosmos. Ancient incantations resounded through the room like gongs, dispelling the shadows like the breaking dawn banishing the night.

She was so damn beautiful.

My darling sister blazed with determination, but it couldn't last.

These shadows were unnatural. Inexhaustible. Sitara had only ever intended to buy us time.

Nani tugged me into the passageway as the shadows slowly, inexorably engulfed her. My eldest sister's brilliant radiance faded into a mere flicker, like a dying star in the expanse of night. She fought until the very end, her hands extended in defiance, but the shadows crept over her like a shroud, consuming her. Her voice, which had echoed with power, fell silent.

A howl of anguish ripped from my throat as Nani closed the passageway behind us just as the shadows sought a new victim. She whispered a hurried spell, and we retraced our steps, stumbling, distraught, experiencing once again how life pivots on a knife edge but never learning, never once learning how to count our blessings when life was tranquil.

The gargoyles were unsatisfied even with our escape, and their warnings came faster still. *The raja is coming. The raja and the mystic know. They will enjoy their vengeance.*

My heartbeat grew sluggish, and my limbs trembled as we pushed on, and I didn't know anymore who held whom up. Only that pounding footfalls approached, too light and too fast to be human, a thundering charge, a frenetic rhythm that told me that Prem Kumar had shifted into his tiger. His roar rattled my bones. I remembered how I had been told he knew the passageways like the back of his hand, and it made sense now that the raja who never shifted in public would need to run off his energy and that maybe this was why there had been skulls and bones in the passageways. He was a monster, and we would encounter him here, in the darkness, in his territory. Nani and I would die here, torn limb from limb, made into dripping pools of gore by the tiger. And my Sitara was gone. Consumed. Those little remaining specks of her essence had been swallowed by the shadows. How fool-hardy I'd been to think my loved one and I could change a kingdom when it was enough to lead a simple life. To live in a rundown old house in a bay on the coast of England and just have each other. That was more than enough. It was perfect.

The roars were almost at our backs. The hair on my nape stood on end, and Nani was saying her prayers.

But there was someone, something, pulling us out of the passageway, though we might have gone further in our fright. Someone with cold, stony flesh, a lion's head and a deep voice that rumbled like distant thunder.

I blinked at the gargoyle leader, who hadn't known Sindhuja's name and always called her Fishtail. Who had come to our rescue once before. "Harya."

He executed a quick bow. "Mistress. I am here to do my duty."

Niceties over, he unceremoniously barrelled past me and turned himself to stone in the passageway, blocking the exit —a grand heroic gesture. Harya's gradual petrification started from his clawed feet. A pale hue of greyish stone spread upwards, enveloping his stocky form, ending at his ridged tail with its pointed arrow tip. I placed my hand on his battle-hardened skin and whispered a thank you as the tiger's golden form rounded the corner, his head low, his eyes steely blue.

My grandmother yanked me onward, advising me to act calm and smile at the guards, even as the tiger's embittered roars stalked our backs. Her words flowed over me, like the water my sister Sitara had channelled, sad and hopeful words stating how not all battles can be won, but to breathe, just to breathe and wait for the new dawn.

CHAPTER 21

In the morning, a contingent of soldiers arrived in the town to hand-deliver invitations to the engagement party. Their starched ivory uniforms with accents of saffron yellow and crimson sashes were a striking contrast to the dusty town. Each soldier rode a horse adorned with embroidered trappings, and the clip-clop of hooves enticed the people onto the streets. The soldiers navigated the winding alleys with finesse, dismounting with an air of formality to deliver the rolled parchment with its gloopy wax seal bearing the raja's emblem.

I unfurled my parchment, revealing its ornate golden script:

You are cordially invited
to the handfasting ceremony and celebration feast of
Maharaja Prem Kumar and Kiya Marlowe
9 p.m. tonight ~ Throne room, The Royal Palace

My stomach was a turbulent sea. I retreated indoors and sagged against a wall. The hare comforted me with his gentle, reassuring hops and soft nuzzle as I retched, away from the prying eyes of those who assumed this was a social triumph for me, even though inside, most had experienced or heard stories of the raja's black heart.

"You can't lose faith now. Hold on a bit longer, Kiya." Merlin's molten gold eyes glimmered, and I remembered how he had wanted our mother to tell us the truth, and later, when Sitara had made us forget our magic, he had cautioned honesty instead. "This marriage won't come to pass. You can't lose yourself amongst all these lies."

By then, the streets had swollen with excitement, and the women hollered over their garden walls about what to wear and how there wasn't time for hair dye or that the children had outgrown their finest pair of trousers. The men talked about how it would be a magnificent feast and the month wouldn't be such a struggle after all if their families would eat their fill and last the remainder of the week on scraps. And maybe the wedding would follow soon after, and there would be an even more splendid feast.

The gargoyles grumbled that they could never partake in the events that mark normal lives and were cursed to observe or disrupt. For a moment, I could see myself in the shoes of the rani, whose statue had been thrown into the deep waters of Boundless Bay. Like her, I was tempted to unleash the might of the gargoyles on my enemies.

"You little minx," teased Farida when a horse and cart arrived to whisk me off to my fitting with the royal tailor. "You make sure you remember us when you are swanning about in that palace."

The horse and cart carried us over the cobbled streets, and the moon was a faint, dusky disc that painted a reddish tint across the azure skies. I was pleased to escape the attention that dawned as the townsfolk realised the raja's fiancée lived amongst them—pleased to leave behind the house that was a yawning chasm without my sisters. An aching hole filled my chest where my heart should have been that couldn't be filled by my grandmother's soft words or fruit teas. Despite the soldier's frowning look, I didn't find it odd to bring Merlin with me to the palace, not when otherwise I would have been all alone with my thoughts. The churning thoughts that Lokesh *Saheb*'s magic enabled him to read.

When the gates opened to allow the horse and cart to enter the grounds, I held Merlin against my chest and whispered into his silken, sooty ears, "Tell Deven what happened in Qasim's chambers but don't tell him about Menon. He is not yet ready for that. Come what may, I will meet him at the banyan tree tonight. And please check on Harya. I worry for his safety. I can't single out his voice from the roar of the others in my head. Please be careful."

That was how I found myself in Lokesh *Saheb*'s atelier, being fitted for a gown worthy of a rani. I'd never been close to an engagement before. Not really. My relationships had always fizzled out before that point. Maybe I was too fussy, or maybe I was just unlucky, but I didn't have any regrets about cherishing my own needs and wanting to find someone who was a good fit and who would make me warm inside even after a lifetime together.

However, I had witnessed the happiness of friends, their glowing faces as they showed off their engagement rings, their excitement at starting a new chapter and the promise of a shared future.

Instead of joy, a heavy sense of foreboding clung to me like a funeral shroud.

Lokesh *Saheb* let out a disapproving tsk at my sombre mood. "Only the rarest beauties can dazzle when their moods are gloomy. Although it is astounding you are managing to stand up at all under the weight of your thoughts."

Dual emotions showed his distinguished face: pride at the chance to finally design a royal wedding trousseau and frustration at my distinct lack of interest. The raja had given him scarcely two days' notice, but the elaborate sketches pinned all over the walls of his atelier revealed that Lokesh *Saheb* had been working towards this moment for years. Indeed, his mahogany eyes twinkled despite the blue-green crescents beneath them, and there was a certain jauntiness to his movements as he snipped with his scissors and prodded me to correct my posture and pressed his palm to his cheek when the material cascaded just so.

A pair of wire-framed glasses perched on the end of his hooked nose, and his usually meticulously wrapped turban was in slight disarray, its pleats less precise as he tended to me. He raised his eyebrow, making it abundantly clear that he had read my thoughts. "There's no time for me to be vain when you require all my attention. You really should have come for an earlier fitting, Kiya. In three hours' time, you will be promised to Prem Kumar, and the entire kingdom will expect you to look the part."

"The servants are working so hard to prepare." I stayed his scissors for a moment. "You told me last time that you stay out of court affairs. I wanted to thank you for not revealing to Prem and Qasim that the shoes left behind in the seer's house were mine."

"I told you I would guard your secrets." The tailor dropped his voice as an assistant passed by. "But I must caution you against your intention to enter the labyrinth. You must think of your safety."

A shard of glass pierced my heart. My sisters and I had made our choices, and it had cost us our safety already. We had lost too much to give up now. My sisters were brave, and I would be too.

Lokesh *Saheb* placed his hand over his chest with a dramatic sigh. "Now, you must reconsider your decision not to wear heels tonight. Crafting this *lehenga* with pockets has already presented a considerable challenge; opting for flat shoes will be a disaster for your silhouette. Both you and

Prem Kumar have planned a night to remember, but I want your swishing skirts to be the star."

I studied his face. "Lokesh *Saheb*, when you fit Prem for his clothes, do you read his thoughts too?"

The tailor sighed. "Cruelty, greed, jealousy. It is emotionally taxing to listen to these things, and I've had to develop meditation techniques and positive anchors to protect myself from their impact. A good facial works wonders for both an external and an internal cleanse." He gave me a shrewd smile. "But there is one thing that I can perhaps relay to you. Prem will offer you an engagement ring tonight, and despite the turmoil in your mind, you must accept it if you are to stand against him."

I expressed my gratitude, but Lokesh *Saheb* shook his head as if even the smallest interventions left him feeling exposed. Undeterred, he continued his adjustments so that in flat sandals, my skirt skimmed the floor without touching it, the blouse hugged my waist perfectly, and the heart neckline revealed just enough of my décolletage to hint at allure without crossing the boundaries of modesty, as befitting an Indian court.

Before he could secure his last pin and finish his last stitch, Merlin bounded up the stairs, prompting me to crouch beside him, though the tailor grumbled at my carelessness. "What is it, Merl?"

The hare's nose twitched. When he whispered in my ear, his voice carried a gravity that could rival the deepest caverns and the oldest mountains. It sucked the air from my lungs.

It was the tailor who lifted me to my feet, his words resonating with quiet resolve. "Go. I will find a way to make do."

I didn't waste a moment. My movements were robotic as I shed my clothes, replacing them with the simpler attire of the tunic and leggings I'd arrived in. Then, I followed the hare deep inside the hidden arteries of the palace.

MERLIN, HARYA AND I WATCHED EVENTS UNFOLD FROM WITHIN the passageway, pressing ourselves against small cracks in the wall.

It had been the gargoyle leader who had found the general and alerted Merlin. Harya had stayed long enough in his stone form for the tiger to grow bored of him. He spent the following twelve hours turning himself to stone at different points along the network of passageways until one courtier declared that it was close enough to a century since the grand pottery master had made the gargoyles, and maybe they were malfunctioning. Pure chance had led him to this particular part of the tunnels, where Deven found himself facing Prem, Qasim and my grandfather.

From my vantage point, I could see only fragments of the room's shadowy tableau, as if peering through a keyhole into another world. Oil lamps burned in the room. This was the room of horrors, not the dungeons where Leena waited patiently to be freed. The walls of this remote, windowless chamber were constructed from thick, unforgiving slabs of cold stone that absorbed any hint of light, leaving it cloaked in an impenetrable, dank gloom. Metallic shelves held an assortment of torture instruments, from rusted pliers and saws to sharpened knives and lighters. Iron shackles hung from the walls, and a scarred wooden table bore the marks of past confrontations. Even outside the room, the lingering residue of despair seeped into my every pore.

The wavering lamplight flickered across Deven's determined face, casting alternating masks of light and darkness on his pained features. His hands and feet were bound, and his dagger belt lay discarded on the ground, tantalisingly close but impossible for him to reach. His shirt was ripped, and bloodied claw marks crisscrossed his chest. The raja had an air of unbridled aggression. Next to him, the mystic turned over a silver claw of torture in his hands. My grandfather watched passively from a chair in the corner, his brows pulled together.

Revulsion knotted my stomach. What kind of man, on the eve of his engagement celebration, chose to indulge in cruelty rather than merriment? How could Prem Kumar subject his own cousin to interrogation and torture? My heart pounded as I strained to hear the muffled voices that emanated from the room. The tone of disdain sent shivers down my spine.

Prem leaned over the general, so close that spit hit Deven's face. "I first suspected when I saw the landscape of Boundless Bay in Kiya's shop that there was something going on. I mean, you are famously buttoned-up, cousin. Even Roshni thought so. A cold fish, she said. Much harder to warm up than I ever was."

Deven flinched. "Take her name out of your mouth."

"You have no rights over a dead woman. Besides, she was mine first." The raja's eyes frosted, and he ground his foot into Deven's crotch. "Isn't it strange how we keep falling out over women?"

Deven gritted his teeth. "You believe us all capable of the same depth of betrayal as you. I sold that painting to the Marlowe sisters and gave the money to my sister to feed her family. Perhaps you should focus your energies on alleviating the hunger in this kingdom rather than chasing imaginary enemies."

I closed my eyes and leant my head against the coolness of the wall. Deven wouldn't betray us, but just that fact left him in terrible danger. I had promised Nisha to protect him, but his every instinct was to protect us.

"Ah, but cousin. That painting did mean something to

you. Just as Boundless Bay always has. Underneath that starched general's uniform, you have a soft core. It's why you come back every time I beat you like a sick dog."

Every step of the way, Prem had thwarted him, but not fairly, always slyly, with crowing glee despite how he had rigged the game. I thought of Menon in the labyrinth and how he could undo the curse if only we could find him. But even without his magic, even carrying all his pain, Deven was the better man.

I forced myself to look again, though I couldn't bear to see the general cowed, and my throat grew thick as the mystic approached with languid, sinuous grace, the sleeves of his gown bulging with shadows.

Qasim's hooded lids lifted a fraction, and his pale green eyes were soulless. When he spoke, his voice slithered through the air with sinister smoothness. "You toy with the general, Prem-*ji*, when my shadow spies have established the facts. The painting is inconsequential. My shadows saw how you–how shall I express it?–brought the raja's fiancée to her pinnacle."

Blood pounded in my ears as I readied myself to intervene if the raja unleashed his wrath. Harya sensed my intention and squared his stance, though Merlin was still soft and cautious at my feet.

My grandfather's voice was a whip. "That particular wording was unnecessary."

"I am merely stating facts." The mystic's voice dripped with dark charisma.

My grandfather turned on Deven. "How could you, General? I know everything that happens in this kingdom. You think I didn't know about you and my granddaughter? You couldn't protect your own wife. What made you think you could protect Kiya?"

"I stood by her. It's more than you've done," said Deven quietly.

Then he ignored the quarrelling courtiers and raised his eyes to meet Prem's. His words were a growl. "Is this about Kiya or about you finally crushing my spirit? Because that's what you want, cousin, isn't it? You couldn't bear for me to freely give you the throne and still find peace with myself when you have all the power you could ever desire and yet still find only the raging abyss in yourself."

Prem's lips curved upwards. "You take things too personally, cousin. It's just a bit of fun. Granted, with parallels… I do find your self-satisfaction amusing." His scorn cut like the sharpest dagger. "A man who wouldn't take the throne. A man who couldn't protect his wife. A man who has devoted himself to a career as a soldier, preparing for an external threat that never comes. Untested. Pathetic. Pitiful."

Deven's coal-black eyes sparked with fury. "I bedded Kiya, and I would do it again."

Prem gave a humourless laugh. "You won't have a chance, cousin. I'm ready to build the world anew with my new wife, and I tire of these games with you. Kiya entered Qasim's quarters last night, but she didn't get what she was looking for."

My grandfather shifted uncomfortably.

Relief washed across Deven's bruised face. "You're not angry with her?"

Prem casually retrieved the silver claw from the mystic's hands. "I could never be happy with a meek wife. That's why I allowed Roshni to become *your* wife. A raja's wife must possess a spirit as fierce as the kingdom she serves. And cousin, Kiya Marlowe is powerful. Her power is revealed in the mystic's tarot over and over again. In time, I will tame her. You see, Roshni taught me that even the deepest loyalty can be eroded. So, Kiya's disloyalty doesn't phase me. At least we both know where the other stands."

Deven strained against his bonds. "I should have killed

you in the battle for the throne, but I still believed in your redemption."

"Is that what broke Roshni's loyalty to me? You filling her head with hope? I always wondered why she couldn't stomach seeing you like that. Why she'd had a sudden change of heart after knowing what she signed up for. Oh, cousin, you gave her hope that she could be unsullied and make a fresh start with you. You really did kill her."

Inky eyes locked onto Prem in disgust. "Why are you like this? Twisted? Craven?"

"Because you try to take what's mine. Twisted is just the nature of this place. You know more than most that even the oaks in our woods are twisted." The raja gave a tiger's smile, dug the claw into Deven's chest and turned it like a corkscrew.

I muffled my scream as Deven let out an anguished groan, and blood poured from his wound, soaking his shirt and trousers and pooling on the floor.

The tiger raja swung my way. "Did you hear that? That blasted gargoyle is still malfunctioning in there. Go ahead. Investigate it, Prakash. One day, I will command concrete to be poured within those passageways and roam this land eating whose flesh I want."

Dread ballooned in my chest. In the kitchens, throne room and gardens of the palace, servants toiled to bring about a wondrous party. The kingdom buzzed with anticipation. Yet, instead of leaning into joy, the raja had once again chosen cruelty.

My grandfather approached the wall until only a brick separated us. He frowned and extended his aged fingers. The air crackled with arcane energy.

"Quick," whispered Merlin.

We darted deeper into the tunnels, but the gargoyle's step was heavier, and I prayed. I prayed that Sitara had been right. That we could depend on my grandfather to come through for us. That he wasn't corrupt, only misguided because he had loved my mother, and he loved my grandmother, and maybe he could grow to love us, too.

Prakash Malini, my grandfather, my blood, invoked his magic, and the wall before him rippled then shimmered as if it were a dissolving mirage. A portion of the wall, just large enough for him to step through, melted away, revealing us in our hiding place. His eyes widened as they settled on me, then found the hare and gargoyle. In his eyes, I read a flicker of fear, like perhaps he wished we would have stayed away from Jalapashu, just like our mother. But then, without missing a beat, he raised his index finger to his lips, turned his back and walked back through the wall. It sealed behind him, leaving the same chinks we had used as our peepholes as if he had never ventured through.

The clamp around my heart eased, and I felt the turning of the tide as if Sitara stood right by my ear and whispered *I told you so.*

"Qasim," said the raja inside the room as Deven hung limply in his chair. "Tell the hunters I will double their price. The parrot shall be the crowning glory of our celebration. The seer and her brother must not be allowed to leave the labyrinth."

Deven emitted a low, desolate groan.

Prem patted his shoulder. "Yes, that's right, cousin. I've known where Menon was all this time. All this time that you've been cursed not to shift." He jerked his head up to my grandfather. "Did you find the gargoyle?"

My grandfather shook his head, a slight quiver in his voice. "It must have moved deeper into the tunnels. I will get some men on it."

The raja nodded. "Give my cousin the healing elixir, Prakash. Clean yourself up, Deven. I am going to give you one last hoorah before banishment. You will dance at my engagement to Kiya. You will make a grand speech praising me. You will eat horseshit if that's what I request of you." He gripped Deven's shirt collar and hauled him upright. "I want you to witness my happiness, cousin."

Deven spat at his feet. He gulped down the elixir my grandfather put to his lips. From the fiery intensity in his coal-black eyes, I knew that the general's last trace of loyalty to his cousin had evaporated like a nebulous dream colliding with harsh reality.

CHAPTER 22

I returned to Lokesh *Saheb*'s atelier in a daze, the hare bounding up the stairs beside me with a rhythmic slap-slap of his feet. My skin was clammy, and my breath ragged as I replayed Deven's ordeal in my head. Aanya's magic or a bottle of rum stolen from the palace kitchens could have numbed my mind, but love and loyalty propelled me further into the shadows.

Deven had been strong, but witnessing his suffering had devastated me. The raja was cruel, callous and fixated on the past. He showed no guilt for killing Deven's wife but played the wounded, demanding to know why Roshni had switched allegiances.

He deserved everything that was coming to him.

It struck me that Prem Kumar was both fuelled and poisoned by his rivalry with his cousin. He needed the general. Deven had become a reference point, a mirror image by which the raja judged his own self-worth. That was why the raja had given his cousin a healing elixir that knitted together his wounds before my eyes. That was why, in that grim torture room, Prem had spoken of Deven's banishment, not death.

His obsession with Deven was his weakness.

That weakness gave us a fighting chance. I formulated my plan around it.

In less than an hour, I was expected to glide into the throne room, wearing a smile and playing the role of the blushing bride-to-be. Even though the raja knew I had been deceitful. Even though he wanted to tame me. To shape me to his will like he was God and I was a lump of clay. He had spoken loftily about my fierce spirit only because he wanted to snuff it out.

I didn't want to be queen-in-waiting. I wanted to vomit at his feet.

After all my lies to sow confusion and gain the upper hand, a fervent compulsion now burned in me to stand centre-stage at the engagement party and voice the truths the people recognised but were too frightened to utter: the raja was undeserving of his kingdom and undeserving of a wife; to him, the people were ants, mere playthings that he crushed at will; he shattered the bonds of family for his own vanity and ambitions.

I hated him. Yet, at the very moment I yearned to be honest, it was crucial to remain quiet. At least until we had faced the labyrinth. If all went according to plan, we would rescue Mahi and Menon from the labyrinth before Prem even realised we were capable of it. Because Prem Kumar's ridiculous reaction to Harya proved one thing: he had no inkling that I commanded the gargoyles or that Sindhuja guarded the parrot for me.

What is more, my grandfather had chosen not to betray us. If I kept my wits and allies about me, Babbu's feather would enable me to free the witch and wizard twins. A possibility that Mahi had foreseen and, therefore, must be achievable.

As if our connection was instinctual, the fishtail gargoyle's voice filled my mind like a bell tolling in a mountainside temple. *The blood moon rises. The parrot and I return.*

I stitched the shreds of my courage together and laid a hand on the cool marble wall at the top of the stairs. "Are you ready?"

The hare would be my emissary while I continued the charade. Gold eyes glimmered. "I am. And so are you."

We entered the tailor's atelier to a chorus of complaints about my harried, wild appearance. Aanya was there, too, singing sweet songs of fortitude. She murmured news of Leena as she helped me shower and applied fragrant oils to my skin.

"Listen carefully, Kiya." She brushed my hair until it gleamed. "There is a heavily guarded annexe to the throne room. It's there you'll be meeting the raja and his jeweller before the ceremony. He'll be showing you a magical vault. It's the talk of the palace staff. The vault holds topaz jewels confiscated from disgraced Jalapashans. You'll be asked to choose an engagement ring. But it holds twin medallions."

"They belong to the seer and her brother." The hare's voice was as steadfast as towering redwood trees in a forest glade. "We'll need to take them into the labyrinth if the witch and wizard are to access their full powers."

The lines had long blurred between expectation, obligation and longing. Were they demanding too much of me, or was I demanding it of myself? Jalapashu had extracted a higher toll from us than I'd ever imagined, pushing us to our limits and wringing out every drop of potential, but amidst the turmoil, it had also revealed our resilience, our gifts, and the depth of our bonds.

"Enough, Kiya. You'll look like a pauper at your own engagement festivities if you don't hurry," came the tailor's voice through the door.

"Aanya, I need you to sing when the eclipse nears, but I am worried it will cost you."

"I'm proud to play my part if it helps bring Mahi home. What about Leena?"

"Leave that to me. Merlin, you'll need to free the animals when the time is right."

The hare inclined his head, and Aanya opened the door as the tailor's team ushered me into the main section of the atelier, tutting and turning me and holding colour palettes of makeup up to my face.

Lokesh *Saheb* had said he would make do in my absence, and he was true to his word. The servants cast me admiring glances as I slipped into the luxurious folds of a silk *lehenga*, and Aanya tied the ribbons at my back. Its emerald tones reminded me of Sitara's eyes before death had muted her colouring. Threads of gold and silver told a story of tradition and grandeur. The whalebone corset thinned my anxious breathing even further. My jewellery–thick bangles, an intricate necklace and pearl moons for my ears–felt like shackles. The necklace, in particular, was heavy against my collarbone, a reminder of the might of the raja. Wrapped gracefully around my neck, the sheer scarf hinted at the bonds that threatened to ensnare me. But the tailor had tried his best to marry the needs of tradition with my authentic style. The servants had tied my hair in a simple high ponytail rather than using a thousand pins. The makeup applied to my face enhanced my features without overwhelming them. He had given me flat sandals to cradle my feet and deep pockets to hide my clenched fists.

When he had finished making his adjustments, Lokesh *Saheb* presented me to his team with a grandiose flourish, waving his feather-adorned walking stick in the air. "In time, this woman will be the next rani of Jalapashu and tonight, her legend begins in the green tones of the earth, the silver of the seas and the gold representing how she will enrich this land." His team burst into applause, but when he turned to me, his eyes were quietly contemplative, as if his eccentricity was a mask. He pressed my hands and simply said, "When you walk into the tiger's den, remember your power."

I hugged him and whispered thank you in his ear and a louder thank you for the rest of his team, playing the rani though my blood thrashed in my ears. Lokesh *Saheb*, Aanya and Merlin gazed at me kindly as I left the atelier. I walked through quiet corridors towards my appointed meeting point with the raja as tradition dictated, wishing my sisters were beside me, wishing I wasn't alone. The moon cast a silvery glow over the palace gardens, where the elephants and peacocks roamed, and a subtle shadow had already begun to encroach on its surface.

A quartet of soldiers guarded the annexe to the throne room. They opened the doors to reveal the raja and a diminutive man who must have been the jeweller. The room was quiet and bare, except for a glass vault filled with jewels. My footsteps were muffled against the thick carpet as I wordlessly made my way to his side. Prem's cold, blue eyes drank up the sight of me like he was a parched man in the desert. Lokesh *Saheb* had dressed him in emerald green also as if we belonged to each other, and he looked every inch the king: tall and broad-shouldered, with a gold turban in raw silk, glittering *mojaris* on his feet and a curved sword at his waist that reminded me of his tiger's claws. When Prem glanced at my rosebud lips, his desire revolted me. I wanted it gone, to destroy it like a cannon taken to a castle.

"Tonight, we make our pledge to each other. Come, Kiya, I have something to show you." He beckoned me over to the vault.

It was constructed of thick polished glass on a metal frame, allowing an unobstructed view of the treasures inside: an array of topaz jewellery, just as Aanya had informed me. My heartbeat sped as I spotted Mahi and Menon's twin medallions: hers, with a violet eye; his, flecked with black. It had neither a door nor a lock.

At the raja's signal, the jeweller stepped forward and held his hands over the vault. I craned my neck to listen, but though the jeweller's mouth moved, I couldn't catch the words. As he chanted, the panels shifted with fluid grace, like the blocks of a 1980s sliding puzzle, allowing access to the display of brilliant jewels.

Prem nodded at the jewels with the nonchalance of a man who was used to riches and power. "You may choose a ring, and my jeweller will fit it for you."

I peered at the collection: a vintage-inspired oval-cut topaz framed by a halo of tiny diamonds; a ring with its jewel suspended within a golden cage; a single topaz flanked by two smaller sapphires set on a minimalist platinum band; a cushion-cut gemstone set in a thick, ornate band with intricate detailing; a princess-cut gemstone, its warm honey hue set on delicate white gold. Though the medallions drew my attention, it was my role to play the bride. The gargoyles roared in my head as I hovered over the rings, but at the fifth ring, they grew quiet, so I chose the honey-hued princess cut band. "This one."

"A fine choice." Sweat dotted the jeweller's bald head. He removed the princess-cut ring from the vault and slipped it onto my finger. "This will sting." His magic tightened the ring around my finger like a noose around my neck. With a satisfied grunt, he tugged it from my finger and placed it in the raja's palm. Words of magic evaporated into the air as he sealed the vault and retreated to a discreet corner.

Prem's glittering eyes met mine as he pocketed the ring. When his eyes darkened, I wondered if he was thinking of Deven's lips on my body. "I won't tolerate disloyalty after this moment. You will add your power and your deviousness to mine."

My throat was tight. "I trust you'll uphold your end of the bargain just as faithfully. Leena regains her freedom tonight."

"I said after our marriage."

"You wish to please your wife-to-be, don't you?"

His eyes hooded, and then he nodded in agreement. "I will send word to the dungeons."

Beyond the doors, *tablas* leapt to their rhythm, and excitement rippled through the waiting throng of our guests.

Prem offered me his arm. "This could be love, as well as business."

I accepted it and took a deep breath. "Love? I don't think you're capable of it."

We entered the throne room to a grand announcement of the betrothed pair and the sound of the *tablas*, their taut, goat-skin drumheads vibrating with every beat. Each rhythmic throb increased the erratic tempo of my heart. The engagement party was already in full flow. Countless candlelit chandeliers hung from the ceilings against the background of the deepening night, lit by my grandfather's magic. All eyes were on us as we progressed to the front of the throne room. I counted my steps, orienting myself, knowing what lay before me and how important it was that I could find my way without fumbling when it really mattered.

The left wing of the room, adjacent to the portrait of Mahi and Menon, had been left clear for dancing. Crates of *dandiya* sticks waited there, wrapped with ribbons and finished with bells, ready for *dandiya raas*. The right wing of the room was filled with an assortment of tanks and cages housing the magical creatures that the hunters had captured: the songbirds, silvery fish, the luminescent rabbits, but also fireflies with tails like miniature stars, iridescent beetles that glistened like jewels, and bees that produced mountains of honey without a flower in sight. One cage stood empty, a golden perch within it, waiting for its prisoner.

In the central aisle of the room, between the pillars, beginning beyond the dais, a dozen long banquet tables were draped with silk tablecloths in burgundy, topped with gilded plates, crystal goblets and silverware. Towering vases filled with roses, lilies and orchids graced the tables, their scent mingling with the fragrant spices and heady perfumes. The raja's throne occupied the middle of the dais, but now, a regal swing waited for us at the front of the stage, decorated with swathes of jasmine buds.

The *tablas* continued their beat until we sat in the swing. Then the ceremony unfolded–though my mind blurred–witnessed by a line of the courtiers and the throng of the people. They studied every inch of me, from the sweep of my hair to the jewellery around my neck, the way my body was angled away from the man who wanted to be my husband and the tightness of my mouth.

Deven approached the dais, resplendent in his general's uniform and neatly combed hair, with not a bruise or a cut on him, except perhaps on his heart, and his dagger belt back around his waist as if nothing had happened. As if nothing had happened. His tone was stilted as he made the speech the raja had demanded. "Brothers, sisters, esteemed guests, we gather here tonight to celebrate a union. We all know the patience required to find the person meant for you. Here we are at last, with the raja ready to tie himself in the bonds of marriage. Some would say this match between Kiya Marlowe and Prem Kumar is a match made by fate. Family, after all, is the cornerstone of a kingdom, and my cousin has always been so loyal to family." He offered a reserved smile as he picked up a flute of pink *sherbet* from the trays circulating the party. "Let us raise our glasses to the couple and our shared future." He lifted his glass, and the guests followed suit, but he didn't sip from the *sherbet*.

His words settled like silt over me, and then my grandfather appeared beside me and applied some sort of volume magic to our voices so that the Raja of Jalapashu could say in front of the kingdom:

"Will you marry me?"

And I could say, "Yes," hoping that would be the end of it, that I would never have to think of it again.

The crowd whooped as if it was a wondrous moment. Though Lokesh *Saheb* had worked hard to make me beautiful, and the *lehenga* brought out the depth of my hazel eyes, clung to my figure in the right places and flowed like a river in others, I didn't feel beautiful. The lie corroded me. It left me a husk of myself. It made me a fraud.

Then the raja forced the engagement ring onto my finger, and in the candlelit throne room, its honey-hued topaz gleamed like the gold on his tiger's coat. My magic responded to the jewel, heightening with the raja's gift, a bubbling volcano, and I knew that I could crack the foundations of the throne room if I wanted.

But I wanted to free Mahi and Menon more.

I wanted to break Deven's curse.

I wanted to knock the raja off his throne and wipe the tiger's smile off his face together.

Prem Kumar held up my hand as if I were a trophy. My grandfather had scarcely finished speaking his words of congratulations when the raja kissed me, long and hard, though I couldn't–I wouldn't–return the pressure of his lips and the temptation to bite down hard made me quiver with anger, even though I knew our time was coming by the hue of the moon. Deven stared straight ahead, a vein throbbing in his jaw as Prem pulled back and sighed in contentment. In the crowd was Nisha, wondering how her brother had been bested again. Wondering how a beast could triumph over a good man.

"Do you see what we can achieve together?" asked Prem, flushed with success, as serving staff circulated with trays of sweet *jalebi* and milky *pera* to celebrate our engagement. "The people wish to hear more from the woman who will be their rani. Tell them what will your first decree be when you are my queen?"

The answer came to me immediately. I'd permit the people to leave the kingdom and improve it so they stayed from love, not fear. But this was a performance, so I made light of the question, and my voice was made strange through my grandfather's amplification magic. "I'd introduce a nap time for all citizens."

The raja's eyes crinkled with mirth. "She surprises even me with her wisdom. An excellent idea that will not dent the kingdom's coffers. Pottery is not a queen's work. She will find a new role as an expert advisor."

I arched an eyebrow, and a murmur went through the crowd at my hint of rebellion. How telling that he thought of pottery as mundane when it encompassed so much of what made a queen: tradition, resilience, humility, transformation.

"Kiya and I are pleased you are here to celebrate with us," said the raja. "Now let us eat."

He helped me from the dais, and our hands hung woodenly together, with no warmth, no affection or moulding to each other. The crowds parted as I arranged my face into a mask, and we strolled through them. Already, I felt separate from the people, as if distance had already set in between us as if I were a mannequin to be paraded. Our guests turned their faces in our direction, clad in their finest clothes. They wore ruby reds and sunshine yellows, determined to show their joy, but a closer look showed fallen sequins, threadbare *churidar* or trousers on young boys that barely reached their shins. There were those I recognised–the librarian Chandini, the dancer Lata, Jilu and Radha from Biryani Junction, the court poet Nitin, our neighbour Farida, and Minesh and Nina with their baby, who hadn't been able to pay their taxes. But there was a critical look in the eyes of some of the women and some of the men, and certainly many of the courtiers. A look that I interpreted as *who is she?* A look evident in the eyes of even my so-called friends as if they questioned why I had received this good fortune and not

them. Each time we neared a particular group, the stares softened, and the grimaces disappeared as if they wouldn't dare
to offend us. As if the real power of the raja, and by default
the rani, was to escape criticism.

But not everyone could hold their tongue.

"We can't trust her. She's more British than Indian," said a
turbaned elder in Gujarati. "The Brits are the originators of
colonisation."

I stewed for a lengthy moment, plotting a retort in our
native tongue, before smiling sweetly. "The British were
known for looting and piracy, too, so you'd better watch out.
I already have a ring from the vaults."

Prem roared with laughter. "You are well-suited to the
role of rani. You see, Jitu," he said to the disgruntled man.
"My betrothed is capable of defending her honour with little
input from me."

I barely ate a morsel during dinner, though Prem had
taken some care to seat my grandparents at our table and
regaled our table with a humorous take on the delinquent
lion-mane gargoyle. The banquet tables were laden with a
multitude of colourful curries, from vibrant spinach *saag* to
deep red *paneer tikka masala*. Gleaming silver bowls held
steaming *biryani*s, their rich saffron hues glistening under
chandeliers. Plates of succulent kebabs, charred to perfection,
released a tantalising smoky fragrance. Bowls of fluffy,
buttered *naans* and flaky *parathas* were piled high.

The moon had almost wholly passed through the Earth's
umbral shadow, causing it to take on a reddish hue that crept
in through the windows of the throne room. I couldn't
stomach any food, and neither could Deven. He sat opposite
me, not uttering a word, simply moving his *paneer* around his
plate as if it were a tasteless stone, but when his inky eyes
flickered to me, I knew that Merlin had passed on my
message. The mystic was there, smirking at the general and
the sorceress with her *jhumka* earrings too, who presumed to

tell me about the history of the ring I wore, how it had belonged to a rani who had once turned against the kingdom. Prem quieted her with talk of how he was having a second throne made for me to slot in beside his own. My grandparents nodded as if he was a good king and could be a good husband.

After dinner, when the palace staff cleared the banquet tables of the food and dirty crockery and prepared the room for dancing, Nani placed a cool hand on my cheek. "Your family and friends are all ready to play their part tonight. Don't worry about your grandfather and me. We can take care of ourselves." Her lips moved as she blessed me and cast her enchantments, enveloping me in a protective white aura. Only she–who understood the deepest bonds of love and protection–could muster such maternal kitchen witch magic. She buffered me against negative energies, and I felt safer after her touch.

By now, the lunar eclipse was moments from happening. The blood moon cast an eerie crimson glow over the landscape, and our guests marvelled at the sight. As planned, Aanya took to the stage to coincide with the celestial event, her rendition of an old Bollywood *ghazal* drifting like a silken breeze through the room.

I leaned my cheek against Nani's hand for a long moment, centring my breathing, feeling the topaz embedded in my thigh and the one on my finger, knowing we had to be quick, or else the raja would turn his most heinous courtiers against us. Then I flicked my eyes to Deven. "It's time."

There, in front of the whole kingdom, Deven stood as the hare had asked him to.

He stood, came to my side and extended his hand to me. "Kiya, would you like to dance?"

For a moment, there was nobody in the throne room except us. I rose to my feet. "I would like nothing more." His warm hand enveloped mine, and my heart raced as if it had slipped its chains and was free to soar.

I remembered the lessons I had learned. How the raja's pride and jealousy blinded him. How you didn't have to be the strongest on a battlefield to win the war. You simply had to use your enemy's weaknesses against him.

The kingdom witnessed our slow walk to the dance floor under the blood moon, accompanied by Aanya's songbird voice. They noticed Deven's familiarity with his cousin's betrothed: the way his arm wrapped around my waist as if he was reluctant to let go, the way I leaned into his touch, the way we gazed into each other's eyes. A ripple went through the guests: a surge of hope and genuine excitement. A wave of *schadenfreude* for a king who had always been focused on his own joy but who caused pain to others for sport. Proof that he wasn't invincible. Proof—on a public stage—that he could be hurt.

Deven stood opposite me on the dance floor. "You kissed him."

My nerve endings tingled, and his hands at my nape made the world spin. "I had no choice."

Inky eyes on mine. "I know. Let me put that right." He lowered his lips to mine.

We kissed, and he tasted of magic and honesty.

We kissed as the raja exploded in rage and the lunar eclipse turned the sky red.

We kissed as my grandfather extinguished the hundreds of candles on the countless chandeliers, blanketing the throne room in darkness, and Aanya released the full force of her magic into her song, and the raja's roar became a purr.

Then we counted our steps back to the annexe, heat pulsing between us, our goal to break into the magical vault. I remembered the spell I had chanted with Nani and Sitara outside the mystic's chamber when we had needed a coven to gain entry. With the ring I wore, my magic thrummed like the steady rumble of tectonic plates beneath the earth, and the spell came easily to me as if my mind could catalogue and sift through even the strangest phrases. I let the spell fall from my lips like a string of pearls, its power building–*āmram naya, āmram naya, āmram naya*–and the vault cracked open as if it were an eggshell. I grasped the medallions, my heart full of wonder, and they felt cool in my hands.

Deven slipped them into his pockets. "He'll kill us if he finds us."

"He doesn't know we have the parrot. Even if Aanya's magic can't hold his anger, he'll be looking for us in all the wrong places." The chorus of creaking voices in my head told me that the gargoyles already waited outside to take us to the labyrinth. "He won't catch us."

His eyes were bleak. "Menon has been in there all this time."

"Let's not dwell on all you've lost. Not right now, when there's so much to gain."

"I've muted my anger, but if I turn into a beast, I don't know if I'll be able to control it."

"You're not *him*. You're your own man… You told Nisha where to meet us when this is all over?"

He nodded. Then he pulled me after him, past guards loyal to him because he had always treated them with care, away from the flowing strains of Aanya's voice towards the palace gardens where the gargoyles stood in formation.

Hope–glorious, dizzying hope–blossomed inside my chest under the crimson sky.

CHAPTER 23

Six winged gargoyles waited in a semi-circle under the eerie light of the blood moon, led by Harya, their grotesque faces contorted into fierce snarls. Moss and ivy clung to some as if they had only just transitioned from their stone forms. At our approach, lips hastily closed over protruding teeth, bulging eyes retreated into their sockets, and menacing spiked tails ceased their slashing. My stomach somersaulted at the sight of a familiar fishtail form.

Sindhuja opened her cupped hands as I rushed over to her. "Mistress. I deliver the parrot."

Babbu flew out, bedraggled, squawking, without a speck of balding on him. "Mahi and Melon. Melon and Mahi."

"Oh, you are brilliant," I said to Sindhuja, but she was already turning at a low rustling in the underbrush.

Out crept Leena, to our common delight. She grimaced at her prisoner garb. "You didn't think I was going to go to a party dressed like this, did you?" said my sister. "After being cooped up, I'm ready to wreak havoc."

"I'm glad you're here." I hugged her. "Did you manage to bring a lighter?"

"Honey, I'm always prepared for an interdimensional jaunt."

"Come on," I tugged her after me. "I'm not sure how long we'll be able to access the portal or how long Prem will be distracted by the trail of my knickers Merlin planted in Deven's chambers."

The general raised an eyebrow. "Now that's something I have to see."

The three of us–Deven, Leena and I–climbed onto the backs of the gargoyles, one apiece, though it was a much easier feat for the general and my sister, given the fit of my *lehenga*. I rode with Harya, Leena rode with Sindhuja, and Deven clambered awkwardly onto a gargoyle with the body of an imp, nimble fingers that ended in sharp claws and a curling tail that strapped him onto its back like a seatbelt.

We only knew glimpses of what awaited us.

I wasn't scared, though I should have been.

Harya took up command. "Passengerless gargoyles, take up position at the outer periphery of the flight formation. Everyone, stay low, and if we come under attack, prioritise the safety of the earth witch. Sindhuja, try to maintain your height."

We pelted through a sky painted in crimson and ebony over the red brick houses and the seer's topsy-turvy one, away from the white-washed palace with its rose garden and roaming elephants. Away from the raja who had slipped the yoke of Aanya's magic and bellowed about his cousin, his honour and his wife. The gargoyles' wings, sinewy and membranous, unfurled and glided through the air, creating a haunting symphony. At the tip was the seer's luminescent green parrot, setting a brisk pace lest we miss our opportunity. His squawks added an eerie soundtrack to the night. I clung to Harya's back, the wind whipping through my ponytail, the scarf around my neck fanning through the sky like a flag. The wind ricocheted around us, and I much preferred my feet on solid ground, but I squeezed my eyes open midflight and spotted the sacred banyan tree before we landed.

Native to the tropics, the banyan tree shouldn't have grown in the British climate, but Jalapashu's magic nourished it somehow. Leathery leaves covered its dark, gnarled branches. Its branches and aerial roots created a canopy that stretched further than the eye could see. They were adorned with jasmine garlands in honour of my engagement to the raja. The sickly-sweet aroma of the jasmine filled my nose as Harya led the formation to the ground, kicking dust into the air with his clumsy landing.

I flung myself off his back with an inelegant thud. Deven had already done a count and ushered everyone to the densest part of the canopy, where the parrot waited, his bright body luminous against the dark branches. I joined the circle of my friends and allies. They turned to me as though I was the anointed leader, though the general was there and Harya too and Sindhuja, whose bravery in protecting the parrot had brought us to this point.

The topaz jewels I wore resonated through my cells as if their energy was in perfect harmony with my own, though the ring had a darker inflection to the jewel in my thigh. I took a deep breath. "When the portal to the labyrinth opens, we know we'll face dark things in there, but we stay true to our intentions–to help the seer and her brother–and we stay together." I held out my wrist.

Babbu came without me calling him, his anticipation evident by the quivering of his lustrous feathers. When he bowed, I plucked a single feather from his wing and held it up for Leena. Babbu tilted his head, staring intently as Leena pulled out the lighter and ignited the feather. My stomach clenched as its emerald tones burned, sending amber flames licking upwards. As the feather grew warm in my hand, it pulsated as if it held the heartbeat of the labyrinth.

Suddenly, the air grew still under the sprawling canopy of the sacred banyan tree, and I heard Nani's words in my head. *God's shelter. The cosmic tree. The tree of blessings.* Then the branches of the sacred banyan tree shivered and shook, and its leathery leaves became the rattle of snakes, and the blood moon seemed to suck all joy from the world. The gargoyles uttered fierce war cries as the portal emerged, starting as a ripple before our eyes that became a shimmering whirlpool of verdant greens, inky blacks, silvery glass and violets like the seer's third eye.

The general grabbed my hand and Leena's, and his grip was strong and warm, though his jaw was clenched. And Babbu had already flown into the vortex, a flash of green that was swallowed by darkness. I dropped the feather and stamped out its last embers. My gaze flitted to the world we knew, then with a nod, the three of us pushed our way into the portal, and it was like stepping through a curtain of warm water, though we didn't get wet.

We found ourselves in a different dimension, in a rough-hewn corridor of the labyrinth, with the portal glowing behind us. The tones of the blood moon had been washed away, leaving a muted palette of colours so that Babbu seemed less green and our clothes monotone. The air carried the scent of damp stone and decaying plants. There was no sun, no moon, no stars. Only the faint flicker of old gas lamps that you found in central London flickered in the distance, barely giving out any light at all. From behind came the song of flapping wings, and the gargoyles emerged from the portal one by one, flying straight into a protective semi-circle around us. Still, the portal didn't close, though I almost hoped it would, because I didn't want to worry about what lay ahead of us as well as behind us.

A demon-horned gargoyle said to the group as if he could hear my thoughts. "I'll guard the portal."

He adopted a fierce stance as we took our first steps into the labyrinth. It was a tangled web of brier and bramble, its dark corridors twisting and turning like the convoluted thoughts of a madman. Such a dense undergrowth should have teemed with life, but I sensed nothing: no worms or microorganisms in the soil, no hooting of owls or fox calls, no thriving ecosystem—only a barren and lifeless void. Even the grass underfoot was brittle, stripped of its lushness.

Leena frowned at the winding path as if it were a web spun by a malevolent spider and not merely root and bark, thorn and branch. "I don't like it." She lit a flame and held it aloft, peering at the tangled corridors as if corruption oozed from the plants themselves. "This place reeks of dark magic."

Deven drew a dagger. "We can still turn back."

"No, we can't." My hands hung loosely at my side, but I was ready to set right all the wrongs that had been done in the name of this kingdom.

I took the lead, my footsteps tentative as I chose our route, anxiety thinning my breath as we ventured deeper into the labyrinth's depths. The grass beneath our feet swallowed our footsteps, even the trudge of the gargoyles. I took solace from how we moved as one, but with every step, my thoughts turned darker, and I wondered why Leena hadn't yet asked why Sitara wasn't with us. I wondered if we would all return from this place unchanged or whether I would chalk up another regret.

All at once, my grandmother's protective aura didn't seem as strong.

Or maybe my desolate thoughts called the darkness to us.

The parrot sensed the change in the labyrinth, too. A dead end loomed before us like a mocking grin. When a vine reached for Babbu with uncanny intelligence, he jerked out of its reach. He squawked Mahi's name in terror, although the labyrinth was silent, and I was afraid that his clamour would waken lurking monsters. Abandoning us, he took flight in an easterly direction towards the heart of the labyrinth, where he disappeared into mist.

"We can't lose him." The darkness seemed to press in on all sides, and there was nowhere for us to turn unless we turned back.

Sindhuja tried to follow the parrot, and Harya commanded a second gargoyle to accompany her, but when they tried to gain altitude, their wings became rubbery and uncooperative, their little jumps pitiful.

The general's voice was grim as he drew a dagger. "That's our hopes of an easy escape dashed. The parrot took the most direct route to Mahi. Our journey won't be so easy."

No sooner had he spoken did the walls of the labyrinth begin to writhe. The vine that had tried to ensnare the bird suddenly seemed to inspire a dozen more. They sprang to life with a cruel elegance, reaching out hungrily to ensnare us like the bony hands of some ancient evil. The serpentine tendrils grabbed at our ankles, waists and necks, threatening to throttle us, stop the blood flow to our limbs, or drag us into the undergrowth to use our bodies as fertiliser. We fought hard. Deven, the tallest of us, hacked with his dagger and took the brunt of the attack. The gargoyles swung clawed fists and tore with fearsome teeth, using their bodies to shield us. Leena howled, waging war with her lighter and calling forth new shoots to cage the evil vines.

I poured my magic into the ground, trying to counter the tainted magic there. I used the spell for repelling darkness that I had poured into the egg cups, which Merlin had distributed around the city. *Tamaso nivāraya, tamaso nivāraya, tamaso nivāraya.* Though the vines resisted, the letters of the incantation roped in my mind, building in power like a coiled spring, spiralling outwards from me until the vines relented against our onslaught and a way forward suddenly yawned before us, a passage carved through the middle of a once-hostile thicket.

We rushed forward, now only eight, when we had entered the labyrinth as a group of ten.

The passage snapped closed behind us like the mouth of a Venus flytrap, and even Leena, who loved plants and could manipulate them, was ashen-faced with fear in the glow of the lighter flame.

"You should conserve the light," said Deven to her.

My sister glared at him. "Hell, no. If something is going to eat me, I want to see it coming."

We ventured deeper into the labyrinth, the cold driving a shiver into our bones. Our eyes had become attuned to the darkness, and we hardly dared to speak, saving our wits and magic for the traps that lay before us. Illusory allies whispered promises of safety: Jilu, the chef from Biryani Junction; Yuvan, Deven's servant; and Lata, the dancer who wanted to be a scientist. When we turned away from them, their faces melted like wax dolls in a fire, and I prayed their screams wouldn't stay with me. We caught glimpses of other humans: echoes of past explorers, doomed to wander the labyrinth forever, seeking a way out. There was a regal woman with a swan-like neck whose ankle bells shimmered despite the darkness, a man who read aloud poems of despair from a book as he roamed the inverted forest and a young boy who carried a rusted sword and whose gaze was pure white.

Treacherous walls shifted at will, closing off paths and revealing new ones, creating ever-shifting routes and forcing us to retrace our steps as if the labyrinth was a perverse lover who wanted to keep us trapped forever. Leena's green witch wisdom helped us navigate our path away from plants that could easily be corrupted by the labyrinth.

But the labyrinth was duplicitous.

Obstacles materialised before us, summoned by the labyrinth: walls of thorns or pits as deep as wells or distorted landscapes that warped our perception of reality. Inverted forests. Shifting sands. Red rooftops so familiar and inviting to a humanoid gargoyle with chaotic energy that he sprang towards them and crumbled to dust, though Harya warned him to stay away.

The gargoyles left him there, though Sindhuja–softer than the rest, perhaps–cast a mournful look over her shoulder. At a junction where multiple paths branched out like the fingers of a spectral hand, I stared down each corridor. Foreboding gnawed at my insides, and every decision seemed too heavy a weight to bear. Overhead, the branches of thorny vines clawed at the sky, their sharp, blood-red thorns gleaming with malevolence. "Left. I think we take the path to the far left."

The labyrinth wasn't finished with us yet. It had us right where it wanted us.

We inched down the left path, exhausted by the wily labyrinth. It was Harya who noticed shadows pouring out ahead, stalking shadows that rushed towards us, born of the darkness and fuelled by our fear. His voice filled my head. *Good luck, mistress. Sindhuja will guard you now.* Then he unleashed a fearsome roar, flanked by the impish gargoyle who had carried Deven and a serpent-winged gargoyle. They spread their wings and became stone with a final whisper of farewell. Their winged formation became an impenetrable shield that safeguarded us from the clutches of the shadows.

Harya's voice faded from my mind, leaving a profound emptiness in its wake. I wailed, overcome with doubt about the heavy toll our goals had exacted. I wanted desperately for them all to survive. My heart wrenched at the unfairness of how their quiet heroism would go unnoticed, how the people would never know what they had given. I stared at them, wanting to learn every rugged fold, distinctive contour and chiselled cut of their stone bodies.

We had come into the labyrinth with ten; now we were only four.

"Kiya, move!" Deven grunted as he half-carried, half-dragged me away.

I only saw him—only felt him—a moment longer before his shout and Leena's scream echoed in my ears, drowning out the labyrinth's eerie silence. In that brief span, the labyrinth separated us. Its sinewy vines coiled around my torso with calculated precision, suspending me in the air. I wasn't a rani-in-waiting. I was a rag doll with torn clothes, muddy feet and hair full of brambles.

For a disorienting moment, I had a bird's eye view of the entire maze.

Pockets of mist clung to the labyrinth's uneven terrain. I spotted the demon-horned gargoyle guarding the portal and the trio of stone gargoyles. A few hundred metres away, tantalisingly close, the seer stroked her parrot. At her side stood a young man who bore a striking resemblance to the portrait in the throne room. There was Leena, Sindhuja and rosy-cheeked Sitara with her cascade of silvery midnight hair, together in one segment of the labyrinth. But deep down, I knew this couldn't be Sitara. I had witnessed Sitara being devoured by the shadows. What is more, the back of the wraith dissolved into black curls of smoke. But Leena wanted so much to believe our sister was alive that she beamed at the unnatural spectacle; even Sindhuja grew fierce. There was the general, my Deven, trapped in a loop, reliving the same events without escape as the tiger mauled Roshni. He threw himself at the apparitions, pleading for mercy, anguish etched deep into his features.

The closer we ventured towards the heart of the labyrinth, the more it intensified its tricks and illusions. Like a cornered rattlesnake, it grew increasingly frenzied and ruthless. If Leena and Deven didn't spurn the apparitions and voice their truths, the labyrinth would never let them go.

I shouted and fought to reach my loved ones, but the coiling vines reacted with seething anger and jerked me back down into the labyrinth's embrace.

It was my turn to face the ghouls.

I caught my breath in a narrow corridor. "Leena! Deven!"

They didn't respond, as if we were insulated in our own hells. The air was thick with an oppressive stillness, broken only by the faint echo of my breaths. The scent of damp earth and decay, tinged with a faint metallic undertone, crept into my nostrils, making my stomach tighten with foreboding. I could feel the texture of the now-worn surface beneath the soles of my new sandals, a reminder of the labyrinth's unforgiving nature.

I flinched as the mystic stepped from a glinting surface nestled within the bushes.

He fixed his pale green eyes on me like a reptile poised to strike. "Prem Kumar might have been taken in by your charms, but did you really think you could best *me*? The seer is staying in the labyrinth, and so are you." With that, he lifted his arms, and shadows poured out of his sleeves, shadows that solidified and became flesh and blood, memory and mayhem.

One by one, the doppelgängers came for me.

Tommy's smile mirrored the one I had adored since we first met at school. Every nuance of his presence was impeccably recreated, from his blonde hair to his loving glance. He reached out a strong hand, his voice reassuring, tempting me to relive more innocent times. "Come with me, Kiya. We're overdue a beach day."

I braced myself as Deven appeared, inky black eyes full of pain and quiet strength. "Kiya, we can explore each other and our magic together. I have so much to show you."

Tears welled as Sitara and Leena appeared, their noses smeared with paint, laughing about a foolish colour choice. "It's about time you did some work," they said, handing me a paintbrush as our house in Boundless Bay appeared behind them.

There was Mum and Dad kissing in our childhood kitchen, so real that I could touch them. Their faces and mannerisms were so finely observed as if the labyrinth had mined the recesses of my thoughts, replaying the moments that were dear to me, as if then I might decide to stay in its clutches. "Kiya, come home. We're waiting for you."

It was tempting to submit to this moment of ease. I yearned for more time with them. Each smile, each gesture, compelled me towards the illusion the labyrinth had woven. It was so much simpler to embrace this fabricated reality. To win time with Mum and Dad and bask in the comfort of their presence once more. To escape the trials that awaited me.

Qasim's sly smile held the anticipation of victory. The gleam in his eye gave me pause.

What would happen to my sister and friends if I gave up now? What fate would befall Jalapashu and its people if I surrendered to the labyrinth's enchantment? So, though my fingers were scrunched as tightly as a paper ball, I stretched them to summon my magic. "I'm sorry. I can't stay."

Oh, the labyrinth wasn't happy.

Briers reached out with their skeletal fingers, snagging my bare skin. The bramble's barbed tendrils writhed, and vines snaked around my ankles. I commanded the earth to reject them, even as the walls of the labyrinth closed in on me and the doppelgängers of my loved ones advanced with unsettling grace, wanting to drag me into the undergrowth. Their smoky eyes judged me for abandoning them, for leaving them all alone.

I trembled with resolve, my chest a leaden weight as I drew on the deep reserves beneath my feet. The earth, my ally, transformed into a weapon. I sculpted the soil beneath my feet, raising mounds and building cavernous pits that the mystic scampered back from. The earth formed jagged shields to protect me from the reach of the ghouls, and I hurtled projectiles towards them. Each act of violence against the twisted apparitions left behind scars I knew would linger if I escaped the labyrinth's clutches.

On I fought as my topaz jewels pulsed in synchronicity with my breath. Sweat poured from my brow as I wrenched the spells from myself and sent them spinning into the labyrinth. Strings of vowels and consonants formed spells that stretched and compressed, folded and unfolded like an accordion. Each incantation felt like a dance of linguistic artistry on my tongue, a kaleidoscope of words and letters that I unleashed into the labyrinth. *Tyāga*, I said to the ghouls. *Krodho nivartatām. Vismar. Tamaso nivāraya.* I used all the spells in my arsenal. The ancient words flowed effortlessly from my lips.

But the ghouls didn't recede. Light didn't blossom to drive them back.

A scream built in me as they regrouped. I renewed my efforts, calling the earth to bury them one by one in a swirling vortex of soil and stone. But as the mounds settled, the ghouls reformed with an eerie resilience. A cacophony of laughter swirled around me as they reformed, and I saw in their malevolent gaze that they never wanted me to leave. They now resembled grotesque caricatures of my loved ones, their features contorted, their teeth sharp and their fingers elongated. Each step towards me was a macabre dance. They were predators savouring the moment they captured their prey.

The pale-eyed mystic grinned at his work.

The ghouls reached for me, and it was the hare's voice that I remembered, the hare who had always encouraged me to be truthful. *Those who dare to enter must confront their deepest fears and desires.* What buried secret could I expel these ghouls with? I had stripped myself of my lies; my family and friends knew who I was. What possible buried truth did I have yet to excavate?

It came to me then. I had known it since I first walked into the throne room since I had seen Mum's portrait in the library and learned of our ancestry. Most of all, since I had witnessed the many injustices the raja had carried out, beginning with Sitara's killing.

My words rang out like a bell, their chime cutting through the silence. "I want to be Rani of Jalapashu. Not as the consort of Prem Kumar. In my own right."

With my words, the ghouls dissipated like smoke, their smiles fading into nothingness, and the labyrinth seemed to have accepted my victory. It shifted and twisted until I stood in the midst of a transformed and purified realm, my mind reeling from the effort. The darkness receded as though the approaching dawn had banished the crimson moon. I heard faraway footsteps, the monotone palette of the labyrinth flooded with colour. The bramble and brier softened into lilac and lavender bushes that reminded me of Mahi's violet third eye.

The mystic's thin body tensed, his features contorting with frustration. "It should have been you in this maze all along after you thwarted the raja at the Summer Soiree, but your grandfather begged him for a reprieve—the soppy old fool. So the raja took the seer instead. A lesson in loyalty. This time, Prem Kumar will not let you live." He walked into the gleaming surface nestled in the bushes.

With the brighter light, I recognised the surface to be a twin mirror of the one I had seen in his chambers. As Qasim stepped into it, I darted towards him to touch the mirror, a spell spilling from my lips. *Tava atītaṃ bhakṣayatu.* I repeated the words, building a vortex of power. It didn't seem like dark magic to ask the universe to let Qasim's past consume him.

It felt like justice.

As the last incantation left my lips, the mirror splintered into a spiderweb of fractures, trapping the mystic in it. His pale green eyes darted, and his outstretched hand strained against the magical prison. The labyrinth around me crackled with residual energy.

With one last look, I turned my back on him, drawn by the voices of my sister and the general.

CHAPTER 24

Leena's sudden tumbling embrace brought a rush of relief, and I surrendered to the familiar softness of her golden hair against my cheek. The cycle of her breath told me she was real, and I buried my head against her like she was my lifeline. Then Deven wrapped his bulky arms around us, smelling like a forest after rain. When Sindhuja leaned her tough cheek awkwardly against my hip, her softening was unexpected but welcome.

The four of us pulled apart, but I kept hold of Leena's hand. "Sitara's gone."

"I suspected when she didn't accompany us into the labyrinth. That thing. It wasn't her." Leena's brown eyes held a reservoir of sadness. "What was the truth that freed you?"

I swallowed hard. "I want to be Rani of Jalapashu. On my own terms, not as an appendage."

"Bloody hell, Kiya. You didn't even want a newspaper around growing up."

I winced and directed the same question to Leena and Deven. "What were your truths?"

"I'm ready to let Sitara go," said my sister quietly.

The gargoyle's stony lips turned downwards. "The labyrinth didn't test me."

The taut line of Deven's lips and his bleak eyes showed what a toll the labyrinth had exacted. "I'm sorry that Roshni died. I forgive her. But I couldn't have saved our marriage if she had lived."

I nodded in silent acknowledgement. Sindhuja glowered at the trapped mystic while the rest of us scanned the serene landscape that had unfurled around us. Our truths had renewed it. Lilac and lavender bushes stretched out in elegant rows. Overhead, the sky had morphed from inky blackness into a tranquil cerulean canvas. The ground beneath our feet, once rugged and uneven, was now a lush carpet of moss and clover. Wildflowers of every hue dotted the landscape, and the distant murmur of a brook met our ears.

Three divergent paths stretched before us.

"Let's find Mahi and Menon and get out of here." As the words left my lips, an archway composed of yellow roses took shape over the central path. I'd seen such roses before in my mother's portrait, and the palace rose garden and our family crest.

Sitara taught us not to underestimate the power of family.

I thought of her then as Leena, and I exchanged glances and darted under the arch. We delved deeper into the heart of the labyrinth, despite Deven and Sindhuja urging caution, guided by velvety yellow roses that sprung up to guide our way in the labyrinth where minutes before only briar and bramble had grown. We gasped with surprise as we came upon a small enclave.

"Mahi," I breathed.

I had missed the sorry sight of her. I had missed her prickly personality and her wily ways.

Most of all, I had missed her wisdom and unparalleled courage.

Her face shone with satisfaction. She was bathed in the diffused light, dressed in black harem trousers and a misshapen Bruce Willis T-shirt that was in dire need of a wash, although she didn't otherwise look worse for wear. Babbu bobbed with happiness on her shoulder, tilting his beady-eyed head every now and then to stare at her.

The general's coal-black eyes turned fiery as he rushed at the stranger standing with the seer, and he clean lifted him off his feet to Sindhuja's delight and Mahi's nonchalant intervention.

"Put him down, General. And let me look at you all. You are a sight for sore eyes," said the seer.

The stranger couldn't be Menon unless time had frozen in the labyrinth, and he hadn't aged at all. He was roughly the same height as the seer–although it was hard to tell with his legs dangling off the ground–and had the same eyes as the seer, but his skin was smooth rather than lined, and his hair was peppered with grey rather than entirely silver. He wore an expression of quiet contemplation to match his tatty wizard's robes.

"I'm sorry," he said to Deven.

Deven let him fall to the ground with a growl. "I don't want to hate you anymore. Just fix it."

His sister helped him to his feet and dusted him off. Her silver pixie haircut had grown wild and was adorned with sprigs of forget-me-nots. "Right on time. You see, brother? Just as I predicted. Although I can tell by their faces how I'm destined to endure many jokes about how women age faster than men. Just think, if I had found you a decade ago, I would have a discernible chin but significantly less wisdom."

Menon tried to regain his composure and bowed, low and deep. "I was always heralded as the great wizard, but my sister is capable of maintaining her integrity and building alliances I could only dream of. Thank you for risking yourselves."

"I've been using our time here to teach my brother how to eat humble pie. He's very serious about making amends."

Clearly, the power stakes had changed between them.

I reined in my delight at seeing her. "Did you manipulate us, Mahi? Did you know when we first met that you needed me to free your brother?" I glared at Menon, brimming with magic. "And *you* won't be leaving here unless you've proved whose side you are on."

The seer grew sombre. "Motives are complex, multilayered. I am loyal to you, Kiya. I know from my visions that you are capable of this and so much more. You carry destruction and creation within your soul. But I also needed to get to my brother. I couldn't let the labyrinth keep Menon forever, so I dragged you into my business."

"I'm all for getting my hands dirty for friends," said Leena. "But I went to prison in aid of this quest."

Mahi's voice was wry. "That was a mini-spa break, and you well know it."

"Quite frankly, while you are worth the trouble, from what Aanya has told me, I'm not sure your twin is."

"You want a thank you, and you are right." Mahi gave a pained sigh. Humility wasn't either sibling's forté. "Without you all, I couldn't have mended what was broken. Menon and I might be old, but we are still writing the end of our story. Thank you for accepting my invitation to come to the labyrinth, taking care of Babbu and giving me this chance to heal old wounds."

I raised an eyebrow. "Your invitation?"

"Granted, it wasn't as ostentatious as a palace engagement notice. I took advantage of my reputation of being a slob and hid the compendium of animals in my lumpy bed. I knew the soldiers wouldn't look there. But you two have such chemistry I thought you might stumble upon it. Yes, I know you were in my bed. And no, I don't mind. As long as you didn't use my stash of dildos."

"What's a dildo?" asked Sindhuja.

"Single women have needs," whispered Leena.

"*All* women have needs," said Mahi.

Deven's voice was grim. "I should ask Menon to curse me again just to escape this conversation."

"You have been quiet, General. You disapprove of my methods?"

Deven's jaw clenched. "I wouldn't have chosen them. You take too many risks, Mahi."

"That may be, but I see what you don't." She inclined her head to his pocket. "You have something for us." It was a statement, not a question.

Deven hesitated before pulling out the two medallions. Their gold chains had tangled. He pried them apart and handed them to the seer. "You know what I want."

I stood by his side. "Undo the curse, Menon. His gift was never yours to take."

Mahi's eyes were bright with anticipation. She touched the jewel with tender hands, then placed the medallion around her neck. A shiver of energy ran through her body, and she straightened her posture as it nestled against her skin. Tucking it into her T-shirt, she looked up with a glimmer of a smile. Then her forehead yawned, and her violet eye came to the fore. Glorious. Strange. Frightening. "Brother?"

The wizard slipped his medallion around his neck, and regret weighed heavy in his words. "I've thought about that day often, General, and what transpired after my part in it. I wronged you. I hope this makes amends."

I snuck a look at Deven. Every sinew in his body was tense, and he held his breath. A shiver chased up my spine. Already, the labyrinth was changing. Gone were the yellow roses and the purples of the hedgerows grew dim with the fading light as if the labyrinth was resetting itself again.

I prayed that we were right to trust Menon.

Menon blinked like the years had indeed had an impact on him, and he needed a visit to the optician. Then he slowly spoke an incantation, stumbling over the pronunciation, feeling his way as if he had been starved of magic in the labyrinth and was a rusty machine that needed to be oiled. At first, nothing happened, and then the tangling hedgerows reached out for Deven from two sides, binding him in the air.

The three of us–Leena, Sindhuja and I–lunged for him, ready to let our magic loose.

The seer held us back with sharp words. "Don't be stupid. I vouch for him. Let him work."

Deven's inky eyes flashed with fear, then fire, and then the golds of the sun, desert sands and tiger coats, and the greens of tropical trees and jade grasses. I shuddered to think of how the curse had taken effect, but this time, his transition was softer, maybe because Menon's magic was this time fuelled by a desire for redemption rather than his desire for power. His bones didn't bend like boughs. No grip of an unnatural tree enclosed him in its bark. This time, the vines twirled him in the air. A radiant magic emanated from them and poured into Deven, causing his clothes to disintegrate into tatters and his dagger belt to plummet to the ground, leaving him bare and exposed. Menon continued his spell, and Deven relaxed, trusting in the process, sensing the honesty of intention, the willingness to set right a great wrong.

With a final thrust of Menon's magic and a tidal swell of energy, the general fell to the earth. I shielded my eyes from the blinding light for a brief second. As the glow receded, we were met by the sight of a lithe Bengal tiger. His golden striped coat was a kaleidoscope of earth tones, and his eyes were as black as midnight skies. I held my breath as Deven padded with enormous paws towards me.

Sindhuja's heavy footsteps sounded as she positioned herself to protect Leena and me.

"It's okay," I said to the gargoyle, my eyes locked on the tiger, instinctively trusting him.

In his eyes, there was a sense of home, of wholeness, of exhilaration. He smelt wild and free.

"Go," I said. "We can take care of ourselves."

He raced past me, muscles rippling beneath his sleek coat as he sprinted across the terrain. His body blurred like liquid poetry, an effortless surge of grace, and I discerned his mandala tattoo mingling with the dark brushstrokes of his stripes on the canvas of his golden fur as if his suffering had made him more than the sum of his parts and not less. A triumphant roar reverberated through the labyrinth as Deven left us in his wake.

I burst with happiness for him. He would prowl through moonlit forests again. He would feel the rush of the wind against his fur and the rhythm of the earth beneath his paws.

He had won back what had been taken from him.

Leena whistled. "Well, I never. Even with my preferences, I'd pay to see that again."

The wizard sagged like a weary, withered traveller. Perhaps he had earned his place in our band of allies, but I didn't know how he would make it out of the labyrinth when he was so drained of his vitality. Especially when change accelerated in the labyrinth.

"Well done, brother. Now come along." Mahi harrumphed as the sky over us grew ominous. "Come on. We must leave before the portal closes."

The labyrinth had regressed as if it had enough of its taste of redemption. It boomeranged back to its sinister state, a place that craved lies and betrayals to fuel its dark self. Elongated shadows slithered at the periphery of my eyes, and Leena clutched me, her fingers trembling in response to the unnerving transformation of our surroundings. Babbu sensed it, too. He flew around us in squawking circles.

I slung the general's dagger belt over my shoulder and

left the remainder of his clothing where it had fallen. I had a feeling he wouldn't be needing it anytime soon.

In my head, there was a faint creaking noise, a familiar strain, a quiet chorus of groans that made me call for Harya, the imp gargoyle and the serpent one. A grinding of stone and bone, a heaving and a shuddering filled my mind, and then they came, the three gargoyles we thought we had lost, flying over the labyrinth towards us. *Hurry, mistress. Time is short. The blood moon is almost gone. The portal closes.*

They landed between the clearing, and already their wings didn't wholly function, already the rubbery effect returned as the noose of the labyrinth closed around us, and we climbed onto their backs. Three witches and a wizard riding haphazardly across the maze, clinging onto the backs of the four gargoyles, with the parrot charging ahead in a flash of muted green. Harya panted beneath me, his voice quiet in my head as he channelled every ounce of his energy. The lion-maned gargoyle leader diverted only briefly, swooping down to the mystic in the mirror, smashing the glass into a thousand glittering shards. He ended Qasim's life with an efficient bloodlust that was alien to me, but I was glad. *You knew that was necessary, and soon you will be capable of such acts yourself,* said Harya's voice in my head as his wings fought to regain elevation and catch up with his team.

I clung to his back as the demon-horned gargoyle guarding the portal called out a warning about a tiger. About two tigers fighting at the entrance to the labyrinth. Suddenly, I couldn't think; I could only react.

The gargoyles' wings ceased flapping, and somewhere, my sister called out. Then I was falling, falling, a tumble of gargoyle bodies and human ones, reaching out my hands to invoke the earth to cushion us with a bed of soil. A cacophony of ground-shaking thuds, agonised moans and breaking stone filled my ears—a maelstrom of chaos and confusion.

Throwing out that desperate net of my magic had eroded me like soil drained of its nutrients. My body wouldn't respond. The seer cursed that shadows poured out of the labyrinth into the kingdom. A tiger roared. A jackalope with liquid gold eyes loomed over me, his face vaguely familiar, his antlers drawn from one of my mother's bedtime stories. Where was Leena? Leena had liked that story the best out of the three of us.

I couldn't hold on anymore. My thoughts disappeared like will-o'-the-wisps floating over a waterlogged riverbank. As my senses dimmed, someone lifted me unceremoniously into his arms, muttering about how he was well past the age for such strenuous adventures.

The edges of my consciousness dissolved, and darkness enveloped me.

CHAPTER 25

erlin brought me back from oblivion with soft chirps of happiness. "Did you see, Kiya? The labyrinth turned me into a jackalope. I had these magnificent antlers crowning my head. I was a masterpiece. Symmetrical, sculpted from shimmering ivory, perfectly in proportion to my body. You did see, didn't you?"

"Dirty hare," said Babbu, unimpressed.

My body ached from the fall, every muscle protesting as I pushed myself into a sitting position. I peeled my eyes open to find splotches of deep blues and purples on my arms and legs, a vivid canvas of pain. I looked around, brow furrowing. We weren't outside anymore. We were somewhere cramped and dark that smelled of magic: Mahi's house.

We were in the seer's kitchen, in the tallest building in the kingdom, second only to the white-washed royal palace. The blood moon had gone, and the skies were lightening. It was sometime pre-dawn. Next to me was a spillage of smelling salts.

"Give her a minute. She's still groggy." Leena positioned me with firm, kind hands. "That's it. Pop your head between your knees. It'll help. And honestly, Merlin, you looked a little imbalanced to me. Like a woman whose breast implants are too big and is in danger of toppling over."

The hare was too focused on his daring feat to be waylaid by her teasing. "I gored the tiger king with my antlers, and he really didn't see me coming." His voice was animated with the thrill of the moment. "I darted through the under-brush, my antlers gleaming in the shadows. The tiger king was focused on the general, so I took my chance, gathered my considerable strength, leapt into the air, and came down with all the force I could muster."

"The jump was about two feet high," said the general, but his gaze was intense, and his body turned my way as Leena fussed over me.

There was a pang near my heart as our ordeal in the labyrinth came flooding back to me, and I recalled his curse had been broken and his pure joy at shifting. I yearned to close the distance between us, and Deven must have sensed it because he knelt down, and his chaste kiss on my cheek was tinged with restraint, gratitude and relief. I shivered at his touch.

But the hare hadn't finished his tale. "My antlers struck true, and the tiger king let out a roar of surprise. He won't recover from his wounds for a long time."

"It was in the leg, not the heart," said Deven. "And it's impolite to muscle in on a duel."

His tone was wry, but I read the dread in his inky eyes. We both knew that the raja wouldn't let this matter lie. He would return our slights and injuries a thousand-fold. Prem's reprisals would be nothing short of brutal, an all-encompassing assault that would test our resilience and unity to the breaking point. He would be ruthless in regaining his honour and asserting his dominance in a way that left no room for doubt. I shuddered just to think of it, but it had been worth it.

For Mahi. And for the sight of Deven as his glorious tiger self.

My friends deserved their happiness. And the kingdom deserved a just ruler.

The kingdom deserves you. A just queen in place of a corrupt raja, said the gargoyle chorus in my mind.

Merlin was on a roll. "You may be Kiya's lover, but *I'm* her familiar. One of those positions is pretty much permanent, and the other is subject to the lady's whims."

My voice was croaky with exhaustion. They'd propped me up on some cushions on Mahi's sticky floor. "There's no need for rivalry."

Deven squeezed my shoulder–flooding me with warmth–and then moved away to form a tête-à-tête with Yuvan and a group of soldiers. Mahi and Menon were within earshot discussing fortification spells. More confusingly still, there seemed to be an influx of people from the kingdom pouring into the seer's house, which was making her shout because she very much preferred a hermit's life and certainly liked to curate the people around her if she was forced to interact.

The hare nuzzled up to me, unabashed, as Leena pressed a cup of murky water into my hand that she had tweaked with an herb for an extra kick. "Drink that up—every last drop. You blacked out after our fall. It'll give you back your strength. It's better if you don't know what it is. Let's just say I got a workout with the mortar and pestle."

I gave her an anxious look. "Did you get hurt?"

"Cuts and bruises," said Leena. "Nothing that won't sort itself out with a little dab of aloe. Aanya's been keeping the gargoyles calm until I can get to them. I think they're going to need a combination of my nursing and your crafting to feel a hundred per cent themselves. We only just about got everyone out before the portal closed. We're lucky that Grandfather was there to heave you out. For a minute, I thought he was going to buckle under your weight. He's more of a paper-pusher than an action hero."

Merlin was a soothing bulk in my lap. "Why does this feel like a command centre?"

Leena gave a sorry sigh. "You didn't think we were going to swan back into Jalapashu without any consequences, did you? He *knows*, Kiya. Prem Kumar knows that you broke Mahi and Menon out of the labyrinth. He knows that Deven's curse has been lifted. And he knows that you can command the gargoyles. He saw it with his own eyes. His rage was so all-encompassing that the shadows surged towards him like he was a magnet, and some of them escaped into the kingdom."

Gold eyes glimmered. "Maybe I can reengage the jacka-lope outside the labyrinth."

My grandfather stalked up to us, his manner gruff. "It is good you are awake. The people are safe because of you, Kiya. You caused trouble in Jalapashu, but the seer tells me that you had the foresight, without her intervention, to distribute enchanted egg cups to every household. They acted as a ward. The people are coming here like you are a beacon, a heroine who can save them from the evil king."

"I delivered the egg cups. And I freed the animals." Merlin poked up his head like a meerkat, but Prakash ignored him.

I grimaced as I swallowed Leena's bitter medicine.

She took the empty cup from me. "Nisha and Ishaan are here, and a courtier called Lata, who is insisting on seeing you. Plus, Farida, who's making me so proud. She said that if you can say no to the raja, she can leave her cheating husband. She's taken off her bangles and is wielding a pair of barbecue tongs with such relish that I think she probably gave him a poke where the sun doesn't shine."

I shooed Merlin off my lap and dragged myself up, not sure if this was what I wanted. Not sure if I could be the leader that Jalapashu deserved. Reality was so much harder than dreaming, and my successes felt surreal, accidental, and impossible to repeat. I wanted other people to make the decisions. It was too hard to make them myself. "What do you think, Grandfather?"

His Adam's apple bobbed up and down in his throat, and he looked frail somehow, scared, even though he had displayed more courage than ever before in helping us. "If I didn't believe in you, I wouldn't have conjured the trail of Hansa's roses to lead you to the seer. I wouldn't have carried you in my arms, as I once carried your mother, to bring you back to Jalapashu. You are family, and I couldn't choose the raja over you. Plus, I found Kavita's tersely worded letter in the wastepaper basket, and her threats about our home life made me think carefully about my choices."

I gave him a weak smile and laid a kiss on his dry cheek.

Maybe we could find common ground after all.

Grandfather's stern demeanour thawed, sensing the fragile bonds forming between us. "I burned my files and relinquished my place and position at court." He blew out his cheeks like he wasn't sure it had been the sensible thing to do.

"That must have been hard," said Leena.

"I think it's wonderful." Mahi swatted my grandfather as she reached behind him for two crystal balls and a tarot deck. "You finally found a backbone, Prakash. And don't worry. I'm not angry at you for colluding to trap me in the labyrinth. It was very kind of you to unwittingly put me exactly where I wanted to be."

Our grandfather stiffened, unsure how to process her insult when she had been forgiving of the harm he had caused. "Kavita is waiting to talk to me." Then he stalked into the bowels of the seer's house, a once-important man, strangely unmoored in a newly-shaped world.

"It's good you're awake." Mahi's violet eye faced me,

unblinking. "Can you believe it? Some women are starting to dust the surfaces in my house like they have nothing better to do. I need you outside. Just a matter of a little vision coming to fruition."

I was no longer in control, just damn exhausted. "Mahi, am I the pawn in this game?"

The seer beamed at me. "Surely you know by now? You're the queen we have been waiting for."

I ACCOMPANIED HER OUTSIDE IN MY TATTERED ENGAGEMENT clothes, and our coven followed suit: Leena, Aanya, Nani and Menon, so that we totalled seven in all, including Merlin as an honorary member, whose knowledge of spells outstripped mine. We stood in a tight circle and held hands, our energies and intentions intertwining. Soldiers loyal to the general took up guard around us.

The gargoyle voices were a storm in my mind.

I hadn't thought our actions would lead to war. But Mahi didn't look surprised, and neither did Menon. It seemed to them that war was inevitable.

I bit my lip at the seer's whispered request, knowing there was no way back, that maybe there never had been. Maybe this moment had been coming ever since our mother ran away from the kingdom, ever since Sitara had been killed on our kitchen floor for a topaz jewel that had turned our lives upside down. That had turned them from mundane into magical. I centred myself and gazed at Merlin, and I didn't know whether the spell was his or mine, only that it came to me ripe, like an apple plucked from a tree.

I spoke the incantation–*kilā nirmāya*–and a subtle vibration coursed through the ground beneath my feet, a gentle hum that built once the coven repeated my words. *Kilā nirmāya, kilā nirmāya, kilā nirmāya.* Our voices were hushed and reverent. The words pulsed through the air like a heartbeat. We closed our eyes in concentration, harmonising in perfect unity. The consonants, with their crisp sounds and distinct vibrations, felt like keystones, each one locking into place as we chanted. Suddenly, the spell wasn't just vowels and consonants in my mind; it was a vivid image, luminous threads forming a drawing that became stone. The hum of our chant intensified, and when I opened my eyes, the spell had etched itself into reality. Clouds whirled across the sky, and the air crackled in response to our magic. The sound of the syllables, with their sharp and sonorous qualities, reverberated like a coiled spring about to be released, and our fortress materialized, brick by brick as if responding to the cadence of our voices.

Walls of earth and stone rose skywards, a fortress constructed from cavernous stones, sturdy towers and battlements that stretched towards the stars in defiant splendour. It encompassed half the kingdom–including the seer's house and our own–its southern wall splitting the sacred banyan tree down its middle so that one side grew inside our fortress and the other half outside it. The gargoyles thudded onto the roof with sighs of pleasure and manned the battlements, war cries building in their chests.

"It's done," said the seer, adjusting her harem trousers.

"Not yet." Leena sent ivy creeping along the walls, blending the structure seamlessly with the surrounding landscape. Then she turned the heart-shaped garlands commemorating my ill-fated engagement into spirals that wound around each other in a continuous loop. "Now they represent our unfolding identities."

My voice was like an echo in an empty cathedral. "I miss Sitara."

Leena touched my face. "I do, too."

"It was very brave what she did," said Mahi cheerfully. "She's not done with you yet."

I stared at her. "Will we see her again?"

The violet eye on her forehead opened. "It's one magical possibility of many."

"That's good enough for me," said Leena.

From the stubborn jut of Mahi's jaw, it would have to be good enough for me, too. Sighing, I glanced over at Deven. He brooded some distance away in borrowed clothes, watching the fortress that had formed around us, then trained his eyes on the palace. He wouldn't be able to go back home. Prem had probably ordered the torching of his belongings.

My sister pushed me towards him. "Sitara would want us to live and not waste a moment. Stop looking at him like a love-sick fool and go to him." Then she ran over to Aanya and flung her arms around her, and nobody cared or batted an eyelid because gossip meant nothing when war and peace hung in the balance.

I went to the general and slipped my hand into his, my heartbeat quickening.

His grip closed around mine as if it were the most natural thing in the world, and he lifted my hand to his mouth and grazed his lips over my fingers. "Do you mind slipping this ring onto another finger, little witch? I take exception to another man claiming you as his when you are so clearly mine."

"I want to see you shift again."

"You want me out of my clothes."

"I want us both out of our clothes. Mine feel like a cage."

He nodded, his eyes darkening. "We should change that."

We walked away, first slowly, then with ever-quickening steps. A luminescent rabbit hopped by. We fumbled with our clothes as we went. Though his soldiers and the gargoyles kept watch, we tossed our clothes away as soon as we reached secluded areas. I flung my jewellery from me, tugging at the necklace and the bangles and ripping at the ribbon of my bodice and the skirt of my *lehenga*. Deven undid my whalebone corset, and I stood before him in just my silk knickers.

I knew from the gleam in his eyes what he intended.

He shifted into his tiger self, and I ran my fingers over his remarkable coat, marvelling at his lithe form, never once fearing his teeth or his claws, even though I was close enough to feel his tiger's breath on my face. He lowered himself to the ground, bending with effortless fluidity. His black eyes invited me to climb onto him. With my heart in my mouth, I straddled his tattooed back, sensing the vitality between my thighs. His muscles rippled beneath me, and I gripped tighter as Deven leapt into motion, his powerful hind legs propelling us forward. We raced through the kingdom under marshmallow skies that promised a new day. The world around us became a blur of colours and shapes, a breathtaking rush of motion and speed that blew the cobwebs from my brain and filled me with wonder. The scent of cool earth and autumn mellowing permeated my nostrils as we sped towards the woods.

I closed my eyes and wrapped my arms around Deven's golden neck, leaning against his fur, knowing he would never let anything happen to me. Knowing I could trust him with my life.

Afterwards, he shifted back into his human self, and we made a pilgrimage to the stump of the oak tree, where he had once been cursed but which no longer held any power over him. At my shiver, Deven reached out abruptly to rub the gooseflesh on my arms and pulled me into his arms. His inky eyes found mine. "He'll try to take our happiness as soon as he has healed from his injuries."

Foreboding mushroomed in my belly. "Was it hard to fight him?"

A vein throbbed in his temple. "I enjoyed making him bleed. Does that make me depraved?"

"It makes you human."

"How did you know you'd choose me and not him?"

"The gargoyles didn't fill my head with warnings when you appeared. And I like your sister."

He laughed and captured my lips with his own. I kissed him back, and our kiss was gentle and full of whimsy, and it washed away the nightmares of the labyrinth. Fireflies with tails like miniature stars darted through the air, and iridescent beetles glistening like jewels scuttled through the blades of grass.

I almost believed that we could achieve anything together.

Not even the distant tiger's incensed roar could wash away that feeling.

"Deven?"

"Yes, Kiya?"

"Who are we now?"

"We're the resistance."

ACKNOWLEDGEMENTS

Faith is currency in the writing world, and I felt that more than ever writing this book.

It's been a busy period in our household. I carved out pockets of time to write and only managed it in short bursts. What brings me back to the page is the sense that the characters are taking on a life of their own and that you can't leave them hanging. Kiya and Deven were so determined to be fleshed out in ink.

On that note: thank you, my readers. I always marvel at seeing familiar names appear in my reader group or in responses to my newsletters. I am so grateful for your support and enthusiasm. A special thanks to Breck for inspiring me with your pumpkin and leaf teacup, which is in Chapter 4. Thanks also to my author friends, especially those in Divining Tales and Seasoned Magic, for your sisterhood and encouragement.

Thank you to my ARC team for your enthusiasm and early story responses. To my beta readers, Debbie and Sherry, I trust your instincts more than my own. I appreciate your honest, insightful critiques and am so lucky we found each other.

Trish and Toni, my editors, your skill elevates my writing, and I am so grateful for your flexibility, professionalism and friendship. Fay, this cover is beautiful and even more so in paperback, with the branches weaving from front to back. Thank you for your art and patience.

A special thank you to Dagmar, my mother-in-law, who

took over kitchen duties on a family holiday so I could sneak away to write. We are lucky to have you, and you never once made me feel like a slacker.

To my own Nani, my maternal grandmother, who doesn't read, although she may read these brief lines. Only after I finished writing this book did I realise how many similarities Kavita has with my Nani. They are both gifted in the garden and kitchen. They are the heart of their families. They have a light spirit and an openness to adventures, even in their eighties. They give sound advice, are fiercely loyal and nonjudgemental about flaws in others. It's hard to love with an open hand, and they both manage it.

To our children, who celebrate my word counts and can tell by the speed of my fingers how much I am in the flow, thank you for your softness and your edges. Watching you grow is a privilege, but laundry is time-consuming. One day, I would love to have a laundry fairy. Failing that, a laundry robot would do. You can go thirds on it with your first salaries.

Most importantly, to my husband Jan, whose belief in me never wavers, even when my own does, and who is currently talking loudly behind me on a conference call. Thanks for all that you do and all that you are. You are my rock in the ocean.

SHARE YOUR READER LOVE

I hope you enjoyed *To Curse a Rival*. Please take a few moments to leave a review online. Reviews are so appreciated. They tell authors which stories resonate and help readers discover our work.

In the next book in the series, *To Trick a Raja*, the rebellion rises and Kiya is its leader. You can pre-order it here.

If you are a book blogger and would like to feature my books, please get in touch at <u>www.NilluNasser.com</u>.

N. Z. Nasser

xoxo

STAY IN TOUCH & GRAB YOUR SHORT STORY

Come and be part of my tribe and join my facebook reader group at <u>Nasser's Book Nymphs.</u>

To receive the short stories in the Majestic Midlife Witch world and keep up to date with my news, sign up for my fantasy newsletter at <u>www.nillunasser.com</u>.

For a close lens into my world, you can get early access to work-in-progress chapters and other goodies by joining my exclusive community: <u>https://reamstories.com/nznasser.</u>

Here's a coupon for the first time you make a purchase in my online store (it's so pretty!) at <u>www.nillunasser.com</u>: NILLU15.

TO TRICK A RAJA
MAJESTIC MIDLIFE WITCH, BOOK 3

My witchcraft made a fortress soar from the earth, fracturing the kingdom in two. Once, the raja pictured me as his queen. Now, I lead the resistance against him. He plots against us in his white-washed palace, leveraging secrets to gain power, and it's only a matter of time before he comes for us.

The kingdom is crying out for justice, but the seer's visions have been off kilter since the reunion with her brother, and not all the rebels trust me. They know that the ancient gargoyles I command once spilled the blood of the people. They know that the raja excels at sinister games and even the brave fall to their knees before him. Like Deven, who has captured my heart, but whose battle to control his shifter self endangers us all.

As betrayal snakes towards us, we discover traitors within the rebel ranks and allies in unfathomable places. I make ever darker choices to protect my loved ones. Am I truly the queen this kingdom deserves if I resort to violence to claim the throne?

To Trick a Raja is the third novel in the Majestic Midlife Witch series. If you are a fan of magic-wielding heroines, swoon-worthy romance and deadly secrets, this book will captivate you.

ALSO BY N. Z. NASSER

DRUID HEIR

Midlife Dawn, Book 1

Midlife Tremors, Book 2

Midlife News, Book 3

Midlife Drift, Book 4

Midlife Portals, Book 5

Midlife Eclipse, Book 6

Midlife Battle, Book 7

MAJESTIC MIDLIFE WITCH

To Save a Sister, Book 1

To Curse a Rival, Book 2

To Trick a Raja, Book 3

COMING SOON

New series: Ink of the Fae

NEWSLETTER EXCLUSIVES

The Magical Grandmother, Druid Heir Short Story 0.5

A First Date in Paris, Druid Heir Short Story 1.5

Midlife Battle, Druid Heir 7 Bonus Epilogue

To Become a Witch, Majestic Midlife Short Story 0.5

Biryani Junction, a Majestic Midlife Witch Cookbook

ABOUT THE AUTHOR

N. Z. Nasser is a writer of fantasy fiction. Her stories are about women who change the world, filled with magic and rooted in friendship.

A lover of barefoot walks along the beach, she is glad to have left behind her career in the civil service and to never wear heels again. Whether she is writing in her garden office or wrangling laundry, she is happiest with a cup of tea at her side.

She lives in London with her husband, three children, two cats and a fox-mad dog.

www.ingramcontent.com/pod-product-compliance
Lightning Source LLC
Chambersburg PA
CBHW050755190726
48285CB00005B/1668